ARTE PERDIDA
A saga of art, love, greed, revenge, and murder

*To Michael /
A fellow /
author /
I wish the /
you the /
best!*

ARTE PERDIDA

A saga of art, love, greed, revenge, and murder

——————

JACK MATTHEWS

Arte Perdida is a work of fiction. Although some real-world names, organizations, and situations are used to enhance the authenticity of the story, names, characters, places, and incidents either are the product of the author's imagination or are used fictitiously. Any resemblance to actual persons, living or dead, business establishments, events, or locales is entirely coincidental. Some historical figures and locations have been used fictitiously, and in some instances have been altered for the purpose of the plot.

This book is protected under the copyright laws of the United States of America. No part of this book may be reproduced or transmitted in any form or by any means, electronic or mechanical, including photocopying, recording, or by any information storage and retrieval system without the written consent of the author except in the case of brief quotations embodied in critical articles and reviews.

Cover design created by:
Val Greco, Greco Design

Cover photograph:
Jack Matthews

Cover sunrise photograph:
Tim Quackenbush

Design Consultant:
Jason Ulm

Copyright © 2019 by Jack Matthews
All rights reserved
Published by Belltown Press
belltownpress@gmail.com

ISBN 978-0-578-22052-9

Printed in USA by 48HrBooks

ACKNOWLEDGMENTS

There are so many people without whose help this book never would have been published. I am grateful to everyone who supported my effort during the years this novel was under construction. To all of you, and to others whom I might have neglected to acknowledge, thanks for being there with me during this wonderful journey.

Alice Simcoe-Matthews
My incredible daughter, to whom this book is dedicated. She is an extraordinary travel planner and tour guide who mapped and led our travels throughout Germany, Spain, and the Azores as we traced the route of this novel.

Co-Editors
Heather Bell, English Instructor, Gateway Community College
Dr. Randy Laist, Professor of English, Goodwin College

Technical advice for military and police sections
Ron Lee
A great friend and fellow Veteran, Ron served as a brownwater sailor in Vietnam and is also a retired deputy police chief. His contributions concerning those aspects of this novel were drawn from his first-hand experience and provided invaluable accuracy and realism. Thank you for your service, to our country and to the development of this novel.

My wonderful BETA readers
Ashley Hanna
Marilyn Nowlan
Kara Simmers
Sandy Wirth

> This talented team read my manuscript, found plotholes, fixed my characters, corrected my grammar, identified unnecessary content, and made *Arte Perdida* a much better novel.

Winston Ruby

> A gracious man who invited me to his home in Portugal Cove, Newfoundland when I went there to conduct research for my book. I spent a delightful afternoon with this published author, talking about writing and soaking up his wisdom and suggestions.

Melanie Cherniak (author Elsa Kurt)

> A good friend, and well-published author, for her encouragement, inspiration and support.

For my daughter
Alice Simcoe-Matthews

Her intelligence and compassion
never cease to amaze me.

ARTE PERDIDA

A saga of art, love, greed, revenge, and murder

PART ONE
1945

*"Earth provides enough to satisfy every man's needs,
but not every man's greed."*

—— Mahatma Gandhi

Museum Island, Berlin

The weather was dreadful.
That's why we chose this night.
Sometimes the worst is the best.

21 April 1945

THROUGH THE HEAVY DOWNPOUR, ULBRECHT HEARD THE
planes droning in the distance and knew he didn't have much
time. The steady hum of the propellers grew louder by the
minute, like a swarm of approaching locusts. The Royal
Airforce Bomber Command had been conducting selected
aerial attacks on Berlin since May 15, 1940. Now, The Battle
of Berlin was underway and with it the bombing had increased
in intensity and had shifted to widespread indiscriminate
bombing.

The streets were deserted as he approached the Kaiser
Friedrich Museum at the northern end of Museum Island. The
Italian Baroque style building, with its high majestic main
dome, appeared to be rising from where the Spree River split
to flow past the opposite sides of the palatial structure. From
the front, the museum looked like the bow of a great cruise
ship steaming through the seas. A small stone bridge, the
Monbijou, crossed the river in front of the entrance to the
stately museum where Ulbrecht was now parked.

◆

1

Admiral Doenitz's Headquarters
17 February 1945 (Two months earlier)

HEINRICH SCHIFFER WAS ONE OF TWO BROTHERS WHO captained German U-boats. His brother Klaus, whom Heinrich hadn't been in touch with for several years, patrolled the North Atlantic, off the coast of Newfoundland.

U-491 brought Captain Heinrich Schiffer to Admiral Doenitz's headquarters near Lobetal, a small town 25 miles northeast of Berlin. From this location Admiral Doenitz coordinated the Battle of the Atlantic for Hitler's Germany. Although he reported to the Naval High Command, Doenitz had considerable latitude in conducting U-boat operations in the Atlantic. He had moved his headquarters here to avoid the heavy bombing that was devastating Berlin.

Admiral Karl Doenitz was an innovator. His superior, Admiral Raeder, didn't like submarines, or U-boats as they were called. However, he respected Doenitz's knowledge and ability to command and gave him free rein to conduct his U-boat operations in the Atlantic.

In 1943, after rising through the ranks of the German Navy, Doenitz succeeded Admiral Raeder as the Oberbefehlshaber der Kriegsmarine, or, Commander in Chief. For his loyalty to Hitler, Doenitz was awarded the Oak Leaves of the Knight's Cross and the coveted Golden Party Badge.

Prior to Doenitz assuming command, U-boat attack strategy consisted of single U-boats looking for and sinking isolated merchant ships transporting war supplies across the North Atlantic from Canada and the United States to England. The U-boats were generally unable to stop the merchant ships from delivering their supplies to Great Britain. Nevertheless, allied ships soon began to travel in convoys, accompanied by escort warships to provide greater protection.

To counter that, Doenitz conceived the idea of Rudeltaktik, or Wolf Packs. This strategy involved groups of U-boats attacking the convoys simultaneously at night, under the cover of darkness. The tactic proved to be highly effective, and for a time turned the direction of the war in favor of Germany.

Doenitz's favorite innovation was U-491. He believed that he could keep his attack submarines in the Atlantic for longer periods of time if they didn't have to return to base to be resupplied with food, motor oil, fuel and torpedoes. He ordered construction of three boats U-491, U-492, and U-493 designed for that purpose. However, construction of the Milchkuhe, or "milk cows," as they were called, was *officially* halted by senior command before it was completed.

Unknown, except to a very few, Doenitz ordered construction to continue on U-491 so that he could test his theory. The boat was outfitted with refrigerator units, a bakery, and additional storage tanks. However, the construction sacrificed nearly all means of defense. U-491 contained no torpedo tubes or deck guns, and the only means of defense in the event of an attack were small anti-aircraft weapons. The more-seasoned sailors referred to the boats as "sitting cows."

◆

The compound was called Lager Koralle, or Coral Camp. Located deep in the pine woods far from any homes or shops, it was a large bunker thirty feet underground. That allowed Doenitz to safely direct U-boat activities from outside the Berlin city limits. It included a communications room from which Doenitz was able to communicate with every ship in his fleet, and a chart room where the positions of his boats were meticulously tracked on a large chart of the Atlantic Ocean. Doenitz took personal responsibility for coordinating all aspects of U-boat activity and was heavily involved in the day-to-day operations of his fleet.

His boat captains reported to him after every operation, and he routinely shared intelligence and strategy with them. As boats reported their new positions, staff members, using long push rods, moved the small-scale replicas of each boat to its new location on the chart on the table. At any time, the position of every boat in the fleet could be identified.

What Doenitz didn't know was that the British had broken the German "Enigma" cipher and decrypted many of the signals between the U-boats and Doenitz's headquarters. His frequent transmissions were often intercepted by the British. That information was analyzed and U-boat operations were tracked in the map room of the Churchill War Room, the underground headquarters of the British Military located just a few blocks from Number Ten Downing Street. At any time they chose, the British could locate and then sink Doenitz's beloved U-boats.

◆

Schiffer was met at the high-walled gate to the compound by two armed guards.

"Heil Hitler," Schiffer snapped with a click of his heels as he was escorted into Doenitz's office.

"Heil Hitler," replied Doenitz.

"Have a seat, Captain."

Doenitz, a tall, thin and energetic man, took a very personal interest in his captains and frequently visited them when they were in port.

"It is good to see you again, Captain."

"And you too, Admiral," replied Schiffer as he shook Doenitz's outstretched hand.

"Have a seat."

Schiffer sat in the chair directly in front of Doenitz's desk, placing the folder he had brought with him on his lap. The folder contained a letter from Doenitz that he had received several weeks earlier, directing him to report to Doenitz's headquarters to receive a special assignment.

"As you are aware, Captain, our U-boats spend a lot of time sailing back to port to resupply. That is time that could be better utilized for increasing the tonnage we sink in the Atlantic. Over a year ago I directed the Deutsche Werke and Germaniawerft to build a different type of U-boat, one that could be used to transport supplies to our boats at sea. Unfortunately, I had to stop their construction due to limited resources, and upon orders of the Fuehrer.

"However," he went on, "I believe these boats could improve our position in the war, so I directed that work continue on one boat, U-491. As you know, that boat was relocated from the Deutsche Werke to slot 2A in the Elbe II pens in Hamburg. Work has quietly continued on the boat. Within a few months it will be ready for a test run. You will be the captain."

"Yes Sir," replied Schiffer, somewhat distracted. His mind raced with divergent thoughts.

"You will oversee the final construction of the ship, its outfitting, including the selection of the crew. I will give you a memorandum to direct all other captains to assist you in getting U-491 underway as soon as possible."

Doenitz opened the drawer on the top right side of his desk, took out a small stack of his official stationery, and set it on the desk. He picked up two sheets then said, "I'll have my clerk type the directive for you."

After he left the room, Schiffer hesitated only a few seconds before lifting two sheets of stationery from the pile and slipping them into the folder on his lap. *What if I'm searched? Is it too risky? Should I put it back on the pile?*

Too late! Doenitz returned to the room and walked over to Schiffer, who stood as Doenitz extended his hand to give him the newly typed directive. Schiffer carefully read it, nodding his head up and down. He raised his eyes until he was looking directly at Doenitz and maintained eye contact with him while quickly sliding the memo into his folder on top of the hidden stationery.

"Let me know when you are ready to put out to sea. I would like to be there to see you off."

"Aye, aye, Sir!"

"Wait a minute! Let me have it," Doenitz ordered, extending his hand towards the folder that Schiffer was holding.

I can't let him see what's in the folder, I can't hand it to him. Schiffer felt a knot developing in the pit of his stomach. He knew that if he handed Doenitz the folder he'd discover the stolen stationery. A guard would march him into the woods, put a bullet through the back of his head, and burn him beyond recognition. Just another person gone missing at the hands of the Nazis.

He had no choice but to assume that Doenitz only wanted the memo, for he didn't know what else was in the folder. Schiffer carefully tilted the top of the folder towards his chest, then reached inside and pinched the top copy, Doenitz's memo, between his thumb and forefinger, making certain to separate it from the other two sheets of stationery. He tried to control his shaking hands. *Would Doenitz notice?*

Schiffer watched him carefully as he took the memo and studied it.

Panic set in. *Doenitz must have suspected something. Should I try to explain it? Should I run? No, I'd be shot before I made it twenty yards.* He resigned himself to a bullet in the back of his head.

Doenitz looked at the memo then laughed. "It will be more effective if I sign it!"

Schiffer let out a stress-releasing laugh as a smile crossed his face and the knot in his stomach quickly dissipated.

Doenitz picked up a pen from his desk, signed the memo, and handed it back to Schiffer.

"And, Captain," he paused, "if you are successful I will see that you wear the German Cross in Gold on your uniform."

"Thank you, Sir," replied Schiffer, aware that very few got to wear that coveted medal.

They exchanged the perfunctory "Heil Hitlers," then Schiffer turned and left the office. He didn't look back as he walked out of the compound and over to his car. His driver opened the door on the passenger side and Schiffer stepped inside. To his driver he said, "Hamburg."

◆

Kaiser Friedrich Museum
Early April 1945

DR. MICHEAL KAHN, CURATOR OF THE KAISER FRIEDRICH Museum, had an affinity for antique model trains. He was a widely-educated man with bushy eyebrows and wisps of thinning gray hair that was perpetually disheveled by the breezes off the streets of Berlin. He frequently toured the museum in his brown corduroy sport jacket and his trademark red suspenders. The glasses perched on the bridge of his nose gave him a scholarly look. He enthusiastically wandered the museum, seeking out visitors and engaging them in extended conversations about things historical and cultural.

Kahn was born in the Charlottenburg district of Berlin and later graduated from the University of Heidelberg. As a history buff, he often boasted that the University, founded in 1386, was the oldest university in Germany as well as the third university established in the Holy Roman Empire. Kahn was widely read in science and technology and had an encyclopedic knowledge of art, European antiquities, and especially model European trains. He had a practical, down-to-earth manner of working with his staff. He had their enthusiastic support when he created a small exhibit of old European trains. The Curator was a perpetual "do-it-yourselfer" and often referred to himself as a "sophisticated crate builder."

Kahn had gathered his staff early on a drizzly Wednesday morning after a particularly heavy week of bombing by the British Royal Airforce. The air carried the smell of smoke and acrid dust from the devastation in the blocks surrounding the museum. Several nearby buildings had been completely demolished. Others were left with only their exterior walls intact, their windows and interiors blown out, leaving them looking like large squares of honeycomb, without the honey. Kahn was grateful that the Kaiser Friedrich Museum had not yet been touched by the bombs, but he knew it was time to begin moving the artwork to safety. It was time to build crates.

"We are most fortunate that our museum has not been hit by bombs, but I fear that day is not too far ahead of us. We need to protect our paintings, and we must begin now," Kahn said, though his staff of twenty-seven gathered around him already knew that.

He paused a minute in thought, looking down at the floor, his thumbs tucked under his suspenders, lightly tugging at them out of years of habit. Few visitors made their way to the museum these days, and so he laid out a plan for moving the artwork.

"Barthold, Karl, Wenzel, you'll stay here at the museum in case we have visitors. I want the rest of you men to go out and find wood for us to use. Check the markets for vegetable crates that have been discarded and scour the area around any buildings that have been destroyed. Bring what you find back here and take it to the upper level. We will close it to visitors so that we can construct crates. Go now, and go every day until we have enough wood to crate 400 paintings or so."

The men left and went out into the streets surrounding Museum Island while Kahn gave instructions to those who remained behind.

"Our Archivist, Iva, and her assistant, Ulbrecht, have prepared a list of the most important works we must save. If we have time we will save others. I reviewed her list and believe it represents the best of our museum. Here's how we will proceed."

For the next ten minutes Kahn circulated the list for them to review.

"Barthold, Karl, Wenzel—you go the entrance, under the great dome, to greet any guests. Do your best to make them feel welcome. Explain that we are protecting the artwork and that some areas of the museum may be closed."

Just then a bomb exploded several miles from the museum. Everyone jumped instinctively and looked up anxiously, hoping the ornate dome was still intact. Streams of plaster dust drifted downward and covered the floor with a light layer of gray powder.

After they recovered, Kahn turned to the eight women standing in front of him and said, "Split into teams of two. Iva has divided the paintings into four lists. Go and carefully measure each painting's length and width, so that when the men return with the wood we can begin building crates to contain them."

Iva gave each group a list of paintings to measure. She was one for great detail, and next to each painting on the list she had written the room number where it could be found.

Iva was a petite, attractive brunette with berry red lipstick that accentuated her pretty smile. She had a passion for learning and was most often seen with a notepad in her hand, jotting down endless information on all aspects of the art in the museum. Three years ago, after she earned her degree in Humanities at the University of Belgrade, she learned about the job as archivist at the Kaiser Friedrich Museum when she was visiting Berlin on holiday. She inquired about it to Kahn when she was there, and after talking with her for more than an hour, he offered her the position. She returned to Belgrade, packed her things, and moved to Berlin where she rented a room from Maddalyn, another woman who worked at the museum.

Iva gave each team a measuring tape borrowed from the woman who ran a tailoring shop next to where she lived. The shop was closed as there was no business to be had, and the woman graciously lent Iva the tape measures. Now, Iva walked from room to room, checking with each group, reminding them to measure each painting twice as they had to perfectly match the crates. By the end of the day the list would be ready for the men to use to build the crates that would protect the precious art.

Ulbrecht left the group and took the small staircase under the rear dome of the museum to the upper floor to prepare an area to store the gathered wood. A few small rooms in the center of the upper level held a number of the lesser works of the museum that were occasionally rotated to the special exhibit room on the main floor. They would close off the upper floor to visitors so that they could crate the art without interruption. He decided on the large courtyard to the left of the stairway for the construction of the crates and dragged several tables from an adjacent room to be used as workbenches.

With nothing more to do upstairs, Ulbrecht went back to the main floor for a far more important task, one that he had been planning for many weeks. He wandered through the rooms until he caught up with the first pair of women, then asked to look at their list so that he could begin organizing construction of the crates. What he didn't tell them was that there would be two crates for several of the paintings. Weeks earlier, after spending several hours walking through each room in the museum in careful study, he had selected some of its smallest, yet most important, paintings.

He looked at the list that Klaudia handed him, found one of the paintings he was interested in, and copied its title, artist, and dimensions: 44 by 48 centimeters. Two more paintings on her list were also of interest to him, and he recorded the same information. He then added his own number next to each painting on his list:

1. Painter on His Way to Work
   Van Gogh

2. Silent Sea with Sailboats
   Jan van de Capelle

3. Portrait of the Venetian Admiral Giovanni Moro
   Titian

He moved on to the next two women and told them the same story about wanting to get a head start on building the crates. Anne handed him their list and he quickly found five paintings he was looking for and recorded the information he needed:

4. Portrait of a Courtesan
   Caravaggio

5. Saint Agnes
   Cano

6. Still Life with Copper Kettle, Bottle, Bowl with Eggs and Two Leeks
   Chardin

7. Virgin Mary and Child and Baby Saint John
   Lucas Cranach the Elder

8. The Murder of Julius Caesar
   Del Sellaio

"We'll start building the crates for these as soon as the wood arrives," he told the two women as he handed their list back to them. "Be sure to measure twice. The crates must be perfect."

He had learned well from Iva.

Ulbrecht had learned other things from Iva. Soon after she had arrived at the Kaiser Friedrich she had mentioned to him that her father had been lost at sea and that her mother still lived in Belgrade with Iva's brother. He had remembered that conversation.

Ulbrecht left the room in search of the third pair of women and found them carefully measuring a painting in room 111.

"Can I look at your list? I want to pick a few for the first crates we will build."

Uta handed him their list of one hundred paintings. Two of the three he was looking for had been measured, and he documented the information he needed:

9. Madame Boone and Her Daughter
   Sir Joshua Reynolds

10. Martyrdom of Saint Lucy
    Beccafumi

The final painting on his list, the most important one to him, hadn't been measured yet. It hung at the far end of the room and he was very familiar with it.

Ulbrecht was sort of a mystery at the museum. Some said he got the job as assistant archivist because his father was a high-ranking officer in the German Military. Others thought that he had just been at the right place at the right time. No one knew for sure. No one dared to ask. What they *did* know was that he had sworn the Civil Servant Oath of Loyalty to Adolf Hitler:

I swear I will be faithful and obedient to the leader of the German empire and people, Adolf Hitler, to observe the law, and to conscientiously fulfill my official duties so help me God!

That information he didn't hide.

13

Ulbrecht was in his early twenties and had lived with his parents in Berlin, until he got his job at the Kaiser Friedrich Museum. Prior to that he had drifted from job to job, not really needing to work since he was well taken care of by his parents.

Ulbrecht considered asking the women to skip ahead to the last painting on his list, but thought better of it. No need to call attention to himself. So, on the pretext of studying other pieces hanging in the room, he moved from painting to painting, looking at them but not seeing them, for his mind was 185 miles away.

Finally, the women approached the painting he was waiting for. He watched as they carefully measured it, twice, and recorded its dimensions. He waited a few more minutes until they had measured two additional paintings, then again asked to look at their list, though he was interested in only one painting:

11. The Vision of Saint Bruno
    Jordaens

Done, he thought, as he slipped the paper into his jacket pocket and headed off to find Iva. He caught up with her under the small dome towards the rear of the main floor. He approached her and tapped the outside of his jacket over the pocket as they made eye contact. She said nothing, but gave a slight nod of her head.

◆

Late in the afternoon Iva tracked down each of the four groups of women, took their completed lists, and thanked them for being so meticulous.

14

"We checked everything twice," Uta said with a hint of pride in her voice.

Just then Kahn entered the room to check on the progress of cataloging and packing the art.

"How is it coming?" he asked the group.

"We've completed the inventory of more than 400 pieces, everything on the list, and the men have already found a good bit of wood and brought it back to the upper floor," Iva reported.

"Do we have enough to get started?" Kahn asked.

"Yes, we do. They will go out for more wood tomorrow."

"Good. Let's call it a day. We'll begin crating tomorrow morning. Thank you for your work. Let's go home."

Kahn headed back to his office and then to the train room. He sized up the collection and planned to come back the following day to remove it to his home. An hour later, after the staff had left the building, he turned the key in the lock of the massive front doors, pulled on the handles to make sure they were secured, then headed down Am Kupfergraben to his apartment.

♦

The rain had let up a little by the time the staff arrived at the museum the next morning. Iva headed off to the rear staircase and walked upstairs to where the men were organizing to build the crates. Stacks of wood were piled high, and a barrel of nails sat on the floor next to one of the benches. Large rolls of brown paper had been brought to the room. It would be crumpled and then stuffed on all sides of the paintings, once they were in the crates. That would prevent them from moving and becoming damaged while in transit to the Flakturm, a large concrete bunker.

"Here are the lists with the dimensions for the crates," she said. "I'll be back in a while to check on your progress. Oh, and make them all thirteen centimeters deep, that will fit the largest painting we bring to you. Build them in the order of the paintings on the lists—we'll bring them to you in that order. And be sure to write the number of the painting on the crate that it's in."

She took duplicate lists out of her pocket and walked back down the staircase and into the courtyard on the west side of the museum.

"Uta, go find Karl and Wenzel and tell them to come back here. Have them bring a stepladder with them."

Uta hurried off to the entrance of the museum. She found the men looking out at the rain falling on the Spree River.

"Iva wants you to bring a stepladder to the Basilica."

Karl went with Uta while Wenzel went to find the stepladder. A few minutes later, ladder in hand, he joined the women and Karl.

"All right. We are going to remove the paintings in the order that they appear on this first list, then bring them to the small staircase where Ulbrecht will take them to the upper level for crating."

The group followed Iva to the courtyard off to the right of the principal staircase, near the entrance to the museum.

"Okay, number one on the list is Caravaggio's *Agony in the Garden* and number two is his *Saint Matthew Writing His Gospel Helped by an Angel*."

Karl set the stepladder next to the first painting and gently removed it from the wall and handed it to the two women standing next to him.

"Let me look at the back," said Iva. "I need to write down the inventory number."

16

She meticulously recorded the inventory number next to the painting on her list.

"Take it to Ulbrecht at the bottom of the small staircase, then come back here."

She directed the group to the second Caravaggio. Karl removed it from the wall, and handed it to two more women who showed Iva the inventory number on the back for her to record. One of the women then carried the painting to Ulbrecht.

Next, they removed Van Gogh's *Painter on His Way to Work*. Iva looked at her list and noted that this piece had a small checkmark next to it. After she recorded the inventory number, she penciled the number 1 on the upper left back corner of the painting.

During the next two hours the staff removed nearly one hundred of the paintings, recorded their inventory numbers, and carried them to the men who were building the crates. Iva documented each piece as it was sent for packing and began preparing the transport manifest.

Eleven of the paintings had an additional number written on the top left corner next to the inventory number. Germans were meticulous about maintaining records for all the art they obtained, and Iva was meticulous.

Iva told the group to continue working their way down the list, in order, while she went to check on the progress of the crate building and packing. Two of the men had just finished constructing the first crate when she arrived at the upper level. She inspected it, looked at her list to confirm the dimensions of the painting that was to go into it, then took the tape measure that she had been wearing around her neck and measured the crate.

"Details, men, details!" she yelled, frustrated by their lack of attention. "The dimensions on the list are the *inside* dimensions of the crate, not the outside like you did with this one. The painting won't fit! Make sure the dimensions of the *inside* of the crates match the dimensions on the lists you are working from. Allow a few extra centimeters on all sides so we can pack paper around the paintings to protect them."

The men, embarrassed, went back to work. Soon they had an efficient system for measuring and cutting the wood to the necessary lengths, and for constructing crates. One man prepared the final slats that would secure the top of the crates to fully enclose the paintings inside. As the day wore on they were able to build crates rather quickly, and Iva continued to record the inventory number of each painting before it was packed.

Ulbrecht spent the day at the foot of the stairs, waiting to receive the paintings as the women brought them to him. One at a time he carefully carried them upstairs and handed them to the men.

As various pieces of art were brought to him, Ulbrecht periodically identified one of the eleven pieces on his list that had a checkmark next to it. Making sure no one was nearby, he quickly moved it into Room 13, a small oval room a few steps from the stairway. It was unlikely that anyone would be going into that room. Once a room had been emptied of its art a large "X" was marked in chalk on the door. A bold "X" was clearly visible in the center of the door to Room 13. By the end of the day, eleven paintings were stacked against the wall in that room and covered with a canvas tarp.

During the next few weeks the staff of the museum constructed and packed more than four hundred crates of art. Once the first fifteen paintings had been crated, the men brought them to the front of the museum and stacked them on end against the wall for Ulbrecht to load onto his truck.

18

Iva was there to help him, under the guise of re-checking the inventory numbers that had been written on the outside of the crates. She was really there, however, to help with the first truckload so that the others wouldn't see the eleven crates, already under a large canvas tarp, in the back of Ulbrecht's truck. They contained no art, but rather a number of boards that Ulbrecht had nailed together to create the perception that a painting was packed inside. He was confident that none of the crates would be opened due to the chaos created by the increased bombing.

They added a few more crates, ones that the men had built and packed, and placed them on their narrow sides next to those already stacked at the front of the truck bed.

Ulbrecht turned to Iva and said, "This is the important trip. I'll be back soon so we can begin moving the rest."

She handed him the first transport manifest, listing the eighteen paintings in the truck.

"Give this to the Major-General when you arrive there."

Ulbrecht jumped into the driver's seat, started the engine and headed off to the Friedrichshainflak tower, or Flakturm, to deliver the art for safekeeping during the bombing raids. The massive concrete structure was one of three anti-aircraft and air-raid shelters that the Nazis constructed in Berlin during the early stages of the war. It would now also be the repository for the art from the Kaiser Friedrich Museum.

Kahn was in regular contact with Major-General of the Luftwaffe, Otto Sydow, the Commandant of the Flakturm. Sydow paid careful attention to the art being delivered to him from the museum because he had to report its acquisition directly to Hitler immediately upon its arrival.

Hitler had long fantasized about creating the world's

largest art museum, the Führermuseum, in Linz, Austria, his hometown. He established special military units that stole important works from throughout Europe that were hidden in a number of places, including salt mines. One mine alone, the Altaussee in the Austrian Alps, held thousands of stolen pieces including Jan van Eyck's Ghent Altarpiece. It was Hitler's most coveted piece. It had been repatriated from Germany to Belgium by the Treaty of Versailles, and he wanted it back.

The Major-General himself met Ulbrecht when he arrived at the flakturm with the first delivery of art.

"Do you have the manifest?" Sydow asked.

Ulbrecht handed it to him, very much intimidated by Sydow's military appearance and authority. The Major-General told his aide to get some men to remove the art from the truck and bring it inside. Fifteen minutes later Ulbrecht was on his way back to the Kaiser Friedrich.

Throughout the week, staff members crated 417 pieces of art and safely moved them to the Flakturm. Unknown to anyone except Ulbrecht and Iva, eleven paintings remained behind in Room 13.

Once the art had been moved to the Flakturm, all of the employees, except Iva and Ulbrecht, quickly fled the museum as bombs landed nearby, shaking its foundation and causing dust and pieces of plaster to fall to the museum floor. The two were standing together in the entrance hall.

Ulbrecht reached into his jacket pocket, pulled out a large envelope, and said, "This is for you, Iva. You kept your promise."

She looked inside and saw a lot of Reichsmarks. She looked back at Ulbrecht, and broke into tears. She sobbed as she threw her arms around him and held him tightly. Months earlier she received a letter from her mother telling her that she had cancer.

20

She shared that information with Ulbrecht, adding, "My brother is no help to her as he drinks all day and can't find work. She is able to make ends meet with the meager savings she accumulated while my father was alive and working. Now, the money is almost gone and she needs medical help."

"I might be able to help you if you assist me with removing a few pieces of art from the museum," Ulbrecht had told her.

She didn't answer him at first. A few days later, having convinced herself that the art would only be destroyed by the bombing or stolen, she informed Ulbrecht that she would help him.

Today, he kept his promise. However, he didn't tell her where the eleven paintings were going or that the plan was to sell them on the black market.

After Iva left the museum, Ulbrecht had one last thing to do. He went out through the main entrance to where his truck was parked and grabbed a measuring tape from the passenger seat. He re-entered the museum and went directly to Room 13. He reached into his pocket and removed the paper with the list of eleven paintings on it and set it on a small nearby table. Very methodically, he measured the length and width of each painting to verify the dimensions. *Better to check and re-check*, he thought, as Iva had taught him.

When he was finished confirming the dimensions he put the paper back into his shirt pocket, looked at the paintings one last time, covered them with the canvas tarp, and left the room. He hurried back through the museum, under the smaller of the two domes and across the basilica. He walked around the large statue of Friedrich Wilhelm von Brandenburg seated on his horse in the entrance hall and exited the building.

◆

Previously, Ulbrecht had meticulously constructed eleven crates. After they were completed, he cut a swastika stencil into a thin piece of wood. Then he took some black paint and stenciled two swastikas on opposite sides of each crate. Now, upon arriving home, Ulbrecht took the list of paintings from his pocket and compared their measurements to the inside dimensions of the crates.

Perfect, he said to himself, confident that the paintings sitting in Room 13 were ready for their journey. He loaded all eleven of the crates onto the wooden slats that he had laid across the back of his truck, covered them with a sheet of canvas, and went back into his house. With all preparations completed, he went to bed, hoping for a few hours rest before the long-anticipated day ahead.

◆

ON THE 21ST OF APRIL, 1945, ULBRECHT AWOKE TO THE sound of pelting rain after a few hours of restless sleep. It was the day after the last of the paintings had been moved to the Flakturm for safe-keeping and the staff had been dismissed. Ulbrecht showered then ate some streuselkuchen, a yeast dough covered with streusel.

He lived on the first floor of a house on Mittelstrasse that was owned by an elderly couple who lived upstairs. The woman was a wonderful baker and often left homemade baked goods in front of his door. The streuselkuchen was there when he returned home the previous night. As a thank you for her pastries, Ulbrecht often left her flowers that he picked up at a market near the house. He regretted that there hadn't been any to buy in recent months.

After he finished eating, he picked up two full gas cans from the entranceway to his house and put them into the back of his truck. He would need them if he was delayed. He went back inside his house, picked up an envelope from a table in the alcove, looked around once more, then left, locking the door behind him.

The rain gathered strength as he climbed into the truck and drove to the museum. The trip was slow as he maneuvered around the remains of numerous buildings the bombs had turned to rubble. Overhead he heard the drone of bombers from the British Royal Airforce and occasionally the explosions from their bombs landing in the distance. A short while later he arrived at the museum and parked in front on the bridge over the Spree River.

After opening the large main-entrance door, he returned to the truck and moved the crates just inside the front entrance. When all eleven were in the entrance hall, he went back to the truck for the eleven strips of wood that would enclose each crate once the designated painting was inside. Each crate was numbered to match the number on the painting it contained.

Back inside the museum, he crossed the entrance hall, continued under the grand curving principal stairway and arrived at Room 13.

Once there, Ulbrecht pulled the list of paintings from his pocket. The first painting lying against the wall, Silent Sea with Sailboats, was to go in crate number 2. He checked the back of the painting and saw the number 2 on the top left corner, picked it up, then carried it to the front of the museum and carefully eased it into one of the canvas bags that he had previously taken from behind a nearby vacant market. Once that was done, he put the painting into crate number 2, then gently wedged crumpled brown wrapping paper around it to keep it from moving inside the crate. Finally, he nailed slat number 2 across the top, fully enclosing the painting. He returned to the remaining stack of paintings, and for the next hour repeated the process until all eleven paintings were secured in their individual crates. Before he sealed the last of the eleven crates, the most important one, he folded his list and slid it inside, along with a letter that he had prepared the previous week.

He then carried the first one out of the museum and placed it in the back of his truck. He repeated the process until all of the paintings were carefully stacked. Then, he stuffed the remaining canvass bags between the paintings and the sides of the truck bed to keep them from shifting and becoming damaged during the trip ahead. He covered them with a large sheet of canvas.

Lastly, he took a length of rope and secured the crates to cleats inside the truck-bed so they wouldn't bounce around and be damaged during the nearly one hundred eighty-five-mile ride ahead.

It was a few hours before daybreak and the heavy rain continued. Everything had gone smoothly, and as planned. Ulbrecht had accomplished what he needed to at the museum, so he closed and locked the entrance door then got into his truck. He sat there a minute holding the steering wheel with both hands. He took a deep breath, then checked the seat next to him to confirm that the envelope with the letter was there. He prayed he wouldn't need it. *Once I get out of Berlin the rest should be easy.* Or so he thought. He shifted the truck into first gear and slowly drove off into the stormy night.

24

To Hamburg

ULBRECHT LEFT THE KAISER FRIEDRICH MUSEUM BEHIND and turned onto the Am Kupfergraben. The windshield wipers could barely clear the rain from the window of his truck as he paralleled the Spree River on his way to Hamburg. After winding his way through rubble from the bombing for a few blocks, he turned east on the Unter den Linden. The streets were lined with debris from buildings that had been bombed by the British Royal Airforce. A few people numbly wandered the streets. Residents had done their best to clear the debris from the streets which were now lined with piles of concrete, glass, steel, wood, destroyed furniture and other household items. People picked through the piles in front of what was once their home, looking for anything they could salvage.

Children wandered the streets, no parents in sight. Nazi flags hung from several buildings, but they were not nearly as evident as they had been a year earlier because the bombing had destroyed many of them. Also, the German people had grown weary of the war and sensed that it would be ending soon, so they were willing to take the chance of not flying the flag. Not everyone had abandoned allegiance to Hitler, however, and he saw several groups of young children wearing red armbands with the black swastika inside a red circle.

Ulbrecht passed block after block of enormous piles of bricks that had been gathered and neatly stacked throughout each neighborhood. Residents undoubtedly planned to use them to rebuild their homes once the war ended. He passed by the Cathedral which, miraculously, was undamaged, even though the buildings on either side of it were hollowed out shells with their interiors mostly gone. Fire billowed out of a building further down the street. The smoke-filled air irritated Ulbrecht's eyes to tears.

Bodies lay on the side of the road. People walked by unmoved, far more concerned about their own lives. He came to a stop in front of a large crater in the middle of the road that blocked his way. He backed up and took several side streets around the impasse.

Just before he turned onto the Charlottenburger Chaussee to head out of Berlin, he saw two women cutting meat from a dead horse that lay on the sidewalk, killed by the concussion of a bomb. Two young boys watched with expressionless faces, numb from the incessant bombing. After they cut off large pieces of horsemeat the women handed them to the boys who carried them down the street to their homes. Meat is meat, he thought.

Although there was little traffic, the rubble that partially blocked nearly every street he traveled slowed his pace. Several times he had to back up and detour through side streets. Ulbrecht had just reached the outskirts of Berlin on his drive to Hamburg when the RAF bombers flew overhead. He was near Konigs Platz, not far from the Deutche Bank, when his truck suddenly shook and bounced sideways from the concussion of a bomb that detonated nearby.

A few blocks to the south was the Fuhrerbunker, Hitler's headquarters. As Ulbrecht drove by, he didn't know that nine days later the Russians would be closing in on Berlin and that Hitler, vowing never to be captured, would put a bullet in his head. His wife of one day, Eva Braun, would also die by taking cyanide alongside him in his bunker fifty feet underground.

Ulbrecht tensed when another large bomb went off nearby. Windows shattered on the buildings next to him, covering his truck with shards of glass. Through his rearview mirror he watched a large fireball rise into the air far behind him, followed by a thick plume of smoke. The few streetlights that remained lit immediately went dark as another bomb struck the main electric generating plant for Berlin. What Ulbrecht didn't know was that one of the bombs had struck the Kaiser Friedrich Museum, destroying part of it, including its ornate dome.

Finally, he left Berlin behind and continued northwestward towards Hamburg. The rain let up and soon afterwards the sun peaked through the clouds to his left. For the next few hours he drove through bogs and wetlands on the main road to Hamburg. He crossed several rivers, thankful that the bombs hadn't destroyed their bridges. Here and there he passed a farm, but the towns he drove through showed few signs of life. Before the war many heads of cattle would have been seen grazing in the fields. Now, apart from a lonely steer or two, the fields were barren.

He made good time. There were few cars on the road and it was in reasonably good condition. The RAF had no reason to drop bombs on the countryside.

The next few hours were uneventful, and Ulbrecht finally relaxed. Soon he would deliver the art to the submarine captain at the pens in Hamburg, and his work would be done. The rain had stopped, the clouds had passed, and the sun was shining brightly as he made his way through several small towns. It was turning out to be a good day.

As he neared Hamburg, he turned onto the main road into the city. Not much farther to go and the art would be delivered. He thought about the past few weeks and how flawlessly the plan had been executed. Even the weather had cooperated.

Now, he was looking forward to meeting up with the captain of the submarine and completing his work.

Ulbrecht nonchalantly glanced at his side view mirror. Involuntarily, his hands tightened on the steering wheel as a convoy of VW Schwimmwagens approached on his left, and then passed by. Four soldiers were in each of the three lead roofless trucks. A staff car with WM clearly visible in large block letters on the front right fender travelled in the middle of the convoy. The initials identified it as a staff car of the Wehrmacht Marine, the German Navy. Emblazoned on the door was the Command Post Flag of the Grossadmiral of the Kriegsmarine. Admiral Karl Doenitz was seated in the right front passenger seat. Doenitz barely glanced at Ulbrecht as he went by.

As the convoy moved away, Ulbrecht slowly let the air escape from his lungs, unaware that he had been holding his breath the entire time that it took for the convoy to pass. He could feel his heartrate decrease as Doenitz and his security force drove off into the distance.

Ten minutes later his hands again squeezed the steering wheel. His heart beat faster than when Admiral Doenitz's convoy had driven past him. Up ahead, two trucks partially blocked the road at forty-five-degree angles, leaving just enough room for a vehicle to pass between them.

Two cars were stopped ahead of him, and as he pulled in line behind them, the lead car was waved through between the two trucks. As the car in front of him moved ahead, he slowly followed it, and then stopped. His hands were shaking, sweat formed on his brow, and a wave of numbness spread throughout his body.

Off to his left was a small building that apparently had been a produce market. It wasn't now. Several official vehicles were parked alongside the building in front of a large, long, rectangular red banner that hung from the roof of the building. In the middle of the banner was a white circle, and centered in it was a black swastika: a German checkpoint.

Two officers of the Schutzstaffel, the German SS, in their intimidating gray/green uniforms approached the car in front of him. Nearby, two soldiers focused intently on the car, their Sturmgewehr 44 assault rifles at the ready. The driver handed some papers to one of the officers who examined them carefully before passing them to the officer next to him. He said something to him, they both nodded, then quickly opened the door and pulled the driver out. They motioned to one of the nearby soldiers to take him to the small building thirty meters away that served as their headquarters, and handed the soldier the driver's papers. A soldier moved the car off the road while another signaled Ulbrecht to pull forward. Ulbrecht glanced at the envelope on the seat next to him, convinced that it would work, but fearing what would happen if it didn't.

He was nervous. *Breathe*, he told himself. *You've practiced for this. Take a deep breath and exhale slowly.* He wiped his hands on his pants to get rid of the sweat, then inched his truck forward and stopped beside the SS officers.

"Papers."

Ulbrecht handed him his civilian identification papers. They looked at them and then at the back of his truck.

Breathe, relax, relax. This has to work.

Ulbrecht reached over and lifted the envelope off the seat next to him. The officer was momentarily surprised as he was handed the envelope, but quickly recovered. He glanced suspiciously at Ulbrecht as he opened the envelope, took out the letter, and read:

Grossadmiral Karl Doenitz
Oberbefehlshaber der Kriegsmarine (ObdM)

By order of the Deputy of the Fuehrer dated 7 April 1945

Strict compliance with this directive is required.

To all who are presented with this letter:

1. On behalf of our Fuehrer, the bearer of this order, Ulbrecht Schiffer, who has sworn the oath for civil servants, is transporting highly secret cargo, that has been confiscated by the Reichssicherheitshauptamt of the SS, to the Kriegsmarine U-boat 491 in Hamburg.

2. All who intercept him are to allow him to proceed immediately and without delay.

3. The cargo that he is transporting is of extreme interest to our Fuehrer and is not to be examined under any circumstances. The Fuehrer himself has directed this.

4. Whenever possible, you are to arrange for safe escort of this cargo so that it arrives no later than 1800 hours 21 April 1945.

5. The passage and destination of this vehicle and driver is to be revealed to no one, by direct order of the Fuehrer.

Heil Hitler!
Signed: Karl Doenitz
Grossadmiral Supreme Headquarters of the Navy

11 April 1945

The officer looked at Ulbrecht and then back at the letter. He compared the name on the letter with the official papers Ulbrecht had handed him. They matched. He then handed the letter to the second officer and moved to the rear of the truck, lifted the tarp and saw the crates with the swastikas on them. Ulbrecht's chest was pounding, his legs were shaking, he was convinced they could see that he was terrified. Then again, they were used to seeing terrified people. The officer pulled the tarp off the crates and directed Ulbrecht to get out of the truck. He was light-headed and wasn't sure if he could stand.

"Come with me," the soldier ordered.

Another soldier moved his truck out of the way as Ulbrecht was prodded towards the building in front of him. His shirt was drenched in sweat even though it was a cold and damp day. He passed under a Nazi flag as he entered and found himself standing in front of a lieutenant in the SS who was seated at a small desk in the middle of the room. Another large Nazi flag hung on the wall behind him. The lieutenant was wearing the black uniform of the SS even though they had recently been replaced by the gray/green uniform. The black uniform was far more intimidating to Ulbrecht.

"What's in the back of the truck?"

"Eleven crates. I don't know what is in them."

"Then why do you have them?"

He was about to answer when one of the officers handed the lieutenant the letter that Ulbrecht had given him. As soon as the officer began to read the letter Ulbrecht heard a terrifying scream from the back room. He tensed and looked at the door behind the lieutenant, who looked up at him casually, then continued to read the letter.

Another scream, then a shot, then silence.

Ulbrecht worked hard to compose himself. His heart raced as he glanced towards the door to the back room. *Don't look overly interested. Focus, focus, as Iva often told me. Don't panic. Don't be too confident. I have the letter. It will work.* He wasn't convinced.

The lieutenant slowly read the letter a second time, then held it up to the light as if to see if there was something written in code.

"How did you get this letter, and," with a pause, "those crates?"

"They were given to me by someone who said it came from high up. I was told that I had to deliver them to Hamburg by April 21st."

As the lieutenant picked up the phone on his desk he said to no one in particular, "I will verify this with the Fuehrer's office."

He listened for a minute then slammed the phone down.

"Damn bombing, the phone lines are down."

Ulbrecht slowly let go of the thought of a bullet going through his head in the back room, though not completely.

After reading the letter once more, the lieutenant said, "Let's have a look at your cargo."

He got up and walked out to Ulbrecht's truck, followed by Ulbrecht and the two soldiers.

The lieutenant looked at the crates and asked, "What's in them?"

"I don't know. They were given to me with orders not to open them. I was told to deliver them to U-491 at the U-boat pens in Hamburg. I wasn't told what was in them and I didn't ask." *Careful, don't be sarcastic.*

The Lieutenant studied the swastikas painted on them trying to guess what they contained. He glanced at the letter again and read, *The cargo that he is transporting is of extreme interest to our Fuehrer and is not to be examined under any circumstances. The Fuehrer himself has directed this.*

33

It was signed by Grossadmiral Karl Doenitz. Doenitz was tough to deal with and the Lieutenant had heard of people who had disappeared after crossing him. He handed the letter back to Ulbrecht and said, "Get to Hamburg."

As much as it disgusted him, Ulbrecht raised his right hand towards the Lieutenant and said, "Heil Hitler."

"Heil Hitler," returned the Lieutenant with little enthusiasm.

Ulbrecht got into his truck and set the envelope on the seat beside him, aware that his hands were still shaking. He started up his truck then noticed the car that had been pulled over was still there. *The driver wouldn't be using it again*, he thought as he slid the shift into first gear, let out the clutch, and slowly pulled away from the interrogation station. Thirty minutes later he arrived at the Fink II U-boat pens on the south side of the Elbe River in Hamburg.

The pens were large concrete structures that were designed to prevent the U-boats from being spotted by air. The Germans learned early that submarines sitting at open docks were easy targets for RAF bombers, and methodically constructed five U-boat pens along the Elbe River. They resembled a row of interconnected two-car garages with an open front, and they protected U-boats from aerial attacks by the British Royal Airforce. They were built at various locations, with Fink II being the largest of them. The captain of one of them, U-491, heard Ulbrecht's truck entering the yard and went out to meet him.

He glanced at his watch, and noted that it was 1715 hours. "You made it," he said to Ulbrecht, extending his hand.

"Yes, but not without some difficult moments."

Ulbrecht took a few minutes to recount his trip, especially his encounter with the SS.

"I knew that if they saw Doenitz's name on the letter they wouldn't harm you. No one wants to be on his bad side. At least the smart ones know that.

"Give me the letter."

Ulbrecht went to his truck, picked up the envelope from the passenger seat, then walked over and handed it to the captain. The captain removed the letter from the envelope, looked at it, then put it back in the envelope as he walked to the edge of the dock.

It worked, he thought as he took a match out of his pocket, struck it against a concrete pillar and touched it to the corner of the envelope. He held it over the water until he felt the heat from the flame on his fingertips, and then released it. It continued to burn as it floated down to the Elbe River below.

"Do we have the special painting?" the captain asked.

"Yes, it's in crate 11."

The painting, *The Vision of Saint Bruno,* was especially significant to the captain and his wife, and they had viewed it every time they visited the Kaiser Friedrich Museum.

"I'm really glad to have that one," said Heinrich.

What neither of them would learn was that in May, 1945, retreating German SS forces would set fire to the Friedrichshainflak to prevent it from falling into enemy hands. The tower was destroyed and fire ravaged all the masterpieces that the museum staff had crated so carefully and shipped there. Only these eleven survived destruction by the Nazis.

"Did you give Iva her money?"

"Yes."

"Will she talk?"

"She knows what the SS will do to her if she does. She

won't talk. Besides, she needs the money for her mother and won't risk it."

"I sail tomorrow, so let's get the paintings aboard."

U-boats have two heads, or bathrooms. Because storage space is so limited, the forward head is usually used to store provisions for the first part of any voyage, and thus is off limits to the crew. It was the perfect place to store the crates.

During the next thirty minutes Ulbrecht and the captain removed the crates from the truck and brought them to the forward head on the U-boat. Occasionally, a bomb exploded in the distance, though none targeted the pens. After the crates had been moved, they used the canvas that had covered them in the truck to pack between one of the bulkheads and the outside crate. That secured them so that they wouldn't be tossed around during the trip.

With that completed, the captain shook hands with Ulbrecht.

"Your trip home should be less eventful than your trip here. You have your official papers and if anyone asks you can say that you delivered cargo here. They won't be bothering me with that."

Another bomb went off to the west, and they both looked towards the center of the city. Neither commented. They were used to it.

Finally, Ulbrecht looked the captain in the eyes.

"I'll see you when you return, Father."

◆

Ulbrecht sat in his truck a minute planning his trip back to Berlin. *I'll get through the checkpoint okay because I can remind them of the letter I showed them on the way here. I shouldn't have a problem. But then, why risk it? I'll go north of the Elbe instead.*

He put the key in the ignition, started up the truck, and headed away from the pens. He drove south for a mile and then turned north to cross the one bridge over the Elbe River that hadn't been destroyed. Immediately after crossing the bridge and turning westward towards Berlin, several RAF planes flew overhead and unloaded their bombs far off to his right. *I'll be safe once I'm outside the city. Certainly, a better risk than dealing with the SS again.*

Soon, he reached the outskirts of Hamburg, and buildings became fewer and farther apart. *Now for an easy ride back to Berlin.*

He heard it a second before he felt it. A bomb. He lost control of his truck and it bounced hard to the right, left the road, and rolled over and over coming to rest upside down against what was left of a small brick building. Ulbrecht felt a sharp, searing pain in his chest—broken ribs had punctured both lungs. Air filled the space around his lungs, putting pressure on them, preventing them from expanding. He couldn't breathe. At the same time, he felt his legs being crushed by the engine that had been blown into the cab by the force of the bomb. His ears rang painfully, and fear coursed through him. He realized that he was in the last few moments of life. His body went into shock which was quickly followed by unconsciousness only seconds before the fire reached him, torching his clothing and charring his flesh. The two gas cans that had been in the truck bed were now split open beneath the upside-down truck. Gas was leaking from the containers, and moments later flames reached them and the truck erupted in a giant fireball.

◆

Aboard U-491

THE SUBMARINE PENS ALONG THE ELBE RIVER IN Hamburg lay seventy miles from where the river reaches the North Sea.

The Finenwerder bunker, or "Fink II," was built with more than 1700 slave laborers, captured during the war. It contained five pens that could house two U-boats each, one on each side, moored against a walkway. The nearby Elbe II bunker was located on the southern bank of the Elbe River. It was used for fitting out new boats, those undergoing last works before setting to sea, and those that returned from the Atlantic. It could accommodate 15 U-boats in its five docks. Pen 2A now housed U-491.

Following his meeting with Admiral Doenitz, Schiffer busied himself directing the completion and final fitting of his boat. Although he was given wide latitude by Doenitz to hand-select his crew from any that were in port, he chose to keep his original crew, minus the torpedomen that would not be needed, since there were no torpedo tubes on U-491. He refrained from taking the best men from other U-boats because he wanted to ensure the support of their captains should he need them in the Atlantic. No sense alienating them, especially since he had a solid crew that trusted him and that he likewise trusted.

This morning he scheduled a meeting with the captains of three U-boats that had been called back to the pens. He had already discussed his plan with Admiral Doenitz, who directed them to meet with Schiffer. Gathered around the makeshift conference table in a room at the rear of the Elbe II bunker were Ernst Mangold, captain of U-739; Hans Falke, captain of U-992; and Klaus Hornbostel, captain of U-806.

"Gentlemen, you are here because you have been specially selected for an extremely important undertaking for the Kriegsmarine. Our orders come directly from Grossadmiral Doenitz. He has been in touch with you and here is his memo directing this operation."

With that he produced the memo from the same folder where he had placed it back in Doenitz's office. He handed it to Captain Mangold. Mangold read the memo and passed it along to the other two officers at the table.

"First, let me assure you that I will not raid your crews. I am very confident that we will fare far better if we leave each of our crews intact. Now, let me share the plan with you."

For the next hour, Schiffer outlined the plan to have the U-boats of Mangold, Hornbostel and Faulke precede him up the Elbe River and into the North Sea. Once in the North Sea they would remain on the surface in order to draw the British fleet to them. They would stay on the surface as long as it was, in each captain's opinion, safe to do so. Then they would dive and split in three directions: Mangold would continue out into the North Sea and eventually pass north of the Faroe Islands. Falke would sail through the Skagerrak Straight that runs between the southeast coast of Norway, the southwest coast of Sweden, and the Jutland peninsula of Denmark. Finally, Hornbostel would turn 180 degrees and return to the Elbe River, making his way back to Hamburg.

If the plan worked and the British Navy and Air Force took the bait and drew their forces to the North Sea, it would open up the English Channel to provide safer passage for U-491.

The U-boats of Falke, Mangold, and Hornbostel were moored in Fink II Bunker, a short distance from Elbe II. Following the meeting with Schiffer, the three captains returned to their boats to begin preparation for this operation.

Each had to make different preparations as their times at sea would vary greatly. During the next few days they brought food and other provisions aboard, completed the final inspections, and practiced emergency drills while awaiting word from Captain Schiffer as to when they would leave port. That word came one week to the day after the meeting at Elbe II.

◆

"AUFMERKSAMKEIT AUF DEM DECK," BARKED FIRST Officer Kirk Mueller, bringing the twenty-six men standing on the deck of U-491 to attention. Few men recognized the officer accompanying Captain Schiffer on this final inspection before the men left port. They could, however, tell by the amount of gold on the sleeves of his uniform that he was important. Very important.

The two officers slowly walked down the front row of men standing at attention. When they reached the end of the row they proceeded to make their way along the second row, carefully looking each man in the eyes and examining their uniform, checking that they were neatly cleaned and perfectly pressed. Each ribbon had to be affixed in the proper order and in the proper place. When they reached the end of the second row, the two men saluted each other and, without a word, the visiting officer walked up the gangplank and stood on the walkway of pen 2A.

Now, with the boat fully supplied, the crew onboard, and, unbeknown to all but one, the art safely stored in the forward head, it was time to sail.

It was late in the afternoon when Captain Schiffer ordered, "Ship's Company, prepare to sail."

The men immediately responded to the captain's order and

scrambled down the conning tower hatchway to assume their positions. The chief engineer had fired up the diesel engines before reporting to the deck for inspection. He was now checking the gauges, making sure there was adequate oil pressure and that all cylinders were firing, duties that he had done so often that he could perform them in his sleep.

"Stow the brow," ordered the captain. Two men moved to the walkway alongside the boat, pulled the gangplank up, and stowed it against the far wall. They then nimbly jumped back onto the deck.

"Cast off bow lines one and two.

"Keep the slack out of the stern lines."

This action allowed the bow of the boat to drift slightly away from the mooring.

"Cast off stern lines one and two.

"Helm to conn, ease her forward, five degrees to starboard," Schiffer ordered from the bridge through the sound powered phone.

U-491 slowly made its way through the dirty, oily water of the pen, easing out towards the Elbe River. Unlike other departures, no bands were playing *Lied der deutchen U-Boot Mann* or *Warte, mein Maedel* (*Wait, my Girlfriend*), the usual Kriegsmarine war songs. No throngs of people were waving goodbye from the walkways on the sides of the pen. Only the solitary figure of Grossadmiral Karl Doenitz stood there in silence, seeing his personal, and secret, project off on its shakedown cruise. He was unaware of its cargo or destination.

Schiffer offered a final salute, "Heil Hitler." It was returned by Doenitz who stood there emotionless, despite the fact that his pet project was becoming a reality. Perhaps he knew that the war would be ending soon and that the test voyage would be all for naught.

41

◆

"Ninety degrees to port," Schiffer commanded as he brought the boat into the Elbe River.

An hour earlier Captains Falke, Mangold, and Hornbostel moved their boats into a single column heading northwesterly up the Elbe River. Now, U-491 was trailing the pack by several miles. Slowly, the boats made their way towards the mouth of the Elbe and the North Sea, seventy miles away. Ten hours later they arrived.

The timing was perfect. Schiffer wanted to take advantage of an ebb tide when running through the English Channel. That tide ran from the northeast corner of the channel, near Norwich, southwesterly towards Falmouth. It would push the sub along much faster than having to fight a flood tide that would be flowing towards the boat. The English Channel has extremely strong tidal flows, especially during the spring tide, when the earth, sun, and moon are aligned. Tomorrow night there would be such a tide, and it would be a favorable ebb tide.

Falke, Mangold, and Hornbostel were surfaced a few miles past the mouth of the Elbe. Schiffer spotted them and brought U-491 nearby and, knowing that they were fully ready to set out, signaled them to get underway. With a wave, the three boats headed out into the North Sea under the light of a full moon.

If all went well, U-739, U-992, and U-806 would draw the British Corvettes—small attack boats, cruisers and destroyers along with British Air Reconnaissance—away from the English Channel and out into the North Sea in pursuit. U-491 could then proceed down the English Channel with less of a threat of being attacked.

42

U-491 floated on the surface of the sea throughout the next morning and afternoon, allowing the men their last breaths of fresh air for what could be some time. The conning tower and galley hatches were open and fresh sea air flowed into the submarine.

Submarine duty is not glorious when at sea. The heavy smell of diesel fuel, blended with the foul air of body odor from men who haven't showered in weeks, compounded by hot and clammy air, made for miserable daily life when below the surface. Conditions were cramped, men were only allowed one change of socks and underwear for the duration of the voyage, and had to tolerate "hot racking," where, when one man was awoken to assume the watch, the man who just relieved him crawled into the same small bunk.

Schiffer gave his men a little more latitude than other captains, allowing them to smoke on the bridge, though not at night when the red tip of a cigarette could be spotted from some distance. Now, the men enjoyed their last few hours in relaxed conditions, knowing that the real work was about to begin.

At sunset, the radioman received radio transmissions from the captains of the other three U-boats. He handed Captain Schiffer the messages from all three captains that informed him that they had drawn several British ships as well as a de Havilland Mosquito, a photo reconnaissance plane. The torpedo and dive bombers wouldn't be far behind.

"Radio them and ask them to keep the British engaged for as long as it is safe to do so, and that we will prepare to sail immediately."

"Aye, aye, Sir."

"Captain to ship's company, prepare to sail."

The men sprung to life, each manning their posts, making

their assigned preparations. The crew had performed this operation hundreds of times and they were ready to get underway.

"Helm, conn, ease her forward.

"Set course for 270 degrees."

"Course at 270 degrees," came the reply.

"Half speed ahead."

"Half speed ahead."

The chief engineer kept the boat precisely trimmed. He had sailed with Schiffer for several years and was considered one of the best at running a U-boat.

U-491 sailed on the surface throughout the night without incident. At 0330 hours they received a wireless radio message from Captain Mangold, who was in the lead boat, U-739. He reported that several British vessels were on the horizon and a British Torpedo bomber had been sighted. He was preparing to dive and head north-northwesterly towards the Faroe Islands as they had planned.

Fifteen minutes later Captain Falke radioed that he was changing course with U-992 to head for Skagerrak Straight and that he would remain surfaced for as long as he could in an effort to draw the British forces away from the Channel. At almost the same time, Captain Hornbostel reported that they had picked up two destroyer masts and several cruisers off in the distance and that he was turning to head back to port.

"Radioman, relay my thanks to the three captains and my wish for a safe voyage."

"Aye, aye, Sir."

Three lookouts were posted on the bridge, searching for any British activity. They swept the seas with their night glasses. So far, nothing. It was dark and they were moving through the sea at fifteen knots, without running lights. Several hours later, as day began to break, there were still no signs of any British ships or planes.

The boat's cook, Otto Weiner, had prepared a meal for the crew. When a U-boat left port, it was well-stocked with fresh food. Every available space was stocked with food, including the forward head. Otto had pulled sausages and potatoes from the forward head, glancing at the tarp and wondering what was under it. He had been informed by Captain Schiffer that it was top secret cargo that had to be delivered under orders of the Fuehrer. It was not to be disturbed for any reason. That was enough for Weiner. He didn't chance looking under it.

They continued sailing southwesterly, making good time on the surface. The decoy seemed to have worked since they hadn't spotted any British ships or aircraft by the time they reached the narrowest part of the Channel, fifty miles between Dover, England and Calais, France.

Just after nightfall, the first officer was on the bridge when the lookout reported, "Ships fifteen degrees off the starboard bow. Planes at one o'clock."

The alarm bell sounded the call to action.

"Make preparations for diving."

"Aye Sir."

"Bridge to con, ship has been rigged for diving."

"Bridge, this is the Captain, I have the con.

"Clear the bridge, on diving stations."

The crew scrambled to their assigned stations with much-practiced efficiency.

The first officer was the last to leave the bridge, heading down the conning tower. With a deft clockwise movement, he turned the wheel to seal the hatch.

"DIVE, DIVE," came word over the announcement circuit.

Three blasts sounded on the alarm and echoed throughout the boat.

"Open ballast tanks," the chief engineer barked.

On that order the ballast tank vents, a series of rectangular openings on either side of the bow of the boat, were opened to allow water in to enable the boat to submerge. However, the relief valve on diving tank No. 7 stuck in the closed position, creating an imbalance in the weight of U-491 and leaving it partially submerged with its stern sticking up into the air. An easy target.

"Captain, we have a problem," shouted Schneider. "No. 7 relief valve is stuck. I've got two men working on it. Hopefully they can get it fixed before the Brits get here."

He knew he should have replaced it before they sailed, but he also knew that the Captain was anxious to get underway, so he decided against it. Now, it could cost him his rank, or worse.

Sometimes mechanical problems send U-boats to the bottom. Other times, the gods are with them. This time the gods were onboard. Schneider picked up a heavy wrench and banged it against the side of the valve. Three more strikes and it worked. Water began flowing, and soon the boat leveled off.

"Captain, the valve is repaired. We can dive."

"DIVE, DIVE," came over the announcement circuit.

The crew quickly finished the dive procedures and soon were 150 feet below the surface of the sea.

Now they waited. Sweat covered the brows of everyone aboard. Every crew member felt his heart pounding. They glanced upward as if they could see if a British ship was overhead ready to roll a string of depth charges onto them. It was silent. Dead silent.

46

The radioman wore the headphones and listened for the 'pings' that would indicate that British ships were approaching or that they had been picked up on Asdic, the British Royal Navy's primary underwater detection device.

The radioman tuned out everything except the silence coming through his headphones. Suddenly he heard the unmistakable slow, steady grinding noise of propellers through the hydrophones. They were approaching from forty-five degrees off the starboard bow. He quickly recorded the information on a sheet of paper and sent it to the captain.

Any other U-boat captain would be excited to be in this position. Under cover of darkness, with British ships approaching the area, and not having been detected yet, they would be looking for a sure kill or two. Schiffer's problem was that they had no torpedoes on board, so all they could do was sit, and wait, and hope they wouldn't be detected. If they were, the British would make short work of them.

They waited in silence. Anxious eyes glanced around the boat. Looking, listening, anticipating the worst. Feeling helpless with no torpedoes. The radioman picked up signals that indicated that the ships were running nearly parallel to them approximately 800 yards away. There were two of them. He sat rigid in his seat, expecting to hear a "ping" at any moment, indicating that they had been detected. He sat, they listened, he waited. Slowly, ever so slowly, the two ships passed by the starboard side of U-491. Their sounds grew fainter and gradually were lost in the night.

After sitting there for nearly an hour, Captain Schiffer gave the command, "All ahead one third."

The boat began to move forward, past the coast of Cherbourg, France, near the end of the English Channel.

"Take it up to periscope depth," commanded Captain Schiffer.

The chief engineer brought the boat to just below the surface. "Up periscope."

Captain Schiffer, looked out at the Channel through the crosshairs of the periscope. Slowly he rotated it 360^0 half expecting to see British destroyers or cruisers through the sight. He saw nothing. It was quiet.

"Down periscope.

"Standby to surface.

"Prepare to surface."

Two minutes later they were on the surface. As soon as Schneider shut off the electric motors and fired up the diesel engines, with the calm seas and the current from astern, they were running at 14 knots.

They made great time sailing throughout the night and on into the next day. They dove once, when planes were spotted far off on the horizon, escaping detection.

Sixteen uneventful hours later they were off Bishop's Rock, on the southwest corner of Britain, heading out of the Channel and into to the Celtic Sea.

Once they cleared the English Channel, Captain Schiffer gave the order, "Set course to 38^0 72' North and 27^0 03' West, full speed ahead. We are heading to the Azores."

Sixty hours later they were two miles offshore of Praia da Vitoria, Terceira, Azores.

◆

PRAIA DA VITORIA, THE BEACH OF THE VICTORY, IS located on the eastern end of the island of Terceira, in the Azores Islands. Two natural barriers that form a narrow entrance from the sea protects its large harbor. Captain

Schiffer was familiar with the harbor and the town. He had been there on numerous earlier occasions when German vessels could freely stop to refuel. This visit was far different from the others.

After safely sailing more than 1800 nautical miles from Hamburg, U-491 was now submerged at 150 feet one mile outside the harbor of Praia da Vitoria. The boat had arrived in mid-afternoon and had remained submerged for two reasons: first, they weren't to send the agreed upon signal until 0100 hours; second, the British/American airbase at Lajes Field was located just a few miles away. They were equally compelling reasons.

◆

The Azores, an autonomous region of Portugal, are a group of nine islands located in the Atlantic 850 miles from continental Portugal. Prior to 1943, under Portuguese Prime Minister Antonio Salazar, Portugal officially maintained neutrality with respect to the war. German U-boats freely entered the Azores and often used it for refueling and resupplying before carrying out their attacks on American and Canadian cargo ships during the Battle of the Atlantic.

Hitler recognized the strategic importance of the Azores, and in 1940 issued Fuehrer Directive Number 18 which outlined a plan to invade Portugal if the British or Americans attempted to establish a foothold there. The Allies developed a plan, called Operation Alacrity, to do just that. The plan entailed setting up bases in the Azores regardless of whatever protests Salazar might make. However, there was no need to implement the plan because in 1943 the British requested, and Portugal agreed, to allow the British to establish bases on the islands. The first one to be built was Lages Field, a broad, flat sea terrace on the Island of Terceira, a mere three kilometers northwest of where U-491 was now submerged.

◆

EVERY NIGHT AT 0100 HOURS FOR THE PAST TWO months Antone Nunes had gone down to the edge of the harbor to look for the lights. Several months earlier he had received a letter from his father-in-law, Heinrich Schiffer, asking him to look for three flashing lights followed by two more outside the harbor of Praia da Vitoria. The letter arrived from Hamburg through the civil post office, rather than the Feldpost, or German Military Mail System. It had been routed through the Netherlands and then on to the Azores.

Antone didn't know why he was asked to sit at the edge of the harbor awaiting a signal, but he knew that it must be important if Captain Schiffer would risk sailing into what was now Allied waters, and so close to the airfield. Night after night he had sat in his truck near the entrance to the harbor waiting for a signal, and night after night he returned home only to return the following night.

Tonight, he expected the routine to be the same, but it wasn't. At precisely 0100 hours he spotted the signal several kilometers out to sea. Three short flashes followed by two short flashes, just as the letter he received had indicated. Taking his flashlight, he replied with two short flashes followed by three short flashes, the agreed upon reply signal. One returning flash confirmed.

Clouds hid most of the stars and the moon played hide and seek behind them as Antone left his truck and walked to the dock where his 28-foot Chris-Craft 557 was moored. The

Bugio, or *Little Devil*, the name of the dog-like servant of Saint Bartolomew, the Portuguese patron saint of sailors and fishermen, was a splendid boat. He had purchased it with inheritance money left by his father. He could not have afforded it otherwise.

He fired up the engine, slipped the mooring lines off the cleats, then flipped the switch to turn on the running lights and pointed the bow towards the exit from the harbor. The onshore breeze carried the fresh sea air to his nose as he passed between the two jetties and headed into the Atlantic. A short time later he approached U-491, pulled alongside, and threw the bow and stern lines to waiting crew members. They dropped a Jacob's ladder over the side of the boat and Antone climbed aboard to the outstretched hand of Captain Schiffer.

"How good to see you after so many years," said Schiffer.

"It has been a long time, but I'm glad you arrived safely. Did you run into any difficulty?"

Captain Schiffer described their encounter in the English Channel as Antone listened intently.

"We hear rumors that the war will end soon. Is that true?"

"The Fuehrer doesn't believe so, but most of the rest of us see the end coming. That's why it was important to make this trip now. We have to transfer some crates to your boat and then to your home."

With that, Schiffer ordered the chief quartermaster to rig a cargo transfer basket between the two boats. Earlier that day the captain had opened the forward head to show him the eleven crates so that he could plan for their transfer. Now, the quartermaster directed two crewmen to go below and retrieve two lines, one of which would stretch between the two boats. He also directed them to bring up the small cargo net.

Fifteen minutes later a line was stretched securely between the two boats with the cargo net fastened to the line with a pulley. A second line was fastened to either side of the cargo net, one that reached to the Bugio for pulling the cargo towards the boat, and the other fastened to the bridge of U-491 for retrieving the cargo net. It was the standard configuration for transferring small cargo at sea.

"Head back to your boat, Antone, I'll have two seamen accompany you to receive the transfer."

Antone, somewhat awkwardly, worked his way down the Jacob's ladder followed by the two seamen. They waited on the deck of the *Bugio* while the quartermaster took several men below to the forward head to show them the crates that had to be moved.

"Be careful," he said, "we can't lose these over the side."

The men carefully brought the crates to the bridge, one at a time. Schiffer himself oversaw the transfer, directing the men to place the first crate into the cargo net and secure it with a short piece of line. Checking that it was secure, he then directed his quartermaster to execute the transfer.

"Haul away."

The seamen onboard the *Bugio* pulled the line fastened to the cargo net and moments later the first crate arrived safely. Antone took the crate and stowed it in the cabin. One by one, for the next thirty minutes, each of the remaining crates was transferred from U-491 to the *Bugio*.

"First Officer, you have the con."

"Aye, aye Sir."

"I will accompany Mr. Nunes to shore with the cargo. Submerge until 0400 hours. At that time bring it up to periscope depth and watch for us. We should be here no later than 0430 so that we can leave before daybreak.

52

"Aye, aye Sir."

The two sailors on the Bugio returned to U-491 and Captain Schiffer left the boat to join Nunes. With a salute to First Officer Muller, Schiffer turned to Antone and said, "Let's head ashore."

Antone took the helm and started up the engine as the crew members onboard U-491 cast off the bow and stern lines. He turned on the running lights and set the course towards the entrance of the harbor. A slight flood tide pushed them along and he held steady at three knots as he approached the entrance of the harbor. Once inside the breakwaters he steered to starboard, went through another smaller breakwater and then made for the dock.

As they approached the dock, Antone swung the boat around 180⁰ as Schiffer dropped the fenders over the port gunwales to keep the boat from getting banged up as it moored. Antone slowly brought the *Bugio* alongside the dock then idled the engine, holding the boat against the dock so that Schiffer could heave the bow and stern lines onto the dock. Once the lines were resting on the dock, Schiffer jumped off the boat and belayed the lines to the cleats, making the boat fast against the dock. Antone cut the engine and looked at Schiffer.

"Now to get them home."

Antone pulled his truck alongside the edge of the dock and in fifteen minutes the crates were loaded into the back.

"Let's head home. Heda will know that you are here because I've been gone for so long. Usually I'm home by 1:30."

He started the engine and slowly drove down Rua da Alfandega, alongside the harbor and towards the center of Praia da Vitoria. A few brightly colored shops lined the street across from the harbor, but they were all closed at this hour.

Two minutes later Antone turned right and slowed the truck as they turned onto a cobblestone street. Immediately in front of them the street divided to either side of what appeared to be a tiny, ornate, white chapel trimmed in blue. It had a white wooden cross on top, and just under the intricate façade was the year 1877. It was no more than fifteen feet by fifteen feet square with a small white fence in front of it.

Antone noticed Heinrich studying the building.

"See the small mosaic on the sidewalk in front of it, with a white anchor in the middle? It says *IMPERIO DOS MARITIMOS*. It is called Empire of the Seafarers, and is dedicated to the seamen of Santa Cruz. It looks like a chapel, but it's not. It's used to store the crowns and flags that we use on Trinity Sunday when we honor the Holy Spirit. We have a parade with bands and celebrate Mass. The Saturday after Trinity Sunday is when we have the tourada a corda, the roped bullfights. It is a wonderful event in Praia da Vitoria and the whole town turns out for it."

Antone took the street to the right of the Imperio, Rua do Conde de Vila Flor. It was a narrow street lined with interconnected small, colorful, single-story, stucco houses. Two-foot wide, stone inlaid sidewalks were the only thing that separated the houses from the street.

Moments later Antone turned right onto Rua Padre Cruz and stopped in front of small white house with salmon trim and green colored window shutters. The door had similar green shutters on either side that ran the entire height of the door. Adjacent to the house was a walled-in yard with a green iron gate leading into it. Schieffer could see a large garden just behind the gate.

"We have one of the few homes in this section of Praia da Vitoria that has any open space attached to it," boasted Antone.

Heinrich wasn't interested in the house, however, because at that moment an obviously pregnant young woman threw open the front door, stepped out, and ran over to him. She wrapped her arms around him and looked up with tears in her eyes.

"Father, it's been so long. I've missed you and Ulbrecht."

"I've missed you too, Heda. And what is this?" he said with a smile as he gently patted her protruding midsection.

"Your grandchild, as if you couldn't figure that out!"

Heinrich grinned from ear-to-ear and kissed her on her forehead.

"How is my brother?"

"Ulbrecht is fine. He came to Hamburg a short time ago, but now he's back in Berlin at the Kaiser Friedrich Museum. He sends his love and hopes we can all get together once this war is over. I would like that."

"So would I," said Heda as she hugged her father again.

"Come in. I know it's early, but let me make you some breakfast, you must be hungry for some home cooking."

"Wonderful, we'll unload the truck while you cook for us."

Fifteen minutes later, ten paintings were stacked against the wall in a small room in the far-right back corner of the house. Heinrich had looked at the back of the crates when they brought them into the room, and set the one with the number 11 on it aside.

The smell of breakfast cooking drew them back to the kitchen.

"Breakfast will be ready in five minutes. Make yourself comfortable in the living room. I'll call you when it's ready."

Heinrich and Antone went into the small living room. A long narrow table sat in front of the far wall, and several pictures were arranged on it. Heinrich walked over and picked up one of his late wife, Grazia. He stared at it for a long time before setting it back on the table next to a vase of fresh, fragrant purple lilacs.

55

"We have several lilac trees," said Antone. "Terceira means 'the lilac island' and the lilacs are in bloom all over the island at this time of year. I always tell Heda that they come out to celebrate her birthday, which is today!"

Heinrich was embarrassed that he hadn't remembered his daughter's birthday, and felt guilty. But then he realized he had a wonderful birthday present for her.

"Breakfast is ready," called Heda from the kitchen.

Heinrich and Antone went to the kitchen and sat down at the table as Heda carried two platters over to them.

"These are ananas. You call them pineapples. We get those when the boat comes from Sao Miguel, which isn't very often these days," she said as she set the platter on the table. "And this is pineapple custard," said Heda, pointing to the three small cups on the side of the platter.

She went back to the stove and brought a teakettle to the table.

"Green tea," she said as she filled three cups.

"And here is some Massa Sovada, a sweet bread. Most people only make it for Christmas and Easter, but I make it all the time. I have some for you to bring back with you."

While they were eating breakfast, Heinrich told Heda the story of how he and her mother met in Reggio Calabria, Italy when he was there on holiday. He also told her about her two sisters, both of whom died in infancy. She never knew about them. Heda was quiet as she sipped her tea, imagining what her relationship with her sisters might have been had they lived.

After they finished breakfast Henrich suddenly exclaimed, "Happy birthday, my daughter, I have a present for you."

With that, he got up from the table, went into the room where the crates were stacked, picked up the one with number 11 on the back, and carried it into the kitchen.

56

Turning to Antone, he asked, "Do you have something to open the crate with?"

Antone went outside, came back with a hammer and a screwdriver, and handed them to Heinrich. Carefully, he removed the slat from the top of the crate, set it aside, then pulled out the paper that was packed around the painting inside.

Slowly, while Antone held the crate, Heinrich eased the painting out, looked at it, and then turned it around to show Heda.

"This is called *The Vision of Saint Bruno,* painted by a very famous artist, Jordaens. It was in the Kaiser Friedrich Museum, where you brother works. Your mother and I often went there to look at it. Your brother saved it from being destroyed by the bombing. It is my birthday present to you!"

The painting depicted St. Bruno kneeling with outstretched hands in front of Jesus Christ, who looked down on him while two angels hovered above. His outstretched hand rested on the left shoulder of St. Bruno. Below and to the right, eight people stood in amazement at the vision in front of them.

"Your mother always believed that the two angels were your two sisters. That is one of the reasons why she loved this painting."

For the next few minutes he shared another—far more meaningful—story about the painting.

"Let's go hang it," said Antone, as he picked it up and walked to the living room.

He already knew where he would place it. He asked Heinrich to help him move the table with the pictures and lilacs on it away from the wall. Two minutes later they moved the table back against the wall underneath where *The Vision of St. Bruno* now hung.

57

"The sun will be rising soon, and we must get you back to your boat," said Antone.

"I have some food and wine for you to bring back," said Heda, as she pointed to two large boxes in the corner of the kitchen.

"My crew will certainly enjoy that," said Henrich as he got up and went over to his daughter.

She stood, wrapped her arms around him, and held him tightly.

"I hope this war ends soon so we can all be together again," she said as tears filled her eyes.

"We will be my daughter, we will. This bloody war is about over, and when it is I will be back to see my grandchild! Perhaps I'll move here since Germany has been nearly destroyed by all the bombing. It will be a mess for years."

"I must go now," he said as he took her head in his hands and kissed her on her forehead. They held each other for several minutes, neither one wanting to let go.

They loaded the two boxes into the back of the truck and headed to the harbor. Soon they were aboard the *Bugio* and underway to U-491.

"The ten crates at your house contain paintings from the Kaiser Friedrich Museum. We have saved them from destruction, and as soon as the war is over I'll be back to take them to Heda's Grandfather's house, my father's, in the United States. They live in the town of Mattapoisett, in Massachusetts."

"Does he know that you will be bringing them to him? And what is he going to do with them?"

"Yes, before I left Hamburg, I sent him a letter letting him know that I would be delivering the paintings to you here in Praia da Vitoria, and that we would get them to him after the

58

war. He has a way to sell them, though I don't know how. If you look inside the crate that we opened you'll find a list of the paintings along with his address in the States. You'll want to save it in a safe place."

"Is it right to keep those paintings?"

"The museum will certainly be destroyed, as would these paintings if we had left them there. Besides, the Russians are looting all of the art that they find throughout Germany, and the paintings would only end up in one of Stalin's many homes, never to be seen again. They'll be safe here until I can come back to pick them up."

Minutes later they drew alongside U-491. The crew dropped a ladder over the side and before he scrambled up to his boat, Heinrich gave Antone a long hug.

As Heinrich drew back and took Antone's hand in a firm handshake, he said, "Take good care of my grandchild. I'll be back to see you all soon!"

Moments later the *Bugio* pulled away from U-491 and headed back to the harbor of Praia da Vitoria. The captain waved one more time as he descended the ladder and closed the hatch behind him. Three hours from now they'd be well northeast of the Azores.

◆

Task Group 22.3

THE USS GUADALCANAL, CVE-60, WAS FOUR DAYS OUT OF Casablanca where it had stopped for refueling and replenishing after crossing the Atlantic from Norfolk, Virginia. The escort carrier, under the command of Captain Daniel V. Gallery, Jr., was the flagship of Task Group 22.3, which had responsibility for searching and destroying German U-boats in the North Atlantic. Task Force 22.3, comprised of two battleships, three cruisers and several auxiliary ships, already had four "kills," evidenced by the four freshly painted Nazi flags on the conning tower. Its hunting ground was the area between the Azores and Gibraltar, the sea lane used by German U-boats coming out of the Bay of Biscay. Now cruising Northeast of the Azores, Radioman Third Class Newman just received a message from the Canadian freighter Saskatoon. The ship was carrying four thousand tons of pig iron from Bell Island, Newfoundland, to be made into steel after it arrived in England.

Newman left the Combat Information Center and approached the bridge to deliver the message to Captain Gallery who, as the skipper, never left the bridge when they were at sea.

"Request permission to enter the bridge, Sir."

"Granted."

"Message received from the freighter Saskatoon, Sir," he said as he handed Captain Gallery the message.

Gallery slowly read,

Detected periscope at N 39 degrees 32 minutes and W 26 degrees and 01 minutes.

Partially submerged, but stern is in the air. It seems to be holding position.

Can you assist?

Handing the message to Lieutenant Commander Scheinberg, he asked, "What's our distance?"

Scheinberg looked at the message, then walked over and gave the coordinates to Sonarman First Class Vaughan.

"Distance?"

Sonar enabled the ship to locate anything below the sea up to forty miles away. Vaughan sent out a signal, directed at the coordinates and waited for the echo to bounce back from the target.

"Ping."

Vaughan had spent many years listening to pings, and he quickly calculated the distance.

He turned to Lt. Commander Scheinberg and said, "Distance 27 miles, Sir."

The 'ping' was also heard on U-491. Without exception, every man aboard froze, knowing that they had been detected. The chief engineer was the first to refocus, turning his attention back to repairing the No. 7 relief valve, which was stuck, preventing the U-boat from submerging.

The rest of the crew stood by helpless, with the exception of the sonarman, who continued to listen for the ominous pings.

"Captain, they have us targeted," said the sonarman after hearing several pings in quick succession.

"What's the status on that valve," the captain asked the chief engineer."

"I can fix it, but I need another thirty minutes."

Reflexively, each man looked at their watch. Thirty minutes was a long time when the enemy had you in their sight. Even though the boat had pulled in fresh air from the surface before they dived, the men were sweating profusely. To a man, they realized their fate depended on getting that valve fixed.

◆

The seas were relatively calm and it was approaching dusk. The bright orange globe of the sun was inching towards the horizon. Above and around it, brilliant splashes of orange and yellow merged with bright reds, then faded into a deep blue sky. Normally, they wouldn't launch an air attack at night because it was extremely difficult to spot a target in the dark. On this night, though, there would be just enough time, and there would be a full moon.

"Radioman, send a message to the Saskatoon. Inform them of our position, and ask them if they have flares aboard. Tell them we will send out our Avengers and Wildcats."

"Aye, aye, Sir."

He returned to the radio and sent the message to the Saskatoon. A few minutes later he received a reply.

We have flares, and there has been no movement by the boat.
What is your ETA?

The radioman returned to the bridge and handed the message to the Captain.

"Send them a message that we are on our way and to watch for our planes. When they spot them, tell them to shoot their flares over the sub to mark its position for us."

"Aye, aye, Sir."

While Newman was sending the message, Captain Gallery gave the orders:

"Prepare to launch—two wildcats and two avengers. Dispatch them to the coordinates.

"Change bearing to 215 degrees."

Below decks, squadron leader Lieutenant Commander Larry Lapidow, along with Lieutenant Rick Nickerson, Lieutenant Mitch Schadtle, and Lieutenant Junior Grade John Murphy were eating the traditional meal served to flight crews before they took off on a mission.

"Nice of the galley to make a last meal for the condemned men," Lapidow said jokingly as he dove into the steak and eggs in front of him.

All four men received their flight training at the Naval Air Station at Quonset Point, Rhode Island, though only Nickerson and Schadtle had been in the same class. They had been serving in the same squadron for a little over two years and were seasoned pilots with numerous "kills" among them. All four were recently ordered to the Guadalcanal.

After finishing their meal, the men scrubbed in preparation for their flight. Thorough scrubbing would reduce the possibility of infection should they be wounded. Now, they were in the squadron ready room getting into their flight gear and going over their instructions.

"Mitch, Rick, you're up first. John and I will be off your left and right wings. We were informed that none of our subs are in the area so we are looking at a U-boat."

Schadtle and Nickerson flew Grumman F4F Wildcats, outstanding fighter planes.

"We'll be right behind you," said Lapidow.

He and Murphy flew Grumman TBF Avengers, highly effective torpedo bombers.

The blaring horn of "flight quarters" sounded over the intercom.

"Pilots, man your planes."

"Pilots, man your planes."

◆

"Can't you fix that valve any faster? We're going to get killed," yelled one of the newer members of the U-boat crew.

"You want to fix it?" snapped the chief engineer.

The man was silent.

63

Crew members of U-boats knew that at any moment their life could end. That was the risk as well as the exhilaration of serving on submarine crew. Some men welcomed the danger while others pushed that possibility from their minds. At this moment, however, every man knew his life was in the hands of the chief engineer. They didn't talk, they didn't scream. Most prayed.

Captain Schiffer had always been aware that things could go terribly wrong on a U-boat. Many of his fellow captains had gone to the bottom of the ocean, sent there by a torpedo or mechanical failure. Usually, he was able to push the thought of that out of his mind. Now, however, he was deeply concerned.

He thought of Heda, who was carrying his grandchild. *Was it a grandson, or a granddaughter? I might never know.* Numbness engulfed him, as if he was in a dream. His eyes looked upward, and before him appeared the painting of *The Vision of Saint Bruno*. He saw Saint Bruno's outstretched hands calling to him. *Is that a sign?*

◆

While the pilots were in the ready room, the Guadalcanal had been brought around to heading 255 degrees so that the bow was now into the wind for takeoff. Massive elevators had brought two Avengers and two Wildcats to the flight deck from the hangar bay, two decks below. They were now sitting on the apron, ready for their crews. The Wildcats were parked ahead of the Avengers since they would take off first to provide cover for the bombers.

"Let's go for a ride," Nickerson said as the pilots left the ready room and headed up to the flight deck.

As they exited the room, each man reached up to tap the

picture of the sea monster Gunakadeit, painted over the door. According to legend, the monster brought good luck.

The catapult machinery room was one deck below the flight deck. Machinist Mate First Class LaBella was in charge of operations, and he and his crew were checking each component of the catapult launching equipment to ready the catapult, a hydraulic cylinder as long as a football field, for the launch. A cable from the catapult was connected to the nose of the plane through a track on the flight deck. During the next few minutes each plane would be hooked up to the catapult and launched.

"Liquid level okay.
"Buffers out.
"Tracks clear.
"Supply level, okay.
"Open supply valve."

During the next few minutes the crew carefully reviewed every item on the checklist to ensure a quick and safe launch.

Meanwhile, on the flight deck, Lapidow and his crew had manned their planes and were going through their own checklist. Lieutenant Schadtle was in the first position in his Wildcat.

"Engine on."

Two minutes later he confirmed:

"Oil inlet temperature good.
"Cylinder head temperature good.
"Engine oil pressure good."

He tested the rudder and brake pedals. *Working fine.*

The Wildcats were designed with a Grumman Sto-Wing folding wing system which allowed more aircraft to be stored on an aircraft carrier. When planes are parked, their wings are folded upward so that they utilize less space on the deck. When they are being prepared for launch the wings are unfolded and locked into place.

"Spreading wings.

"Wings locked."

Moments later the intercom blared:

"Stand by to launch planes by catapult.

"Stand by to launch planes by catapult."

Schadtle received the order to taxi his plane down the guideline over the catapult track.

Here we go. Weather looks good. We should be back in short order.

Schadtle pushed forward on the throttle and slowly moved his Avenger forward until the front wheel hit the positioning stop that indicated that the plane was in the proper alignment for takeoff. The towbar was connected to the plane's nosegear and the hydraulic piston system would soon propel the plane forward off the bow of the Guadalcanal towards its target.

With the first plane in position on the catapult track, Murphy was given the signal to move his plane into the number one spot, ready to taxi onto the catapult. His wings were down and locked, and his engine had been running for several minutes. He pushed the throttle forward and moved his Avenger into position, ready to advance to the launch position as soon as Schadtle was airborne.

With the holdback and towbar attached, the stop chocks were removed and the countdown began. Below, the catapult officer was opening the valves to fill the catapult cylinders with high-pressure steam. They would drive the pistons forward at high speed and throw the plane into takeoff over the bow of the Guadalcanal. Schadtle sat in the cockpit, and in his great baritone voice sang the song he sang at every launch:

Yank her away, my boys, yank her away.
Straight off the bow we fly to fight another fray —ay —ay —ay;
Nothing can keep our boys, from victory.
We'll hunt those Nazi boats and send them to the bottom of the sea.

Petty Officer First Class, Don Larson, the control board officer, was sitting in the catapult control pod, a small, encased command station with a transparent dome protruding above the flight deck on the port side of the Guadalcanal. From there he exchanged signals, through a dual light system, with the catapult machine crew below deck.

A petty officer stood on deck just off the plane's starboard side and held up a chalkboard that listed the final safety precautions. As Schadtle ran down the list, he checked each instrument and setting on the control panels in his cockpit. When he finished, he gave a thumbs up to the petty officer.

Soon, he was given the signal to advance the throttle to full, or military, power. He eased his feet off the brakes and the Wildcat strained hard against the holdback unit.

Satisfied that his plane was ready for launch, he saluted the catapult officer, who in turn signaled "all set for launching" to the bridge. A green flag was displayed at the bridge, a warning horn sounded, and the command "launch aircraft" blared from the speakers on deck.

Schadtle braced in his seat, knowing that in just moments his Wildcat would rapidly accelerate and launch him over the bow of the Guadalcanal. The throttle was wide open and his straining plane reminded him of his pet lab pulling at its leash, nearly taking him off his feet.

Larson checked the flight deck signal receiver, used to exchange signals with the catapult room. Three lights could be lit on the receiver, first ready, standby, final ready.

The machinery room was ready and announced, "**Standby to check signal light**."

"**First Ready**" was sent from the machinery room to the catapult control board topside, illuminating the "first ready" light.

"**Flight deck standby**," signaled Larson to the catapult room

"**Final Ready**," sent topside where Larson made a final check of the catapult settings, the wind speed and direction, and the ship's heading, and then gave the signal to launch:

"**Fire**."

Below deck the catapult operators activated the catapult that rapidly dragged Schadtle and his Wildcat forward by the launch bar and off the bow of the Guadalcanal, accelerating them from zero to 150 miles per hour in just over two seconds.

"Flaps up, thanks for the lift," said Schadtle as he raised the nose of his plane upwards and away from the ship.

In short succession Lapidow, Nickerson, and Murphy were launched, and they soon caught up with Schadtle. The four pilots quickly maneuvered into formation, with Schadtle and Murphy in the lead in their Wildcats, and Lapidow and Nickerson off their port and starboard sides in their Avengers.

Lieutenant Commander Lapidow was the Squadron Leader and directed operations.

"Pico One to squadron, maintain course at 255 degrees. We should be there quickly.

"If it's on the surface, Schadtle and Murphy, you go in first to take out any deckguns. Nickerson and I will follow with the torpedoes. Otherwise, we'll reverse positions. Maintain radio silence until we reach our target."

For the next ten minutes they flew towards the target. Although the sun hadn't quite reached the horizon when they spotted the conning tower of the sub, the *Saskatoon* had launched its flares as soon as the planes came into view. The pilots flew in a wide arc around the target so they would be approaching from the west, with the sun behind them and directly in the eyes of any crew members on deck manning antiaircraft guns.

"We have target."

The boat's stern was in the air and the bow was submerged. It appeared to be diving, but it wasn't creating a wake or turbulence.

"It looks like it's dead in the water," Lapidow said over his radio. "This could be an easy one, but be alert. Maybe they have a problem. They haven't dived."

"Well, if they don't have a problem already, they are about to," replied Nickerson.

"Approach at 90 degrees off their starboard beam."

Lapidow and Nickerson dove and began their strafing run to knock out any antiaircraft fire. They expected to see tracers from the deck guns on the boat below. None came.

This is too easy!

They dropped to three hundred feet and ran straight at the sub, broadside.

Still no fire.

At 400 yards they opened up their .50-caliber machine guns and strafed the deck from bow to stern with armor piercing slugs. Sprays of water kicked up the full length of the sub.

No return fire.

They shot in bursts rather than streams of fire so they wouldn't heat up the guns or use up their ammunition.

After unleashing their firepower, the pilots pulled their aircraft up and flew directly over the boat, making a wide looping arc as the bombers began their descent.

Lapidow and Nickerson followed the fighters in. Normally, when dropping a torpedo, they aimed where the sub was going to be, not where it was. Nickerson had lots of practice with that, developed on his many duck hunting outings when he was growing up in Maine. Newer flyers needed to use a Launching Data Chart to determine the "aiming point," but Nickerson had enough experience that he could use his "seaman's eye" to determine the radar slant range, or how far in front of the boat he needed to aim so that the torpedo and boat would meet at the same point. That wouldn't be necessary on this mission, however, as the boat was stationary in the water.

♦

Below the surface, the chief engineer spoke to the captain. "Another two minutes and it'll be fixed."

"Good work," replied the captain. "Man your stations and be prepared to dive as soon as I give the command," he ordered the crew.

Relieved, the men scrambled to their assigned stations and readied the boat to dive. The seconds ticked by with agonizing slowness as they awaited the captain's order. They were in a race, but were now confident that they would win it.

♦

Straight in and let 'em fly.

Nickerson went in first, dropping from 5,000 to 3,000 feet at a 70-degree angle. When he leveled off, he ran through the bombing checklist:

Mixture control, full rich
Rudder tabs, one and half units right
Bomb doors open
Diving flaps open

He pointed the nose of the plane directly at the target. There was a saying among pilots, "The plane is the gun and the bomb is the bullet." He didn't need to look at the bow wave and wake to determine the boat's speed. There were neither. He dove again, then leveled off at 800 feet. Fifteen hundred yards from the target, he released the torpedo. It hit the water four hundred yards from the boat and ran hot, straight and normal.

Moments later the boat exploded, sending plumes of water hundreds of feet into the air. Nickerson didn't see it immediately, as he had pulled back on the stick and quickly gained altitude as he flew over the destruction below.

Lapidow was right behind him and dropped his torpedo on what was left of the boat. Water again burst into the air, though not nearly as high as when the first torpedo hit. As the eruption slowly settled back into the sea, Lapidow and Nickerson brought their Avengers into sweeping turns in opposite directions, then flew back over the target for one final look. All that remained was an extensive debris field floating in a large pool of oil and air bubbles. No bodies were visible.

The two pilots pulled back on the throttles, quickly caught up with Schadtle and Murphy, then headed back to CVE-60 to paint up the score, another Nazi flag, on the Guadalcanal's conning tower.

PART TWO
1970

"The sea does not reward those who are too anxious,
too greedy, or too impatient."

— Anne Morrow Lindbergh

Atlantic Crossing

HURRICANE EDWIN FORECAST/ADVISORY
NUMBER 17
NWS NATIONAL HURRICANE CENTER MIAMI FL
1800 CDT TUE AUG 25, 1970

A HURRICANE WARNING IS IN EFFECT FOR
PUERTO RICO. INTERESTS ALONG THE COAST OF
NEW ENGLAND AND IN THE CANADIAN
MARITIMES SHOULD MONITOR THE PROGRESS OF
EDWIN.

HURRICANE CENTER LOCATED NEAR 17.26N, 65.30W
POSITION ACCURATE WITHIN 10 NM

PRESENT MOVEMENT TOWARD THE NORTH-
NORTHWEST OR 340 DEGREES AT 10 KT
MAX SUSTAINED WINDS 100 KT WITH GUSTS TO
130 KT

HURRICANE FORCE WINDS EXTEND OUTWARD
UP TO 115 MILES . . . 185 KM . . . FROM THE CENTER.

EDWIN IS A SLOW-MOVING HURRICANE THAT
WILL PRODUCE SIGNIFICANT DAMAGE.

FORECASTER EISNER

A THIN RED LINE SEPARATED THE SEA FROM THE SKY
announcing the sun and the start of a new day.

Red sky at night, sailor's delight; red sky at morning, sailors take warning, thought Antone as he pulled his pickup truck up to the dock where the *Bugio II* was moored.

"A storm's a coming," he said to his nephew Caetano, "but we'll be well out to sea by the time it hits here."

Caetano owned a winery on the Island of Pico and had built quite a reputation, not to mention a substantial fortune, for the excellent Vinho Verde that he produced year after year. His mother inherited it two years after his father deserted the family and was declared dead. It became his a few years ago after his mother passed away. A case of the latest vintage of the white wine sat in the back of the pickup truck.

Several hours earlier the two men had carefully loaded ten crates into the truck along with several boxes of food that Heda had packed for them: chourico, a spicy local sausage; fresh pineapples, bunches of grapes, and dried figs, grown on the nearby Island of Sao Miguel; vaquinha cheese; bacalhau, dried salted cod; green tea; and, some fresh baked masa souvlada, a light airy sweet bread. Antone kissed Heda and his daughter, Anna Grazia, goodbye and drove the short distance to the dock.

One-by-one Caetano lifted the crates from the back of the truck and carefully handed them to Antone, who was standing at the stern of the Bugio II. He took each crate below deck and stowed it forward in the cabin. When all ten crates were onboard he secured them with rope attached to the cleats on either side of the hull.

After the wooden crates were unloaded, Caetano handed down the boxes of food. Antone put the food in the refrigerator, with the exception of the fruit and masa souvlada. *We should have more than enough*, he thought.

As they had planned weeks earlier, once the truck was

unloaded Caetano drove it back to the house while Antone remained on the boat to go over the final checklist for the trip. He watched the truck turn up Rua da Alfandega; then he looked eastward. The top half of a bright red sun had climbed above the horizon and was slowly making its way into the morning sky.

During the next half hour Antone ran through the checklist and confirmed that the Bugio II was seaworthy. *The screws are tight and the heads are snug and level in their holes.* He methodically checked every switch and lever and verified that they were functioning properly. *The hatches and doors all latch properly. Fuel and water are at capacity. Bilge pump is working. The red port side running light, the green starboard side running light, as well as the white light at the top of the boat are all working.* Once they were underway he would have Caetano check that everything on deck was properly stowed and secured.

Antone had purchased the Bugio II a year earlier as a replacement for the smaller Bugio I that he had inherited from his father. The Bugio II was a Meridian Trojan, a 48-foot long range cruiser with a cruising speed of ten knots, and more than enough fuel capacity to carry them the 1600 nautical miles from Praia da Vitoria to their destination. He had fitted it with a diesel generator and a larger alternator to increase the amount of electricity that could be produced.

Antone was in the wheelhouse studying a chart of the North Atlantic when Caetano returned to the boat. A shiny gold chain was draped around his neck and an oval bronze medal of a man holding a crook in his left hand hung from it. Around the edge of the medal was the name *S. Francesco Di Paola.*

"Heda gave me this to wear for our trip. She said he's the Patron Saint of Boatmen and Mariners, and that it would bring us good luck."

Antone looked at the medal and recognized it as the one that his mother always wore when his father, John, went to sea. He hadn't seen it since his mother passed away and his father moved to the United States with one of his sons, Antone's older brother. That was many years ago. Another brother, Carlos, had left the Azores years ago and was never heard from again.

Antone reached into his vest pocket, pulled out a sheet of paper, and carefully read it. *Mattapoisett, a funny name for a town.* Antone had been corresponding with him for several months now to arrange for the delivery of the art. As years went by without hearing from Captain Schiffer, Antone had grown increasingly concerned about having the paintings in his house. He considered calling the authorities and surrendering them, but he knew they would ask a lot of questions. *Why do you have them? How did you get them? What did you plan to do with them? Why did it take you so long to get in touch with us? The war's been over nearly twenty-five years!* The same questions kept coming back to Antone: *What if they don't believe me? Will they send me to prison, away from Heda and Anna Grazia?* After agonizing for many months, he decided to get the paintings out of his house and to Mattapoisett.

He contacted his brother, who developed a plan for him to meet a fishing boat, the Theresa M, and transfer the art to it. Antone replied with a letter informing him of his departure date from Praia da Vitoria and his anticipated arrival date. Everything was in place, he thought, as he folded the paper and put it back into his vest pocket.

"Get ready to get underway," Antone said to Caetano as he slid into the center console in the wheelhouse.

Caetano was standing on the dock, ready to cast off the lines securing the Bugio II to the dock. Antone started the ventilation blowers and then flipped the battery switch. He then turned the key to start the twin diesel engines. He listened carefully for a few seconds, checked the gauges, and then, convinced that the engines were running smoothly, gave the order to Caetano. "Cast off the bow line."

Caetano removed the bow line from its cleat and tossed it onto the deck. With the throttle in idle, Antone moved the clutch to forward, nudging the bow of the Bugio II slightly away from the dock. After casting off the stern line, Caetano threw it onto the boat and jumped aboard as Antone advanced the throttle, pulled the boat away from the dock, and pointed the bow towards the breakwater that led to the Atlantic Ocean.

He brought the Bugio II's speed to four knots, just under the limit for the harbor. As they cruised towards the entrance of the breakwater, he glanced at the brilliant red sky overhead and knew they'd be driving through a heavy storm before the day was done.

"Secure the lines and then come to the wheelhouse," Antone shouted to Caetano over the loud hum of the engines.

Two minutes later Caetano entered the wheelhouse.

"Take a tour of the deck and make sure everything is secured. We'll be running into a storm before long and we don't need to lose anything before the Azores disappear over our stern. And check the crates below deck to make sure they are tied fast."

Caetano left to conduct his inspection as Antone steered the boat through the breakwater and into the open sea. As soon as he cleared the breakwater he pushed the throttle forward until the boat reached its cruising speed of ten knots. Seagulls flocked off the stern hoping for any scraps of food, or better yet, fish chum, that might be tossed overboard. They'd be disappointed.

"All right, so where are we headed?" asked Caetano.

Antone had deliberately kept him in the dark so that he wouldn't inadvertently slip and let Heda know their true destination. She assumed they were going on a lengthy fishing trip and to visit friends on several of the Azores Islands—Pico and Faial. Since he hadn't had the boat very long, she assumed he wanted to take it for a good test run. *It's good that she doesn't know the truth.*

"Newfoundland."

"That's across the Atlantic! Why Newfoundland?"

"Let me set our course and then I'll tell you."

Antone already knew the course they would be taking, as he had studied the chart for months prior to their departure, but he checked it one more time.

"We'll start off heading northwest, but we'll make several adjustments along the way."

He turned the wheel slightly to port until the compass read 293 degrees, then straightened out the Bugio II as Terceira grew smaller in the distance off the stern. The sky had turned from a brilliant red to a dark gray as storm clouds rolled in from the southeast.

"Go below and get the foul weather gear out and bring it up here. We'll need it soon. Then I'll fill you in on what's happening.

A few minutes later Caetano returned with two sets of foul weather gear and set them on a bench in the corner of the wheelhouse.

"Now, why are we going to Newfoundland?"

For the next half hour Antone told him the story of the crates that were stowed below deck.

"Near the end of World War II, during the bombing of Berlin, Heda's father, Captain Heinrich Schiffer, and his son,

80

Ulbrecht, took some paintings from a museum in Berlin that was being bombed. They said the paintings would have been destroyed or stolen by the Russians if they hadn't taken them. Heinrich was the captain of a German U-boat during the war. He met my father and frequently saw him here in the Azores when he stopped to refuel during his patrols of the Atlantic.

"Heda's father and my father became good friends, and that's how Heda got here. Heinrich asked my father to look after her because the war was going badly, and on his next trip, he brought Heda here to live with us. I don't know how he was able to take her on the U-boat, but I know that he was very high up in the German Navy. Heda was a beautiful girl, and I knew the first time I kissed her we would marry, and eventually we did."

Antone paused to check that they were still on course, holding at ten knots. They were. He glanced at the sky.

"The storm will be here soon and our visibility will drop. I'm going to turn on our running lights. Keep an eye out ahead, though I doubt we'll see anyone."

He continued with the story.

"Many years ago, after Mother died, my father and my older brother left for the United States. I never heard from them again, until recently. Captain Schiffer had apparently stayed in touch with my father over the years, though I never knew that.

"Decades ago, near the end of World War II, Heda's father, Captain Schiffer, sent me a letter telling me that he would be coming to Praia da Vitoria with some important crates. He told me to wait at the entrance to the harbor and look for two flashes of light from offshore. I went there many nights, watched and waited, and then returned home. Finally, one night I saw the flashes and took my boat out to meet him. His men loaded eleven crates from his U-boat onto my boat,

81

and we took them back to my house where they've been ever since. Those are the crates that we have onboard, except for one. Captain Schiffer was supposed to get back to me about what to do with them, but I never heard from him again.

"Before he left to return to Hamburg he gave me my father's address in the United States, in a town called Mattapoisett, in Massachusetts. I wrote to my father, but he never wrote back. After many years without hearing from Captain Schiffer, I again wrote to my father. My brother wrote back and said that my father had gotten mixed up with a gang that sold drugs and was murdered. He was aware of the paintings and told me that I should get them to him. I agreed, knowing that would solve a problem for Heda and me.

"He's arranged for a fishing boat to meet us off the coast of Newfoundland that will take the crates to him. We'll radio them when we are near Newfoundland. The paintings are of no use to us and I don't want them around. I'm sure people wouldn't be too happy with us, knowing that we had those missing paintings all these years. So, that's where we are headed, but for now we have to get through this storm."

Rain had begun falling, lightly at first, but soon the raindrops turned into a steady downpour. Visibility was reduced to twenty feet and the waves swelled as the Bugio II rode over the crests and down into the troughs. Rain and sea water washed the deck but were quickly drained back into the sea through the scuppers, drains along the sides of the boat.

An hour later the rain suddenly stopped and the sky turned bright blue. The seas calmed and the clouds moved away to let the sun shine down on the Bugio II.

"Hey, we haven't had breakfast yet," Antone said to Caetano. "Go below and get a pineapple and some masa souvlada."

Caetano left the pilot house and returned a few minutes later with the food. He cut the pineapple into chunks and sliced the bread. Putting it on plates, he handed one to Antone and began eating his breakfast.

"Aunt Heda makes the best masa souvlada. Even my mother's wasn't this good."

Antone checked the compass and was satisfied that they had maintained their course throughout the storm. They pushed on through the day, each taking a turn at the helm.

"Newfoundland is about 1600 nautical miles from Terceira, so at our speed we should be there in about seven days, assuming we don't run into problems."

They ran the Bugio II 24 hours a day, taking turns at the helm, eating, and sleeping. The weather was uneventful, the waves relatively calm, and the days were filled with sunshine and warm weather. Antone was an excellent navigator and one of only a few men who still knew how to use a sextant. Several times, after looking at the stars, he adjusted their course as Caetano watched and learned from the master captain.

Antone knew that they would soon be approaching land and instructed Caetano to keep a good watch off the bow. Sure enough, in the early afternoon of the seventh day at sea, a small dot of land appeared on the horizon.

Antone checked his chart and then told Caetano, "That's St. Pierre and Miquelon, just off the southern coast of Newfoundland. The area of the Atlantic we're in now is called the Grand Banks. It's one of the best fishing grounds in the world."

They began to see fishing boats—draggers and trawlers from the ports of New Bedford, Gloucester, and Boston. Antone assumed the boat he was looking for was among them. He changed course to the northwest to avoid the boats, and as land grew closer they passed by St. Johns, the capital of Newfoundland.

"Where are we headed?" asked Caetano.

"We're going around the Northeast corner to a town called Portugal Cove. There are a few things we need to do there and we have to contact the Theresa M."

He checked the fuel level and was pleased that he had calculated correctly. They had more than enough to make it to Portugal Cove where they would refill the tanks and take on more fresh water and food for the return trip.

A few hours later they entered Conception Bay, passed Bell Island off to the starboard side, then turned to port and prepared for their arrival at Portugal Cove. Antone cut the speed to three knots and slowly made his way to the dock. Caetano dropped the bumpers over the side of the boat while Antone shifted the engines into reverse to bring it neatly to a stop. Caetano threw the bow and stern lines onto the dock where a local fisherman tied them to the cleats. The worst was behind them. Or so they thought.

HURRICANE EDWIN FORECAST/ADVISORY
NUMBER 26
NWS NATIONAL HURRICANE CENTER TAUNTON MA
1000 EST TUE SEP 1, 1970

AT 1000 AM EST A HURRICANE WATCH IS IN EFFECT FOR THE CANADIAN MARITIMES.
THE CENTER OF HURRICANE EDWIN IS LOCATED 690 MILES EAST OF NEW YORK CITY MOVING NORTHEASTERLY AT 12 KTS.

INTERESTS ALONG THE CANADIAN MARITIMES
SHOULD MONITOR THE PROGRESS OF EDWIN. AS
IT IS EXPECTED THAT A HURRICANE WARNING
WILL BECOME IN EFFECT IN THE CANADIAN
MARITIMES.

HURRICANE CENTER LOCATED NEAR 39.48N,
64.30W

POSITION ACCURATE WITHIN 10 NM

MAX SUSTAINED WINDS 110 KT WITH GUSTS TO
135 KT

HURRICANE FORCE WINDS EXTEND OUTWARD
UP TO 125 MILES . . . 185 KM . . . FROM THE CENTER.

EDWIN HAS THE POTENTIAL TO PRODUCE
SIGNIFICANT DAMAGE.

FORECASTER BYRON

Portugal Cove, Newfoundland

Day 1

ANTONE AND CAETANO WALKED UP THE FRONT STEPS OF the Beachy Cove Café and stepped inside where they were greeted by a young, vivacious waitress whose nametag announced she was Kady. She had tattoos on her left arm and her curly, sandy-brown hair reached below her shoulders. She took them upstairs and seated them at a table by the window where they could look out at Conception Bay and Bell Island off in the distance.

"Where ya 'longs to?"

She could tell by their expressions that they must not be from around there.

"I haven't seen you here before, what brings you to Portugal Cove?"

Antone thought about it briefly then answered, "We're Portuguese, from the Azores. We decided to stop here on our way to Massachusetts to visit some relatives."

She accepted his explanation with a smile and handed them two menus.

"We have cod tongues on the menu today."

Seeing the looks on their faces she added, "Some people like them and some people don't. I like the smaller ones because they tend to be crispy. The larger ones can be a bit slimy."

The two men ordered baked haddock and washed it down with several cold, locally brewed beers followed by generous slices of chocolate raspberry cake. They paid for dinner with a credit card and left a generous tip for Kady.

Just before leaving, Antone asked, "Oh, by the way, do you know where the Holy Rosary Church is?"

Kady paused a minute, then said, "Yes, it's just down the road," pointing to the left down Beachy Cove Road.

"Is there a cemetery there?"

"Yes, I believe there is a small one. I haven't been there in a long time."

They thanked Kady, left the Beachy Cove Café, and walked back across the street to their boat. The Bell Island ferry was just pulling away from the dock and was steaming across the tickle to Bell Island. The ferry ran regularly and transported residents back and forth between the tiny island and Portugal Cove for work and shopping.

"I have to try to raise the Theresa M on the radio," said Antone. "While I'm doing that, see if you can find out how we can refuel and where we can get food for our return trip. We should have asked Kady."

Antone went into the pilot house while Caetano went off on his appointed errands. He returned thirty minutes later and informed Antone as to what he had learned.

"There's a small store just up the street where we can get food for our return trip. They have a lot of fresh fruit and produce, and with the refrigerator, the fish they sell will last us a few days. And, one of the fishermen on the dock said the man who runs the fuel station is here early in the morning and then again in the late afternoon. We can refuel either time."

"Good. That takes care of that. We'll do both in the morning. I spoke with Captain Domingo Medeiros, on the Theresa M. He's out in the Grand Banks. He said there's a hurricane on its way and that he would be coming into Conception Bay to ride it out. We'll head back home right after we transfer the crates to them. The storm will be behind us and we'll leave it in the distance. They usually die out when they get this far from the Caribbean."

Antone slipped an old tattered letter into his pocket and told Caetano they had something important to do. They stepped off the boat, turned right onto Wharf Road, and walked up the hill to where it met Beachy Cove Road. At the intersection, they turned right, passing the Beachy Cove Café, and followed the road along the bay. As they were walking, the ferry pulled into the dock to discharge the cars and passengers it had brought over from Bell Island.

"Where are we going?" asked Caetano.

"You'll see in just a few minutes."

Large clusters of pink, lavender, and purple lupines lined the road along the way. They passed an unnamed cemetery that was overgrown with long brown weeds. Most of the forty-eight gravestones were toppled over and several were broken into pieces. Had they stopped, they would have noticed that everyone buried there was a man. They would have also noticed that they all had German names. And they would have been particularly interested in the headstone near the center of the small cemetery where a Kapitanleutnant was laid to rest surrounded by his men.

◆

Bell Island is rich in iron ore, and during World War II extensive mining operations were conducted there. Deep shafts were excavated, including lengthy ones under the sea on the north side of the island. Countless English-built merchant ships transported the ore from Bell Island across the Atlantic to England where smelters turned it into steel for the war effort.

German U-boats frequently patrolled the waters of Conception Bay during the war, and on September 5, 1942, a German U-boat, U-513, sank the *SS Lord Strathcona* and the *SS Saganaga* off Bell Island. Another U-boat fired at the *Ana T*, but missed and blew up the dock. It was the only direct attack on North American soil by the Germans during the war.

In late 1942, U-796 was submerged on the bottom of Conception Bay just offshore from Bell Island. Its plan was to stay there overnight and then attack ore-carrying cargo ships the next day, as they left Conception Bay. However, it was spotted, and a Canadian frigate came over from St. John's and dropped a depth charge on it, forcing it to the surface where the crew surrendered. Kapitanleutnant Klaus Schiffer and his crew of 47 were captured and jailed in Portugal Cove. Captain Heinrich Schiffer never knew what became of his brother. No one ever inquired about the forty-eight men or how they came to be buried in Portugal Cove.

◆

Antone and Caetano continued along Beachy Cove Road, following the shoreline. After a walk of a half mile, they passed a cluster of houses on the left and came to Church Road. They turned left and walked up the short hill to Holy Rosary Catholic Church. It was a small church with a cross prominently sitting on top of its round dome. A few old gravestones, most in disrepair, were clustered in an area to the left front side of the church. They were surrounded by a low white fence that had several sections missing. They walked over and looked at each grave.

"What are we looking for?" asked Caetano.

"Hopefully, you will see soon enough."

Not finding what he was looking for, Antone led Caetano along the side of the white church to the back where they discovered a larger cemetery. As they walked towards the Southwest corner Antone began reading the headstones. They slowly moved up and down each row, then suddenly Antone stopped. He found it.

They both looked at the headstone. Caetano sensed that something was different, but didn't say a word. He stared at it, trying to comprehend its significance. Finally, Antone reached into his pocket and pulled out the old yellowed letter that had been folded and unfolded so many times that it was beginning to tear along the creases. He slowly read the letter, then handed it to Caetano.

"This will explain everything," he said as his eyes moved back to the headstone.

Caetano slowly opened it and read . . .

August 8, 1964
Dear Antone,

I am writing to you from Portugal Cove in Newfoundland. You don't know me, but I know a little of you. You see, your brother, Carlos, was my husband. We were married in 1956 by Father Squire at Holy Rosary Church here in Portugal Cove. Like many people who live in Portugal Cove, Carlos worked on the boats that fished the Grand Banks. We met at a bakery shop in town and were married a year later. Carlos told me he came here because of the name of our town. He shared little else about his reasons for coming here.

Carlos was very silent about where he came from, but often spoke very fondly of a son, Caetano. I know it was very painful to him when he spoke of him, and that he missed him. He never mentioned any other children. I assume he had been married when he lived in the Azores, but he never shared that information with me or the reasons why he left the Azores.

Carlos was killed in an accident on the wharf a few weeks ago. He was attempting to drop a bumper between the fishing boat and the wharf. The sea was rough and he slipped overboard and was crushed between the boat and the wharf. The men on the boat did their best to try to save him, but were unable to do so. Father Ward held his funeral and we buried him in Holy Rosary Roman Catholic Cemetery off Beachy Cove Road. He is near the southwest corner, next to our son. That is where I will be buried.

Carlos told me he was born on November 1, 1924, but I have no way of knowing that as I never saw any records of his birth. We had a good life together, though at times it was a struggle to make ends meet.

90

Carlos was a good provider and worked many long hours on the fishing boats and we had a small garden. We had one child, James, who died when he was very young. He was named after my father, James Tucker. He is buried next to Carlos at Holy Rosary.

After Carlos died, I was going through his things and came across a piece of paper in the bottom of a drawer that had your name and address on it, and so I write. I hope this letter reaches you as I have no way of knowing if you still live there or not. Carlos shared very little about you, and he never told me where you lived, other than in the Azores. He never told me much or I would have written to you much sooner. I hope you forgive me for not doing so.

I'm sorry that my letter brings such sad news, but I thought that it was right that I let you know about your brother, especially after so many years. He was a good man, and I miss him terribly.

Fondly,
Elisabeth (Tucker) Nunes

They looked back down at the headstone:

Carlos Nunes
1924-1964

Tears ran down Caetano's cheeks. "My father," he said.

"I received that letter several years ago, but didn't want to tell you. Perhaps that was a mistake. I never knew what happened to my brother. He had gotten into a lot of trouble back in the Azores and said he was going to Canada to start a new life. He never told us exactly where he was going and we never heard from him.

"There was no return address on the letter, it only said Elisabeth Nunes, Newfoundland. I suppose I could have tried to contact Elisabeth to find out about my brother, your father, but I respected his wish to move away and start a new life. If he wanted to stay in touch he could have written, but he never did. Now, we've found him."

They stood there in silence for a few minutes, wondering what might have been had he not left, or if he had stayed in touch from Newfoundland. There were no answers.

"It's time to go," Antone said.

Before they left they looked at the two other headstones one last time:

Elisabeth Tucker Nunes
1924 – 1969

James Nunes
1958 – 1960

They walked in silence back to the Bugio II

Day 2

Early the next morning Antone caught up with the dockmaster and had the boat's fuel and water tanks filled for their return trip home.

"Where are you headed from here?" asked the dockmaster.

"The Azores."

"Well, you don't want to be leaving any too soon. It's gonna be a mad ruff and blowin' a-gale."

He looked at Antone's puzzled face, then laughed as he said, "The wind and seas will be kicking up due to the hurricane that's on the way."

"We'll get out in front of it and put it behind us in short

order. It won't be a problem. I've sailed in some pretty rough weather off the Azores."

"Do you have hurricanes there?" asked the dockmaster.

"We've had a couple, but they usually start farther south, near Madeira."

"Well, they're nothing to mess with. You'd be smart to stay right where you are until it blows over. If you go, you'd better have a fast boat and a hold full of good fortune. Most people who fight a hurricane end up on the losing side."

He handed Antone's MasterCharge Card back to him and, with a shake of his head, said, "Fair weather to you and snow to your heels."

"Thanks, we'll be fine."

Turning to Caetano, Antone said, "Let's go get our supplies."

They walked up Beachy Cove Road in the direction of St. John's. The wind had picked up and was blowing directly into their faces as they headed uphill towards the store. They pulled their jackets a bit tighter, and a few minutes later they arrived at the Whale's Tail convenience store.

As they stepped inside, a friendly young woman with bright red hair greeted them.

"Hi, stocking up for the storm?"

"Kind of," Antone answered. "We're heading back home in the morning, so we are getting a few things for the trip."

"Where are you headed?"

"The Azores."

"By boat? There's a hurricane coming!"

"Yes, but we'll be out in front of it and moving away from it."

"Doesn't sound like a good idea to me. What can I help you with?" she asked, changing the subject.

93

"Fresh fruit, produce, bread, meat, fish. We have a refrigerator onboard."

During the next thirty minutes they filled two shopping carts, then went to the cash register where the girl with the red hair rang up their order and put it into several large boxes. They looked at the boxes and figured they'd need a few trips to get them back to the boat.

An older man, who had been talking with the clerk at the next counter asked, "Need some help with those? I can run you back to the wharf if you want."

The red-haired girl nodded at Antone as if to say *he's okay*.

"Thanks, that would be much appreciated."

The three men carried the boxes out of the store and set them in the back of his battered old pickup truck.

"Jump inside," he said to Antone. "The kid can ride in the back."

"I'm Emile. See you're come-from-away. Heard you were heading out tomorrow. I've lived here all my life. These new guys, they get shitbaked in this weather. You won't have any problem, if you have a decent boat. I've worked fishing boats out in the Grand Banks. Rode out many a storm with no problem. Ya, you'll get bounced around a bit, but if you're a sailor it's no big deal."

A few minutes later Emile brought his truck to a stop on the wharf next to their boat. He helped them unload the boxes, then extended his hand.

"Good luck."

"Thanks for the lift, and your words of encouragement."

Antone turned to Caetano and said, "Let's get this stuff stowed away."

94

They brought their provisions below deck and readied them for the trip home. Fueled and resupplied, they went over to the Beachy Cove Café for one last meal.

Kady greeted them when they walked in.

"Hi, joining us for dinner? We were about to close early due to the storm, but come on in, we'll serve you."

She showed them to a table near the window on the upper level. From there they looked out at their boat moored to the wharf. The waves were a bit stronger and the boat was pitching gently from side to side.

"Going to finally try the cod tongues?" Kady asked with a smirk on her face.

"Maybe on our next trip," Caetano shot back with a grin on his face.

"We're heading out in the morning and we'll be back in the Azores in about a week."

"Aren't you afraid of the hurricane?"

"No, we're sailors."

After Kady took their order and left for the kitchen, they listened to a verse from The Provincial Anthem of Newfoundland which was playing through the speakers:

> *When blinding storm gusts fret thy shore,*
> *And wild waves lash thy strand,*
> *Thro' spindrift swirl, and tempest roar,*
> *We love thee windswept land.*

They ate, paid their bill, and said goodbye to Kady.

"Let's get back to the boat. I want to radio Captain Medeiros to confirm that everything is still good for tomorrow morning."

When they were back on the boat, Antone got on the radio and raised Captain Medeiros, who confirmed that he'd be at the east end of Conception Bay early in the morning.

For the next hour they thoroughly checked the Bugio II from stem to stern. When they were finished, Antone was confident that they were ready to depart.

"Let's call it an early night. We have a busy day ahead tomorrow."

Antone and Caetano settled into their berths and soon the waves rocked them to sleep.

Day 3

They woke up just before the sun broke the horizon. Their boat was rolling considerably more than it was when they turned in the night before. Antone went up to the wheelhouse, picked up his binoculars, and scanned the horizon near the east end of Bell Island. A fishing boat appeared through the lens and he knew it had to be the Theresa M.

"Hey, rise and shine," he called to Caetano. "We're going to get underway."

Caetano woke from a deep sleep, sat up and pulled his boots on. He headed up to the deck.

"Are they here?" he asked.

"I think that's them out at the end of Bell Island," Antone said, pointing towards the entrance of Conception Bay.

Antone started the boat and listened for a minute. Everything sounded fine.

"Release the bow line."

Caetano scrambled up onto the wharf, unwound the line from the cleat and tossed it onto the deck.

Antone inched the bow away from the dock and shouted, "Get the stern line."

96

Quickly, the stern line and Caetano were back on deck. Antone pulled the Bugio II away from the dock and pointed the bow eastward toward what he hoped was the Theresa M. After they left the dock, Caetano coiled and secured the bow and stern lines, then joined Antone in the wheelhouse.

"We'll make one turn around its stern just to make sure it's the right boat. Grab the binoculars so you can check."

Antone pushed the throttle forward and a short time later swung the Bugio II around the stern of the fishing boat.

"It's the Theresa M," Caetano said excitedly.

Antone picked up the radio and called.

"Who the hell else do you think would be out here?" came the reply from Captain Medeiros.

"Bring your boat along our starboard side. Drop your bumpers or you'll end up a pile of driftwood."

Caetano dropped the bumpers as Antone maneuvered the boat slowly towards the Theresa M. When they were alongside, Antone shifted the clutch to neutral as Caetano threw the bow and stern lines to crew members on the deck of the Theresa M. Once their boat was secured, they dropped a Jacob's Ladder and the two men climbed aboard.

"You picked a good time for this," said Captain Medeiros looking at the sky. "It better be worth the trouble," *though he's paying me a pretty good sum when I get these crates to Mattapoisett.* "Let's get them onboard."

For the next thirty minutes Antone and Caetano brought the crates to the deck and carefully passed them across the gunwales. When they were all onboard the Theresa M, Antone climbed up the ladder, went over to Captain Medeiros, and handed him an envelope.

"Please give it to him when you deliver the crates."

"You heading out now?" Medeiros asked.

"Yes, we're going to get going. We'll beat the storm out of here."

"Not sure I'd do that. You'd be smarter to heave to and wait it out. We're going to stay right here. If we head out now we'll be driving right through it on our way back to New Bedford. It's not the first hurricane we've been through, but they ain't fun. This bay will give us some protection. We've dropped both anchors and will head into the wind and ride it out. If you're going, you'd better leave now or we'll be pulling you up in our nets on our next trip. And if I lose a hold full of yellowtail because of this I'm coming looking for you. If the sea doesn't get you, I will."

Antone and Caetano climbed back onto the deck of the Bugio II. Antone went to the wheelhouse, shifted the clutch to forward, advanced the throttle, and pulled away from the Theresa M. A sense of relief came over them—they were finally rid of the paintings. Now, Antone just wanted to get back home to Praia da Vitoria, and Heda and Anna Grazia.

◆

Homeward Bound

FQCN17 CHLU 170900
MARINE FORECAST FOR THE MARITIME
PROVINCES ISSUED BY ENVIRONMENT CANADA
AT 4:00 A.M. NDT
TH SEP 3, 1970

A HURRICANE WARNING IS IN EFFECT FOR THE
MARITIME PROVINCES

AT 0600 AM EST THE CENTER OF HURRICANE
EDWIN WAS LOCATED NEAR LATITUDE 45.49N
LONGITUDE 56.15W . . . SOUTH SOUTHWEST OF ST.
PIERRE AND MIQUELON AND NEWFOUNDLAND

A GENERAL NORTHEAST DIRECTION IS
EXPECTED OVER THE NEXT 12 TO 24 HOURS

THE CATEGORY THREE HURRICANE IS
TRAVELLING AT 19 KM/H . . . MAXIMUM WINDS UP
TO 98 KNOTS AND EXTEND OUTWARD UP TO 200
KM

STORM SURGES RAISING WATER LEVELS AS MUCH
AS FIFTEEN TO TWENTY FEET CAN BE EXPECTED
WITH BATTERING WAVES NEAR THE CENTER OF
THE HURRICANE.

FORECASTER SIMMERS

———————

THE DARK BROWNISH-GREEN WATER IN THE BAY WAS
choppy, churned up by the wind and waves that announced
the advent of hurricane force winds. The wind was blowing a
light rain across the Bugio II as Antone circled once around
the Theresa M. He gave a long blast on the horn, then quickly
brought the boat to twelve knots, its maximum speed, and
headed east out of Conception Bay. Twenty minutes outside
the bay, rolling waves were cresting at ten to fifteen feet and a
steady stream of sea water washed over the deck and flowed
out the scuppers.

Caetano returned to the cabin and asked, "What's our
heading?"

"We're going to go due east as fast as we can to get the storm as far behind us as possible. We should be in smoother seas in a couple of hours."

The boat rolled heavily over the waves, and they braced themselves each time it slid over a crest and dropped into the trough between waves. Although the boat shook every time it sank into a trough, Antone was confident that they would weather the storm.

As Newfoundland grew smaller off their stern, the seas became rougher and the wind was now gusting to thirty-five knots. They bounced hard over the waves and Antone kept the bow straight into them to keep it from broaching, or turning broadside, which could push it over and sink them.

An hour out of Conception Bay Antone began to question his decision to leave before the hurricane passed through. The sky grew darker overhead and rain began to fall more heavily. He checked the barometer, which continued to drop, and cut the speed back to ten knots to maintain better control of the boat. He had turned the bilge pumps on when they left Conception Bay, and they were doing a good job pumping seawater out of the hull.

A few more hours and we'll be out of this.

"It might be my imagination, but it looks a bit clearer out on the horizon," Antone said to Caetano. "Hopefully we'll be out there soon."

Then, as they dropped over a crest he saw it. Too late! Ten feet in front of them a piece of fishing net half the size of the boat floated on the surface. It had most likely been tossed over by one of the fishing boats in the Grand Banks. Antone held his breath as they ran directly over it.

Five seconds later, warning lights lit up on the console. The net had gotten caught in the prop. Moments later, the engine

100

abruptly stopped. Antone could no longer control the boat. It was at the mercy of the wind and waves.

"What happened?" Caetano asked anxiously, sensing that whatever it was, it wasn't good.

"We drove over a piece of fishing net and it wrapped itself around our prop and propshaft. We have to free it, and quickly. Damn fishermen who throw stuff like that overboard rather than taking it home with them."

On the outside Antone appeared calm, as if he had encountered this situation many times before. He didn't want to alarm Caetano, but inside, his heart was racing, his adrenaline was pumping, and a sickening feeling of grave concern slowly spread its way up from his stomach into his chest. Despite the cold, he was sweating profusely. At the forefront of his thoughts he was considering how to free the net, but just behind those thoughts loomed the question, *what if I can't?*

"I'm going to tie a line around me and fasten it to the boat. I'll go over the side and cut the net loose. It won't be easy with these waves, but we don't have a choice."

He took a large knife out of a drawer in the wheel house, opened a storage box, took out a length of rope, then carefully made his way to the stern. The boat was pitching heavily and he had to hold on and inch his way to the stern.

"You stay here by the stern in case I need your help."

Antone wrapped the rope around his chest and tied it with a bowline knot. He looked at the dark water. It was rough and he knew it would be cold.

"If I give three tugs on the line, pull me up right away."

Holding the knife tightly in his hand, he slipped over the stern. The cold water instantly numbed his skin as he dove below the surface. After being slammed against the boat several times, he finally reached the prop. The boat was bouncing roughly in the waves and he had to hold onto the prop with one hand so that he could stay close to it. He would have worked far more efficiently if he could have used both hands to free the prop, but with the turbulence, that was impossible. *I don't know how long I can handle this cold and beating, but if I don't . . .* with his knife he began cutting away the netting that was tangling the prop.

He returned to the surface for air. The transom banged against his head as the boat pitched and rolled on the sea. Pain seared through his head and he knew it had been split open. He dove back under the pitch-black water and resumed cutting, more by feel than by sight. *At least there doesn't seem to be any damage to the prop.*

Antone was nearly out of breath, and once again returned to the surface to fill his lungs with air. The sea was rougher on the surface than below, and he repeatedly slammed into the boat. *I can barely feel my body. I'm losing my strength.* Taking a deep breath, he once again slipped below the surface. He felt his way to the prop and cut away another strand of the net.

With the limited visibility and constant churning of the water he was only able to free one strand per trip below. It would be a long, slow process of cutting a strand, surfacing for air, then returning to cut away more netting. He suppressed a thought that floated in the far recess of his mind—*this is all futile.* Twenty minutes later he freed the last remaining piece of the net from the prop, surfaced, and with the help of Caetano, struggled to climb back aboard the Bugio II.

There was no time for Antone to rest and regain his strength. The rain had increased in intensity and was now falling at 3-4 inches an hour. Winds were gusting at 50-60 knots and the seas were cresting at fifty feet. The swells had switched from rolling to breaking. For the first time since they left

Conception Bay, Antone acknowledged to himself that he was afraid. His heart raced as fast as his mind. He knew that he had made a mistake in trying to outrace the hurricane. *And for what purpose?*

Slowly, he worked his way forward along the starboard side until he reached the wheelhouse. Once inside, and after several attempts, he was able to start the engine. *At least some good news.*

Caetano had followed him and collapsed on the deck. He sat there and watched Antone attempting to steer the boat.

Gradually, he brought the boat around to head directly into the waves. It shot upward to the crest of the next wave, then balanced at its crest before diving down the back side. He prayed that the water crashing over the bow wouldn't push the windows in.

"We need to put on lifejackets." *Why didn't we put those on when we left?* "I have to send out a distress signal," he said reaching for the microphone for the VHF radio. "We'll need to be lifted off, we aren't going to make it in these seas."

Caetano never heard him. The noise of the sea was too loud and he was nearly in shock.

Antone pulled two lifejackets out of one of the storage boxes. After he put one on himself and Caetano, he turned the VHF radio on and adjusted it to the highest power setting. Spreading his legs to brace himself so he wouldn't fall, he called:

"Mayday, Mayday, Mayday. This is the Buggio II."
"Mayday, Mayday, Mayday. This is the Buggio II."
"Mayday, Mayday, Mayday. This is the Buggio II."

"We are located at 47^0 31' north and 51^0 82' west."
"We are on a Meridian Trojan, a 48-foot long range cruiser."

"There are two on board."

"Our prop was fouled by fishing nets, which we have cleared. Our bilge pumps are not keeping up and we are taking on water."

"I don't believe we have much time left."

"If you hear this, please contact the Coast Guard and tell them we need to be rescued."

"Over."

Antone squeezed the microphone in his hand and prayed for a response. Caetano hadn't said a word for minutes, and he seemed to sense the inevitable. Waves crashed over the bow and the scuppers were no longer able to clear the water that flooded the deck. Below, the bilge pumps couldn't keep up with the sea water that was pouring in from above.

Moments later a voice came over the radio. The watchstander on duty at the Coast Guard station had heard their distress call and responded. "Switch your radio to Channel 16." Antone switched to the channel used internationally for sending distress signals, and said:

"This is the Buggio II."

"We are located at 47^0 31' north and 51^0 82' west."

"We are a Meridian Trojan, a 48-foot long range cruiser."

"There are two on board."

"Our prop was fouled by fishing nets, which we have cleared. Our bilge pumps are not keeping up and we are taking on water."

"We need to be rescued as soon as possible."

"Over."

"Sending assistance as soon as possible. Maintaining communication on Channel 16."

"Over."

As best he could, Antone steered the boat directly into the waves. Though he felt helpless, he refused to accept what likely lay ahead. The wind speed was increasing as were the height of the waves. Visibility was so poor that he could no longer see the bow of the boat. The waves were breaking hard and the boat was crashing through walls of water. Every five minutes an ever-larger wave hit the boat. Now, when the boat reached the crest of the wave it was lifted out of the water and wouldn't obey the rudder. Antone no longer had control of the Buggio II. It was in the hands of the angry sea.

The hatch cover was torn loose. A wave crashed onto the deck, snapping off the antenna, ending any possible communication with rescuers. Antone stayed at the helm, although he no longer commanded the boat. It was out of fear that he couldn't move. Another large wave swept the boat from bow to stern, knocking out the windows of the wheelhouse. Seawater shorted out the electrical system. Without electricity, the bilge pump ceased to operate, though in reality it had long ceased to function effectively.

Wave after wave battered the boat and the two men were thrown backwards against the bulkhead. Caetano grabbed his right arm. Because he was in shock he was unaware that his humerus bone was protruding from his shirt just below the shoulder. Antone hit the back of his head hard against the bulkhead. He felt a sharp pain and was no longer able to see.

Greenish-black water poured over the bow, ran the length of the boat and spilled over the stern, leaving a long stretch of white frothy foam trailing behind.

The boat was tossed like a cork. The waves had grown even higher, now reaching more than eighty feet. The Bugio II started to climb the next wave, but the midship didn't clear the top of it. Almost surrealistically the boat slowly came to a stop, then slid backwards down the wave. The stern dove deeply into the ocean behind it and the boat flooded. Waves flipped it over and over until it came to rest upside down on the sea. Caetano was washed overboard and swallowed by the turbulence.

Antone didn't drown immediately. Air was trapped inside the boat. He was floating in a pool of seawater in the upside-down wheelhouse. It was pitch black, though he had no vision to know that. He no longer thought of Caetano, but, as panic set in, his thoughts were of Heda and Anna Grazia.

Slowly, the water in the wheelhouse rose until Antone's head was no longer above the surface. He held his breath, but soon his body called for oxygen and he involuntarily took a breath. He inhaled saltwater, and then some more. Most of the water went to his stomach, but some also began to fill his lungs causing a burning sensation. Just before he lost consciousness, a strange peace came over him. He was done.

Let the last breath out and then I go to sleep.

♦

Aboard the Theresa M
One day later

THE THERESA M LAY AT ANCHOR IN THE MIDDLE OF Conception Bay. Captain Domingo Medeiros was in the wheelhouse getting the weather forecast from the weather service at St. John's:

"There's a small craft advisory with waves stacked up ten to fifteen feet. Winds are gusting to 35 knots."

Not a problem, we've been in far worse.

"We've got 70,000 pounds of yellowtail in the hold. It's time to get it to New Bedford," thought Captain Medeiros.

106

The first boat in usually gets the best price, and that can mean a difference of thousands of dollars in each crew member's pocket.

Commercial fishing is a wet, cold, hard, and dangerous occupation. It can also be very lucrative. After expenses are deducted, each crew member gets a percentage of the profit based on their seniority and contributions during the trip. Senior crewmembers can often make more than ten thousand dollars a trip. Most of them save it, though Ellis Vaughan, a younger, but reliable crewmember, often quoted W. C. Fields, "I spent half my money on gambling, alcohol and wild women. The other half I wasted."

The Theresa M was a 125-foot trawler that fished the Grand Banks, a large area of the Atlantic to the Southeast of Newfoundland. The underwater plateaus are a lot shallower than in other areas of the Atlantic, and when the cold Labrador currents mix with the warmer waters of the Gulf Stream, rich nutrients are pulled to the surface to provide food for marine life, like the yellowtail laying in the hold of the Theresa M.

When fishing, trawlers let out hundreds of feet of net behind the boat. Fish swim into the net, get caught by the gills, and then get hauled aboard the boat. Crewmembers pick the fish out of the nets and throw them onto the tons of ice in the holds below deck. That keeps the fish fresh until the boat returns to port and the catch is unloaded at the commercial fish processing plants at the edge of the harbor.

Captain Medeiros went below deck to check the ice on the fish in the hold. He could always stop at St. John's to pick up some more, but that would mean time and money. Satisfied that there was enough ice so they wouldn't lose the fish, he returned to the wheelhouse and picked up the microphone.

"We'll haul anchor in fifteen minutes."

The smell of breakfast worked its way up to the main deck and Medeiros followed the smell to the galley where he grabbed a plate and filled it with scrambled eggs, bacon, and baked beans. After breakfast, he made his way to a forward cabin where he checked on the wooden crates. They were securely lashed to the bulkhead and sat on several thick boards that raised them off the deck.

Satisfied that they would be safe during the trip, he returned to the wheelhouse and announced, "Haul in the anchors. We've got a thousand nautical miles to cover. We'll be driving out of the storm so we should be back in port in four or five days."

Medeiros knew it would be rough sailing at first, but gradually the storm would be moving further out into the Atlantic, behind them, and things would calm down.

Wally Morgado, the senior deckhand, entered the bridge.

"We're ready to go. Anchors are hauled and the lines are faked."

Medeiros drove the boat out towards the end of Conception Bay, then gradually swung it around and headed towards St. John's at the southeast corner of Newfoundland. It settled into a steady roll from port to starboard, then back again as it made its way down the East Coast of Newfoundland. Once they reached St. John's, Captain Medeiros brought the boat to a southwesterly heading, passing below St. Pierre and Miquelon.

Just after midnight, four and a half days after leaving Newfoundland, Nantucket came into view. Two hours later the Theresa M passed Martha's Vineyard and Captain Medeiros navigated through Woods Hole and then across Buzzards Bay towards the red and black buoy near Nye Ledge, a rocky outcropping about a quarter of a mile wide. It's located about two miles across from Ned Point Lighthouse, which sits at the entrance to Mattapoisett Harbor.

Captain Medeiros slowed the boat as he approached the ledge. He looked at the chart on the table next to him, and decided he was close enough. He didn't want to run aground, and since his was the only commercial fishing boat to be seen, he shouldn't be hard to find.

A couple of locals were night fishing. Some say that's when they run the best. They glanced at the Theresa M then dropped their lines back in the water, hoping to catch tomorrow's dinner.

"He'd better be here," Medeiros said to no one. "He'll be paying for a hold full of yellowtail if he isn't."

◆

His boat was red. It was unusual, not just because of the color, but because he really wasn't interested in calling attention to himself. Yet, it was the only red boat in the harbor. He inherited it from his father, along with all of its stories. Now, it was about to become part of another one.

He pulled away from the ledge and headed towards the Theresa M. Medeiros watched him; then, convinced it was his contact, went out on deck. He didn't know if this guy was the final destination for the crates, or if he was just a delivery man. He didn't care, as long as he got his money.

He motioned for the boat to pull alongside, and two minutes later they were tied together. A crew member dropped a ladder over the side and the visitor climbed aboard.

Captain Medeiros was all business.

"Do you have the cash?" he asked.

"Yes," he said, taking a large envelope from inside his vest pocket and handing it to the captain.

"Let's go up to the wheelhouse. A little privacy."

Once there, Captain Medeiros counted out the hundred-dollar bills and confirmed that it was the amount that had been agreed on.

"I was asked to give this to you," he said, handing the visitor an envelope who opened the letter and scanned the list that was written on it.

"Let's get the crates onto your boat. I've got fish to get to New Bedford."

They went out on deck and Captain Medeiros called Morgado over.

"Get some men and bring up the crates that are in the forward hold."

"And be careful with them!"

During the next thirty minutes they moved the crates onto the red boat. Had its captain been alert, he would have noticed that only ten crates were transferred to his boat, not the eleven that were on the list.

"We never met," yelled Captain Medeiros after the crates had been transferred.

The guy in the red boat nodded as he pulled away and headed towards Mattapoisett Harbor.

PART THREE
1970

"While seeking revenge, dig two graves—
one for yourself."

— Douglas Horton

The Beginning

More than 300 million years ago . . .

earth consisted of a large land mass that incorporated the now existing continents of North and South America, Africa, and Australia. This supercontinent was called Pangaea, from ancient Greek words meaning "all the earth."

More than 100 million years ago . . .

Pangaea slowly split and drifted apart, creating four continents: Europe and Africa to the East, and North and South America to the West. The area between them filled with seawater forming the central Atlantic Ocean between northwestern Africa and North America, and the southwestern Indian Ocean between Africa and Antarctica. This movement occurred during the Jurassic period when dinosaurs roamed the land.

At that time, the Appalachian Mountains were far more formidable than they are today. White quartz was abundant throughout the mountains, and over the course of millions of years was eroded by wind, rain, and continual cycles of freezing and thawing. Gradually, the white quartz became finely ground and rivers flowing out of the Appalachians carried much of it southward to form the white sandy beaches along the Gulf Coast of Florida.

A smaller amount of the ground white quartz was carried by a river flowing northward along the ridge of the Appalachians, leaving deposits along the way. One branch of the river turned eastward and left a small amount of white sandy quartz near what would later be called Buzzards Bay.

Fourteen million years ago . . .

The two old Megalodons swam slowly along the coast, feeding on whatever small whales or fish crossed their path. They had been moving northward for weeks and were tired. Disease wracked their 50-foot long bodies and they struggled to keep enough water running through their gills to keep them alive. They reached the entrance of an inlet and turned into it. They swam past a rocky outcropping about a quarter of a mile across. The water around the ledge was shallow and their bodies rubbed against the sharp rock. They didn't feel it. Nearly exhausted, they continued on until finally they could go no more. They settled on the sandy quartz bottom as their strength slowly slipped away from them. Finally, one at a time, they rolled onto their sides and their lives ended. Large fish soon moved in and began feasting on the Megalodons, tearing the meat from their sides. Smaller fish grabbed fragments that floated free, and within a week there was nothing left of the Megalodons but their teeth and cartilage. During the next few years the fragile cartilage deteriorated as the ebb and flow of the tides washed over the remains. Their large teeth settled on the floor of the inlet where they would lie undisturbed for millions of years.

Mattapoisett Harbor

HE PULLED AWAY FROM NYE LEDGE AND THE THERESA M, then headed towards Ned Point Lighthouse at the entrance to Mattapoisett Harbor. A short time later he picked up green can buoy number 7 and, farther away, red nun 10. He turned the boat to port, passed between the two markers, entered the channel of the inner harbor, then steered the boat towards the wharf. Even though it was after midnight, he kept his speed under five miles per hour. It wasn't worth irritating the harbormaster for a few extra minutes.

The harbor was tranquil. Behind it, a few lights were shining from houses along Water Street. A quiet night, he thought, until he saw light coming from the harbormaster's office on the wharf. The door was open and the lights were on. *What the hell's he doing here at this time of night?*

He didn't have much choice. He couldn't stop in the middle of the harbor because if the harbormaster was there he would most likely check to see why he stopped, so it was safer to pull up to the wharf and dock at his assigned mooring space. He slowed his speed to a crawl, dropped the bumpers off the port side, then swung the boat around and pointed the bow back out towards the harbor. He eased into the outermost space on Makuch Wharf, then cut the engine. *We'll see what happens. Hopefully nothing.*

♦

Eddie Tinkham, the harbormaster, was highly respected by the residents of Mattapoisett. Even though he worked far more hours than his contract called for, he still found time to volunteer at the many charity events that are held in town. He was regarded as an expert on the history of whaleship building in Mattapoisett, and often spoke on the subject to students at the town's public schools. Kids often stopped by his office on the wharf and he always found time to talk with them.

♦

He threw the bow and stern lines of the red boat up onto the wharf, then climbed the wooden ladder that was bolted to its side. Once up top, he secured the two lines to wooden pilings, one forward and one aft of his boat. With the boat secured, he headed to the parking lot to get his truck. *So far, no harbormaster.*

He unlocked the door to his black pickup truck, stepped inside, turned the key in the ignition, then slowly drove out onto the wharf and parked next to where his boat was moored. A quick glance towards the harbormaster's office eased his fears. *No sign of him. Now to get the crates.* He climbed down the ladder, but just as he stepped onto the deck he looked back at the harbormaster's office and froze. The harbormaster was heading his way.

In panic, he picked up a belaying pin that he had saved from his father's sailboat just before it was sold. He kept it on his boat to give any fish he caught a rap on the head to stop them from flopping around. A lot easier to fillet that way. He shoved the hard, wooden club-shaped pin deep into his side pocket and climbed back up the ladder to meet the harbormaster. His mind was racing. *If he finds out what I have onboard I'll be in jail tomorrow. Will he check? What's my story if he does?*

"What are you doing out here at this time of night?" asked Eddie Tinkham.

He was wearing tan slacks and a neatly pressed black shirt that sported a gold harbormaster's shield above the left pocket. A large patch on his left sleeve also announced his title.

"Just coming back from some night fishing."

"What's in those crates down there?"

"Nothing."

"Well then, let's have a look."

The captain of the red boat was known around town as a bit of an unsavory character, and he occasionally got unwanted attention from those in authority, like the cops and the harbormaster. He'd been in more than one police lineup, and had been fined for over-fishing on several occasions.

116

As Tinkham turned and stepped towards the ladder he felt a blinding pain in the back of his head. His eyes squeezed shut and stars exploded in his head moments before everything went dark. He collapsed onto the wharf, blood flowing profusely from the wide crack in the back of his skull.

Now what do I do? Damn. Hit him too hard and now he's probably going to die. Throw him in the harbor? Maybe they'll think he fell and hit his head on the way down.

He thought for a minute, then picked Tinkham's body up and wrestled it into the back of his truck.

What about the blood on the wharf?

There were hoses on the dock for boat owners to use to wash the salt, old bait, and fish entrails off their boats when they returned to port after being out on the water. He quickly walked over to where one was attached to a faucet, picked it up, and turned on the water. He dragged it back to where Eddie's blood had pooled and hosed the area down, washing it over the side of the wharf. After rinsing the wharf down, he turned the water off and coiled the hose near the faucet.

I know, he thought as he looked around and confirmed that the wharf was still deserted. A few more of the homes along Water Street had gone dark since he docked, and there was no activity on the wharf or the street.

I have time.

He climbed down onto his boat and picked up the lone bluefish that he had caught while waiting for the Theresa M to arrive. He climbed back up onto the wharf, pulled a knife out of his hip holster, then sliced the head and tail off the fish and threw them into the harbor. He then ran the knife up its belly, spilling bluefish guts and blood onto the wharf on top of Eddie's blood. *That should fool 'em.*

117

He threw the rest of the bluefish into the harbor. Someone would grouse about the damn inconsiderate fishermen before hosing it all over the side.

Now to get out of here.

During the next thirty minutes he carefully made ten trips up and down the ladder, bringing the crates up and stacking them in the back of his truck. Once they were loaded he made one last check of the wharf next to his boat.

The belaying pin! It's got blood on it.

He picked it up and tossed it into the truck bed. Then, satisfied he left no clues behind, he stepped into his truck and drove across the wharf to the harbormaster's office.

He left his truck running. The door to the office was open. He went in, turned left into the small, wood-paneled inner office, looked around, and found what he was looking for lying on the desk—a ring of keys—a few for buildings on the wharf and the key to Ned Point Lighthouse. He picked them up, glanced at the clock on the wall, then turned and walked out. He reached into his back pocket and removed his handkerchief. Then, holding it in his hand, he closed the door and turned the key in the lock. Looking around once more, he was confident that he hadn't been seen. He let out a sigh of relief as he got into his truck, drove up the short hill, turned right onto Water Street, and headed home.

♦

Fall

THEY CALL HIM WHARF RAT. NOT TO HIS FACE OF COURSE. His actual name is Freddie Texeira and he lives on the family pig farm up on Crystal Spring Road. Freddie often hung around the wharf, picking up odd jobs here and there. He was excellent at filleting fish, and always carried a knife on his belt. Often, when fishing boats took charter parties out, Freddie was hired on to fillet their catch of blues, stripers, and cod. When he wasn't working on the pig farm, he spent most of his time at the wharf.

Freddie was a loner. When he was young, he was an easy target for the town bullies on the school playground who often taunted him about living with the pigs. As a result, he became withdrawn and avoided the other children, preferring the solitude of taking his small skiff out into the harbor for some extended fishing. A few years ago, he bought a Mako 23, a center-console boat with an inboard motor, and he frequently sold the fish he caught off it to local restaurants. He was considered one of the most knowledgeable boat owners in town.

Some say he earned his nickname from an incident that occurred when he was in the first grade at Center School. His teacher, Mrs. Hickey, announced that it was time for recess. When Freddie asked her what that meant, she told him he could go outside and do anything he wanted to do. When he didn't return from recess, Mrs. Hickey informed the principal who went out and searched the school grounds for him. When he couldn't find Freddie, he notified the police. Three hours later they found him fishing off the end of the wharf.

When they asked him what he was doing there he explained, "Mrs. Hickey said it was recess and we could go outside and do anything we wanted to do. I wanted to go fishing, so I went home and got my fishing pole then came here."

Freddie rarely saw soap and water. His thinning hair was long and scraggly, and rumor has it that he occasionally cut it himself with his filleting knife. About ten years ago he spent some time in jail for stabbing a guy who had been bullying him.

The judge was lenient on him because he had been repeatedly provoked by the guy for a number of years. As a result of his incarceration, however, he was often rounded up with the "usual suspects" by the Mattapoisett police when they were investigating crimes such as break-ins at summer homes out on Mattapoisett Neck.

Freddie was up and out of the house before the sun rose this morning, the first day of the annual Tri-Town Fair. For more than twenty years his family sold pulled pork at their booth at the fair. Theirs was one of the most popular food items, and over the years had earned them quite a bit of money along with numerous ribbons for "Best Fair Food."

Three days earlier he had begun preparations for the event. It was a long and bloody day. He grabbed his .22 caliber Winchester rifle off the gun rack and headed out of the old family farmhouse. It was cool and breezy outside, and the sun was just starting to poke over the trees at the Eastern edge of the farm. He walked out to the barn, backed the tractor out, and hooked the flatbed wagon behind it. Pushing it into gear, he drove around the barn and out to the pig fields.

He stopped to open the gate leading into the biggest of the fields, where several hundred pigs fed and spent their fall days. He drove the red Farmall 706 through the gate, then stopped to close it behind him. Most of the sounder of swine were on the far side of the field, basking in the sun. The field was muddy from the recent rain, much to the delight of the pigs that were wallowing in it.

He drove over to them, shut the tractor off, picked up his rifle and scanned the field. He needed about one hundred pounds of meat, and knew that would take about three pigs. He quickly identified three that were the right size.

120

He slowly approached the first one. The pigs were used to him and didn't bother to look up as he got closer to them. He stood for a moment in front of one of his picks, raised the rifle, and put a bullet through the center of the pig's skull. It dropped to the ground instantly. At the sound of the gunshot, the remaining pigs scrambled ten or fifteen feet away from the dead sow, as if that moved them to safety. He spotted his next target and methodically dropped it to the ground. Finally, he spent one more bullet on his third selection. *That was easy.*

He walked back to the tractor and drove it over to the nearest dead pig. The tractor was fitted with a small gasoline-operated winch that Wharf Rat started up. He laid a wide board from the back edge of the flatbed to the ground just in front of the pig and payed out the chain from the winch until it was near the pig. He then took a piece of rope from the flatbed and used it to tie the rear legs together. After they were tied, he hooked the chain to its legs then kicked in the winch to slowly drag the pig up the plank and onto the flatbed. Once the first pig was resting on the flatbed, he moved along to the two remaining pigs. He hauled them up, then jumped on the tractor and took them to the slaughter house.

The slaughter house was a small, old wooden barn with a large heavy beam running across one end with several hooks hanging from it. A three-foot deep trench ran the length of it, and a few planks stretched across the trench for the person who was doing the slaughtering to stand on. Flies feasted on the decaying pig remains that lay in the bottom of the trench, and the stench of rotting flesh hung in the air.

He drove the tractor through the wide double doors of the slaughter house, then killed the engine, stepped off the tractor, and grabbed a chain that was attached to a winch connected to the beam above. After hooking the chain to the first pig, he activated the winch, raised it off the flatbed, then swung it towards the trench. He guided the pig under the beam then slipped a hook between its tied legs before releasing the winch, leaving the pig suspended over the trench. He repeated the procedure with the remaining two pigs then drove the tractor back to the barn.

Now for the good part. A long, blood-stained wooden table ran along the far wall of the slaughter house. He walked over to it, looked at the collection of various knives in the wooden knife rack, selected one, ran his thumb across the blade, then walked back over to the pigs. He stuck the knife several inches into the front of the first pig's throat, twisted it, and then pulled it out. A stream of bright red blood spurted from the pig. In less than a minute it slowed to a trickle, then continued to drain into the trench below while he repeated the procedure on the other two pigs. *It will take a while.* He spent the next ten minutes sharpening the knives that he would use to butcher them.

After the pigs had drained, he picked up a saw and cut their heads and front feet off. Once they were decapitated, he began removing their skin. With quick smooth strokes, honed through years of practice, he stripped the skin from the first pig and dropped it into one of the fifty-five-gallon drums next to him, which already held the three pig heads and their front feet. A few years back he would have saved the heads, removed the brain, ears and eyes, then brought the heads up to the house for his mother, Madalena. She'd use the meat from them to make sausages. Freddie hated them, and when his mother passed away her sausage recipe died with her.

He moved on to the second pig and then the third, repeating the process. Once their skin had been removed, he wiped off the knife, returned it to the rack, then picked up a large hacksaw. One-by-one, with a steady sawing motion, he opened up the chests and bellies of the pigs, then eviscerated their entrails into the trench below. He'd shovel them out into the drums after most of their bodily fluid had been absorbed into the ground.

He let them drain for another thirty minutes, then began slicing off the thick layer of fat that enveloped each pig. When he was finished, he took a hose that was connected to a cold water tap and thoroughly rinsed the pigs inside and out. All that work had made him hungry so he let the pigs hang to dry while he went back to the house to grab some lunch.

It wouldn't be ham, as he hated it. Instead, he took some linguica, a spicy Portuguese sausage, from the refrigerator, cut off a piece about five inches long, sliced it in half, and put it in a frying pan on the stove. While it was cooking he took a hotdog roll from the freezer, buttered both sides, and set it in the frying pan next to the linguica. The roll browned quickly and he turned it to toast the other side. When the linguica was cooked, he put it in the roll and spread some spicy mustard on top. He grabbed a beer from the refrigerator and went out to the porch to eat his lunch.

He wasn't a happy man, and hadn't been for years. Between the constant bullying he received when he was younger, and what he saw as harassment from the police every time they needed someone for a lineup, he felt targeted.

I need to retire and move away from this town. I'm sick of getting called in by the cops every time there's a break-in. Maybe I should really give them something to think about.

As he took a sip of his beer he thought about the task ahead of him.

After he finished his lunch he returned to the barn and moved the pigs to the walk-in refrigerator in the corner of the slaughter house. There, he hung them off the ground so that they could continue to drain overnight.

The following day he butchered the pigs, placing the meat into large pots that sat on a metal grill over a wood fire in the back yard of his house. He added the ingredients from a decades-old family recipe, covered the pots, then let the pork cook over a very low heat for the next twelve hours. When it was done, he easily pulled it off the bone and packed it in large containers. It was the best pulled pork around, and it was ready for the fair.

He had one more thing to do. He went into the house and a minute later came back out carrying a large bag that he put into the back of his truck. *I might as well get this over with.* He climbed in and headed to River Road.

◆

Saturday morning. Late September. I woke up—slowly. Not all of me at once. My hearing was first. I heard the shower running. Carla was up before me. Thought I wore her out last night. Guess it was the other way around.

My nose was next. Filled with the scent of vanilla, parfume de baunilha. Portuguese. It lingered on her pillow.

My brain was waking up. Remembering last night. Vanilla on her neck and her long black hair tickling my face as we spooned ourselves to sleep.

Finally, my eyes opened. I saw the bright blue sky through the picture window across from my bed that overlooks Mattapoisett Harbor. A perfect day for the fair. I love the excitement of this annual fall event.

I rolled over and sat on the edge of the bed for a minute, shaking the cobwebs out of my head, trying to decide whether to head to the shower or the window. I decided on both, though not in that order.

I wasn't going to put my leg on just yet, so I grabbed my crutches and swung my way over to the window. I checked the thermometer fastened to the outside window casing. Sixty-two degrees, a perfect day for the fair. It would warm up a bit more.

I cranked open the window and breathed in the fresh salty air that filled the room. Then, out of habit, I glanced at the plaque on the wall to the left of the window:

Mattapoisett Volunteer of the Year – 1969
MANNY PEREIRA

I was presented with the award mostly for raising money and pulling together local tradesmen to build a home for a Vietnam Veteran who was experiencing battle fatigue, or shell-shock.

Upon returning home, following my discharge from the Navy after I lost my leg in Vietnam, I too had suffered from battle fatigue. I was often depressed and frequently had nightmares and flashbacks that so consumed me that I lost interest in the things that I had once cared about. I felt emotionally cut off from others.

For nearly a year, I participated in weekly group and individual counseling sessions at the Veterans Administration, and eventually found peace. I was grateful for the help I had received while I was recovering from my amputation and its residual effects, and wanted to pay it back. That opportunity came when I learned about a Vietnam Veteran who was experiencing battle fatigue and needed a home.

I organized a Kiss-A-Pig contest to raise money for the project. Town notables, including the police chief, fire chief, first selectman, high school principal, and the editor of the *Presto Press*, a weekly town newspaper, all agreed to kiss a pig at a public forum, if they received the most votes.

Five-gallon water jugs were set up at each candidate's workplaces as well as other locations around town. Each jug had the candidate's name and picture taped to it. People voted for the person they wanted to see kiss a pig by dropping money into their candidate's jug. One dollar equaled one vote. The teachers and students at the town high school, Old Rochester, stuffed enough dollar bills into the jug in the principal's office to ensure that he won.

Freddie Texeira was convinced to provide one of his large sows to be the recipient of a kiss from the winner. At noontime, on a bright, early summer day, with lots of tourists and townspeople gathered at Shipyard Park, the principal, Dave Hogan, climbed onto the bandstand, took a bottle of mouthwash out of his pocket, gargled with it, then, as the cameras flashed and the television cameras rolled, gave the pig an effusive kiss.

I guess they also decided to give me the award for a number of things I was involved with, including helping the scouts to earn their fingerprinting merit badges, serving for a term on the town planning board, and playing trumpet in the town band. However, I think the pig thing put me over the top.

◆

A few sailboats were anchored out in the harbor, though many had already been pulled for winter storage and were sitting at Whitehall's Boatyard out on Acushnet Road.

Far out at the end of the harbor, Ned Point lighthouse shone bright white in the morning sunlight. Tonight, as on most Saturday nights, cars occupied by hormonal teenage couples would be parked along the retaining wall at the lighthouse while they watched the submarine races.

I heard the shower turn off and headed to the bathroom. I walked in without knocking. Timed it perfectly. Carla had just stepped out of the shower. She stood barely up to my shoulders, and her long black hair hung well past hers. Water drops covered her body. I examined every one of them.

"Couldn't be bothered to put on your leg, huh? Had to hurry to catch me stepping out of the shower." She was smiling.

"Just how the timing worked out," I said.

She knew I was lying.

"Diner at the Weir for breakfast?" Carla asked.

"Unless you have other ideas," I said with a smirk.

"You're too worn out. Let's go have breakfast before the fair."

Attending the Tri-Town Fair had become a fall tradition for us. It was one of the oldest agricultural fairs in the country and had been held every year since 1856. That was a year before Mattapoisett split off from Rochester and became separately incorporated. The neighboring town of Marion joined the fair a few years later. It became an annual event, organized by farmers as a way for them to show off their yokes of oxen and steer, and to wind down after a hard summer of tending their crops.

The Tri-Town Fair Society was formed a few years later and has held the fair every year since then. Over the years it was expanded to include exhibits and contests for the best sheep, swine, chickens, flowers, vegetables, largest pumpkin, apple pies, tallest sunflower, quilting, and the products of numerous other hobbies. Nearly every contestant went home with a ribbon. Horse riding events and tractor pulls were added more recently along with a small midway with rides for the kids. Their favorites, however, were the "frog jumping" and "the biggest frog" contests.

Fair-goers flocked to the food booths that ran the length of the fairgrounds and feasted on food they knew they shouldn't eat. After rotating the fair among the three towns during the first few years, the Society settled on a permanent location on River Road in Mattapoisett. That's where we were headed, after the diner.

"Let me grab a quick shower."

I did that while Carla fussed with her hair and makeup.

After showering, I sat on the bed next to her and put on my prosthetic leg.

"Shake a leg," she said with a mischievous grin. "We want to get there before the cows go home."

I didn't respond. I was used to her leg jokes.

I put my left leg on, then took her hand in mine. *I'm going to try again.*

"Carla, let's get married."

Her face answered my question.

"Manny, you know I . . . I care about you. A lot. But I just can't."

She felt the shield coming up, then added, "You know the top three things that need witnesses are crimes, accidents, and marriages. Need I say more?"

Her therapist had told her that making light of my proposals was a defense mechanism to help her cope with her anxiety over a developing relationship. It was painful, and she had been working on it for quite some time.

My head dropped in resignation. This wasn't the first time I asked her to marry me. It wasn't the first time she said no. It didn't make the sting of her rejection any less painful.

Carla changed the subject.

"C'mon, let's go have breakfast. The fair awaits."

"All right, let's get going."

Ten minutes later we pulled out of Mahoney's Lane, turned left onto Main Street, and shortly took another left onto Route 6 on our way to the diner. A few minutes later we passed the herring weir, at the intersection of River Road, near the mouth of the Mattapoisett River, and turned into the parking lot of the diner. It was packed. I guess our idea of breakfast before the fair wasn't original.

It was noisy inside, filled with townspeople catching up on the latest gossip, reading the *New Bedford Tribune*, and kids antsy to get to the fair. The booths along the front of the diner were filled, so we took two seats at the far-left end of the counter. Lisa, an energetic young woman with black-rimmed glasses, bounced over with two menus.

"Hi Carla, hi Manny. Going to the fair?"

"Yes, along with the rest the town, judging by the crowd here," said Carla.

"Well, have fun. I'm stuck here until this afternoon. I plan on going tonight. What would you like?"

We didn't even have to discuss it.

"A linguica and cheddar omelet, home fries and wheat toast. We're going to share it. Save room for fair food. Oh, and coffee."

"Coming right up."

I listened to the chatter of the other customers. Much of it was speculation about the harbormaster. He hadn't been seen or heard from for several weeks. No conversations with town officials, no notes. Nothing. Just gone. Since it was past peak activity time in the harbor, some assumed he had gone on vacation and must have thought he had informed the selectmen of his plans. But he hadn't, at least according to the selectmen. If it was July or August they'd be more concerned, since he'd be busy making sure visitors weren't anchoring in unauthorized spots in the harbor, adding names to the long waiting list for a coveted mooring spot at one of the wharves, and occasionally dealing with an intoxicated boater exceeding the speed limit in the harbor. But at this time of year things were slowing down in Mattapoisett Harbor.

"Refill on your coffee?"

"Keep it coming."

"Your breakfast will be right up. Want the paper?"

"Sure, let's see how many corrections and retractions they had to print today," I said.

She brought the paper over. Coffee and egg stains on the front. And a little bacon grease.

An article below the fold caught my eye, "Yale Grad in Town to Discuss Children with Disabilities." A recent Yale Law School Graduate, Hillary Rodham, was in New Bedford as a volunteer for the Children's Defense Fund. She and other volunteers were going from house to house trying to find children with disabilities who weren't attending school. What they discovered was quite startling. Hundreds of children were not going to school simply because they had a physical or mental disability. All the politicians were scrambling, talking with the media, vowing to investigate, vowing to fix the problem, mainly to get re-elected.

I flipped to the sports section. Old Rochester's football team was playing Wareham in the annual Cranberry Bowl Game. Wareham won last year and was a big favorite to win again this year. A good day to go to the fair.

Our omelet came and I put the paper down.

Three eggs stuffed with Portuguese sausage and cheddar.

130

Carla ate a half slice of the wheat toast and picked around the edge of the omelet. I ate the rest.

I waved at Lisa, letting her know we were ready to leave.

"Have fun at the fair," she said as she handed us our check. "Maybe I'll see you there tonight." She winked at me.

"Probably not, but have fun if you go."

Hundreds of teenagers descended on the fair every evening. A good reason not to hang around.

We left the diner, headed out of the parking lot, and turned left onto River Road in front of the herring weir. The herring weir is a thirty by thirty foot raised concrete platform that sits a few feet above and directly alongside the Mattapoisett River. It's enclosed on all sides except the one facing the river. Every spring, herring return from the Atlantic Ocean and swim upstream to spawn. The town's herring inspector is busy during the month of April, dropping a large net into the water and hauling up some of the herring that were heading upstream. He'd empty his net onto the concrete platform behind him where a helper sorted them out. Most of the fish were sold, while the coveted red roe was removed from the females and sold in quart containers. Some locals considered it a delicacy. I didn't.

It was a crisp fall day. The kind where you have to decide between the warmth of a sweater or the invigorating nip of the cool air on your skin. The leaves on the sugar maples, at their peak of radiant reds, oranges, and yellows, reflected on the Mattapoisett River.

"It reminds me of Monet's painting, *The Bridge in Monet's Garden*," said Carla.

Colorful dried leaves had fallen from the trees onto the river and were being carried downstream by the current, towards the herring weir. Up ahead, the old stone arch bridge, one of two in town, crossed over the river. On the other side, the road turned left and continued to follow the river. Most of the houses along the road belonged to families who had lived in them for generations.

Soon after crossing the bridge, I turned right into a big field that served as the parking lot for the fair. I found a spot a few rows from the gate. We were among the early birds. In another hour, cars would travel up and down the rows looking for a place to park. We headed to the ticket booth, bought two tickets, were handed a program of events, and entered the fairgrounds.

"Do you think the police chief will call you in on the harbormaster situation," Carla asked as I was looking through the program to get an idea of the early events.

"Well, I imagine they'll wait to see if he's just away on vacation. Not much to investigate right now."

I served in Naval Intelligence during the Vietnam War, and after being discharged, I moved back to Mattapoisett. I had a busy practice doing private detective work. Mostly wives wanting me to find out if their husbands were cheating on them, or vice versa. Lousy work. Nobody won. Except me. I made good money tracking down philanderers.

There weren't too many questionable deaths in this quiet harbor town, but two years ago the police chief asked me to assist them with one.

Wolf Island Road is a gravel road that runs a few desolate miles along the northern border of Mattapoisett, along its boundary with Rochester. Few houses are found on the road, and those that are, are mostly occupied by people looking to escape civilization. The road connects Long Plain Road on the west and North Street to the east. It's lined with pine and a few holly trees. An old small cemetery, named after the Ellis and

Bowles families whose members occupy many of its plots, lies a few tenths of a mile in from Long Plain Road. A three-foot high square stone wall surrounds the hundred or so people who are buried there, and probably a few more who aren't identified by grave markers.

The cemetery is believed to have been a sacred burial ground of the Wampanoag Indians before it became a Christian burial ground in 1872. Because it is so isolated, it was an occasional site of ambushes during King Philip's War. One legend has it that a group of prisoners were hung from trees behind the stone wall at the rear of the cemetery. Depending on which storyteller you listened to, those swinging from the trees had once been members of the Wampanoag Tribe, or locals.

Every once in a while, someone travelling the road would be convinced they saw a body hanging from a tree behind the cemetery. The police would make their usual run to check it out, and find no evidence of a hanging. Except for two years ago.

The cops expected to find nothing—again—but that time a guy *was* hanging by his neck. The police called me in to help with the investigation. I had far better training than the cops did, and it made it easier for them if I did the work.

A large patch of ground directly beneath the body was wet. Just after death, muscles relax, causing people to urinate. His pants were wet, but he didn't lose enough bodily fluid to soak the ground that thoroughly. It hadn't rained for a few days, so I had work to do.

When conducting an investigation, you look to find little pieces then try to connect them. You never know where you'll find them. Or what they might be. Or what they might mean. We were in the middle of a heat wave and beads of sweat formed on my forehead as I walked along the back

133

wall of the cemetery, not looking for anything in particular. Fifty feet from the body I found an empty prescription bottle with a few stones in it. No label on it. Odd, I thought. Good chance it was from a druggie hiding behind the stone wall, popping pills, escaping reality, easing his pain. I used a small stick to roll it into a plastic bag that I always carried with me so I wouldn't destroy any possible latent fingerprints, then dropped it into my pocket. You never know.

I walked out to the road and followed it back towards Long Plain Road. For no particular reason. More just to think. I turned around and walked in the other direction. A few hundred yards past the cemetery a pickup truck was parked on a narrow path that led into the woods. No plates. Surprised the cops hadn't picked up on it. Probably thought it belonged to a hunter. I walked over to it and looked into the bed. Except for a few oak leaves and pine needles, it was empty. The passenger side door was unlocked. I opened it and I stuck my head in. A few empty coffee cups on the floor and some burger wrappers. A receipt on the dashboard was for some ice from the Fairhaven Ice Company. They supplied ice to the fishing boats when they were heading out to the fishing grounds, usually the Grand Banks off Newfoundland. Preserves the fish until they returned to port. I picked up a straw that was on the floor and used it to slide the receipt into another plastic bag. I made a mental note to tell the cops about the truck.

I searched around the area a bit longer and didn't come up with anything else, so I headed back into town to the police station. I walked into the chief's office, Lu Fernandez, and filled her in on what I had found. I asked her to run a test on the residue in the prescription bottle, and to see if they could lift any fingerprints from it. I also told her about the truck and gave her the receipt for the ice. I inquired about an autopsy report. She told me that the body had been taken to the medical examiner's office in New Bedford, and they should have the results within the week.

There wasn't much more I could tell her at this point, so I drove over to Fairhaven to the ice company. A young guy, Cape Verdean, wearing a heavy coat and black watch cap, was standing behind the counter. I told him about the receipt and gave him a description of the truck. He confirmed that he had loaded quite a few blocks of ice into one just like it two days earlier. Said the guy was acting a little strange. Seemed anxious. I thanked him and went home.

Three days later the chief called, confirming that the residue in the prescription bottle was Seconal, and that the prints on it matched the victim. I mulled over my findings during the remainder of the week, waiting for the autopsy report. Chief called on Friday. She told me that the report had arrived, so I walked over to the police station on Church Street, diagonally across from Mahoney's Lane, where I lived.

As soon as I sat down, Chief slid the report across her desk to me. The description of the ligature marks on the neck was interesting. They didn't run the length of the neck, which is typical in hangings where there is a sudden drop and the tightening rope slides up the length of the neck. Instead, they circled the neck in a tight, neat circle. The toxicology report sealed the case for me. The corpse had enough Seconal in it to kill him five times over.

"You can wrap this one up," I told the chief. She just looked at me, clearly puzzled.

"You don't have a murder on your hands. You have a suicide."

I explained my theory to the chief.

"The victim stacked blocks of ice under the tree where his body was found. He then parked his truck, with the receipt for the ice still in it, down the road. He came back to the cemetery, threw a rope with a noose on it over a branch above the blocks of ice, then tied it around the trunk of the tree. He climbed onto the ice, then swallowed the Seconal. The small stones in the bottle enabled him to throw it a good distance from the tree, to the spot where I had found it. He slipped the noose around his neck then sat on the blocks of ice and waited for the Seconal to kick in. Before long he was unconscious, and over the next few hours the ice melted and the noose slowly tightened around his neck until his esophagus constricted *to the point where he could no longer breathe."*

The chief just looked at me.

"I don't know how you do it. We wouldn't have gotten that one. Thanks. I'll write it up and close the case as soon as we identify the victim."

"Who says naval intelligence is an oxymoron," I said with a laugh.

That was the last time I worked for the Mattapoisett Police Department.

◆

TOM AND CAROL WILLIAMSON TURNED ONTO RIVER road. Their two girls, Sandy and Erica, were in the back seat, reading, oblivious to the brilliant colors of fall outside the car windows as they crossed over the arch bridge. Some townspeople say this bridge was built in the 1700's and that still, today, more horses than cars have passed over it.

"Are we there yet?" asked Erica.

"Is our car parked?" asked Carol.

"No."

"Then we aren't there yet."

They followed the river for a tenth of a mile then pulled into the parking lot of the fairgrounds. The layout of the fair was pretty much the same every year: exhibits, rides, competitions. Lots of food vendors. The Fair Society leased the land that abutted the back of the fairgrounds to the Almeida family, who used it to grow corn for their cattle. In exchange for a low annual leasing fee, the Almeidas agreed to cut a maze into the cornfield as an attraction for fairgoers. When the fair ended, they harvested the corn for silage for their cattle.

136

"Let's go watch the parade," said Tom.

The girls groaned in unison, "Can't we get some fried dough first?"

"No, it's too early."

They walked over to the road and joined a large group of excited fairgoers who were waiting for the parade to come by. A few minutes later they heard the high school band playing *The Stars and Stripes Forever* just before the queen of this year's fair, a senior at Old Rochester Regional High School, came into view sitting on the back of a '57 Thunderbird convertible. She was followed by the usual hoard of politicians waving for votes; a long line of old tractors—Allis-Chalmers, McCormick Farmall, Massey Harris; little girls with their hair in pony tails twirling batons; scout troops; and a float packed with members of the high school drama club who were promoting their fall musical—Oklahoma. It was a short parade, and ended with a town fire truck and police cruiser blaring their horns and sirens.

"Now can we have some fried dough?" Erica and Sandy asked in unison.

Against her better judgment, but to quiet them down, Carol gave in.

"Okay, but only a small one."

They spent the morning walking through the animal barns, admiring the Jerseys, Holsteins and Herefords. Numerous blue, red, and white ribbons hung on the walls behind the cattle, proudly displayed by the teens who were sitting on bales of hay near their livestock. Chickens, rabbits, goats, pigs, and other animals were exhibited in several other barns along the edge of the fairgrounds.

◆

Carla and I spent a few hours wandering through the various craft and vegetable displays, and now I was headed to my favorite food stand while Carla went off to buy an apple. For years, the Congregational Church had run a large food booth, selling barbecued chicken and homemade pies. It was good, but I walked on by. Three booths later I came to the one I was looking for. The sign over it proclaimed, **"Our Wurst is the Best!"** I was greeted by Berta, a large German woman with a smile that stretched from ear to ear.

"Hi Manny. Good to see you again."

"How have you been, Berta?"

"Well, I'm a tough Fraulein. I had bronchitis for a few weeks, but I'm doing fine now," she said with a hearty laugh. "The usual?"

I had ordered the same thing every year since Berta set up her booth at the fair—knockwurst, sauerkraut, and German potato salad.

"The usual."

Tom Williamson was in line behind me.

"Hi Manny, how are you doing? Anything new on the harbormaster?"

"Not much, there's little to go on. We're still hoping he's away on vacation and will show up soon."

"Probably the case. He'll have some explaining to do, though. Most of the town is pretty concerned."

"Time will tell. Are your girls enjoying the fair?"

"Now that they've had their fried dough they are. I'm getting a bratwurst sandwich from Berta and Carol and the girls are going to get some pulled pork. We're heading over to the corn maze after that. We'll probably kill a few hours in there."

Berta handed me my plate, piled high with delicious German food. The smell instantly activated my salivary glands.

138

"Enjoy your day, Manny, and say hi to Carla for us."

"You too. Have fun, and say hi to Carol and the girls for us."

"Will do."

After putting a generous amount of spicy brown mustard on my knockwurst, I walked over to the picnic tables and joined Carla. She was eating a MacIntosh that she had bought at the Roberts' Farm fruit stand. Behind Carla, I watched the long line at the pulled pork booth.

Freddie Texeira and his family had sold pulled pork plates and sandwiches at the fair for fourteen years. Since his mother died two years ago, Freddie had prepared the food and worked the booth alone. Customers could buy plain sandwiches or, for fifty cents more could add cheese and cole slaw. Pulled pork platters that included baked beans and potato salad were also available. A variety of sauces with names like *Wimp Juice*; *Lethal Ingestion*; *Sudden Death*; and, *I Told You It Was Hot* sat on the counter for use by customers to enhance their pork. The sign over his stand read "Let Us Pull Your Pork!" Fair management had received a number of complaints about the sign over the years, but hadn't done anything about it. Freddie was used to the jokes, and had heard them all. He didn't care as long as they kept buying his pork.

◆

After they ate lunch, Tom bought four tickets to the corn maze. The paths were enclosed in chicken wire fencing to keep fairgoers from trampling down the corn. Sandy and Erica rushed ahead, turning down a path that quickly led to a dead end. Then they backtracked.

"Stay with us, girls. I don't think you want to get lost and

139

spend the night out here," threatened Carol.

For the next fifteen minutes they followed various paths through the cornfield, often hitting a dead end or circling back to where they started.

"What's that?" Erika asked, pointing into the corn stalks.

Tom went over to Erica and looked. It appeared to be a human leg, or, more likely, a mannequin leg. As he stared at it more intently, he suddenly realized it wasn't a mannequin.

"You stay with the girls. Get them out of the maze," he shouted at Carol. "I'm going to go report this."

Carol, spotting what Tom had been looking at, fought against the urge to scream and choked back the breakfast that had started to ascend from her stomach.

I have to mark the spot, Tom thought as he reached into his pocket and pulled out his handkerchief. He stuck a corner of it into the fencing to mark where the leg rested on the ground fifteen feet into the cornfield.

Carol grabbed the girls by their hands and hurried them back to the entrance of the maze while Tom ran to the fair's office building.

He burst through the door and hollered to the woman behind the counter, "Call the police! There's a problem in the corn maze!"

Puzzled, the woman just looked at him.

"Call the police, now! There's a human leg in the corn maze."

Her face blanched as she picked up the phone and quickly dialed the emergency number.

Tom left the office and ran to the entrance of the fairgrounds so that he could direct the police to the body part.

◆

140

Carla and I sat at the picnic table by the entrance to the maze, enjoying the warm sun and swatting away yellowjackets. I was savoring every bite of my wurst while Carla worked on her apple. In the distance I heard the faint sound of a siren, but paid little attention. However, my ears perked up as it grew louder and sounded like it was heading up River Road towards the fair. Moments later, a Mattapoisett police cruiser turned into the fairgrounds, and I stood as it approached. Several fairgoers hastily emerged from the maze. I spotted Rich and Karen Price in the group and hurried over to intercept them.

"What's going on?" I asked.

"It looks like there's a human leg in the corn, a few feet in from the path," said Rich.

As Officer Townsend and Detective Aiello stepped out of their cruiser, Tom approached them and said, "Follow me."

He led the officers through the maze to where his handkerchief was stuck in the fence. The group of people that had gathered cleared a path for the officers.

"Right over there," said Tom as he pointed to the leg.

"Please leave the maze, now," Officer Townsend ordered as he corralled the gathering crowd of spectators and herded them out of the maze.

Police Chief Fernandez heard the call on her radio and also rushed to the fairgrounds, arriving moments after Townsend and Aiello had pulled up.

Chief's family members were long-time residents of Mattapoisett and were well-known for their service to the town. Her father, Joe, served on the school committee for many years, and was instrumental in many of the improvements to the town's education system. Her mother, Frances, had been a

141

volunteer at the Mattapoisett Historical Society, and for two years served as president of the high school's Band Parent's Association.

Following her graduation from college, Chief took a job as a police officer in Keene, New Hampshire, the first woman to serve on the force. Four years later, the chief's position opened up in Mattapoisett and she was encouraged to apply. She, and many others in town, were surprised when the selectmen hired her for the job. Because of her work ethic and communication skills, she soon won the respect of the town's residents.

Chief parked her cruiser, saw me, then said, "You might as well come with me. We'll probably be using you on this one."

My brain immediately kicked in. It always did when I went on duty. *I guess I'm reporting for duty.* My eyes and ears quickly toggled from the fun and relaxation of the fair to the intensity of an investigation.

I followed the chief through the maze to where the two officers peered into the cornfield. As we approached the scene, Detective Aiello pushed the chicken wire fence down and walked through the corn to examine what appeared to be a human leg, oblivious to any evidence he might be trampling.

"Looks like a leg, Chief," he shouted.

I stood next to the chief and surveyed the scene. I noticed a distinct path of trampled corn that went in a northwesterly direction away from the spot where the leg lay on the ground.

For years I had a habit of carrying my camera with me. I never knew when I might need it. I pulled it out of my pocket and snapped a few pictures. I then stepped into the corn and carefully walked towards the leg, searching the ground along the way and stopping every few steps to take pictures.

I stooped to examine the leg and photographed it from

several angles. It was a left leg, neatly severed just below where it would have been attached to the hip. There was no blood on the ground under the leg, suggesting it was probably not separated from its owner here. The cut was too neat for the leg to have been chopped off, torn off, or eaten off the body. Certainly not an accident. I looked around to see if there were other body parts or possible evidence, but saw none.

I carefully backtracked out of the cornfield and went over to where the chief was standing.

"I'm going to take a look around," I said to her as I headed out of the maze.

Once I reached the entrance, I turned right to follow the perimeter around to the far side of the field. Rows of corn stalks stood nearly nine feet high, each sprouting a half dozen large ears of corn.

I had a good idea what I was looking for. At the edge of the cornfield I turned right to follow it along the northwest side. A dirt road skirted the perimeter, travelled by the farm vehicles, and I was careful not to walk in the tracks, but stayed along the grassy edge farthest from the field. Fifty yards down I spotted an unmistakable path of trampled cornstalks going in the direction of the leg.

When you come upon a crime scene it's important to gather as much evidence as you possibly can, as quickly as you can. Otherwise, it might be lost for good. I needed to confirm my suspicion. I moved several yards to the left of the path through the trampled corn, and walked parallel to it, taking pictures along the way. Soon, I heard the voices of the police officers up ahead. I spotted the leg, still lying on the ground, and the officers standing behind it. I was confident I knew how it ended up in that spot.

I retraced my steps out of the cornfield while methodically

scanning the path on my left. As I approached the road I spotted something and stopped. *How did I miss that on the way in? I'm slipping!* Something small and pink was lying on the ground in the middle of the path, just before where it exited the cornfield. I carefully walked over and stooped to examine it. It was the distinctive wrapper from a stick of Teaberry gum. I recognized it because it was my favorite gum, though I had a hard time finding it. I pulled another plastic bag out of my pocket, picked up the very corner of the wrapper between the nails of my right thumb and middle finger, then dropped it into the bag. *Hopefully we can lift some prints off it.*

I went back to my path then followed it until I exited the cornfield. Two furrows were created by vehicles that had travelled the road along its perimeter. Most likely from tractors and farm vehicles. Fresh tire tracks turned slightly to the right and off the road directly in front of the path. A few feet further the tracks turned back onto the road and continued down the middle of the furrows. Drivers often subconsciously pull their vehicles over a little when stopping.

They stopped here. I spotted some fresh footprints beside the tracks. *Possibly left by the driver.*

I pulled out my camera and took close up pictures of the tire tracks and footprints from several angles. If we found a suspect we could compare the photos to the tracks from their vehicle and their shoes. I was careful not to disturb them as I took one last picture of the trampled cornstalks before heading back along the edge of the field to the entrance of the maze. I arrived there just in time to see the officers exiting with a plastic bag that obviously contained the leg.

I caught up with the chief and filled her in on what I had found. She asked if she needed to send a detective out to where I found the entrance to the path and the tracks. They wouldn't find anything that I hadn't already found, but I suggested she have the detective make plaster castings of the footprints and tire tracks in case we located a suspect.

"While you were on the other side of the cornfield, Ralph Barstow shared some information with me on a possible suspect. My detective will follow up on it and see what develops," she said.

"Why don't we get together Monday in my office to figure out a plan. In the meantime, I'll have my men do some more investigating. I'll fill the selectmen in on this and prepare a news briefing. The press has probably already started calling them.

"See you on Monday. Eleven o'clock?"

"I'll be there."

I re-entered the maze, looked around the crime scene and took a few more pictures. I heard footsteps behind me. Officer Townsend returned with a roll of yellow plastic tape that had "CRIME SCENE – DO NOT ENTER" printed on it. It had never been used. Probably been in the trunk of the cruiser for a few years.

After one of the fair employees verified that no one was left inside the maze, Townsend tied one end of the plastic to some corn stalks on the left side of the entranceway, stretched it across the entrance, cut the ribbon, and tied the other end to stalks at the right side of the maze. It was shut down for the foreseeable future, much to the disappointment of hundreds of families that had planned on spending hours exploring its various paths on this beautiful fall day.

Detective Aiello arrived back at the entrance, and I watched as he and Townsend slipped under the ribbon to continue their investigation. I had already searched the area thoroughly and was confident that I had seen everything there was to be seen.

I rejoined Carla who was eating a maple walnut ice cream

cone from Frates Ice Cream stand. I'd touch base with Aiello and Townsend when they came out of the maze to see what they came up with and to fill them in on what I had found. I doubt they discovered anything that I hadn't.

"Want one?" Carla asked as she waived her ice cream cone at me.

"Sounds like a plan."

She knew I would need a few minutes to think about what I had seen, and would leave me alone with my thoughts.

"What kind would you like?"

"Surprise me. Is Deb working at the booth?"

"Yes, she is."

"Tell her I'll stop by later to say 'hi'. For now, I need to process what I've learned."

Deb owned the ice cream stand. Everyone liked Deb because she was so vivacious and always had a smile on her face. She did a great business as she always went out of her way to make people feel welcome and happy, though it certainly didn't hurt that she and her brother Mike made the best ice cream in the area.

Carla got up and headed over to buy me a cone. On the way, she passed Freddie Texeira's pulled pork booth. Though many in town called him Wharf Rat, she hated that name and never used it. She continued on to the ice cream stand, then she returned to where I was sitting and handed me an orange-pineapple cone.

"Nice pick. My favorite."

"You think I don't know that?" She smiled.

"What do you think happened? Do you think it could be the harbormaster?"

I spent the next ten minutes filling Carla in on what I had discovered.

"Do you think they'll ask you to work on this case?"

"Yes, Chief already asked me to be involved."

"If anyone can figure it out, you can. They are so lucky you are around to help them. The whole town is."

◆

Word about the leg spread quickly among the fairgoers. Ralph Barstow, who runs a charter fishing business, had just taken a bite out of his pulled pork sandwich. It was loaded with *I Told You it Was Hot* sauce.

"Hey Wharf Rat, are you sure there's only pork in here?" he said with a sneer as he pointed at the pulled pork in the warming tray behind the counter. "The cops might be stopping by for some samples, but not to eat," he snarled with a sarcastic laugh as he turned and walked away.

Ralph hated Texeira ever since he turned him in to the shellfish warden for taking oysters from the beds in the harbor that were less than three inches long. In subsequent weeks, the warden had made it a point to observe Barstow, and he caught him with undersized oysters and also harvesting more than the allowed one peck per week. As a result, Barstow had his shellfishing privileges revoked for a year.

Just as I finished my orange-pineapple cone, I spotted Townsend and Aiello walking out of the maze. I got up and went over to intercept them.

"I have something to show you that I think might help your investigation. Come with me."

I led them back into the maze, then said, "Look over there," as I pointed to behind where the leg had been found.

"See how the cornstalks are leaning towards the ground,

creating a path?"

Detective Aiello took out his notepad and began writing. He clearly had missed the obvious.

"Follow me."

I led them around the perimeter of the cornfield until we reached the opposite side.

"This is where the path begins. I followed alongside it until I came to where you were conducting your investigation. I didn't disturb the path."

"Also, look at these tire tracks and footprints," I said as I pointed at the road.

"See how the tire tracks pull off the road a little bit right here, then pull back onto the road up ahead there? It looks like the driver stopped here. The footprints next to the tracks are probably from the driver."

Aiello scribbled a few more notes. No pictures, no talk of lifting the tracks, just a few notes. The three of us returned to the fairgrounds. I didn't mention the gum wrapper. No sense complicating the chain of custody. I'll give it to Chief on Monday. Townsend and Aiello cordoned off the area with crime scene tape and an auxiliary officer was assigned to preserve the crime scene.

I walked over to where Carla and I had been sitting. She wasn't there.

She must have gone to the porta-potty. I waited a few minutes, but she didn't return. *Probably wandered off to explore the fair. I'll go find her.* I spent the next thirty minutes scouring the fairgrounds looking for her, figuring she must be checking out some more exhibits while I was talking with the police. I couldn't find her.

On a hunch, I walked over to the parking lot to see if she had gone back to her car. I arrived at where we had parked, but her car wasn't there. The space was occupied by a '61 Chrysler DeSoto. My heart beat faster. My detective instinct kicked in.

148

Something seemed wrong. *This isn't like her.*

I went back to the fairgrounds and sat down at the picnic table where we had enjoyed our ice cream cones a short time ago. *This is where she'll look for me. She must have a good reason for leaving. I'll give her a half hour.*

For the next thirty minutes I watched several children who were sitting on the backs of ponies, circling a small pen as their parents stood behind a snow fence snapping pictures. The smell of fried onions filled the air.

I was becoming more worried about Carla. Thirty minutes went by and still no sign of her. *I'll ask the police to check on her house to see if she drove home, though I'm not sure why she'd do that without letting me know. I was always nearby.*

I walked over to Detective Aiello.

"I know you're busy with the investigation, but Carla is missing and I'm a bit worried. Her car is gone too. Could you radio the station and ask if they could send a car by her place on Pearl Street to see if she's there?"

"I sure can, I'll do it right now," he said as he started towards the cruiser.

But before he was halfway there, Carla appeared.

"Where did you go? I was worried about you."

"You weren't around and I saw a man walk out of the cornfield over there," she said as she pointed off to her right. "I thought that was unusual and I knew you were tied up, so I followed him," she said with a hint of pride in her voice.

"You had me pretty worried. I'm the detective, remember? It's not fun investigating *your* disappearance. So, where did he go, detective?" I said with thinly disguised sarcasm.

"He went to Ned's Point Road."

"Well, that leg was there for quite a while, certainly since before the fair opened today, so your 'suspect' wouldn't just be

149

coming out of the cornfield. He probably had to relieve himself, and with the long lines at the porta-potty he probably just stepped into the cornfield to take care of it. Besides, where you saw him was on the other side of the path from where the leg was found."

"Let's go watch the ox pull. There's nothing more I can do about the leg or the investigation right now."

Halfway down the left side of Ned's Point Road, towards the lighthouse, a black truck was parked in the driveway of a small house. Its only distinguishing feature was a large sticker of a fish on the window behind the driver's seat.

In competition, teams of oxen are hitched up to a sled to which an increasing amount of weight is added for each consecutive pull. To start the pull, the driver cracks a whip, urging the oxen to pull the load forward. A chalk line marks the required distance for the pull, and the goal is for the team to pull the load across the line. After each pull, additional weight is placed on the sled. Teams that can't pull for the distance are eliminated until only one team remains. That team and its driver win a large blue ribbon.

What I find impressive about ox pulling is the teamwork between the oxen and the handler. Long before tractors were introduced to farming, oxen pulled plows, skids loaded with blocks of ice cut from ponds, and bales of hay—all very effectively for their owners. Though some people feel they are being mistreated during competitions at fairs, oxen *are* work animals doing what they do best—pulling as a team. I like teamwork.

"Are you getting hungry?" I asked.

"Getting there," replied Carla. "Do you have any more

work to do here?"

"No, nothing until I meet with the chief on Monday."

"How about going to the Holy Mackerel? I'm up for some swordfish," said Carla.

"Sounds like a plan."

Before we left the fairgrounds, we stopped by the ice cream stand so I could say hi to Deb.

"Did you come for another cone?" she asked.

I laughed and patted my midsection. "I think I'm carrying enough of your ice cream for now, so don't tempt me."

"Well, you know where you can find me when you have a craving for some."

"I sure do. See you soon."

We left the fairgrounds and drove over to Fairhaven for dinner.

♦

CARLA WALKED TOWARDS CHURCH STREET, ON HER WAY to A Brewed Awakening. She and Kendra were long-time friends who usually got together once a week to catch up on the town gossip and to talk about relationships. Five minutes after leaving her house, she walked through the front door and spotted Kendra sitting at a table reading the latest copy of the *Presto Press*. Carla gave her a quick hug and joined her. They had been there so many times that their waitress, Melissa, no longer had to ask what they wanted, and moments later she set a cup of coffee in front of Carla—cream, no sugar.

"Hi Carla, like something to eat?" she asked.

Kendra had a blueberry muffin in front of her that was packed with blueberries.

"I'll have one of those," she said, pointing at the muffin.

"Fresh out of the oven. Be back in a minute."

"How was your weekend?" Carla asked.

Kendra raised an eyebrow, grinned, then asked, "Why, did you hear something?"

Carla just shook her head. Their get-togethers were often punctuated with such quips.

Kendra is a real looker. Leggy, redhead, green eyes, and a great figure. When Carla and Kendra were out together, Kendra was usually the one who got the elevator scans—from men and from women. Some of the attention, undoubtedly, was because her attire was usually cut low on the top and short on the bottom.

Melissa brought Carla's muffin. She watched steam escape as she split it apart, then put on a dab of butter on it that melted instantly.

"Better wait a second before you eat it," said Melissa as she turned and left their table.

"Manny and I went to the Tri-Town Fair. You probably heard about the leg that was found in the corn maze."

"Oh no," exclaimed Kendra.

"There's speculation that it belongs to the harbormaster, but there is no evidence of that. Manny was asked to help out with the investigation."

"Oh my God! That's awful! I *didn't* hear about it. Do they have any idea what happened?"

"No. Manny is meeting with the police chief in a few days. They were supposed to meet today, but I guess they don't have much to go on right now. Tell me about your weekend."

Carla braced herself.

"It was wonderful. I went on a date with an attorney. We had dinner at the Dockside Grille over in New Bedford. We finished a bottle of wine and had an Irish coffee for desert. We ended up back at his place."

"Details, details. Let's hear 'em."

Carla knew that Kendra would tell her anyways, so she might as well ask her.

Kendra filled her in on all the details as she savored her blueberry muffin. Actually, her stories were similar to the details she had shared with Carla about nearly all of her previous dates.

"I meant to behave, but there were so many other options!"

"Really? And what were they?"

Kendra just winked at her.

They chatted for a while. Kendra was aware of Carla's challenges and listened without interrupting as she rehashed them with her for the umpteenth time. Carla felt fortunate to have such a close friend who was familiar with what she had been through. She had experienced it herself, though her experiences affected her differently from how Carla's affected her. That happens.

They finished their coffee and muffins and made a date for the following Monday, same time, same place.

◆

WE HAD POSTPONED OUR MEETING FOR A FEW DAYS SO that Aiello and Townsend could do some more investigating. It was late Thursday morning and we were sitting at a table in a quiet corner of the Whaler's Inn. The chief wanted to drive over here as soon as I got to her office. Coffee and a house-made donut in front of each of us. I guess cops really do like donuts.

"It hasn't even been a week since we found the leg and the papers are already slamming us. Reporters from the *New Bedford*

Tribune have been calling every hour asking for an update. Suggesting we aren't competent. Channel 6 has filmed the front of the station a half dozen times. How much footage do they need of a police building? Must be nice to have a job where all they have to do is take potshots at people whose jobs they couldn't do themselves."

She paused. I didn't interrupt her silence. Chief is usually pretty calm when she's under fire, though she's more used to investigating break-ins and traffic accidents than murders.

"Chief, I learned not to worry about criticism. God knows I got enough of it when I returned from Viet Nam. Spit in the face. Called a baby killer. All by people who had nowhere near the experience I had. I learned to let it roll off my back. At the end of the day we'll all be heroes. It's just that the path in that direction will be a bit rocky. So, where are we?"

She was quiet for a minute.

"Well, to start with, we haven't found any witnesses, other than Ralph Barstow, and I'm not sure how credible he is. He lies as easily as he breathes. Remember I told you that he caught me at the fair and told me he had seen Freddie Texeira, the guy they call Wharf Rat, leaving the fairgrounds the night before it opened? We brought him in for questioning, and he's sure Texeira must have left the leg there. But, those two guys have been at each other for years, so his comment is suspect. On the other hand, Texeira does have a record and did jail time for stabbing a guy a few years back, so I sent Townsend out to talk with him. Texeira told him he went to put a new sign up over his booth. Said the old one had ripped. Townsend checked, and said the sign looks new, but who knows.

"No one else has come forward with anything. We were hoping that with so many people attending the fair someone would have seen something. But, nothing. Probably means it was there before the fair opened," she said.

Chief continued, "We're trying to see if there's a link to the harbormaster's disappearance. Detective Aiello knocked on every door on Water Street and spoke with all the residents on the street. No one reported hearing or seeing anything unusual.

"They also checked with most of the boat owners with boats moored at any of the three wharves—nothing.

"The leg is over at forensics in New Bedford, but I doubt it will tell us much," the chief continued.

Maybe, maybe not. "It looks like it was deliberately cut off," I said. "The cut was too straight, too perfect. Maybe with a saw. Probably not an accident, but we'll have to see what the forensic report tells us."

"Our men went back and searched the fairgrounds foot-by-foot, but found nothing to add to the investigation.

"We're walking through a search warrant so we can get into Tinkham's house. The Fourth Amendment slows us down a bit. We're trying to persuade a judge over at the courthouse in New Bedford that we have probable cause. We dropped off an affidavit and are waiting for permission to get inside. We'll be on that as soon as we can. His truck is in the driveway, so we can search that as soon as we have the warrant.

"Also, we're in the process of rounding up our town's usual suspects and questioning them. Don't expect to get much out of them, but who knows. Has to be done. At least it's something I can report to the press."

I waited a minute to see if she had anything else. She didn't.

"I picked this up at the far side of the field," I said, as I held up the plastic bag containing the Teaberry gum wrapper. Might not be anything, but worth tagging as evidence and checking for prints."

I slid it across the desk to her.

"I took pictures of the tire tracks and footprints at the back of the field," I said as I handed them to her.

I had duplicates back at my house.

"As you know, tire tracks leave unique patterns, so I sent the pictures off to several of the databases that tire manufacturers and the FBI maintain to see if we can get an ID on the type and brand of the tire. It probably won't help us now, but if we develop a suspect, it could help to place them at the scene by matching the tires on their vehicle with those we found at the maze."

Chief looked at me. "Are you sure you don't want to join our force?"

"Positive."

"Anything else?"

"Not unless you've got something."

"Well then, I guess that's all we have for now. We've got a few things to follow up on. Let's meet here next week to see where we stand. Oh yeah, and the selectmen approved this," she said as she opened the folder in front of her and handed a sheet of paper to me.

It was a contract for me to work with the police on the case. A nice amount. It would pay a few bills. I read it, signed it, and handed it back across the table to the chief. She gave me a duplicate copy, minus my signature.

"Next Thursday at eleven?"

"Unless something develops before then. See you next Thursday," she confirmed.

"Here?"

"Works for me."

She must like the donuts.

FRIDAY FINALLY ARRIVED. IT HAD BEEN A HECTIC WEEK for both of us, so over breakfast Carla and I made plans to have dinner that night at Stuffies, a popular seafood restaurant over in Marion, one town closer to the Bourne Bridge and Cape Cod from Mattapoisett. The two towns have a friendly rivalry as to which is better, which is the richest, and which has the best harbor. That debate has been ongoing for generations, even after the two towns and the neighboring town of Rochester joined forces to establish Old Rochester Regional High School in the early 1960s.

Both towns are popular summer destinations for wealthy out-of-state vacationers who have money to burn. The license plates on the cars filling the parking lot at Stuffies attested to that: New York, New Jersey, Pennsylvania. We walked through the front door and ran the gauntlet of waiting customers who occupied the benches on either side of the lobby. After making our way to the reservation desk we were greeted by Mary, a pretty blond woman with an infectious smile.

"Hi Manny, Carla. For two?"

"Yes, and in a quiet corner."

We all laughed. There were no quiet corners at Stuffies.

Mary and her husband Dennis moved to town from Rhode Island many years ago and opened the restaurant. They quickly earned a reputation for having the best stuffed clams and clam chowder in Southeastern Massachusetts. Dozens of certificates lined the walls attesting to that, earned in competitions with most of the other well-known seafood places in the region. The first-place certificates for "Best Stuffed Clams – Southeastern

Massachusetts Seafood Competition" formed a long line down an entire wall, winner for each of the past nine years. The same was true for the best clam chowder. Both were made in-house, from scratch. During the summer months, Dennis made more than a thousand stuffed clams a week, using a closely guarded secret recipe. On more than one occasion he'd been offered money for his recipe, but he staunchly refused to give it up. When they lived in Rhode Island, stuffed clams were called "stuffies," thus the name of their restaurant.

Mary's specialty was the clam chowder, made from an old family recipe. Certificates for her award-winning clam chowder rivaled the number of Dennis's for his stuffies. The two items were the most popular on the menu.

"Grab a seat in the lobby, if you can find one. I'll come and get you as soon as a table opens up."

We went back to the lobby and stood near the entranceway. While we waited, we read a review of the restaurant that was in a large frame on the wall. It had appeared in the *New Bedford Tribune*. The article raved about the restaurant and gave it five scallops—its highest rating.

Before long, Mary came out and told us she had a table ready. We followed her into the restaurant and over to a small table against the wall.

"Will this work?"

"Any table you have works for us. The food's the same, right?"

We all laughed.

"Do you need menus?"

I glanced at Carla who shook her head, and then said, "No, we know what we're having. Two bowls of clam chowder and four stuffies."

"Oh, and I think we'll need some oysters for tonight," I said as I winked at Carla. "A half dozen should work—let's

158

make that a dozen."

Mary just smiled and said, "They'll be right up. Would you like the oysters first?"

"Sure, bring 'em on. Still serving Wellfleet's?"

"Only the best! Trish will bring them right out to you."

Trish was Mary's sister, and along with their other sister, Linda, they comprised the front-of-the-house staff and also filled in as cooks during the really busy times, which was the entire summer. Both were attractive and personable women with the same beautiful smile as Mary's. The three sisters were all working tonight.

The room was filled with nautical décor: a pair of crossed oars, some fish netting, large sea-glass float pendants. Quite a few local lobstermen had given them one of their distinctive lobster buoys. A buoy floats on the surface of the water and is attached with rope, called a potwarp, that runs to the bottom where it is secured to a lobster pot.

Most lobstermen set numerous pots, usually up to the limit allowed by law. The captain of each boat creates his or her own unique combination of colors and patterns for their buoys. That makes it easier for them to identify the location of their pots, and also helps the harbormaster to identify the rightful owner of a pot, reducing the chances of theft. More than a dozen colorful buoys from local lobstermen hung on the walls at Stuffies.

"Here's your oysters," said Trish, drawing us back from our study.

She set a platter in front of us with a dozen plump oysters camped on ice. The house cocktail sauce was a blend of fresh horseradish, ketchup, and a dash of another hot sauce, the name of which they wouldn't reveal. It was unique, and a great compliment to the oysters. Several lemon wedges surrounded the oysters.

"Trish, would you bring me a glass of sauvignon blanc, please?" asked Carla.

"Sure thing. Anything for you Manny?"

"I'll have iced tea, unsweetened, with lemon please."

"You've got it," she said as she headed over to the counter that served as their small liquor and raw bar.

Five minutes earlier Trish had shucked a dozen Wellfleet's for us. Now, she poured a glass of the chilled white wine.

"Here you go," she said as she set the glass in front of Carla.

"Thanks Trish."

I just looked at Carla. She knew what I was thinking.

"Any progress on the investigation?" she asked, deflecting my look.

"No, and it's very frustrating. Often, I find clues right away. The longer it takes the less likely we are to solve it. And, the cops are taking a lot of flak from the press and the locals. Seems like they think we can just walk in, look around, then arrest the person who did it. We aren't finding much to go on."

Linda walked out of the kitchen and set two bowls of chowder in front of us.

"Would you like some ground black pepper?"

"Sure would, please," said Carla, "and can you bring me a refill on my wine?"

She didn't make eye contact with me.

Linda came back and ground a generous amount of black pepper onto our chowder. The steam rising from the bowls carried a mouth-watering seafood aroma to our noses, olfactory bliss that made the first taste even better.

Trish returned with Carla's wine and asked, "How is everything?"

160

"Award-winning," I replied.

"Glad you are enjoying it. Your stuffies will be right out."

While we were savoring our chowder, Linda came over and set a plate filled with six large shrimp on the table between us. They sat on a bed of kale, and were joined by two lemon wedges and a small cup of cocktail sauce.

"Here's a little something for you—on the house."

"Thanks Linda. Keep it up and you'll have to wheel us out to our car," Carla said with a laugh.

Linda's hair was blonder than her sisters', but they all shared the same beaming smile.

"Busy tonight, isn't it?" I asked.

"It's been like this all week. Great, considering it's not our peak season."

"How's John doing?" I asked.

John was their brother. A tall, lean, handsome man. He owned a fishing boat, the New Gent, and supplied Stuffies with most of their cod, haddock and bluefish. During the busiest of weekends, if he wasn't fishing, he filled in wherever he was needed. He was known as the fastest oyster shucker in the area.

"John's doing great. He was in earlier this morning, dropping off some fresh fish for us. They are running really well right now, so we can offer more specials than usual. You'll have to try our Parmesan-Crusted Cod."

"You mean we'll have to get out of our rut?"

We all laughed.

We had just finished our chowder when Dennis walked out of the kitchen carrying a plate of his famous stuffies.

"How are you guys doing?" he said as he set them down.

Dennis was a big guy, with swatches of gray hair on both sides of his head that matched his gray beard. Judging by his enthusiasm and cooking he was in the right business.

161

"Good, and we'll be even better after we finish your stuffies."

"Glad you like 'em. Do you need hot sauce?"

"Absolutely," I said.

He returned a minute later with a large bottle and said, "We're trying a new one, it's called habanero orange. Tell me if you like it. If you don't, let us know and we'll bring you something different."

The stuffies were delicious, and the habanero orange worked perfectly with them.

Our conversation shifted as we picked the delicious mixture of clams, chourico, breadcrumbs and secret spices off large sea scallop shells.

"Weeks like this are tough, frustrating. No witnesses have come forward. No more clues have turned up. Not much to go on. And it gets harder as time goes by. The longer it takes, the safer it is for the criminals. I'm beginning to think that maybe I should retire."

"Be patient, Manny. You are good at what you do, and I know you'll figure it out. I believe in you."

"Enough about my week, I know yours has been challenging too," I said, looking at Carla as she took another sip of her sauvignon blanc.

"I have a new client whose situation is really bothering me. A young girl. Possible abuse. I can't tell you much about it. You know that, but this one has me especially concerned."

I knew she couldn't discuss much with me about any of her clients, protecting their confidentiality. She never wavered on that, and it was the right thing to do. Another reason I love her.

Linda came by and asked if we wanted dessert.

Carla looked at her and asked, "Really? No, but I'll have another glass of wine."

I looked at Carla. She knew the look. "Never mind," she

said.

We paid our bill, said goodbye to the sisters, and headed for the door.

Just as we were leaving, Art Nunes pushed his way through the entranceway, bumping into Carla.

"It might be nice to hold the door for a woman," I said. I have little tolerance for rude people. No civility.

Nunes was a local fisherman who I knew had done some jail time years ago. He was a little rough around the edges, as had been his father, and most people avoided him.

"Screw you," he said as he pushed past us into the restaurant.

We walked to my car, and as I went to open the door for Carla I noticed a long scratch down the side. Someone had keyed my car.

"Damn. Some obnoxious kid with nothing to do. Another project on my list."

I wasn't happy. Carla knew it. She also knew that she might be able to fix that.

I closed Carla's door and got in on the driver's side. Then I pulled around the black pickup truck parked next to us and headed home.

◆

I WAS SITTING AT A TABLE AT THE BACK OF THE WHALER'S Inn, sipping an iced tea and reviewing my notes as I waited for the chief to arrive for our scheduled meeting. I keep detailed notes on my investigations on a steno pad, and have learned that I see something new every time I read through them. I was on my second run-through when the chief walked in. She came over, and before she sat down she looked at the table and asked, "What, no donuts?"

"I'm not a cop," I answered.

She knew better than to spar with me, so she just sat down.

"So, what have you got?" she asked as she looked at my notebook then waved for a waitress.

"Unfortunately, not much," I said, as our waitress arrived.

"Could I get a cup of coffee, black?" Chief asked.

"Can I get you anything else?"

"That's it for . . . oh, and could you please bring some menus?"

"What, no donuts?" I asked.

"No, I can't handle your abuse."

She changed the topic.

"I'm still waiting for the search warrant, so we can get into Tinkham's house. Hopefully they'll issue it in the next day or two. I'm also waiting to hear back from forensics about the leg. I know they're backed up over there, but I'm guessing they'll have something for us soon. I brought in some more of our town's shady characters, but didn't get anything out of them. We still don't have any witnesses, so we can't do a lineup."

"Any prints on the gum wrapper?" I asked.

"There were prints on it, but they were too smudged to be useful."

I was disappointed. I was hoping they'd find a good print, though I knew that there were several factors, in addition to smudging, why prints might not show up: rain, high humidity, air temperature, obliteration by being stepped on, or having been exposed to dusty or dirty surfaces. Or, the guy could have been wearing gloves.

Our waitress brought us two menus and coffee for the chief. A few minutes later she came back and we ordered lunch.

164

We didn't have anything else to discuss about the case, so we ate our lunch and talked about the upcoming elections. Town politics are always fun. New candidates promising to fix problems that the guy they replaced had promised to fix, which were created by the guy in office before him. Little ever changes, especially the campaign promises.

♦

OFFICER TOWNSEND AND DETECTIVE AIELLO WERE ON their way to the pig farm on Crystal Spring Road. Chief Fernandez had given them the go ahead to search the farm for evidence of the harbormaster. They didn't have a search warrant, but there are exceptions to needing one; for example, when there is consent, when items are in plain view, or when there are exigent circumstances. They were going to try for consent.

Shortly before noon they pulled into the driveway of the farmhouse. The large white house appeared to be well-maintained. There were numerous flower beds in the yard, and a long row of yellow and maroon chrysanthemums ran along the entire front of the house. Not the kind of landscaping they expected from a pig farmer.

They parked the car, then walked up and knocked on the front door. A moment later Freddie opened it.

Aiello immediately spotted the knife in his hand and asked, "Is that what you used?"

"Used for what? Why are you here?"

"Used to kill the harbormaster."

"I don't know what you're talking about. I didn't kill the harbormaster. I'm just sharpening my knives. I need them for my business."

Officer Townsend took over.

"Mr. Texeira, he's been missing for a while, and we have to investigate. Your name came up so we need to look into it. We're not saying you did anything, and if you let us look around a bit that will probably be the end of it."

They had decided to play good cop/bad cop. Aiello wanted to be the bad cop, and that was fine with Townsend.

"Don't you need a search warrant to do this?"

"Not if you give us permission. If you let us search now it might make things a whole lot easier for you down the road," said Townsend.

Freddie thought for a minute. *If I throw them out, they'll think I'm hiding something and they'll be back with a search warrant and tear up the place. If I let them look around and they don't find anything, maybe they'll leave me alone. I might as well let them search now.*

"All right, you can look around, but you won't find anything."

"If something's here, we'll find it," said Aiello, though he had never investigated a murder. "Why don't you put that knife down and come with us."

Minutes later they were standing inside the slaughter house. A dozen fifty-five-gallon drums lined the far wall. They walked over to them and looked inside. Aiello immediately gagged from the stench of rotting flesh and entrails.

"What the hell is this?" he asked through a series of dry heaves.

"That's the part of the pigs that I don't use. I collect it here, then every once in a while I bury it at the back of the farm."

"We're going to have to look through this stuff," said Aiello as he swatted away the flies that were buzzing around the drums and his head.

"Just don't make a mess."

"We'll do what we want to find what we are looking for."

Let me get him out of here. We don't want him to chase us off his property, thought Townsend.

"Mr. Texeira, how about you show me around the rest of the property while Detective Aiello looks around in here?"

"All right, but like I said, don't make a mess."

After Freddie and Townsend walked out the back door of the barn, the officer asked, "Why don't you take me to where you bury the pig remains?"

"It's this way," Freddie said as he headed towards the far side of the field.

"You seem like a nice guy, Freddie, so why don't you just tell me what happened with the harbormaster. I'm sure it was an accident and if you cooperate I will do my best to make sure they are very lenient with you. I know you have a record and did some jail time, so they are going to look at you pretty carefully as a possible suspect. If you help me, I'll help you."

"I didn't do anything, and I wish you cops would believe me. I'm sick of being a suspect every time something happens in town."

"I believe you Freddie, but we have to do our job. I'm sure you understand that."

We reached the back of the field and Freddie pointed to a long, wide trench. Three feet down a layer of loose soil covered pig remains.

"That's where I bury it. This is my newest spot. There's another place farther down my property line."

"Let's go look at that one."

He led me a few hundred yards down the property line to another trench.

"Right here. I closed this one up more than a year ago."

I made a mental note that we'd have to look at these

167

trenches a little more thoroughly.

"Why don't you show me the rest of the property, then we'll get out of your way?"

For the next thirty minutes Freddie and I walked the perimeter of the farm. At the back edge there was a long stretch that dropped off and bordered the Mattapoisett River.

"Catch anything there, Freddie?"

"It's a pretty good spot for perch and pickerel. Once in a while I get a brown trout, but not very often. I eat everything I catch."

We followed a dirt road back to the barn and went inside.

"What the . . . ?" Freddie screamed.

All of the drums containing the pig heads, feet, entrails and blood had been dumped onto the floor and spread around. A bloodied rake lay in the middle of the pile. Detective Aiello's shoes and pants were covered with blood and other fluid from the drums.

"Why did you do this?" Freddie asked.

"You gave us permission, Wharf Rat. Just doing my job. I got some samples in those jars," he said, pointing to a half dozen jars sitting on a table near the door. "We'll take those back and see if any of them contain part of the harbormaster."

"I don't suppose you're going to clean up the mess?"

"Not my job, Wharf Rat."

"Detective, why don't you take the jars out to the car? Give me a minute with Mr. Texeira."

Aiello grabbed a wooden box and put the jars in it, then carried it out to the cruiser.

"I'm really sorry, Mr. Texeira. I didn't realize he was going to do that. Just so you know, they may want to come back and dig up those trenches, but if they do, I'll ask them to fill them back in when they are done. I do thank you for

168

cooperating with us. Here's my card," Townsend said as he handed it to him. "Give me a call if there's anything else you think I should know."

Freddie and Townsend walked back to his house, then Townsend shook his hand before he got into the cruiser and backed out of the driveway.

"What do you think," Aiello asked as they turned onto Crystal Spring Road on their way back to the station.

"I don't know. He didn't seem too nervous. Usually, if someone is guilty of something their voice and body language give a good indication of that. He seemed angrier and more inconvenienced than guilty."

"Yeah, but good criminals know how to be convincing. Let's see what the stuff in the jars tells us."

♦

MY WEEK HAD BEEN FRUSTRATING. I SPENT A LOT OF time thinking about reasons why Carla should marry me, and I came up with quite a few—I'm honest, respectful, make a decent living, and I communicate pretty well. I'm also a good listener, which is how I learned what women look for in a serious relationship. I thought I had a compelling argument, and I presented it to Carla as we walked along Nauset Beach out at the Cape Cod National Seashore. She had cancelled her Wednesday appointments so that we could go there for a little get-away. The summer crowds were gone, and even though we were in the midst of an Indian Summer, few people were on the beach. I thought it might work this time.

I don't like talking about myself, and actually felt a little uncomfortable as I presented Carla with all the reasons why we should get married. I was encouraged that she didn't answer right away, as she usually did, but thought about my proposal as we walked hand-in-hand farther along the edge of the water. Then, when I was as hopeful as I've ever been that she would say yes, she rejected me. Hope exploded out of my heart and through my chest, leaving a painful vacuum.

◆

I ALWAYS SEEM TO ARRIVE BEFORE THE CHIEF, AND TODAY was no exception. I was sitting at our usual table at the Inn, reviewing my notes. I really came up empty this week, both with Carla and the investigation. Chief finally arrived, twenty minutes late, and I was hoping that she'd have some good news.

"Hi Manny. Sorry I'm late. The first selectman called me in and wanted an update on the investigation. The press is going after him now, and he isn't being so subtle in pressing me for answers about the harbormaster. I gave him all I know and he finally backed down a bit. I have to meet with him once a week to keep him updated. Anyways, did you order yet?"

"No, I didn't."

I picked up one of the menus our waitress had left at our table and handed it to the chief. I opened the other one and quickly decided on a bowl of lobster bisque.

Our waitress returned, and after we ordered lunch the chief asked, "Making any progress?"

"Not much, unfortunately. I was hoping I'd get a report back on the tire tracks so we'd know what brand we'd be looking for, but I haven't heard yet. That's all I've got. It's a bit frustrating, but hopefully we'll catch a break soon. How about on your end?"

"Well, a little better news, I guess. Aiello and Townsend convinced Texeira to let them search his property. They tossed it pretty good, but came up empty. They did take a few samples to have checked for any trace of human remains. We haven't got the report back from the lab yet. Also, we got the search warrant to get into Tinkham's house and went through it pretty thoroughly. We didn't find a thing. It hadn't been broken into, there were no signs of a disturbance inside, and nothing we found indicated any travel plans. We discovered an address book and contacted the people listed in it. None of them were relatives. His truck was parked in the driveway. We went through it and lifted some prints. They were all his. Also, I didn't hear back from forensics regarding the leg. I'll put in another call tomorrow to see if they can give me a tentative date for the report."

I thought back to my military training and all the classes I had sat through on conducting investigations.

"As you know, Chief, sometimes it's as important to rule things out as to rule them in. At least it shortens our list. We're not at a dead end yet. We still have the lab report on the samples from the pig farm, the forensic report, and, hopefully, identification of the brand of the tire that left the tracks."

I tried to be optimistic, though I was anxious to move this investigation forward. You always feel the pressure in these kinds of cases. Sometimes the internal pressure is greater than the external pressure. We were feeling a bit of both, and I knew the internal pressure was self-imposed. It always is, and it can be draining.

◆

AT NINE O'CLOCK I WAS ALREADY IN BED. THIS IS MY least favorite time of year, and this year was even worse. The investigation is going far too slowly for my liking. Carla keeps refusing my marriage proposal, and the days are getting shorter. Every day has more darkness than the previous one. It swallows me up every year at this time. That, along with my history, can be a lethal combination. I pray the nightmares won't return, though they probably will.

◆

Winter

CARLA AND I HAD GONE TO HEAR THE BOSTON

Symphony Orchestra to try to get me out of my funk. Armando Ghitalla, the principal trumpeter, played a masterful rendition of Haydn's *Trumpet Concerto in E-flat*, and it had helped improve my mood. I had just dropped her off at her house and was exhausted when I finally arrived home after midnight. No *parfume de baunilha* tonight. Quite some time ago she had told me that she likes a man in her life, but not in her house. I had always taken that figuratively, but now it seemed like it was much more than that.

I took the mail out of my mailbox, turned the key in the door lock, and went inside. After dropping the mail onto the growing pile on my desk, I headed straight to the bathroom and turned on the shower to let it warm up while I brushed my teeth. I stepped in, hoping that the hot water beating down on my neck and shoulders would wash away the stress that had been accumulating. Steam filled the bathroom. I closed my eyes and all the events of the past three months rolled through my mind like a one-minute news summary. Not much of it was good.

After fifteen minutes of shower therapy, I turned it off, stepped out, dried myself, grabbed my crutches, and walked to the bedroom. I leaned the crutches against the wall near the bed, then slid under the covers. A light sat on the table next to me. I reached over, paused a second, then turned it off. More darkness.

◆

Manny had grown up in the village of Mattapoisett, Massachusetts and was accustomed to the sights and sounds associated with the harbor in his small hometown, not those of the Mekong Delta in Vietnam where he was a "brown water sailor." His mind drifted back home as he breathed in the cool salty air of the night and smelled the odor of diesel fuel from the boats moored in the bay. He felt the soft, nighttime breeze as he listened to the crickets playing their song off in the distance. Suddenly, he was startled back to reality with a deafening KABOOM! - KABOOM! - KABOOM! coming from the fuel storage area on the pier.

Three mortar rounds had landed near the fuel tank farm, one of them hitting its mark and erupting a storage tank into a ball of fire. A cloud of heavy black smoke drifted upwards from the burning fuel. It was another of the nightly Viet Cong attacks on the Naval Support Activity Base in Nha Be, South Vietnam where Manny had been stationed for the past three months while serving with Task Force 117.

The blare of the air horn, an all-too-familiar call to General Quarters, sent Manny and his fellow sailors scurrying to their battle stations to defend against yet another assault. The crew ran to the pier and jumped into their River Patrol Boat, or PBR, manning their positions. Manny was at the .50 caliber gun mount in the bow of the boat. GMGC Don Lee, the boat captain, fired up the engines and cast off. As he pulled the boat away from the dock, he checked the river for swimmers who might be trying to place mines or explosives on other watercraft during the distraction of the mortar attack. Lee directed the 32-foot PBR up river and then towards shore. There, they concealed themselves in the thick growth of nipa palms and silently regrouped and regained their composure following the fury of the explosions.

After things settled down, Chief Lee decided that they should drift back downstream towards the base. As the boat approached a small stream that fed into the river, the eerie silence was broken by the sound of people moving along the bank. Chief Lee attempted to pop a flare for illumination, but it didn't work. A cover boat that had been trailing them by fifty feet then popped a flare that briefly blinded Chief Lee's crew. Then, all hell broke loose.

The bow of the PBR took a direct hit by a rocket-propelled grenade, knocking Manny semi-conscious and filling his legs with shrapnel. His eardrums burst. The concussion stunned Engineman Second Class Stark and Chief Lee, knocking them both to the deck just as a heavy salvo of automatic weapons fire peppered the boat. Recovering quickly, Gunners Mate Seaman Goodwin got to the rear .50 cal. deck gun and began returning fire. The cover boat was also receiving fire from the bank while returning fire with all they had. Chief Lee crawled to the radio and called for a Seawolf helicopter gunship for support. He then moved to the coxswain station, reached over, and slapped the throttles forward to quickly propel the boat out of the ambush zone. Both boats put down a wall of fire as they cleared the area. The attack had taken its toll on the PBR. It was on fire and taking on water. The engines came to a halt. PBR 750 was ablaze and dead in the water.

While drifting in and out of consciousness, Manny realized that the Seawolf gunships had arrived at the firing zone and were strafing the area with their rockets and mini-guns. The cover boat pulled alongside and began helping the crew off of the sinking vessel. The strong smell of burning cordite hanging heavily in air was the last thing Manny remembered as one of the Seawolf gunships hovered over the boat to extricate and medivac him to treat his shattered legs.

I bolted upright in bed, drenched in sweat, my heart racing. Another nightmare. An agonizing reminder of my battle fatigue.

I recalled how, after the attack, I awoke and found myself in the hospital alongside rows of other bandaged casualties. I felt an excruciating, burning pain in my legs and yelled out for a corpsman to administer aid. It was only then that I became aware that my left leg had been amputated just below the knee. The pain I often feel now is the phantom pain of my missing limb. Losing it had been my ticket out of Vietnam and back to "*The World.*"

Unfortunately, my military days ended after repeated surgeries, rehabilitation, and extensive treatment for battle fatigue that occasionally tormented me with flashbacks and nightmares. At the time it happened, I had no idea that the intensive training in military intelligence that I had undergone before being assigned to a PBR in Nha Be would affect the remainder of my life.

◆

THE CHIEF CALLED ME FIRST THING IN THE MORNING TO change our meeting to her office. She also moved the time up to nine o'clock, explaining that Larry Benham, the first selectman, wanted to meet with her later that morning. I walked into her office a little before nine. I was up early and had gone to A Brewed Awakening for two cups of coffee, one for me and one for the chief. I knew they had a coffee maker at the station, but I was convinced that all they did each morning was add some new grounds to the old ones. Just like the lifer-chief petty officers did when I was in the Navy. I couldn't drink coffee like that back then, and I wasn't going to now.

" 'Mornin' Manny. Sorry for the short notice."

"Not a problem," I said as I set a cup of coffee in front

of her.

"What's this for," she asked. "We have a pot going all the time."

"Oh, I know, and it tastes like sludge. When was the last time you threw out the old grounds?"

"We do it occasionally."

"I rest my case."

"Larry wants an update on the investigation. He's getting more and more heat, and has an interview with Channel 6 this afternoon. Going to try to convince the reporter that we are actually doing something and making progress, even if it's slow."

"Well, I've got some good news. The report came back on the tire tracks. They're Bradstone BZ 300s, truck tires. Should be pretty easy to match, if we find the truck. I went back to Almeida's farm and they let me check all their vehicles. None of them had BZ 300s, which means someone else was back there."

"That's progress. I've got a few more pieces too, one good, one not so good. The samples from Texeira's farm came back negative. No traces of human remains."

"Well, absence of evidence isn't necessarily evidence of absence."

"We did get some good news. The pathologist's report came in. It's the left leg of a male. The report indicates that it had been cut off with a fine-tooth saw, so it was deliberate. They tested the blood, and it was B-negative, one of the rarer types. The report also said that there was evidence that the leg had been frozen. We haven't had any consistent temperatures below freezing yet, so that begs the question as to how and why it was frozen? Did the murderer keep it in a freezer? Is that where the rest of the body is? At least we have something

176

to work on."

My thoughts were the same as the chief's. The fact that the leg was deliberately cut made me immediately wonder about a mob connection. *Drugs?* He must have got someone pretty angry.

"Chief, I think we ought to check into whether it might be drug related. We both know this is the kind of thing that big-time crime families do to people who cross them. Maybe it was a drug deal gone bad, though I can't imagine he was into that. Why don't you pull in the known dealers and users in town? See if you can get anything out of them. In the meantime, I'll visit Chief Barboza over in New Bedford to see what he might be able to tell us about any connection. New Bedford is a lot bigger than Mattapoisett and they have a lot more experience dealing with these kinds of situations. There was a big drug bust over there a few months ago and maybe they picked up something. Besides, he owes me lunch."

After I left the chief's office, I went home and took a nap. I needed it.

♦

CARLA HELD A PURPLE UMBRELLA OVER HER HEAD AS SHE walked along Church Street to A Brewed Awakening and her weekly get-together with Kendra.

She stepped inside and looked for her, but she wasn't there yet. She took a seat at the table near the window. Marcia was working today, and as soon as Carla sat down she set a cup of hot coffee in front of her.

"Hi Carla, can I get you something else?" she asked.

"Not right now, I'll wait until Kendra gets here."

"All right. Holler if you need me."

A few minutes later Kendra walked in and gave Carla a hug.

"I missed seeing you last week," said Kendra.

"Me too. How have you been?"

"Good, but busy with school."

Kendra was a second-grade teacher at Mattapoisett Center School, right next to A Brewed Awakening. She had taught there for several years since earning her degree in education at Bridgewater State.

"How about you?" Kendra asked.

"I had to go out to Chatham. The mother of a friend of mine passed away. I went to her funeral then spent the night with Janice."

"Better to go to someone else's funeral than yours," said Kendra.

"Same for weddings!" Carla replied.

They both laughed. Kendra knew the reason for Carla's challenges with commitments. She had shared most of her history with Kendra over countless cups of coffee. Kendra was a good sounding board, and often provided Carla good insight. She trusted her.

"Anything new on the investigation?"

"Well, it's coming along slowly. Manny is frustrated that they aren't making better progress, but they do have a few new leads they are working on. Obviously, I can't share them with you."

"How are you two doing?" Kendra asked.

'We're kinda walking side-by-side, but on two different paths. He really wants to get married, but I just can't do it. The thought of marriage makes me feel like I'm stepping into a cage, and I know I won't thrive in captivity."

"Do you think your therapist is helping?"

Kendra knew that Carla had been seeing a therapist on a

178

weekly basis for quite some time. Trying to work through some childhood issues and their impact on her relationship with Manny.

"It's been slow, but steady. Certainly not at the pace Manny would like. I'm not sure what's going to happen with us. I keep hitting a wall."

Kendra looked down, then picked up her spoon and slowly stirred her coffee.

She smiled slightly before she looked up at Carla and said, "Well, time will tell."

"I guess it will."

◆

CARLA RECEIVED HER BACHELOR'S AND MASTER'S degrees in counseling psychology from Radcliff, then went on to earn her doctorate in child psychology at Yale University. After graduating, she worked as a psychologist for the Massachusetts Department of Child Protection and Advocacy for two years before moving to Mattapoisett to start a private practice. Her specialty was providing therapy for victims of child abuse. She had transformed one of the rooms in her house on Pearl Street into an office. She skipped the formal desk in favor of a small table and had several chairs of varying sizes placed around the room.

Her therapy space was filled with a variety of items that provided children an opportunity to express themselves and their feelings. Paper doll body figures that she used to help her clients recognize appropriate and inappropriate touch, a tub for bathing the dolls, puppets, cars, trucks, airplanes, doll houses, various plastic and cloth animals, doctor kits, a sandbox for children to create various scenes, art supplies, and many other items were available for the children. Often, she introduced certain "toys" into their play in order to observe their interaction with and reaction to them.

Colleen Donovan had made an appointment with her daughter, Kate, for ten o'clock. Colleen was a single mom who worked as a bank teller at Fairhaven Bank and Trust. Kate attended the town's elementary school. At exactly 10 a.m. Carla's doorbell rang.

"Good morning Colleen, Kate."

"Good morning Dr. Vierra."

"Oh, please call me Carla," she said as she motioned them inside.

"Come on in, my office is right here," she said as she pointed to the large room to her left. "There are some toys over there, Kate. Would you like to play with them while I talk with your mom?"

Kate nodded, then walked over to the corner and sat down on the floor with the toys.

"Would you like some coffee, tea, water?" Carla asked Colleen as she motioned her to a chair.

"No thank you, we ate just before we came here."

"Why don't we start by getting some of the paperwork out of the way?" Carla said, as she handed Colleen several forms.

After Colleen completed the forms she handed them back to Carla, who reviewed them briefly before putting them in a folder.

"What brings you to see me, Colleen. What can I help you with?"

"I'm concerned about Katie, she hasn't been herself lately."

"How old is she?"

"Seven."

180

"And what grade is she in?"

"First."

"Will you share with me what's been happening?"

"Well, there's been some recent changes in her behavior."

"Can you tell me about them?"

"Yes. For starters, she's been potty-trained for quite a few years now, but she recently began wetting her bed. She's also been acting babyish in other ways, like sucking her thumb."

"Anything else?"

"Yes, her teacher called me to say that she wasn't paying attention in school like she used to, and that she was concerned. But my biggest worry is we were watching a television show a few weeks ago, and a man and woman were kissing. Katie turned to me and said, 'that man is going to touch her down there.' I asked her about it, but she wouldn't talk. Two days later I mentioned it to her pediatrician when I took her for her annual checkup. When he tried to examine her, she threw a fit and wouldn't let him. He's the one who suggested that I call you."

Abuse.

Carla had to fight back the anger that was welling up inside her.

Her pediatrician should have reported it. I'll have to find out if he did. His name would be on the intake form, and she signed a release form that would let me speak with him.

Carla questioned Colleen for several minutes, evaluating her using a standard protocol to determine if *she* might be a possible abuser. Sometimes a parent's behavior or responses send up a red flag. Carla didn't see one.

"Would you mind waiting in the foyer so that I can talk with Kate alone?"

"Okay, and she prefers to be called Katie."

181

"Thank you, that's good to know."

"Mommy's going to be right outside while you talk with Miss Carla, okay?" Colleen told Katie as she stepped out into the foyer and closed the door behind her.

"Hi Katie, can I come and join you?"

Katie nodded her approval as she occupied herself with two dolls.

Carla sat on the floor next to her.

"Is it okay if we talk?" Carla asked in a calm, reassuring voice.

"About what?"

"Well Katie, first I want you to know that I'm going to believe whatever you tell me."

Carla waited a bit before continuing.

"Has anything happened to you lately that you haven't liked? Anything at school or somewhere else?"

Katie quickly darted her eyes away from Carla to the dolls. Another pause.

"If it did, you know it's not your fault. And, I'm going to believe you."

Carla paused.

"If something did happen, it doesn't mean that you are a bad girl. Or that you did something wrong."

"I don't want to talk anymore."

"It's okay Katie, we don't have to talk any more. Maybe some other day?"

"Maybe."

Carla got up and went out into the foyer, leaving the door to her office open. She had already learned a lot.

"Colleen, I think there's a good chance that Katie's been abused. Possibly sexually. Some of the signs are there. I really should report my suspicions to the Massachusetts Department of Child Protection and Advocacy. It really is for Katie's

182

protection."

Carla watched Colleen's reaction carefully. Abusers often dart their eyes in panic and fidget when they think they are under suspicion. Colleen did neither. That was good.

"I'll call them as soon as you leave. They will be in touch with you to conduct an investigation. There's a good chance they will recommend that Katie continue to see me for help. Of course, I'll be glad to do that. But let's wait for the results of the investigation."

Colleen began to cry. "Who could have done this? And Why? Why my Katie?"

"That's what they'll try to find out, and then we'll help Katie. You are doing the right thing. I'm glad you came to see me. Please call me if you need to," Carla said as she handed Colleen her card.

Carla stood in the doorway of her office as Colleen went and got Katie. Angry thoughts seeped into every corner of her mind.

"Bye Katie, I'll see you again soon. The next time we'll both play with the toys, okay?"

Katie looked at her and nodded.

Carla closed the door behind them and then slammed her fist on the door casing to her office.

Damn pedophiles.

♦

THE RAIN PICKED UP AS I CROSSED THE ACUSHNET RIVER into New Bedford on my way to meet Chief Rafael Barboza. He headed up the largest police force in the area and was a wealth of information. I often called on him when I hit a roadblock in an investigation, though it usually cost me lunch

183

at a local restaurant.

Ten minutes later I parked on Rockdale Avenue, across the street from Tia Mary's, which was regularly voted the best Portuguese restaurant in the area. I skipped an umbrella because I usually ended up leaving them behind after I finished my appointments. I dashed across the street, stepped inside the restaurant, then took out my handkerchief and wiped the raindrops off my face and arms.

As I had guessed, Chief Barboza was already there. I knew food was the perfect bribe to get him to meet with me, and he was devouring the last bite of a Portuguese roll. The half-empty basket in front of him told me that it wasn't his first.

"Hi Chief. I see you started without me."

I had to give him a dig or he'd be disappointed.

"You owe me lunch, just reminding you," I said.

"Not happening, Manny. You called the meeting, so it's on your dime."

"It's always on my dime. The only way I can get you to meet with me is to feed you."

He smiled, and knew it was true. Thing is, I could turn this one in on my expense account, so it was no big deal.

Our waitress came over to our table and announced, "Hi, I'm Maria. I'll be your waitress today."

I couldn't resist, and replied, "And we're Rafael and Manny, and we'll be your customers."

She laughed.

"I know the chief, he's in here often. I think it's his second office."

"I think you're right."

Rafael made no bones about the fact that he liked to eat, and that he was on the portly side.

"What can I get you?"

184

"What do you have for a red wine?" asked the chief.

"We have a nice full-bodied Tinto Transmontano."

"I'll take it."

"And for you, Manny?"

She was good. She remembered my name.

"I'll have the same thing. The chief's sampled everything in New Bedford so I'll go with his recommendation."

"Do you know what you're having or should I give you a minute?"

I took the lead on this one. "I'll have a bowl of kale soup, and some Portuguese rolls."

"Make it two," said the chief. "You make the best in the city."

Rafael reached for the last roll in the basket as Maria left to turn in our order and get our wine. He stuffed it full of butter, bit off a third of it, then reached for his glass of water. I waited for him to finish. I wasn't interested in watching him talk and chew at the same time.

Maria came back and set two glasses of red wine in front of us.

"Your soup will be right out."

"So, what can I help you with this time?" Rafael asked.

"Well, as I mentioned on the phone, I'm working with the Mattapoisett police on the missing harbormaster situation."

For the next few minutes I filled him in on where we stood with the investigation.

"We're trying to see if there's a connection between the leg we found and the harbormaster. So far, we don't have much to go on, so I'm looking into whether there might be a drug connection. A long shot, but we need to check it out."

Maria brought our soup and asked if we wanted refills on our wine. I had only taken a sip or two, but Rafael had finished his, and replied, "Yes, your glasses are small."

185

Maria smiled, knowingly.

"I'll be right back with your rolls and wine."

The kale soup smelled wonderful. It was thick and hearty, filled with pieces of linguica, beef, potatoes, onions, white beans, and a generous amount of kale.

Maria returned with our bread and Rafael's wine.

"Let me know if you need anything else."

She paused, and when we didn't reply, she left to wait on another table.

We both took a spoonful of soup before Rafael spoke.

"We had a big raid on our major drug dealers last year, coordinated with the State Police and Federal Agents. We'd had a lot of drugs coming in from the harbor and through New York. We nabbed the kingpin and a number of his underlings. They've all been sentenced to federal prisons. Our biggest dealer was part of Joseph Palermo's family out of New York. Palermo is big-time. Before Palermo got involved with drugs, he was an enforcer for Lucky Luciano and Vito Genovese. He ran his operations out of Little Italy and several of the restaurants on lower First and Second Avenue. The raid here put a big dent in our drug traffic, and it hasn't really recovered since then, though there obviously is still some activity."

We worked on our soup and finished the basket of rolls. *This job is going to kill my waistline.*

"Are you aware of any drug connection to Mattapoisett?" I asked, as I tipped my soup bowl to scoop out the last spoonful.

"Not for a long time. Whatever existed is pretty well dried up, at least for any major activity. Once in a while we pick up someone from Mattapoisett who's trying to buy some pot up in the North End, but no big dealing. I'll ask my detectives if they are aware of anything and give you a call. I doubt I'll be able to be much help on that angle."

"Well, ruling it out is as significant as ruling it in, so that helps."

Maria returned with our check and looked back and forth at us to see who was going to reach for it. Rafael didn't hesitate, "Give it to him, information always comes with a price."

The rain had let up, and as I walked back to my car I knew I would have left my umbrella at Tia Mary's. I'm not sure why I own one.

Before returning home, I stopped at B&A Seafood near the New Bedford-Fairhaven Bridge to pick up some swordfish. *I'll overwhelm Carla with my culinary skills tonight.*

◆

THE FAR-NICER HOMES ARE ON THE HARBOR-SIDE OF Ned's Point Road. Almost all of them are large, stately, turn-of-the-century, summer places with expansive gardens and landscaped lawns that serve as carpets leading to the edge of the harbor. During the summer months, rows of blue hydrangeas accentuate the grandeur of nearly all the estates. Most are unpainted, other than the trim. Instead, they are clad in white cedar shingles that have been weathered by years of sun and salt air. Many of the estates have been in the same family for generations, and they are left vacant during the winter months when the residents return to their permanent homes in other states. That's when trouble often starts.

The short, wiry man knew that many of the homes were unoccupied at this time of year, and he also knew that their owners had money. It was the perfect time and place to go to work. He had just returned to his truck with some jewelry and antique dishes that would fetch him a good price at one of the shadier antique dealers in New Bedford. He took them out of the box he was carrying and put them on the front seat of his truck, then covered them with a sheet. *One more house and I'm out of here.*

Officer Townsend was on his way down Ned's Point Road, the lights on his cruiser flashing, but the siren off. The dispatcher sent Townsend there after she received a phone call from Carrie Crowther, who, with her 91-year-old husband Harry, had been a year-round resident for nearly fifty years. She reported seeing a suspicious person walking along the shoreline in front of her house, carrying a cardboard box, and going in the direction of the lighthouse.

A few minutes later, he walked by again, heading back from the lighthouse. She had followed him and observed him on the porch of the unoccupied house two doors down from hers. That's when she called the cops.

Officer Townsend parked his car near the lighthouse and turned off the flashing lights. There was only one other vehicle in the parking lot, a pickup truck, and he walked over to inspect it. It was locked, and the only thing visible inside was a sheet covering the passenger seat. He walked down the beach to the Crowther residence, and a few minutes later knocked on the back door. Carrie and Harry both answered.

"Oh, come on in," said Carrie.

"Thank you," said Townsend as he stepped inside. "Thanks for calling us. What did you see?"

"We know some of the homes near here are empty during the winter, and we kind of keep an eye out for our summer neighbors. I spotted a man walking down the beach that way," she said, pointing away from the lighthouse. Ten minutes later he walked back the other way, carrying a box, and I was suspicious, so I called you—I mean your office."

"I'm glad you called. So, as far as you know, he hasn't come back this way?"

"Not unless he just walked by."

"How long ago did you last see him?"

"Just before you got here."

"All right, I'm going to check the houses heading down that way and see if I can find him. It was a man, correct?" asked Townsend.

"Yes, definitely."

Townsend left and walked a short distance to the back yard of the house next to the Crowther's. A small window pane on the door was broken and the door was unlocked. He had reason to believe that a crime had been committed, so he opened it, drew his gun, and stepped inside.

"If you're here, I have a gun. Come out with your hands up." No answer, no one appeared.

He spent a few minutes searching the house, but it was unoccupied, so he left and locked the door behind him, making a note to notify the owners.

Just as he stepped off the porch, thirty yards away a man carrying a box was walking towards the lighthouse.

"Stop where you are," Townsend shouted as he quickly ran towards the man with the box.

"Put the box down and keep your hands where I can see them."

The man looked guilty. Townsend could tell by his eyes. Darting, dancing, trying to figure out an alibi.

"What have you got there? Lie on the ground and spread your hands and feet."

Once he had complied, Townsend stooped and looked into the box. It contained dozens of old coins, each in its own holder.

189

They were all labeled, and some were from the early 1800s.

"I suppose you've got a good reason why you are walking along the beach with a box of old coins."

He said nothing. He knew he was caught. He had nothing plausible to say. He was too calm. *He's gone through this before. We'll find out.*

"Stand up and turn around. Put your hands behind your back."

Townsend cuffed him, picked up the box, then said, "Start walking, towards the lighthouse."

The man stumbled along until they reached the cruiser. Townsend put him into the back seat and set the box on the front passenger seat.

"That your truck?"

He just nodded.

Townsend radioed the station and asked them to send a tow truck out to haul it back to the station. Easier to do that than finding a way to drive it back.

"When the truck gets there, inventory the contents. It's probably stuff that's been stolen. Anyway, I'll be back in before the truck arrives, and I'm bringing a suspect with me."

Ten minutes later Townsend pulled into the station, took the suspect out of the back, brought him inside, processed him, then locked him in the small holding cell. His driver's license identified him as Raymond Alves, from Fairhaven. Townsend knew the chief over there and decided to call him.

"Hi, may I speak with Chief White please? Officer Townsend calling from the Mattapoisett Police Department."

"One minute please."

"Hi, what can I do for you?"

"Officer Townsend with the Mattapoisett police. I just picked up one of your finest, breaking into homes out on Ned's Point Road. His ID says he's from Fairhaven. I thought I'd see what you have on him. Name's Raymond Alves."

Chief White didn't hesitate.

"Oh, we know him. Way too well. He's spent more time in a cruiser than I have, and more time in jail than some of the people who work there. This is a parole violation. He was released about six months ago after serving fifteen years for murdering a Fairhaven woman. She didn't get time off for good behavior. He'll be going back to prison, for a good long time. Hopefully, the judge will get him out of our hair permanently."

"All right," I said, "Glad I checked him out with you. We'll be taking him over to New Bedford later today. They'll hold him before he goes to court. You can catch up with him there. Then we'll coordinate what we want to do with him."

"Sounds good. At least I won't have to be investigating him for a while. Talk to you soon."

It took two hours for Alves' truck to be towed to the station. One of the downsides of a small town. Not much for services.

Alves was read his Miranda Rights and he said he wasn't interested in an attorney.

Townsend decided to obtain a search warrant to look through his truck because although most things were in plain view, they were covered by a sheet, so a search warrant was necessary.

Once Townsend obtained the search warrant he took the keys and opened the passenger side door of the truck. He discovered some jewelry and antique dishes under a sheet. It was unlikely that they belonged to Alves. Townsend picked them up carefully, brought them inside the station, and logged them in as evidence. On his next trip he removed several ships' compasses that were lying on the floor, covered with another

191

sheet. Again, he was pretty certain they didn't belong to the man he arrested at the lighthouse. Townsend went back to the truck one more time, but found nothing, except for a wooden belaying pin in the back. He carefully picked it up and examined it. Part of it was covered with a reddish-black stain. Almost looked like dried blood. It raised some questions. Probably nothing, but they'd still have to check it out, so he brought it into the station and logged it in. Then Townsend went back to the holding cell and asked Alves a few questions, although he wasn't very talkative. When asked about the belaying pin, he said he found it in the rocks at the lighthouse.

Aiello took Alves over to New Bedford to be locked up, while Townsend spent an hour writing his report. The dispatcher had called Chief to let her know of the arrest. She liked to be kept informed of things like this, and came into the office just as Townsend was finishing up his report. He filled her in on the details, including his conversation with Chief White over in Fairhaven. Chief didn't like surprises.

"What have we got for loose ends?" Chief asked Townsend.

"Well, we have to get a court date. We also have to notify the residents of the homes that he broke into and let them know about it, and inform them that we'll have to hold their property as evidence until after he goes before the judge. We have to check with our boaters to see if anyone is missing a compass. There were three of them in his truck, and my guess is they were stolen. Also, the belaying pin should be sent out for some tests, especially in light of his history. It looks like there could be blood on it, though probably from fish. Still, we need to check it out."

"Good work, Townsend."

They made some decisions on who'd do what, then the

chief told Townsend to clock out and go home. He earned it.

♦

I knew the chief had to be busy when she cancelled our lunch meeting at the Inn and asked me to go to her office instead. I was sitting in front of her desk, sipping a hazelnut coffee that I had picked up on my way. She seemed to like the sludge they made at the station, so I didn't get one for her. She didn't complain.

"Hi Manny, we have to make this one fast. I have another meeting with the selectmen. This time with all three of them. They want me to fill them in on the break-in on Ned's Point Road.

"Townsend caught a guy stealing stuff from a few of the vacant summer homes out there. Some dishes, jewelry, and old coins. He also had three ships' compasses in his truck and three boaters have already come in to claim them. We told them that we had to hold them for evidence. They were just glad that they had been recovered. One of them mentioned that he had chased a guy off a boat tied up at Mello's Wharf that matched the description of the guy we caught. We'll follow up on that and set up a lineup.

"Townsend also found a belaying pin in the back of his truck," said the chief. "Looked like blood stains on it. We sent it over to the lab to be checked out. Probably fish blood."

"Wish we knew if he had any run-ins with the harbormaster," I said.

"Well, since he stole some items off some of the boats at the wharf, chances are Tinkham ran into him. He's definitely not a good guy. Chief White over in Fairhaven told Townsend that he just got out of prison about six months ago for committing a murder over there resulting from an argument with a girlfriend who dumped him."

I filled her in on my meeting with Chief Barboza over in New Bedford. He had called me two days ago after talking with his detectives. Just as he thought, they weren't aware of any big drug connections to Mattapoisett.

"We spoke with several of our known dealers, users, and sources, but no one had any information for us. A few said they hadn't heard that he did drugs. Probably as good as we'll get out of them," said Chief.

"Well, we can at least move that to the 'not likely' list. That's still progress," I said.

"I'll be glad when we solve this thing," said the chief. "I took this job because Mattapoisett was supposedly a quiet little harbor town. So much for that. I have to get ready for my meeting, so unless you have anything else, let's plan on next Thursday at eleven, this time with lunch."

I nodded, then picked up my empty coffee cup and dropped it in the trash can before leaving her office.

◆

WINTER WAS UNUSUALLY COLD THIS YEAR. DURING THE past eight days, temperatures had hovered near zero degrees, but today they had inched their way up near the freezing mark. The cranberry bogs on Acushnet Road were frozen solid, and it was a perfect Sunday afternoon for nearby families to enjoy some ice skating and a bonfire. A half dozen large bogs cover several square acres in the Tinkhamtown neighborhood of Mattapoisett. Thick vines spread out in the bogs and produce cranberries that are harvested late in the fall by migrant workers. At the peak of the growing season the bogs look like deep red football fields. Severe winter weather can harm or kill the cranberry vines, so in order to prevent that, the bogs are flooded with a foot of water, introduced from nearby streams, to protect the vines and newly-formed buds from the cold weather. Since the water is only knee-deep, when it freezes it's ideal for kids to safely skate on.

It hadn't snowed since the ice formed on them, and there hadn't been any wind to cause ripples on the ice. It was perfectly smooth, an excellent condition for skating. A dozen families were enjoying the day at the cranberry bogs. The adults had started a bonfire on the ice and some were cooking hotdogs and toasting marshmallows. They had set up lawn chairs around the fire where they sat and shared the town gossip as they kept half-an-eye on their kids.

Nearby, a group of boys had created a makeshift hockey rink and were embroiled in a game featuring the Bruins versus the Blackhawks. Farther down, at the back corner of the bog, girls in their white figure skates were working on their Olympic moves.

The conversations around the bonfire were interrupted by a group of girls who raced back towards the adults, screaming, "Come here, come here. There's something frozen in the ice."

Frank Randall and Don Scott went out to meet the excited girls, then followed them as they skated towards the far end of the bog.

"Probably a fish frozen in the ice. Sometimes they swim in when they open the dams to flood the bogs," said Scott. "It doesn't take much to get these kids excited."

As they neared the end of the bog, the girls stopped, and they all pointed down at the same spot. There, frozen into the ice, was unmistakably the leg of a human being.

Stunned, they looked at it for a few seconds before Scott

shouted, "I'll go call the cops."

He raced back down the ice, crossed the street to his house, and called the police.

Detective Aiello was warming up over his third cup of coffee at A Brewed Awakening when he got the message on his radio. He put down his coffee cup, left a dollar bill on the table, then got into his cruiser and headed towards the bogs.

He arrived ten minutes later and spotted the men motioning him down the road that ran between two of the bogs. He drove down and parked his car next to where a crowd was gathered on the ice. After getting out of his car, he cautiously stepped onto the ice, then gingerly slid his feet over to where the kids, Scott, and Randall were standing. When he got there, he looked down and saw a leg, frozen into the ice.

"Don't touch it," he shouted instinctively, as if someone could. It was imbedded in six inches of ice.

He went back to his car and called Chief Fernandez.

♦

I was watching the football game between the Boston Patriots and the Miami Dolphins when I received the phone call from Chief Fernandez. I didn't mind the interruption, since the Patriots were in the process of losing their tenth game of the season. She told me it appeared that a human leg had been found in the ice out at the cranberry bogs and asked if she could pick me up and take me out there with her. I told her yes, and I was back on the clock.

Out of habit, I stuck a couple of plastic bags in my pocket and grabbed my camera. Questions started running through my mind while I waited for her to pick me up. *Was the leg from the same person as the one we already found? Why were they showing up in different parts of town? Could it be the harbormaster's? Has to be a psychopath. What's the motive for this? Why was someone dismembering the body? Where's the rest of the body?* Lots of questions. Not many answers.

The chief picked me up in her cruiser, "POLICE CHIEF" painted along both sides. I guess that's a perk of the job, though I'm not sure why.

"Hi Manny, looks like we've got another body part. You might as well join us on this one too."

"Well, let's see what we've got. Hopefully, there's not many people there so we don't lose evidence. I'm guessing it's connected to the other leg we found, at least figuratively. Forensics will be able to confirm that for us."

Chief flipped on the blue and red lights overhead, and ten minutes later we pulled up alongside the bogs. We spotted Aiello's cruiser on the road towards the back of the bogs, and the chief turned and followed the dirt road in that direction.

After she parked I said, "Clear the people out of here. Move them away, so that they don't disturb any evidence. I'll go see what we have over there."

Chief hollered and motioned for people to move away from the leg, in the opposite direction from where she was standing.

It's hard enough to walk on ice, never mind with a prosthetic leg. I stepped onto the ice and carefully waddled like a duck to get to where the crowd was gathered. When I got there, the right leg of a human being was clearly visible through the ice.

"Can anyone get a chainsaw?" I asked.

"I've got one," said Randall, as he turned and headed off towards his house.

The chief was standing next to her car. I guess she didn't want to waddle like a duck, so I went back to where she was standing.

"A guy is going to get a chainsaw. Let's have Aiello direct him to cut a block of ice around the leg so we can remove it. I'm going to look around and take some pictures before they start cutting."

I went back to where the leg was encased in the ice and snapped some pictures. It had a rope tied around the middle of it and a brick tied to the other end to hold it below the surface. *This was very deliberate. Someone wasn't just discarding the leg. They thought it out.*

Randall returned with the chain saw and Aiello directed him to cut around the leg, and to be careful not to touch it with the saw. Officer Townsend arrived just after they pulled up the leg, encased in a solid block of ice. He helped carry it to where his cruiser was parked and sat it on the ground while Aiello opened the trunk and pulled out a large evidence bag. They worked the leg into the bag, sealed it, and put it into the trunk.

The chief spoke with Townsend, "Run it over to New Bedford. Let them know what we know and tell them to give me a call when they have something. Ask them to check if it's connected to the other leg they examined for us. Give them my card," she said as she handed Townsend her business card.

While they were cutting the leg out of the ice and loading it into the car, I had slowly walked up the road between the two bogs, looking for anything that was out of the ordinary. Tire tracks were frozen deep into what had been mud before the ground froze. I took some pictures. They were probably from trucks used by the bog workers, though they were mostly migrants who lived in a large dormitory at the back of the bogs during the summer months. Few, if any, had a car. Bog owners no longer took the cranberries out by truck since it was faster and easier to empty them into large wooden gaylords, large pallet boxes, that were airlifted by helicopter to the Ocean Spray cranberry processing plant in Middleborough.

I walked a little farther along the road, then stopped. On the ground, a few feet in front of me, I immediately recognized a wrapper from a stick of Teaberry Gum. *A connection?* That changed the direction of the investigation. *Just a coincidence? Could be, but not likely. Teaberry gum is hard to find. Left in both places. Deliberately?*

Before picking up the wrapper, I carefully checked the ground around it. There were clear footprints frozen into the ground, so I pulled my camera out of my pocket and took pictures of them. I'd have them compared with the prints I found at the fair, along with those of the pictures of the tire tracks I had just taken.

I pulled the plastic bag out of my pocket, turned it inside out, then placed my hand inside. I reached down and carefully picked up the gum wrapper, then turned the bag right-side out, with the wrapper inside, without touching the evidence. I was getting good at this.

I looked around a bit longer. I didn't find anything that seemed significant, so I walked back to the chief's car. She was sitting in the driver's seat, writing notes on a pad attached to a clipboard. Chief's work.

"Find anything?" she asked.

"Some tire tracks and footprints. I took pictures of them and you should have Aiello take castings of them.

"I think we've got a connection to the leg we found at the fair," I said as I pulled the plastic bag out of my pocket and handed it to her. "Another Teaberry gum wrapper."

"Geez, in both places. Could the leg be the harbormaster's?

And where's the rest of the body? The press will really be on my case now. Why couldn't they have done this over in Marion? I don't need this."

As she drove me back to my place, we reviewed what we learned at the scene.

"We can't do much until we get the forensic report, and that will take a few days. In the meantime, we'll run the wrapper for prints," she said.

"While you're doing that, I'll work on the tire tracks and footprints. Call me as soon as you hear from forensics and we'll get together to figure out where to go next."

I had more to sort out, but the chief had enough on her plate for now. This was becoming a challenge. Maybe I should renegotiate my contract.

◆

I WAS SURPRISED TO GET A CALL FROM THE CHIEF THE following Tuesday. She had received the forensic report and asked me to swing by her office. I had just sat down when she handed me the report. I already knew it was the right leg from an adult male that had been neatly severed just below the hip. The report indicated that the leg had been frozen. I had a good idea of that since it was inside a block of ice when we removed it from the cranberry bog. No way of telling if it was already frozen when it was dumped there. Also, the blood type was B-negative.

"This certainly is deliberate," I said. "It almost seems like someone is taunting us, leaving the parts in pretty public places."

Made me wonder what the motive might be. There's always a motive to a crime, sometimes complex, sometimes simple. I was hoping that the motive for this case would reveal itself to us sooner rather than later. Make it easier to wrap things up.

"We sent the gum wrapper off for prints. Hopefully that comes back with something," said the chief.

"And I'm following up on the tire tracks. If they come back with a match for the tracks we found at the fair, it will be a big step for us. Likely suggest the same person is responsible for both, and give us some good evidence when we find the person who owns the truck that the tires are on."

"We've got another break. The belaying pin had human blood on it, B-negative. The lab report says that it's one of the rarer blood types and that only about two percent of the population has that type."

"That doesn't necessarily mean it's the murder weapon, but we can't rule it out. Do we know what blood type the harbormaster has?" I asked.

"We're following up on that now," said the chief. "Checking with local physicians and dentists to see if he's a patient of theirs, and if so, to see if they have a record of his blood type. Might have to subpoena the information because of confidentiality, but we are on it."

"We had a lineup for the Ned's Point break in. Brought Alves back from New Bedford, picked up that Texeira guy and two of our other problem children. Lined them up for Todd Schlosser, the boatowner who chased a guy off a boat down at the wharf, to take a look at them. He picked out Alves. I'm going to have a talk with him. Ask him one more time how he happened to have that belaying pin."

I didn't expect him to tell us anything, but she had to check.

"Got anything else?" the chief asked.

"No, that's it from my end. We've got some work to do.

Touch base again next week?"

"How about a week from today. Nine o'clock. Let's meet here in case the selectmen stop by. That way I won't have to convince them that I'm having a working lunch."

"See you here."

◆

ON A WHIM, I CALLED CARLA AFTER I LEFT THE CHIEF'S office. I hadn't seen her for nearly a week and I missed her. Besides losing my leg overseas, my battle fatigue affected me in several other ways, and I found comfort in our closeness. I felt safe when she was with me, more so than when I was with anyone else.

"Hey beautiful, any plans this evening?"

"Hmmm. Maybe, maybe not."

I could tell by her sing-song voice that she was teasing.

"I know a handsome guy who'd love to take you out to dinner and then to the Zeiterion Theater in New Bedford to see a Broadway show."

"Oh yeah? What's his name?"

"Manuel," I said, like I'd trip her up telling her my given name.

"Maybe. Where does he want to take me to eat and what's playing at the theater?"

"He was thinking about Emile's French Kitchen, and *Oh! Calcutta!* is playing at the Zeiterion. I guess he thinks the nudity in it might give you some ideas."

"What time does he want to pick me up?"

"I believe he was thinking around five o'clock."

"Tell him I'll be ready."

"I will certainly let him know."

We had a lovely dinner at the quaint little French Bistro out near the New Bedford-Dartmouth line. My coquille Saint-Jacques was excellent, and Carla raved about her lobster thermidor. The avant-garde musical worked perfectly, and later that night I fell asleep with the scent of parfume de baunilha on my nose.

◆

IT WAS FOUR O'CLOCK, AND MEGAN HAD JUST FINISHED restocking the bar at the Whaler's Inn when Hope strolled in to relieve her. After Megan put her tips in her purse, she left and walked across the street to her mom's gift shop, ArtSea.

After receiving her Master in Fine Arts degree from Williams College, her mom, Bella, worked for many years at the Museum of Fine Arts in Boston before retiring and opening her store in Mattapoisett.

As soon as Megan opened the door it struck a small bell hanging by a string from the ceiling, letting her mom know someone had entered. Bella came out from her tiny office in the back of the store and walked over and gave Megan a big hug.

"Hi Megan, how are you?"

"I'm doing fine. I just got out of work and thought I'd stop by to say hello. Many customers today?"

"I sold a small painting of the lighthouse to Jan Furnans. It's a present for her sister for her birthday. That's about it, but it's always slow during the winter. As soon as we get some warm weather things will start to pick up, and then it will get crazy when the summer tourists start to arrive."

"It's the same at the Inn. During the winter we serve a

slow stream of locals who don't even need a reservation to get a table. Then when the summer folks arrive they'll need them a week ahead of time. I don't mind the crowds though because the tips are great."

"Well, even though the tourists can be obnoxious at times, they help us pay our bills for the rest of the year."

"Anything new or interesting, Mom?" Megan asked as she looked around her store.

"Lots of the 'same as usual.' " A few original oil paintings by some of the local residents, wampum jewelry, cute nautical signs that get grabbed up for the summer homes, and I have some new scrimshaw, though it's not that good. I call it 'fakeshaw' since it's not hand carved. It's machine-made. I can tell when it's fake because the lines carved into them are all the same depth when it's done by a machine. With hand-made scrimshaw the lines carved to create ships, mermaids and other nautical scenes vary in depth. It's rare that I see a piece like that, but once in a while someone comes in with a piece of the real stuff, carved by a crewmember on a turn-of-the-century whaleship. Although I have to pay a pretty good price for it, if it's good, I can sell it quickly and at a profit. It's just hard to get good stuff."

"Is it hard to give something like that up?"

Bella laughed. "No, I'm happy to see stuff walk out the door, as long as it's been paid for."

"What time will you be closing today?"

"Probably in an hour or so, unless I get a rush of customers, which isn't going to happen. I have to pay a few bills for merchandise I bought, and I'd like to finish up the project I started this morning. I've been looking through some of the new catalogs and I want to see if there's any items that I can pick up to sell to the summer tourists."

"Why don't you stop by for dinner after you close? I'm in a cooking mood, and that will give me time to put together some bouillabaisse. I've never made it before, but I've been wanting to try it."

"Making me a guinea pig, huh?" asked Bella.

"Well, I'm going to eat it too, so that's both of us. I'll see you in a bit."

Just as Megan turned to leave, her mom said, "I almost forgot to tell you this. That guy they call Wharf Rat was in here yesterday. He came in when I was in the back. He was here for about five minutes and didn't say much when I offered to help him. He was looking pretty carefully at my displays. He didn't smell good and he had blood on his clothes. He also had a knife. I felt a little uncomfortable, but he didn't take anything or threaten me or anything like that. I just thought I'd tell you."

"Well, I guess you could call the police and let them know, but if he didn't take anything or make any threats or do anything to you, they probably can't do anything. If you run a business, anyone can come in, as long they behave. Call me if he comes back. If I'm working I can get someone to cover for me for a few minutes so I can run over. I wouldn't worry about it. Probably just had nothing to do. See you soon."

◆

CARLA CALLED ME AND INVITED ME OUT TO DINNER. I LIKED that, because usually it was the other way around, me inviting her. She even offered to pick me up and drive us, but she didn't tell me where we were going. I like mysteries, but I like them even better when they are solved, and this one was solved thirty minutes after we pulled out of Mahoney's Lane.

We were sitting at a table at Moby Dick's, a popular

205

seafood restaurant overlooking the Cape Cod Canal. I took a sip of my porter beer as I looked out the window at a large freighter inching its way under the Sagamore Bridge, the northern of the two bridges that connect the mainland to the Cape.

Carla looked especially nice tonight. She had done something with her hair, putting it up rather than carrying it off her shoulders, and she looked like a model. She was downright elegant in her black dress, a single strand of pearls contrasting so beautifully against it. I wished she was my wife.

"I need to share something with you," she said, pulling me back to our table.

I knew that her job as a child psychologist was demanding, and that occasionally she worked with clients whose situations created a lot of stress for her, especially since they were almost always victims of abuse, a topic that was close to her heart. Sometimes she just needed to talk, to help her purge her personal turmoil and refocus on her professional responsibility. She knew I was a good listener, and I was beginning to suspect that's why she invited me to dinner.

"You know that a lot of my clients have been abused, sexually and otherwise. Almost always they begin therapy with me after the person who did it has been convicted and is in prison. Well, I'm working with a young girl now who I suspect is the victim of sexual abuse. All of the signs are there. I've reported it to Protection and Advocacy and I know they followed up and interviewed her and her mother. You know that I can't share too much with you, professional ethics, but I strongly suspect the abuser lives in town and obviously hasn't been caught and arrested. Because of that, I'm seeing her in individual therapy instead of with a group of children, so that she doesn't begin to mimic their stories. I'm making progress

206

with her, and I hope that she will reveal something that can be used to arrest the person who hurt her. It's so hard for me to know what most likely happened, but not be able to do something to put the guy away, assuming it was a guy."

We both knew what we wanted from the menu, and when our waitress came back to our table Carla ordered baked scallops and I ordered fried clams. Carla asked for another glass of wine, and I didn't call her out on it.

"Carla, you know you are helping that child more than anyone else on earth. You need to believe that and somehow find a way to separate her experience from yours. And I know you know that. And I also know it's something that is very hard to do. You might be the only person with the potential to identify a suspect, and if you do, the police will be on that case in a heartbeat. Until that time, you should feel incredibly proud of yourself for all the children you help. I sure am proud of you. Enough of my sermon, okay?"

"Yes, and thank you. You are a special man."

I felt my face getting warm as she spoke, and fortunately our waitress arrived with our orders.

"No more business tonight, agreed?"

We touched our glasses together and both took a sip.

The Snow Moon was high in the sky as we crossed into Mattapoisett hours after having dinner at Moby Dick's. A local band, The Sand Dunes, was playing at the restaurant, and we had stayed to dance. We hadn't done that in a long time, and it was wonderful to hold Carla in my arms as we moved around the floor to some of the old classics, *At Last, Moonlight Serenade, Begin the Beguine*—music I occasionally played with the town band during our summer concerts on the wharf. It was also nice to be one of the youngest couples on the dancefloor.

Carla surprised me when she turned onto Pearl Street. I had expected her to drop me off at my home. She pulled into her driveway and turned off her car. This hadn't happened in a long time. Maybe she was having second thoughts about what she had told me about wanting a man in her life but not in her house.

◆

THE CHIEF CALLED AND ASKED ME TO STOP BY HER office. She said she had a lot of new information about the harbormaster case. She seemed far more elated than usual, and I was optimistic that she'd have good news, and more importantly, some useful information. I didn't bother to shave, and ten minutes later I walked into her office.

"Hi Manny. Want some coffee?"

"Ummm, thanks, but I think I'll pass."

"Before I tell you what I have, have you come up with anything new?"

"Yes, actually some good progress. I got the report back on the tire tracks we found at the cranberry bogs and they were Bradstone BZ 300s, the same as the tracks we found at the fair. That gives us a stronger case as there's a good chance that both legs were put where they were found by the same person. Now, if we can find the truck they came from . . ."

"That's excellent. The report on the gum wrapper came back, and again they couldn't lift any prints from it. So not much help there."

"Other than we have a small connection between the two scenes. That's important," I added.

"I've got three more things," she said. "I talked with Alves over at the prison in New Bedford. He told me that he found

208

the belaying pin in the rocks down at the lighthouse. Same as he told Townsend. Says he picked it up just before he was arrested and threw it in the back of his truck. We have him with possession of it, and that brings me to the next piece of news."

Chief was as animated as I've seen her in a long time, and I was about to learn why.

"Townsend tracked down Tinkham's doctor, Dr. Bernier, over in Marion. She was a little reluctant to give us his blood type, but ended up telling Townsend that it was B-negative, the same as what was found in the legs and on the belaying pin."

◆

Spring

I PICKED CARLA UP AT NOONTIME, AND A SHORT TIME later we crossed the bridge over the Acushnet River into New Bedford. Once on the New Bedford side, we turned south and drove along Front Street until we came to the Dockside Grille. The restaurant is one of the best seafood places in the area and we came here often. We parked on the wharf, then entered the restaurant where we were greeted by a young hostess.

"For two?" she asked as she picked up two menus.

I looked at Carla and asked, "Miss, would you like to join me for lunch?"

She elbowed me in the ribs.

I nodded, and our hostess led us to a table next to a window that looked out onto Homer's and Leonard's Wharves. Two rows of fishing boats were tied next to each other along each wharf. A waterway between them led out into New Bedford Harbor. They were docked there to unload the cod, yellowtail, and scallops that would be sitting on plates in restaurants around Southeastern Massachusetts by the next day.

I held Carla's chair for her, and just before she sat down I looked around, saw that no one was looking our way, and spanked her on her butt.

"Hey, don't start something you can't finish."

I put my innocent look on.

Our waitress came to our table.

"Hi, I'm Taylor. I'll be your waitress this evening. Can I get you something to drink?"

Carla ordered an iced tea with lemon. I was proud of her for not ordering wine. It was a good step in her effort towards sobriety.

"What do you have for a dark beer?"

Taylor glanced at a small notepad she was carrying and read, "We have a Bowsprit Porter. Want one?"

"That'll work for me."

"Great, I'll be right back with your drinks."

We studied our menus, and I quickly decided what I'd be having, Orange-Ginger Scallops. The menu described them as pan-seared in scallions and orange-ginger sauce. I'd had them before and they were good. Carla chose the Fisherman's Salad—seared shrimp, scallops and lump crab over mixed greens with carrots, cucumbers, red onion, and tomatoes; served with soy-ginger vinaigrette.

Taylor returned with our drinks and took our dinner order. "Good choices," she said to both of our picks.

"And could you bring us a half dozen oysters and four shrimp, please?"

"I sure can. I'll be back in a minute with them."

While we sipped our drinks, we looked out at the dozens of fishing boats moored several hundred feet from us. *Ilha*

210

Trader, Mariah, Gail M. Many were named after their mothers, wives, girlfriends, or daughters: *Kara S, Theresa M, Lady Jane*. Colorful trawlers and draggers in reds, blues, greens. Most of them made regular runs between New Bedford and the Grand Banks off the coast of Newfoundland.

"Here's your oysters and shrimp. Can I get you anything else for now?"

"A few more lemon wedges would be great, please."

"I'll be right back with them."

We stuck our forks into the middle of our lemon wedges and squeezed generous amounts of the tangy juice onto our seafood. The cocktail sauce that was served with them had just the right amount of horseradish and perfectly enhanced our appetizers.

While we ate, we watched the activity on the docks. Mostly men working on their boats, repairing nets, checking equipment, getting ready for the next trip. I had always wanted to go on a commercial fishing trip, but never did. I think it was the adventure of it that excited me, until I thought about the extreme cold, perpetual dampness, and real danger it presented. It's probably just as well that I never went.

Nearly every year it seems a fisherman is lost at sea. A few years back, "Snooky" White died when he became entangled in a line while hauling in a net on the dragger *Ellen Marie*. He joined the league of other fishermen who had been claimed by the ocean.

My attention shifted to a crowd that was gathering on Leonard's wharf, off to our right. A dozen or so people were standing in a circle next to where the Theresa M was docked. They animatedly pointed toward something in the middle of the group. That got my curiosity.

"I'm going to go see what's going on out there," I said to

211

Carla.

"Don't be too long or your food will be cold," she shrugged.

"Be right back."

I went out the front door of the restaurant and then walked around the left side towards Leonard's Wharf. Seagulls squawked overhead and the air was heavy with the smell of brine, seaweed, and dead fish—surprisingly, not an unpleasant smell. One that reminded you that you were in a fishing port.

No one turned to look at me as I approached the group. I waited at the outer edge of it until a few spectators left, then inched my way forward until I saw what they had been looking at. A large man with a long scar on his left arm was holding a skull: a human skull. I'd seen enough of them to recognize that. I listened to the speculation of the bystanders. All acting like private detectives. A few minutes later the crowd began to dissipate, and I approached the man holding the skull.

"Where'd you get that?" I asked. "Looks like it belonged to a human."

"Pulled it up in my nets," he said.

"You work on one of these boats?"

"Yeah, I'm the Captain of the Theresa M. I own most of the boats you see here," he said as he swept his arm down the length of the dock.

"I'm Domingo Medeiros, but they call me the Codfather."

"Where did you pull it in?"

"Off the Grand Banks."

"Pretty unusual to bring a skull back to port," I said.

"I've brought a few things besides fish back here. Comes with the business."

"Oh yeah? What else?" I asked. He seemed to like the attention, so I took advantage of it.

"A year ago, we pulled up four pieces of luggage. Mostly

212

clothes. Turned them over to the police when we got back to port. They said they came from a boat that had disappeared off Nova Scotia. Must have floated for months to get to Newfoundland.

"Last fall I picked up some crates off a boat in Portugal Cove, in Newfoundland, just around the corner from Saint John. Dropped them off in the middle of the night to some guy in Mattapoisett. Met me in the outer harbor and paid me a good price for delivering them. I have no idea what was in them. Not my business to know. He almost cost me a hull full of yellowtail because I got stuck in Newfoundland while a hurricane was passing by. Fortunately, my ice held out."

My detective instincts were kicking in. I looked at the skull and knew it probably didn't belong to the harbormaster if he found it off the coast of Newfoundland, but the Mattapoisett connection piqued my curiosity.

"Do you remember the name of the guy or what his boat looked like?"

"Depends on why you're asking."

"Well, I'm a private detective and while I can't give you all the details, if you provide information that helps us solve a case we are working on there could be substantial reward money in it for you."

Codfather thought for a minute, then he said, "I might have some information on him back at my office. Stop by tomorrow, and I'll see if I can find it."

I could tell that Codfather was an opportunist and knew more than he was sharing. He reached into his pants pocket and pulled out a stained and wrinkled business card that had his address and phone number on it.

"Thanks. I'll see you tomorrow. Will one o'clock work?"

"Yah. See you then."

213

Just as I turned to leave, he tossed the skull into the water in front of the bow of the Theresa M.

When I re-entered the restaurant, I asked the receptionist if I could use the phone.

"Sure," she said, pointing to it on her receptionist podium, even though it was obvious where it was.

I had the number memorized, and three rings later it was answered.

"Officer Carlos, can I help you," the woman who answered said.

"Yes, I'm Manny Pereira. I'm a friend of Chief Barboza and I'd like to speak with him please."

"One moment and I'll connect you."

"Hi Manny, what's up?" asked the chief when he came on the line.

"I'm at the Dockside Grille. There was a commotion out on Leonard's Wharf and I went out to see what it was all about. The captain of the Theresa M had a human skull that he said he pulled up in his nets when he was fishing off the Grand Banks. He just tossed it into the water in front of his boat. I know it's legal to own human skulls, unless they were acquired through illegal means, like murder, but the police in Newfoundland might be interested in it, so I thought I'd give you a call."

"Thanks, Manny. I'll have one of our divers go over and see if we can find it. We'll have to run it through our system first, but most likely we'll send it up to the authorities in Newfoundland. I'll keep you posted."

I rejoined Carla who had asked Taylor to keep our dinners under the warming lights in the kitchen until I returned. Taylor was on her game and came over to us as soon as she saw me sit down.

"Shall I get you your dinners now?" she asked.

"You sure can, and thanks for keeping them warm for us."

Two minutes later she set our food in front of us. While we ate, I filled Carla in on what I had learned on the dock.

"Do you think it has anything to do with the harbormaster?" she asked.

"He says he pulled it up in his nets off the coast of Newfoundland. And, I don't think he'd be flashing a skull around if he was responsible for it being detached from the person whose neck it had previously been resting on. So, no."

I told her that I had called Chief Barboza to report it and that I would follow up with him in a few days to hear what he learned.

Taylor stopped back and asked if we wanted some more bread. It was good, but my waistline didn't need it and Carla waved her hand to say she didn't want any either, so I said, "No thanks."

Just as we finished our lunch, we watched a police car pull onto Leonard's Wharf. A man got out, opened the trunk, and pulled out a wetsuit and scuba gear. Once he had it on, he walked over to where the Theresa M was docked and jumped into the water in front of the bow. Five minutes later he surfaced with the skull. I'd check in with Chief Barboza later in the week.

As we walked out of the restaurant I turned to Carla and asked, "What do you say we go over to the Whaling Museum?"

"I haven't been there for years, let's go!"

◆

We drove over to Johnny Cake Hill and parked around the corner from the New Bedford Whaling Museum. The museum exhibits artifacts and art that focuses on the history of the whaling industry, and in particular whaling that occurred in Southeastern Massachusetts. The museum's holdings include the world's largest library of whaling logbooks, prints, journals, and vintage scrimshaw. Several complete whale skeletons are also exhibited in the museum.

Whaling was at its peak in the area during the late 1800s and early 1900s. During that era, New Bedford had the world's largest fleet of whaleships, thus its nickname, the Whaling City.

After we paid our admission, we headed straight to the showcase of the museum, a half-scale model of the whaling bark *Lagoda*. It was built in 1915-16 and is the largest model ship in existence. Its three masts with full sails reach upwards towards the ceiling of the museum. During its service, the original boat was so successful catching whales that it made its owner, Jonathan Bourne, one of the wealthiest citizens of New Bedford.

We climbed up the steps onto the deck of the *Lagoda* and spent the next twenty minutes exploring the whaleship, its rigging, and equipment used for harpooning and processing the whales to retrieve the blubber and whale oil. I envisioned myself out in the Atlantic, standing next to Captain Ahab.

We left the *Lagoda* and walked over to a small room that displayed scrimshaw. To pass the time at sea, when they weren't chasing whales, sailors carved designs into the teeth and bones from the whales they caught. The ivory teeth from sperm whales was the most popular for carving, and sailors would use their knives or discarded needles from the sailmakers shop to create intricate pictures of their ships, mermaids, girlfriends, and marine life. Once a design had been scratched into the tooth, black soot was rubbed into the grooves, bringing the pictures to life. More modern scrimshanders use ink to fill in the grooves on their carvings, though it is no longer legal to buy or sell teeth from sperm whales as they are on the endangered species list. Illegal trafficking in the teeth can earn the violator thousands of dollars in fines, and jail time.

We left the room displaying the scrimshaw and walked into a large art gallery that featured dozens of paintings of the whaling era. As we walked along and studied the paintings, we encountered a staff member who was looking at *Sealers Crushed by Iceberg*. This painting showed a sailing ship being crushed in an iceberg in the Arctic and the crew abandoning the ship onto the iceberg.

The person studying the picture, an attractive woman with berry red lipstick that accentuated her pretty smile, was in her early fifties. Carla was the one who noticed that she had tears in her eyes, and, ever the therapist, made an effort to console her.

"Hi, are you okay?"

"Yes, this picture just brings back old memories."

"Painful ones, yes?"

"Yes. When I was young, my family lived in the Faroe Islands. They are out in the North Atlantic, halfway between Norway and Iceland. My father was the captain of the whaleship, *VAGAR*. In 1940 my father went on a whaling expedition to the Arctic Ocean and he never returned. We learned a year later that the ship had been crushed in the icebergs, and no survivors were found. This painting always reminds me of him."

Carla opened her purse and handed her a tissue. The woman dabbed the tears from the corner of her eyes.

"I'm so sorry to hear that," said Carla. "It must have been very hard on you and your family."

"It was a long time ago, but I still miss him. I wish I really knew what happened to him."

"How did you end up in New Bedford?" Carla asked.

"It's a long story. When we lost our father, we knew we had to leave the Faroes. My uncle, my father's brother, lived in Serbia, so we moved there. I went to the University of Belgrade, and after I graduated I went on holiday to Berlin. While I was there, I visited the Kaiser Friedrich Museum and saw that they had a job opening for an archivist. I spoke with the curator, Dr. Micheal Kahn, about it and he hired me. My mother stayed in Belgrade with a cousin, but she developed cancer not long after I went to Berlin."

She paused and stared blankly at the painting for a minute. Carla waited for her. Finally, the woman wiped the corner of her eyes with the tissue and continued.

"I worked at the museum for a while, but when the heavy bombing began during the Battle of Berlin, I returned home to Serbia and my mom. Soon after the war ended, we sailed to Boston so that she could have treatment for her cancer at Boston General Hospital."

Tears again formed in her eyes, and Carla took her hand to comfort her.

Once the woman had composed herself, she continued, "While we were there I saw an ad in the *Boston Times* for an archivist position here at the Whaling Museum and I applied. I was hired, and my mom and I moved to Fairhaven. She passed away last year."

"That's quite a story," said Carla. "I'm sorry about your mom. I'm Carla by the way, and this is my . . . friend Manny."

"It's so nice to meet you. Thank you for listening. I'm Iva."

We wandered through the museum for another hour and left at closing time. We drove back to my place. After we got

218

there, and after we 'finished what I started' with the spank on her butt at the Dockside Grille, we drifted off to sleep.

◆

IT WAS SHORTLY AFTER NOONTIME THE DAY AFTER I MET the Codfather. I was parked on Walnut Street, a hundred feet from where it intersected with South Second Street, a short walk for the Codfather to get to his boats down on the wharves. Judging from the look of his ornate Victorian house, he had money, and probably lots of it. The house sat high enough on a hill so that it overlooked the harbor. Several towers and turrets added to the stateliness of the ornately painted home. Tan window sashes and porch railings complemented the rose-beige clapboards and sage green shingles.

Promptly at one o'clock I walked up the steps and knocked three times on the cerise-colored front door. A plaque to the left of the door identified the house as having been built in 1846 by Captain Bartholomew Hawes.

"Come in, it's open," shouted a voice from inside.

I opened the door and stepped into an opulent foyer. Two elegant curved stairways arched around both sides of the room and led to a common landing above. Colored light from large stained-glass windows was reflected on the walls. A large crystal chandelier hung from high above and was centered over a Persian rug that covered most of the floor in the foyer.

Codfather was seated in a room straight ahead, between the stairways. He was on the phone, but motioned me into his office. I entered it, and before taking a seat I looked at the pictures on the wall. He had an extensive collection of photographs and paintings of New Bedford whaleships that had been lost at sea: *Awashonks, Massachusetts, Reindeer, Elizabeth*

Swift, and dozens more. Perhaps they reminded him of exactly how unforgiving the ocean can be.

I took a seat in front of his desk and tried not to appear like I was eavesdropping.

"Damn processors keep skimming fish off my haul and underpaying me. They think I'm an ass and don't know what they're doing. I've been around long enough to know the weight of my catch. I'm going to go pay them a visit," he said as he slammed the phone onto the receiver.

"I'm about ready to sell my fleet," he said to me. "I get screwed at both ends. The government limits how much fish I can catch on each trip and the processers steal some of what I do catch. Then they've tightened up their inspections and I get fined if I'm over the limit in my hold. They've done that twice already."

This guy will be willing to talk. Especially if he thinks I'm with him.

"Sounds like the business has changed from what it used to be."

"Damn right it has, and not for the better. They're killing my profits."

I didn't argue with him. I needed him to be on my side.

"I've got other ways to make money in this business. Don't have much choice."

Overfishing has seriously depleted many species, and governments have tried to address the problem by establishing quotas and other rules. However, some unscrupulous or desperate fishing boat captains operate in restricted areas, ignore quotas, catch prohibited species, misreport their catches, or sell fish on the black market. My guess is that Codfather has done all of that.

His comment was a good segue to my interest.

"You said you might have a name for me—the guy from

Mattapoisett you delivered some crates to." It was a statement, not a question.

"I'm not sure I can find it. Why do you need it?"

"Well, I can't tell you too much, but I'm a private detective working on a case with the Mattapoisett Police. There's a reward fund, and if your information helps us solve it you might be entitled to some or all of it."

He's greedy. That should motivate him.

Codfather thought for a minute, and then maybe a bit too long. Didn't seem to be searching for the answer to my non-question.

"Let me look in my log," he said as he got up, went over to a tall file cabinet behind his desk, and opened the top drawer. He pulled a logbook out, set it on the other files, and began turning the pages.

"It was last fall, early," he said as he thumbed through the logbook. He didn't seem to be looking too carefully.

"Naw, nothing here. Sorry I can't help you with it."

"Can you tell me about his boat?"

"It was a small fishing boat. It was night, and I wasn't paying much attention to it. I just wanted to get the crates off my boat so I could get to New Bedford and unload my catch. Time is money, and I was already late getting back into port."

"Where did you get the crates from in the first place?"

"Up in Newfoundland. Transferred them from some guy's boat in the middle of a hurricane. No idea who they were. I got paid for delivering them to Mattapoisett. Didn't ask a lot of questions. Didn't really want to know."

"You won't be in any trouble for telling us what you know. You only delivered some freight as far as we're concerned. Nothing illegal about that."

I didn't think I could get any more information from him,

221

and I didn't want to push him too far in case he remembered something else. No sense alienating him.

I stood and handed him my business card.

"Thanks for giving me a few minutes. If you remember anything else I'd appreciate a call. Don't forget about the reward money."

I turned and walked back out through the opulent foyer. He didn't bother following me to the door.

Codfather pulled the top left drawer of his desk open and removed a small slip of paper. He looked at it, then picked up his phone and dialed a Mattapoisett number. *This might get me a lot more than any reward money.*

A man answered, but before he could say a word Codfather said, "Listen, don't talk. We need to meet to discuss the crates I delivered to you. Be at Ned Point Lighthouse at 8 a.m. tomorrow. Wear a red shirt so I can spot you. If you don't have one, get one. Trust me, you want to be there."

Before the person on the other end of the line could reply, Codfather hung up the phone. He sat at his desk, folded his hands under his chin, and planned the meeting.

◆

CODFATHER ARRIVED AT THE LIGHTHOUSE AT 8:15 THE next morning. *Make him wait. He'll be there.* A row of picnic tables lined the trees along the edge of the park across from the lighthouse and the water. It was early, and the only person in the park was a man sitting at the farthest picnic table from the entrance to the park. He was wearing a red shirt. Codfather pulled up near the table, turned the engine off, then deliberately sat in his truck for a minute. *Let him get a little anxious. It will*

222

make my work easier.

He stepped out of his truck and slowly walked over to the picnic table, sizing the guy up.

"You here about the crates?" Codfather asked.

"Yes," he replied, a little bravado in his voice, but also a noticeable tremble.

Codfather sat down and stared into his eyes.

"You know there's a reward out for you? Only they don't know it's you—yet!"

His bravado went away. He remained silent.

Codfather waited. *Let him sweat.*

"I don't know what was in those crates, and I don't care. But, I know it must be worth a lot of money if there's a reward out for you. I have a very fair deal for you that can prevent them from finding out."

Make him wait, make him sweat some more.

"Think it's worth a hundred thousand dollars to stay out of prison, or worse? I'm not asking you, I'm telling you. You have sixty days to come up with the money. Not a day longer. Cash."

Codfather took a large knife out of his pocket and opened it to reveal the blade.

"Put your hands on the table—now!"

His hands were shaking as he slowly slid them onto the table in front of him. Codfather ran his thumb across the blade of his knife, testing its sharpness. He looked into the frightened eyes that were staring back at him, then, without warning, he slammed the point of the knife into the table between the two hands.

"I'll call you and tell you when and where to deliver the money. If you don't show up, I'll find you. And if I have to do that you'll end up as chum in the Grand Banks on my next trip there. That should help us attract 100K worth of fish. You decide how you want to pay me. Now get out of here, you have work to do."

When he stood up to leave, Codfather noticed that the front of his pants were wet.

Codfather sat there for a while, contemplating his next move as he watched a large ketch with full sails leaving the harbor. Even with a slight breeze blowing onshore, it was a hot day and getting humid. Summer was right around the corner.

I need a beer.

◆

A LIGHT DRIZZLE OF RAIN WAS SPECKLING THEIR windshield. Carla and Kendra were stopped in traffic while waiting for the bridge over to New Bedford to close. It had been opened to allow the passage of a fishing boat from a fish processing plant on one side to the docks on the other. They were on their way to a book talk and signing at W. Fielding's bookstore on Purchase Street. While they were having coffee yesterday, they read an article in the *Presto Press* announcing the talk and decided to go. Elsa Kurt was going to discuss her newest book, *The Whaling Captain's Wife,* and then sign copies. Kendra had told Carla that most of Elsa's books were about strong females who didn't always follow the rules and the male characters who were attracted to them. It was right up Kendra's alley, and she talked Carla into going.

The bright blue trawler, *Imigrante,* passed down the river in front of them and the bridge slowly began to close to allow traffic to cross.

"Manny still pressing you to get married?" Kendra asked.

"Well, he hasn't for a while now, but I'm sure he hasn't

forgotten the subject. He's pretty persistent. I don't know how many times I have to tell him 'no.' "

"Do you ever think about just giving up and walking down the aisle with him? He really is a good catch."

"The only aisle I'm interested in walking down is the one between the cabernets and the sauvignon blancs." Kendra knew both reasons behind that.

"Have you thought about dating someone else who's not so intent on marrying you?"

"I have, but most likely the topic of marriage would come up somewhere down the road and I'd be right back in the situation I'm in now with Manny. So, what would I gain? Manny knows I don't want to get married, but I know he won't give up asking. So, what do I do? Throw him away only to end up in the same situation with someone else? And, they certainly wouldn't be as nice as Manny. He is so good to me."

We parked on the street in front of W. Fielding's. It was an old brick building with dark green trim that had been there since the days when Portuguese men from the islands of Cape Verde and the Azores walked down the cobblestone streets of the city to board the whaling ships *Charles W. Morgan, Rosseau, Wanderer, Desdemona,* and a hundred others.

"Carla, maybe, just maybe, there's a nice guy out there who wants a relationship that doesn't involve marriage."

Carla didn't respond.

"Let's go inside before the rain picks up," Carla said as she opened the door and stepped out of the car.

Kendra sat on the edge of her seat, transfixed by every word of Elsa's talk. Carla, however, was preoccupied by her conversation with Kendra on their way to the book talk.

Maybe Kendra's right. It's like I've come to a fork in the road, but have no idea which path to take. I'm at a roadblock without a direction, never mind a destination.

After Elsa finished her talk, Carla and Kendra each bought a copy of her book. When Carla asked her to sign hers, Elsa opened it to the title page and asked Carla her name.

Elsa wrote "Carla," then underneath it,

"Wherever your voyage takes you, may the seas be smooth."

♦

CARLA CLOSED AND LOCKED THE DOOR TO HER HOUSE after she decided to walk over to Manny's. He was expecting her. Carla's training taught her that she should leave her work at the office, but her sessions with Katie were weighing heavily on her mind. She was very confident that her client had been sexually abused and had informed the Massachusetts Department of Protection and Advocacy of her suspicions. Ethically, she felt obligated to prevent further harm to her clients, and was hoping that through their sessions Katie would reveal her abuser. More than anything, Carla wanted to see that person behind bars—for good.

Carla inserted her key into the lock on the side door of Manny's house, stepped inside, and hollered, "I'm here."

"I'm upstairs," replied Manny.

She walked up the stairs and found Manny lying in bed reading the *New Bedford Tribune*.

"Anything interesting?"

"Just more editorials knocking our cops for not solving the murder. Like they could solve it any quicker."

As he turned the page to the sports section, Manny thought, *I don't know why I read that stuff, second string quarterbacks.* He wasn't

226

referring to the football teams.

Manny peeked under the newspaper and watched Carla as she unbuttoned her blouse and dropped it on the floor. Then her jeans.

Hmmmmm. My favorite, white lace.

"Don't think I don't see you looking," Carla said as she walked into the bathroom and turned on the shower.

She reached behind her back, unhooked her bra, and hung it by a strap over the doorknob. *I'll know where to find it in the morning.* She slid her panties down her legs and left them on the floor before stepping under the steaming hot water.

As it cascaded over her head and down her body, she took a deep breath then exhaled, and another, then another, trying to release the tension in her bones. She turned her back to the shower, raised her arms and rested them against the shower wall, letting the hot water beat down on her neck and shoulders. Slowly, she stretched her neck to the left, then the right, forward then back. She shrugged her shoulders then quickly dropped them. She repeated the motion several more times. Twenty minutes later she climbed out, dried off, and wrapped a towel around herself.

Better, but not gone. I know what will work.

Carla returned to the bedroom and glanced over at Manny, who was still reading the paper. She went over to his bureau, opened the top left drawer, found what she was looking for and took them out. She turned, walked over to the side of the bed, and dropped them on Manny's stomach.

He jumped, then looked down to see his cold metal handcuffs resting on his naked skin. He looked up at Carla just as she dropped her towel.

With an impish grin she said, "I've been bad!"

◆

EASTER CAME AT THE END OF MARCH THIS YEAR, AND AT mid-morning on Easter Sunday, Bobby Frates, the town Herring Inspector, got a call from someone reporting that a man was scooping herring out of the river at the herring weir on River Road. He was not happy as he jumped into his truck and went to investigate. As he approached the mouth of the Mattapoisett River, he spotted the man standing on the walkway above the dam. He was dipping his net into the water below where the herring gathered before swimming up and over the dam on their way upstream to spawn. A bucket of fish was on the ground beside him.

Bobby parked across the street and walked over to where the man was netting herring. He recognized him as Ralph Barstow. Knew him because he'd had a few run-ins with him in the past.

"What are you doing, Ralph?"

"Just catching a few herring for bait for my charter trip tomorrow. You got a problem with that?"

"As a matter of fact, I do. You know it's illegal to catch herring so I'm giving you two choices—you can dump them back in, or the cops will be here in a minute to give you a ticket. Your choice. If you're smart, you'll dump 'em."

"Why the hell do you have to interfere with me making a living? You don't own these damn fish," he said angrily. "You'll be sorry you messed with me!"

Just then Officer Townsend arrived. "What's happening Bobby?"

"I caught Ralph netting herring. That's illegal. I asked him to dump them back in, but he refused."

Turning to Barstow, Townsend said, "Be smart and throw them back in, Ralph. Then we can all go home and enjoy our Easter dinners."

Ralph picked up his bucket. Suddenly, he grabbed the bottom of it and heaved the fish and slimy water onto Bobby.

"Here's your damned fish," he yelled.

Officer Townsend reacted quickly.

"You're under arrest for assault. Put your hands behind your back. Don't make things any worse for yourself than they already are."

"I'll make things worse, don't you forget it," shouted Ralph.

Townsend cuffed him, prodded him towards the cruiser, then pushed him into the back seat.

"Guess you're spending Easter in lockup. Not too smart of you. Must be starting to feel like home there."

"I'll show you who's smart."

"On your best day you aren't as smart as I am on my worst day," said Townsend as he slammed the door.

With Barstow locked in the back of the cruiser, Townsend walked back over to Frates.

"I might need you to come down to the station later today or tomorrow so I can take a statement. I'll see what the chief wants to do and give you a call. Happy Easter," he said as he rolled his eyes.

◆

I SPENT THE MORNING PRACTICING MY TRUMPET. I'VE played off and on since the second grade—high school and college bands, a brief stint with the Navy Band in Newport, and more recently with the Mattapoisett Town Band. We perform concerts on Wednesday evenings during the summer at the bandstand at Shipyard Park. During the off-season we rehearse on Tuesday evenings in the large meeting room upstairs at the town hall.

We'll be starting our concerts at the end of May, and one of the first pieces we'll be doing are some selections from *South Pacific*. I had just finished practicing *I'm Gonna Wash That Man Right Outta My Hair*, a pretty easy piece for the trumpet. While I was looking through my music, trying to decide what to practice next, I couldn't help but think that that was what Carla was trying to do with me—wash me out of her hair. She had rejected another marriage proposal last week, and I was beginning to think I should give up trying.

I had just set the sheet music for Sibelius' *Finlandia* on my music stand when the phone rang.

"Hey Manny, Chief here. We've got a problem. Can you meet me at the herring weir?"

"I'm on my way. See you in a few."

Now what?

I grabbed some plastic bags and my camera. *Probably need these if the chief called.*

Ten minutes later I walked down the steps and into the herring weir. I was standing on a concrete platform just above the edge of the Mattapoisett River. At this time of year, herring begin their annual run from the sea up the river to spawn, or lay their eggs, twelve miles upstream.

Bobby Frates had been the town's herring inspector for many years, and at this time of year he'd usually be dropping a large net into the river and pulling up herring that were swimming in the swirling water in front of him. That's where they gathered their strength before swimming up and over the dam. On a normal day he'd be dropping nets full of fish onto the concrete platform behind him. But, this was not a normal day.

Chief was already there, as were Frates and Freddie Texeira. Freddie worked there when the herring were running.

230

After the fish had been caught, Freddie would identify the females and cut a slit from their back to their belly, halfway through the body, just behind the gills. Then he'd make another slit along the length of the fish, just under the backbone, creating a flap that he could then peel back so that he could pull out the red roe, or eggs. He put that into pint and quart cardboard containers that were then sold as a delicacy.

I stepped inside and immediately knew why I had been called. It wasn't to buy some roe. Lying on the floor in the middle of the platform was a severed arm, minus its hand. Chief, Frates, and Texeira were standing in a circle looking at it.

I walked over and looked down at the arm. A left arm. There was a clean cut right at the wrist. I looked around the platform to see if the hand was there somewhere, but it wasn't. *Could have been thrown into the water. But why? Fingerprints?*

I knew it was connected to the two legs that we had found, since taped around the forearm was the pink wrapper from a stick of Teaberry gum. The murderer had a calling card, and I had a lot of questions.

"Who discovered it and when?"

Frates answered, "Freddie and I got here about the same time. We came to check the amount of water coming over the dam to see if we needed to raise or lower it. Also, to see how the herring were running. When we unlocked the door and came inside it was lying there. That was around eight o'clock."

"Was there anyone around outside?"

I expected the answer to be 'no,' and it was.

"Did you touch or move it?"

"No, we didn't. I went across the street to the Diner at the Weir and had them call the police."

Just as I finished taking some pictures, Officer Townsend and Detective Aiello arrived. I gave them a quick review of where we stood. They didn't need all the details, at least for now.

Aiello looked at Freddie and asked, "You know anything about this, Wharf Rat?"

Still playing the bad cop.

"No."

"We'll see."

Chief looked at Aiello and he stopped his questioning. He knew he had pushed it a little too far.

"But if the hand was still on the arm, we'd know if it was the harbormaster or not," said Freddie.

We all turned and looked at him in surprise.

"He had four letters tattooed on the fingers on his left hand. When he made a fist and held it towards you it spelled L-O-V-E. I always thought it was pretty neat."

"Are you sure?" I asked.

"Yes. We used to talk a lot. I'm positive."

Aiello started to say something, but thought better of it.

"Thanks for that information, it could be very helpful," I said.

Another piece, though I wasn't sure where or when it would fit into the puzzle.

"By the way," said Townsend, "I don't know if this might be helpful or not, but Bobby had a problem with Ralph Barstow a few weeks ago. Caught him netting herring illegally on Easter. He ended up in cuffs and got himself locked up. Made a couple of threats along the way, so it might be worth talking with him."

Bobby chimed in, "Yeah, nice way to spend Easter morning."

I saw the chief taking note of that so I didn't follow up.

I looked at the gum wrapper on the left arm and decided to leave it there. Between the tape and body fluids, it was pretty unlikely that it would yield any prints. Might be something for

232

the folks in New Bedford to look at.

"We should get this over to forensics," said the chief, to Townsend. "Let him know that it's probably from the same person as the two legs they previously examined for us."

"Before you move it, I want to check something," I said to Townsend.

I carefully lifted the arm so that I could look at the side that was resting on the concrete. There were some slight abrasions along the entire arm. I glanced up at the walkway over the dam and then back down at the arm, tracing an imaginary line between the two. I knew I had one part of the investigation solved.

"The arm was thrown here from the walkway up there. That would explain the abrasions right here," I said, pointing to the underside of the arm. "When it landed on the concrete, it slid, causing the skin to be roughed up."

I took a few more pictures, then nodded to Townsend that he could take the arm over to New Bedford. He was getting used to that run.

I was getting a clearer picture of what was happening, but there was no need to share it with Frates and Texeira.

"So, when are we getting together, Chief?"

"Tomorrow, my office, at ten."

When you're on the payroll, you show up for meetings.

"See you then."

As I drove home, *Finlandia* was running through my head.

Be still, my soul, thy best, thy heavenly friend
Through thorny ways leads to a joyful end.

It certainly wasn't a joyful end for whoever that arm belonged to.

◆

CARLA LOOKED UP FROM HER COFFEE AND SAID TO Kendra, "I like everything about him."

"But you don't want to marry him," Kendra replied.

They were sitting at the window table at A Brewed Awakening. It was their Monday morning spot. The regulars knew it, and it was almost always available for Carla and Kendra around ten o'clock. The smell of cinnamon drifted from the kitchen, the best marketing they could have. It worked on Carla, and she was enjoying a big slice of sweet bread swirled with the gooey stuff and a cup of coffee.

"How many times has he asked you now?" asked Kendra.

"Lots," Carla replied.

Kendra knew more about Carla's ghosts than anyone. About her being abused when she was young, her challenges with alcohol, her ongoing therapy, former relationships that crashed and burned, her relationship with Manny. Carla had shared a lot with Kendra over the past few years.

Carla trusted Kendra. Everyone needs a confidante, a best friend with whom they can share things openly and honestly, a friend who doesn't judge, but rather listens, helps clarify things, and cares. Kendra was that person for Carla.

"Okay, Miss Expert, and how many husbands have you had?" Carla asked.

"Two, but I didn't find out until after I broke up with them."

They both laughed, even though Kendra had told that one at least a dozen times. It put Carla back in control of the subject of marriage.

"I want things to stay just the way they are. He's a really good guy, but I just can't give him any more."

234

"Do you think he'll stay with you if you don't accept his proposal?"

"I don't know. I don't know."

Carla stared into her coffee cup.

Kendra was quiet. Things were moving in a good direction. Kendra waited until Carla said, "I - just - don't - know."

"Have you ever thought about breaking up with him?"

Carla sat silently for a minute, then said, "Sometimes."

"If you know it's not working, it might be best to end it. The longer you wait, the harder it will be to walk away. It can hurt a lot to let someone go. But it can hurt even more if you realize years later that staying together was the wrong decision. You know you're smart and attractive. I'm sure there's a guy out there who would want you for that, but who wouldn't insist on marriage. Who would want you just the way you are—no constant proposals. How many more of those will Manny make before he moves on? You know how badly he wants to be married."

Carla picked up her spoon and stirred her coffee. Staring into her cup, watching the coffee swirl in a clockwise direction. Conflicting thoughts running over each other in her head.

Kendra waited a minute before she said, "Carla, you know that as much as you two have a lot in common, and he's a really nice guy, you really aren't a good match—he desperately wants a wife. Maybe, just maybe, it's time to let him go."

Kendra knew the word "wife" was a very hard one for Carla. That's why she used it. She had to help her move on. Or convince her to.

Small tears formed at the corners of Carla's eyes. She didn't bother wiping them away. She was quiet as she processed what Kendra had just said. Not making eye contact. *Maybe she's right.*

They sat in silence for five minutes. Kendra knew what was going through Carla's mind. She didn't interrupt. She hoped Carla would reach the conclusion that she was looking for. Sadness painted Carla's face. The deep sadness that appears on the face of a person who just lost a loved one. It's part of the grieving process. Carla was grieving.

Finally, she looked up.

"You're right. I know it. But it hurts, and I'm so damn tired of being hurt. It's not fair!"

She took the napkin from her lap, shredded it, and threw it onto the table.

"It's just not fair! I'm a good person."

Tears streamed down her face. She banged both of her fists on the table. The coffee cups rattled and coffee sloshed onto the table.

"Why me, why me?"

Then she was quiet. Kendra handed her a napkin and she wiped the tears off her cheeks.

"I have to go."

After Carla walked out the door, Kendra sat and reflected on what had just happened. Carla was breaking up with Manny. It was a good thing. For everyone. She smiled.

◆

EVERY PROFESSIONAL HAS A TOOLBOX. CARPENTERS have hammers, saws, and planes in theirs; mechanics have wrenches, screwdrivers, pliers; secretaries have typewriters; doctors have scalpels and stethoscopes. *My toolbox has words in it. Words are the tools of my trade,* thought Carla.

While working on her doctorate in child psychology, Carla took a course in linguistics. Her professor discussed the idea of "meaning," which is the information or concepts that a sender intends to convey, or does convey, in communication with a receiver. She learned that the words she chose to use when working with a client determined, to a large extent, whether her work with that person would be successful or would fail. She had become pretty good at choosing and using the right words. Today, however, she was struggling.

Words almost never failed her. Her brain and her vocal chords, more often than not, worked well together. Process, speak—usually exactly what was appropriate for the moment. She almost never used a prepared script, but she had run a bunch of them through her mind during the past few weeks, and none of them were working. Today, she didn't know what to convey, or perhaps more accurately, how to convey it. She'd have to go with her gut, and her heart.

Carla told Manny that she'd pick up some Thai food and meet him at his house for dinner. Residents were fortunate to have a Thai restaurant in town, considering its small population. *Thai Dim Up* was located next door to the duck pin bowling alley on Route 6. Lots of jokes about the place circulated around town.

Carla had called ahead and ordered some Gaeng Keow Wan Kai, or Green Chicken Curry. It was Manny's favorite and was made with small pieces of chicken and eggplant, bamboo shoots, green curry paste and hot creamy coconut milk, seasoned with coriander and basil. The other item Carla ordered was Gaeng Daeng, Red Curry, her favorite. With shrimp, red curry paste, coconut milk, with a hint of lime, it served as a nice contrast to the Gaeng Keow Wan Kai.

At 5:45 Carla walked up to the receptionist station, gave them her name, and was handed a large bag of food. Carla paid the woman behind the counter, then left, started up her car, and drove to Manny's.

He was looking for her out the front window, and before she reached the front door he opened it and took the bag from her, then gave her a kiss.

"Hello, beautiful."

Carla blushed. She always blushed when he said that. This time she was nervous about it.

"Hungry?" Carla asked.

"Let's eat," he said.

He had already set plates and utensils on the table that looked out the front window at the harbor. They sat down, pulled the cartons of Thai food out of the bag, opened them, and scooped some food onto their plates.

"This is delicious," Manny said after his first bite.

It was hard for Carla to concentrate on the food, or the view, or his comment. She was trying to rein in the thunderstorm in her mind so that she could think clearly. She kept recalling her linguistics course. Words. *I'll wait until after we eat.*

Carla craved a glass or two of wine, but Manny never offered it to her. He knew that she had struggled with excessive drinking over the years. He understandably didn't want to be an enabler. Carla knew she should be grateful for that, but she really wanted some wine. They finished their dinner, then brought their plates and the leftover food to the kitchen.

"Let's go sit on the porch," Carla suggested.

They walked out to the porch and settled into a comfortable bench that faced the harbor. The tide was coming in, and high above, seagulls squawked as they scanned the harbor below looking for dinner. Every once in a while, one would spot its prey and dive to the surface, more often than not lifting back off the waves with a fish in its bill.

I have to do it.

Carla closed her eyes and took a slow deep breath, hoping the right words would come to her.

"Manny, we've been together for a while now."

"I know. More than two years." *Perhaps she's finally going to accept my proposal. Be patient.*

"And I know how much you want to get married."

"Well, I've certainly asked you enough times."

He's smiling—damn.

Carla took a deep breath, then turned and looked at him.

"Manny, I can't marry you. I've thought about it long and hard, and as much as I really care about you, it's me—I just can't do it. You are such a wonderful man—everything a woman could ever want, and you deserve a good wife. It just can't be me. We both have to move on. I'm so sorry."

Manny's shoulders dropped, and so did his head. He was quiet. He dabbed a tear from the corner of his eye and then reached into his back pocket and pulled out his handkerchief. He covered his eyes with it and sobbed.

Carla cried too. For the both of them. They both hurt; they both hurt a lot.

They held each other for a long time. The sun had gone down and the moon was rising over the harbor. They hadn't noticed it. They were both grieving. Carla felt awful, and knew that Manny must feel at least as bad as she did.

We can, and we will, move on, as difficult as it might be, thought Carla.

Finally, Carla said, "Manny, I should go now. We can remain friends if you'd like, and I so hope we can. I'm sure you don't feel very good about me right now, but please, let's remain friends. You are a good man and I enjoyed every moment that we shared."

She squeezed him a little harder, then stood up.

"Good night, Manny. I won't say, goodbye."

Manny's lips formed the words *good night*, but there was no sound.

◆

THE CHIEF AND I WERE SITTING IN HER OFFICE, DISCUSSING the arm that was found at the herring weir, trying to sort out where we were on the case. It was moving slowly and was very frustrating. So far, solving this case was like trying to put a picture together with parts from six different jigsaw puzzles. Nothing fit, and all of it was made far worse by the depression that had engulfed me since Carla left me. Surprisingly, our breakup has actually helped me to focus on this case. It gave me purpose in the midst of emptiness.

"The forensic report came back and indicates that the two legs and arm we sent over to them are all from the same person. The report suggests that since there was very little decomposition, the parts most likely had been frozen soon after they were separated from the body. And, the blood type is B-negative. We've got a pattern there, but I don't know what else that really tells us," said the chief.

"Well, it probably tells us that there's a right arm out there somewhere that has been sawn off the body and is sitting in a freezer, most likely in town. The question is, where is it? And more importantly, who committed this crime? And, why? I also think it means that someone is taunting us. This is deliberate. The question is why?"

"Forensics sent the gum wrapper over to the New Bedford police, but as you thought, there weren't any legible fingerprints on it. We also questioned Barstow, but didn't get a thing out

240

of him. He even let us into his house to look around, but we didn't find anything. He either didn't do it, or he's hiding something from us that we didn't uncover."

"Well, the absence of evidence isn't evidence of absence," I reminded her.

I didn't have much else to offer the chief on that one.

"Keep him on the list. It's kind of like a symphony, sometimes instruments come in at different times. Let's go over what we've got, maybe there's something right in front of us that we've missed."

I continued, "We've got two legs and a left arm with the hand missing, all from the same person. Someone sawed each part off the body and froze it. We know that wasn't done at the three crime scenes. We found Teaberry gum wrappers at each scene, and the same tire tracks were found at the first two scenes. We also have two sets of footprints that may or may not belong to the guy we're looking for, if it is a guy. We have a belaying pin with B-negative blood on it, the same blood type as for the body parts and Tinkham's. If we find the missing hands, we know that if the left one has L-O-V-E tattooed on the knuckles it belongs to Eddie. We have three people who rise above the level of suspicion, but not to the level of proof—Freddie Texeira, Ralph Barstow, and Raymond Alves. We know Barstow is a stranger to the truth, Alves was convicted of murder, and Texeira served time for stabbing a guy. And, I got that story from the captain of the Theresa M, but that doesn't seem to be leading us anywhere. Did I miss anything?" I asked the chief.

"Yeah, who did it?"

"Don't we wish we knew that?" I was pretty confident that the pieces would ultimately come together and we'd catch the guy we were looking for. I was also pretty sure that more would happen between now and then.

◆

THE BELL RANG OVER THE DOOR TO ARTSEA'S,
announcing a customer. Bella looked up from examining the
new shipment of jewelry that had arrived in the morning mail
to see Wharf Rat enter.

He's back.

He was carrying two bags, and that made her nervous.

Is he going to steal something?

She thought about going back to her office and calling
Megan or the police, but decided not to. It was the middle of
the day, and there certainly were people nearby if he caused
any problems.

"Hi Bella. I want to show you something."

It had taken Freddie months to gain the courage to visit
Bella. He had difficulty engaging with people, a problem that
had its roots in his childhood. Today, however, his desire to
visit her outweighed his apprehension.

He set both bags on the glass display case that held custom-
made jewelry, reached into the larger bag, pulled out an artist's
sketchbook, and carefully set it on the counter top.

"What do you think of these?"

Bella carefully opened the sketchbook and gasped.

"Where did you get these?"

"I drew them."

"They're beautiful," said Bella as she examined page after
page of fine pen and ink drawings.

Most were nautical scenes: tall ships, whaleships, whales,
and other seascapes. Several were scenes from Mattapoisett,
the harbor with the swordfish weathervane at the end of the
wharf, Ned Point lighthouse, cottages along the beach.

242

"Where did you learn to draw like this?"

Freddie took a deep breath and began.

"Miss Hirons was my art teacher in the fourth grade at Center School and I really liked her. Besides Miss Hickey, she was the only teacher who ever took an interest in me. I hated my other classes. She really encouraged me to practice my drawing. One day we took a class trip to the New Bedford Whaling Museum, on Johnny Cake Hill, and I saw all the scrimshaw they had there. There was a whole room full of it. There were whale teeth and bones and some walrus teeth that men who sailed on whaling ships had carved on to make different scenes. When I got home, I borrowed a book from the library that had a lot of pictures of scrimshaw in it.

"One time when we went to New Bedford we stopped at an art supply store on Kempton Street and I bought some pens and ink. I began drawing pictures like the ones that were on the whale teeth and in the book. Miss Hirons helped me to draw better, and sometimes I would stay after school and she would teach me how to use the pens and how to make the scenes seem real."

"You were fortunate to have such a wonderful teacher. You are a fine artist."

Freddie continued, "When I got to high school, they ended the art program because of budget cuts, so I dropped out of school. But I kept drawing in this book."

"These are beautiful, so professional," Bella said, excitement rising in her voice. "Would you like me to sell some for you?"

"Do you think anyone would buy them?" Freddie asked, quite surprised at the idea.

"I think they would," said Bella knowingly.

"Which ones do you think you might be able to sell?"

Bella spent a few minutes carefully looking through the book and pointed out five that she thought would be of interest to her customers.

Freddie said, "If you think you can sell some, that's okay with me."

Bella carefully removed the five drawings from the pad and said, "I'll have these matted so that they will be more like what my customers are looking for."

"How much will you charge me to sell them?" Freddie asked.

"I won't charge you anything for these," said Bella. "If they sell, we can talk about a price for your other sketches, if you want to sell them. I'd like you to write your name on the bottom of them," she told him.

"Why do you want me to do that?" he asked.

"Because you are the artist, and it will make them more valuable if you sign them."

"My name on them will make them more valuable?" Freddie asked incredulously.

"Yes, it will," she replied, enjoying the look of amazement on his face.

She went back to her office, found a fine black pen, then came back into the shop and handed it to him. She looked at each painting and pointed to where he should sign his name. When he was finished, he beamed with pride, put the pen down, shook his head, and said, "I never thought my name would be worth something."

"Maybe more than you know."

As she was saying that, he reached into the other bag and took out a quart-sized plastic container.

"These are for you," he said. "They're scallops. I dug them this morning out at Brandt Cove. I thought you might like them."

244

"Thank you so much. That's real nice of you," Bella replied, surprised that he would bring her such a nice gift.

"I dig a bushel a week, that's the legal limit. And, I do have my shellfish button. I can bring you more if you'd like. I sell most of them to restaurants, but I'm not supposed to."

Bella thanked him again and said, "Let me put these in the refrigerator, I'll be right back."

Bella went into the back room that she used for her office. She opened the door to a small refrigerator and set the container of scallops on the top shelf. *That will make a nice dinner for Megan and me tonight.*

While Bella was out of the room, Freddie moved down to the next case and examined the scrimshaw. Bella returned and walked over to him.

"You seem interested in scrimshaw," she said with a question in her voice.

"Yes," he said, "I think it's very beautiful. Where do you get it?"

"Well, I usually buy from catalogs. It's not real scrimshaw. Most of these are made by machine. These three pieces over here," she said, pointing to three large whale teeth with intricate pictures of ships on them, "came from an estate in New Bedford. The designs were carved into these teeth by sailors on an old whaling ship. They did that to pass the time while they were at sea."

"I have to go now," he said as he turned and started for the door.

Bella was embarrassed that she only knew him as Wharf Rat, and she certainly didn't want to call him that.

"I'm glad you dropped in, and by the way, what's your name?"

"Freddie Texeira," he replied.

Then Bella realized that she could have learned his name by looking at his signature on his drawings.

"It's nice to meet you Freddie, and thank you for the scallops. Feel free to stop by anytime. Come back soon to see if I was able to sell any of your drawings."

The bell over the door rang as he opened it and left ArtSea. Bella stood there a moment, staring at the door as she thought about her visit from Freddie.

◆

"YOU KNOW, I DON'T THINK WHARF RAT, I MEAN Freddie, is such a bad guy," Bella said as she placed a casserole dish of baked scallops on the table.

"This smells wonderful," said Megan as she leaned over the dish and inhaled the rising aroma. How did you make them?"

"Well, Freddie brought them into my store today and gave them to me. They're bay scallops, the smaller, sweeter ones. You have to be careful not to overcook them," she said with authority.

Bella was highly regarded as a cook, especially for her seafood dishes.

"My secret is adding some grated Parmesan cheese. And not baking them too long! You don't want to overcook them or they'll be tough and chewy."

"Why would he bring you scallops? They think he might have killed Eddie Tinkham."

"Well, he's been very nice to me, and he's very talented. Let me get the rest of our dinner and I'll tell you."

Bella walked to the kitchen and returned with two baked sweet potatoes, a fresh salad, and a chilled bottle of rubica branco.

246

"So, tell me about Wharf Rat."

"Please call him Freddie. Wharf Rat is such a mean thing to call him," Bella asked as she took a bite of the baked scallops. "They need some lemon," she said as she again got up from the table and headed to the kitchen.

A minute later she was back with a bowl of fresh lemon wedges that she set on the table between them.

After she squeezed some fresh lemon juice on her scallops, Megan asked, "Freddie?"

"Freddie's been in ArtSea several times, and he's always been very polite. He seems genuinely interested in the art and other merchandise. He asked questions about a lot of things that I had for sale. The day he brought me the scallops, he brought me something else. Any guesses?"

Megan thought for a minute and came up empty.

"He brought me a book of sketches that he had drawn. They were very professional. As good, if not better, than the majority of the ones that I have for sale. I offered to sell some of them for him, and he was amazed that someone might actually buy them. I kept five of his better ones, what I thought my customers might like, and had them matted. I already sold one and got a good price for him. I'll give him the money the next time he comes into the store. I know he'll be surprised."

"Wow, I never would have guessed."

"Me either. I sure learned that my assumptions about people may not always be accurate. Maybe I need to rethink how I feel about those New Yorkers."

"Do you think you'll sell a lot of them?"

"I think I will once we get into the heart of tourist season. They are as good as the art that you see in the galleries on Cape Cod."

Megan was quiet as she lifted a scallop from her plate.

"And you feel safe when he's around?"

"Yes, I do. I think he's a nice guy who is just misunderstood. Hey, how about some dessert? I made a key lime pie."

After they both finished a slice of pie, Megan hugged her mom then walked to her apartment above the Inn.

♦

I'D BEEN AWAKE FOR AN HOUR, BUT I JUST COULDN'T push myself out of bed. It had been like that since Carla broke up with me several weeks ago. I felt like I was swimming against a riptide and losing ground. I lost Carla because my impatience for wanting more ended up getting me less. I'd run into a wall trying to solve the disappearance of the harbormaster. Not a clue since the last body part showed up.

I fought the temptation to just stay in bed. I knew the longer I lay there the harder it would be to get up. I also had to get moving because I had a lunch meeting with the chief to review our progress. I had a little more than an hour before I had to meet her at the Inn. We really didn't have anything new to discuss since the last time we met. I think it was more an excuse for her to eat some good cooking rather than to work on the case. She could rationalize another meal out if she convinced herself that it was for a meeting to work on the murder.

I got up, took a shower, then checked my mailbox outside the front door. A couple of bills and the latest issue of the *Presto Press*. I made a cup of coffee, dropped a dab of vanilla ice cream into it, then settled into my recliner to catch up on the town news. There was a small article about the harbormaster,

248

basically no news. I glanced at the report of the selectmen's meeting. Mostly discussions on the number of new large houses being built by wealthy out-of-town summer residents. Complaints about how obscene wealth is changing the character of the town. I read the list of honor roll students at Old Rochester, lots of familiar names. The back pages were filled with small ads for local businesses. Lobsters on sale at Hal's Meat Market, ten percent off all jewelry at ArtSea's, and a book signing at the General Store.

An ad announcing a ham and bean supper at the Congregational Church caught my eye. Sittings begin at 5 p.m. tonight. That's my dinner. Suppers were held there every few months, and the baked bean dishes were homemade. They were soaked overnight and baked in the oven with various combinations of molasses, ketchup, honey, mustard, onions, salt pork, and bacon. Most of them were old family recipes that had been passed down from generation to generation. Each with their secret ingredients. No cooking for me tonight.

I put my leg on and got dressed. I thought about driving to the Whaler's Inn, but it was a nice day and wasn't that far so I decided to walk. It would give me time to clear my head and organize my thoughts. I locked the door behind me and headed up Water Street. Ten minutes later I passed the short road that led down onto the wharf and glanced at the harbormaster's office at the bottom of it.

I'll find you.

I walked through the front door of the Inn and was abruptly bumped into by Art Nunes.

"Any luck finding the harbormaster?" Nunes asked.

His voice had a hint of sarcasm to it.

"Not yet, but we will."

I gave it right back to him. I don't like wise guys.

Noelle was tending the bar that stretched across the front of the restaurant.

"The chief is already here."

I guess we'd been there often enough so that she knew our routine. I spotted the chief at the back table, where we always sat.

"Thanks Noelle, I'll have whatever porter you have in your cooler."

"Coming right up."

I walked over and sat down with Chief. She was sipping a vinho verde, a light, fruity, Portuguese wine. Two menus sat on the table, though we'd eaten there so often that we had them memorized. Noelle brought a dark porter beer over.

"This is a new one, *Any Porter in a Storm*. Hope you like it."

I took a sip and nodded my head.

"Ready to order?"

Chief ordered a lobster roll with the fries, and I ordered a bowl of quahog chowder. A few minutes later Noelle set our food in front of us. I tasted the chowder. It was good, even better after Noelle ground some black pepper on it. The chief had already taken two bites out of her lobster roll by the time I took my next spoonful.

"Well, there's really nothing new from our end," said the chief. "I assigned Aiello almost exclusively to the case, but we aren't making any progress. Do you have any thoughts?"

I had many thoughts, but I began with the basics.

"Solving a murder generally means finding a motive. Most murders are committed during cases of domestic or gang violence, in situations involving jealousy or a personal dispute between people who know each other, to prevent discovery after committing a crime, or to get revenge."

"We can probably rule some of those out. Chief, you told me that Aiello looked into the possibility of domestic violence and didn't come up with anything. Eddie isn't married and doesn't have any close family members in the area, doesn't have a girlfriend. It seems unlikely that it's a case of domestic violence. Agree?"

"I'm with you on that one."

"We can probably also rule out gang involvement, since there's only one small gang in the area, and they are over in New Bedford. It cost me lunch to get Chief Barboza to look into the drug angle. He was pretty confident that there wasn't any drug connection, at least with the bigger dealers in the area. That leaves us with four possibilities."

I went on. "Jealousy is probably out too. Nothing or no one to be jealous about concerning the harbormaster, unless someone really wanted his job, which is unlikely. I'd move jealousy way down the list.

"That leaves us with a personal dispute, covering up a crime, or vengeance for something. I think we should focus on those three possibilities."

The chief nodded, her mouth filled with the last bite of her lobster roll.

"I'll have Aiello work on the personal dispute angle. He knows most of the people in town and that should help."

I thought that was a good call. At least we were making progress. My riptide was easing up. Except for the Carla part.

Noelle came over and asked if we wanted dessert. I was tempted to ask the chief if she wanted a donut, but thought better of it. I glanced at her and she shook her head.

"I guess we are all set."

We paid our bill, and on the way out I told Noelle she should stock up on the porter.

"It's a good one," I said as I walked out the door and turned down Water Street.

When I got home I grabbed a pad of yellow-lined paper and a pencil. A pencil, not a pen, because I can erase a pencil mark. I sat on the front porch and looked out at the harbor. There was a soft onshore breeze that carried the pungent scent of seaweed. The mid-afternoon sky was bright blue with only a few white, fluffy cumulus clouds scattered here and there. They looked like giant heads of cauliflower.

I sat and thought. I jotted down notes, but they were vague. Unlike what many people think, most of the time detectives aren't kicking doors down and arresting people. Much of our time is spent sitting. And thinking. And more thinking. That's what I was doing now.

Committing a crime? Covering up a crime? Or revenge? Or all of them? It could be more than one. Are the body parts Tinkham's? We don't know. Forensics over in New Bedford wasn't able to come up with anything to help us with that one. *And why leave body parts all over?* That one puzzled me. It seems like taunting. *But, for what?* That was the primary question. I needed to find the motive.

Mental work is more exhausting than physical work. Even with one leg. The afternoon had passed too quickly. I got ready to go over to the ham and bean supper. I shaved and showered again. I was feeling better, at least about solving the murder. Carla was another story.

◆

I WALKED UP CHURCH STREET, PAST THE TOWN HALL AND the Historical Society. A short time later I arrived at the Congregational Church and entered the parish hall. I smelled the aroma of baked beans and heard the lively conversations of locals who knew a good meal when they found one.

Adele Heuberger was sitting at a small card table just inside the entrance to the hall.

"Hi Manny. It's good to see you."

Adele was well into her eighties, but had the energy of a forty-year old.

"Hi Adele, nice to see you too. How have you been?"

Her face beamed as she replied, "I'm still on the right side of the grass!"

I gave her a thumbs up with my left hand and three singles with my right.

"Best meal in town for three bucks."

I picked up a plate, put a napkin wrapped around utensils in my pocket, and started down the buffet line. I took a scoop of beans from each pot, red kidneys, pintos, and black-eyed peas. I added some brown bread to my plate. At the end of the line Fred Reynolds sliced off a couple pieces of ham and dropped them on top of the beans.

Long rows of tables ran the length of the hall. I decided to sit at the far end of one. I wanted to be by myself. No questions about the missing harbormaster. No questions about Carla. I sat down and dove into the kidney beans. They were good. Even better with a bite of brown bread.

I was enjoying dinner when a voice behind me asked, "Can I join you?"

I looked up and saw Kendra Johnson. "Sure, have a seat."

I knew Kendra was a teacher at Center School, the elementary school across the street. She was tall and attractive. Most people in town knew her. Some better than others. I also knew she was a friend of Carla's.

We made small talk. Talked about the upcoming band concerts at Shipyard Park.

"I went to every concert last summer. I know you play the

253

trumpet. I liked the solo you played last year. What was the name of it?"

"*Malaguana*. It was a tough piece, but fun to play."

We had a pleasant conversation during dinner, and I was glad she didn't mention the investigation or Carla. Her leg brushed against mine a few times under the table. I didn't mind that either.

"I don't know if you know, but my dad was named 'Volunteer of the Year' this year. The same award you won two years ago."

She put her hand on my arm and asked, "The award ceremony is at the Harbor's Edge again. Will you go with me? You really should, since you're a past award recipient. I know my dad would like it if you were there."

I thought about it for a minute, very aware of her hand still resting on my arm, then said, "Sure. It will be fun. Just let me know when it is."

She must know about Carla and me.

"I sure will."

We finished eating. I was going to skip dessert until I saw slices of Helen Roberts' lemon meringue pie. After we finished our pie we dropped our dirty dishes off at the kitchen window before leaving through the side door. Before she headed to her car, Kendra gave me a big hug. A very big hug, and a long hug. Touch was nice.

"See you soon," she said as she got into her car.

I watched as she drove away. Mixed feelings. I had enjoyed Kendra's company, but it only served to remind me of how much I missed Carla.

I walked home and sat out on the porch for a while. Watched the moon rising over Ned Point Lighthouse, reflecting on the harbor while I was reflecting on my life. The masts of sailboats silhouetted against the darker distance. It was quiet. I needed that. I needed to think about the investigation. I needed to think about what had happened with Kendra at the ham and bean supper.

◆

TORRENTIAL RAINS HAD HAMMERED SOUTHEASTERN Massachusetts the previous week, but today the sun was shining and the sky was bright blue. It was a hot, sunny Memorial Day and Freddie headed to one of the silos to get some food for his hogs. He and his brother grew acres of corn, and every fall they harvested it with a tractor that had a combine attached to the front. The combine reaped and ground the corn, stalks and all, and then blew the resulting feed through a shoot into the back of a large, wooden-sided truck that his brother drove alongside the tractor. The silage was then emptied into one of the large bunker silos that were used to store feed the pigs would eat throughout the year.

Freddie had just finished feeding them when he looked at his watch and thought, *it's almost time*. He walked over to a small shed near the edge of the cornfield, then went inside and took a lawn chair off a peg on the wall. An hour earlier the first two contestants in the annual Mattapoisett River Memorial Day Boat Race had paddled their boat across Grandma Hartley's Reservoir alongside Snipatuit Road in Rochester, to begin the twelve-mile paddle down the river to the herring run in Mattapoisett. The race had been held every Memorial Day since 1934 except for a few years during World War II. Most of the entrants were locals who had built their own boats out of plywood, as called for by the race committee rules. The boats, resembling canoes, were twelve to fourteen feet long and were called Hudson Bay flat-bottoms. At the end of the race, the team member at the bow of the boat tapped the concrete wall of the dam at the herring weir and the race committee members recorded their time. The fastest teams would be awarded ribbons and small cash prizes at a dance in Rochester later that evening.

Freddie carried his chair down to the river that formed the back boundary of the farm. The fields were muddy from all the rain, and he had to weave a path through the mud and puddles to get there. He planned on watching the race from the bluff that overlooked the river, a perfect vantage point to watch contestants paddling the final four miles to the finish line.

As he approached the river, he abruptly stopped, shocked by the sight of the damage the rains had caused. Although the river had receded a bit, he had never seen it this high. It had washed away several feet of the bluff where it had spilled over its banks during the storm. What was left was an expanse of fine white sand more than fifty yards long. Freddie stepped onto the sand, reached down, picked some up, and let it sift between his fingers. It reminded him of the pictures he had seen of the white sandy beaches in Florida.

He surveyed the vast expanse of sand, then stood when he spotted something sticking out of it a few feet away. He walked over to it, stooped down, and brushed the sand away.

"What the . . .?" he exclaimed.

It was a pure white giant tooth, nearly six inches long. He looked at it in awe. It reminded him of the whale teeth he had seen at the Whaling Museum in New Bedford, but it was much bigger. He saw the tip of another one a few feet away and went over and pulled it out of the sand. It was nearly identical to the first one he found. He stood there, transfixed for a minute, looking back and forth between the two teeth he held in his hands. *Where did they come from? How did they get here? Are there more?*

He set the teeth down and dug around in the sand. *Three more teeth!* These were smaller than the first two, about four inches long. *How many more can there possibly be?*

He got up and ran to the nearest barn, grabbed a couple of boxes, then went back to where he had found the teeth. When he got there, he put the teeth he had uncovered into one of the boxes, then continued to dig for more. Before long he uncovered enough teeth to fill both boxes.

He spent the next two days carefully sifting through the white sand, and when he was finished, he had collected nearly five hundred teeth.

◆

KENDRA HAD INSISTED ON PICKING ME UP, AND PROMPTLY at 4:45 in the afternoon she pulled her red convertible, top down, into my driveway. After parking, she walked up the front steps and knocked on my door. I was ready for her and opened the door before her third knock. She looked stunning in her form-fitting long black dress. A strand of pearls hung around her neck and looked radiant against the tanned skin of her chest. I felt an upsurge in my heartrate as I looked her up and down. She followed my eyes with hers. And smiled.

"Do I pass?" she asked.

I didn't hesitate, "You most certainly do. The question is, do I?"

Kendra made eye contact with me, smiled a flirty smile, and nodded her head.

"Would you like to come in, or do we need to get going?"

"Let's get over there. I'd like to have a few minutes with my dad before the crowd arrives."

Harbor's Edge is a spacious and elegant banquet facility and restaurant that sits on the beach at the end of Reservation Road, a quick left off Route 6. It had been the venue for countless weddings, anniversary celebrations, proms, and other special events since the turn of the century. The front of the building was anchored by a long row of large blue hydrangea bushes. A lineup of seagulls perched along the peak of the roof. Mattapoisett harbor formed a perfect backdrop for the grand and picturesque setting.

I held the front door open for Kendra, and as soon as we stepped inside she slipped her arm through mine. It was nice but unexpected, and a bit awkward. A few couples were mingling in the spacious foyer, drinks in hand. She spotted the first selectman and his wife, Larry and Linda Benham, and gently pulled me in their direction.

"Hi Kendra, hi Manny. You must be very proud of your dad."

"I certainly am, and I'm proud of Manny too. You remember that he was the volunteer of the year two years ago."

I wish she hadn't said that. It's his night, not mine. I certainly don't want to upstage him.

"Well, we certainly are in distinguished company tonight," said Linda.

"Can I get you a drink?" Larry asked Kendra.

"Sure, I'll have a cosmopolitan. Thanks."

"Let's go get the girls' drinks," he said to me.

"I assume you need a refill?" he asked Linda.

She nodded.

Larry and I passed through one of the sets of French doors and into the banquet hall. The large windows that spanned the opposite side of the room offered a breathtaking view of the

258

harbor, all the way across to the lighthouse. We stepped up to the bar and ordered a cosmo for Kendra and a porter for me. Larry ordered two sauvignon blancs.

"So, Manny, fill me in on the investigation."

While I brought the Selectman up to date, Linda was grilling Kendra back in the foyer.

"I heard that Manny and Carla broke up. Now he's available?"

"Oh no he's not! He's *my* boyfriend now."

"Well, that was fast."

"You can't let the good ones get away. She really wasn't right for him. Her loss, my gain."

Kendra was enjoying the attention she was getting from people seeing Manny at her side. It was a rush.

"Well, you sure captured the town's trophy guy."

They chatted another few minutes, then Kendra said, "I have to go find Manny and then my father. We'll catch up with you later."

I had just finished giving Larry an update on the investigation, at least what I could share with him, when Kendra approached.

"I hate to break this up, but I'd like to go find my father."

I nodded to Larry, handed Kendra her cosmo, then walked alongside her out to the veranda. I was quite aware that she had once again slipped her arm through mine.

Dick Johnson, Kendra's dad, was surrounded by people congratulating him.

Her father spotted us, excused himself from the group, and came over to greet us.

Most people in town knew Dick. I knew Dick. He had helped with the fundraising for the home-building project I organized that landed me the "Volunteer of the Year"

259

award. He attended the award banquet held for me two years ago.

He gave Kendra a hug and a kiss.

"How's my girl?"

"I'm doing wonderful. You know Manny. We just started dating."

I hadn't thought of it in those terms, and wasn't sure where to go with it. So, I said nothing.

"Congratulations on your award. You certainly deserve it for all the good things you've done for our town. I should have shared part of mine with you for all the money you helped raise for that Veteran's home. The Vet still lives in it and is doing well. I give him a ride to the VA once in a while for his therapy."

"Well Manny, I'm following in great footsteps. Thanks for coming tonight, it means a lot to me. And be sure to take good care of my little girl."

We touched glasses before he said, "I have to circulate, but I'll see you before you go."

For the next half-hour we wandered around and chatted with the guests. We knew most of them, and more than one stole a quick glance at Kendra's arm linked with mine. It was discomforting, but I didn't want to make a big deal of it.

Promptly at six o'clock, a staff member walked through the crowd striking a small chime with a mallet, inviting us to take our seats in the banquet hall. Seats were pre-assigned, and Kendra and I found our place cards on a table in the front row, directly in front of the head table. Our server promptly asked for our meal preferences. Kendra chose the blackened swordfish while I selected the filet.

Dinner was excellent. I made a good choice in the filet. After the plates were cleared, the master of ceremonies, a radio personality from a station over in New Bedford, began the award presentation. He welcomed those in attendance and went on to say, "We have some dignitaries with us tonight, three previous award winners. Please stand when I call your names so that you can be recognized."

Here we go, I thought. *I really hate being in the spotlight.*

"Walter Sherman."

"Roger Holmes"

"Manny Pereira."

I stood and gave a slight nod before quickly sitting down. Kendra hugged me a little too long. I'm sure I blushed. But just like when you squeeze toothpaste out of a tube—once it's out, you can't put it back in.

Dick was then introduced as this year's award winner. The master of ceremonies went on for several minutes, describing all of the things that Dick had done over the years before presenting him with a plaque, similar to the one that hung in my bedroom.

He received a standing ovation that lasted more than a minute. Then, after being invited to say a few words, he pulled a prepared speech out of his suitcoat pocket but hardly glanced at it as he modestly deflected credit for his accomplishments to others.

Another standing ovation and then the MC closed with, "Now, let the music begin."

The Harbortones was a popular local band, and after offering their congratulations to Dick, they began playing dance music. The dance floor quickly filled, and Kendra and I watched couples move around the hardwood floor. Some were good, others were entertaining. After two fast numbers, the band began playing a slow one, *At Last*.

"Dance with me. I like this song," Kendra said as she took my hand and pulled me to the dance floor.

I was a pretty good dancer, at least I thought so. We held each other and began moving with the music. Her left hand started out on my shoulder, but quickly moved up until it was behind my neck. She pulled me close, her cheek next to mine. Her fingers slowly tracing patterns on the back of my neck. I liked dancing. It was nice to be held by someone, but I couldn't get Carla out of my head. I recalled our talk on my porch when Carla made it clear that we both needed to move on. That made it a little easier to hold Kendra in my arms.

In between dances Kendra and I visited with the other guests, making small talk. Talking about her dad. Gratefully, no one asked about the investigation. This was a polite crowd. They didn't comment about the two of us either, though, by their glances, I knew they were gossiping about us, probably more than as just two friends attending an event.

When the Harbortones announced the last dance, Kendra took me by the hand and led me, not out onto the dancefloor, but rather to the veranda. The sky was cloudless and speckled with bright stars. The reflection of the moon painted a yellow line on the water that stretched the length of harbor towards us. The wharf was visible off to our left. My thoughts drifted to the harbormaster. The investigation began to creep into my mind. Kendra brought me back to the current moment.

"The stars are beautiful tonight, and you are one of them."

I knew I was blushing. She couldn't tell because of the darkness.

"Thank you for coming with me. It meant a lot."

She put her hands around my neck and pulled me towards her. She kissed me. It was more than a thank you kiss. Much more. I kissed her back and didn't feel guilty for doing so.

262

Kendra finally said, "Let's go, before they lock us up out here for the night, though that wouldn't be so bad."

We walked back inside, found her father, and congratulated him one more time. Another hug for Kendra and a firm handshake for me.

"Hope to see you both again real soon. Maybe for dinner?"

Kendra looked at me, then replied, "Definitely."

We walked to her car and then headed up Reservation Road.

A few minutes later she drove past Mahoney's Lane without turning into it.

"Where are we going?"

"My place. The night is young."

◆

I JUST LEFT MY REGULAR THURSDAY MEETING WITH THE chief. We were hoping to find a link or two that would move us in the direction of solving the case. We didn't. We were stalled. Aiello and Townsend had revisited all the homes on Water Street, asking if anyone had seen or remembered anything. Nothing. They interviewed most of the boat owners, including some they hadn't gotten to earlier in their investigation. Nothing. They brought in the likely suspects and grilled them again. Nothing.

About the only good thing that had happened was that the reward money was substantially increased by a longtime resident of the town who wished to remain anonymous. Hopefully, that would jog some memories. Sometimes it does. Sometimes it doesn't.

◆

IT WAS A TOSSUP BETWEEN THE GEANG KEOW WAN KAI and the Gaeng Daeng. Carla had called ahead and just now walked into Thai Dim Up to pick up her order of the red curry.

"Hi Carla," the woman behind the counter said as she greeted her.

"I'll get your order," she said as she turned and walked towards the kitchen.

Carla casually glanced around the red and gold decorated restaurant. A small gong and mallet sat on the receptionist's desk. A creative way for customers to let the staff know that someone was there if the desk was unattended.

Carla looked at the customers in the restaurant, then stopped. Kendra and Manny were seated at a table in the far-right corner. Holding hands.

They hadn't seen Carla, who stood there and glared at them. They were too busy staring into each other's eyes. Carla could tell from the counter that this was far more than a couple of friends out for dinner. *How could she do that to me? That's one hell of a friend. Moving in on him so soon after we broke up, and not even talking with me about it first. Bitch! Some friend.*

The receptionist brought her order and Carla handed her a twenty-dollar bill. She rang her up, then handed Carla her change as she slid the bag containing her Gaeng Daeng towards her. Carla thanked the receptionist, forcing a pleasant voice, before glancing back into the restaurant. *Still holding hands. Still making goo-goo eyes at each other and finger dancing.* She thought about going over and confronting them, but Carla knew she'd be the one who would look bad if she did.

Carla picked up the bag with her food in it, then turned and rushed out of the restaurant. She got into her car, set her food on the seat next to her, then swore at the top of her lungs, using words she had never before uttered during her lifetime.

264

She beat her fists on the steering wheel until they hurt. *I can understand Manny. I can't accept or forgive Kendra.*

Carla backed her car up then drove to Ned Point. She needed to think.

◆

CARLA WALKED INTO A BREWED AWAKENING AND spotted Kendra sitting by herself reading the *Presto Press*.

I thought she'd be here, out of habit.

Two other people, a couple, were in the restaurant, obviously tourists. The man was wearing boat shoes without socks, and white slacks with a white belt. His blue shirt was dotted with large lobsters and a tacky boat captain's hat with scrambled eggs on the visor completed his ensemble. Probably from Long Island. Carla really didn't care.

She walked up to the counter and was greeted by Melissa.

"Hi Carla, what can I get you? I'll bring it over to the table."

"That's okay, just a cup of coffee, with cream will be fine."

She filled a white porcelain mug with coffee, added some cream, then set it on the counter while Carla reached into her purse for some money.

She put a dollar on the counter and said, "Keep the change."

"Thanks Carla."

Carla picked up the mug slowly, walked over to where Kendra was sitting, and sat down in the chair across from her. Carla didn't say hello as she slowly set her coffee on the table and held it, feeling the warmth on her hands. She was hotter inside than the coffee in her cup.

Carla looked up at Kendra, who put the *Presto Press* down and looked back at her. Kendra wasn't smiling. She had an idea what might be coming.

Carla's eyelids narrowed and she felt her face tighten as she glared at Kendra.

"You," Carla yelled, as she pushed her index finger to within an inch of Kendra's eyes. "How could you go out with my. . . my . . . you broke the girl code! You broke the friend code! After all these years!"

Carla picked up her coffee mug, her hands shaking, and took a sip. She slammed it on the table, spilling half of it onto the placemat.

"And I thought we were best friends. How could you do this to me? My best friend! Were you setting this up all along?"

"Do you love him?" Kendra asked.

"I . . ."

"Is he your boyfriend?"

Carla looked down at her coffee cup and said nothing. Kendra was using everything that Carla had shared in confidence with her to her advantage. Carla felt so betrayed.

"No, none of the above, right?" asked Kendra.

She knew that a person who had been abused often had difficulties with relationship issues, often couldn't use relationship words like 'love' or 'boyfriend.' The two of them had discussed that so many times. Now, Kendra was using it against Carla.

"Did you make a commitment?" Kendra asked.

She already knew the answer.

Carla's eyes were tearing up. She avoided looking at her. It felt like a knife had pierced her heart, stuck there and twisted by her best friend.

"You bitch," Carla said as she got up, stormed out, and slammed the door behind her.

♦

266

Summer

THE BLACK TRUCK WAS SLOWLY ROUNDING THE CURVE on Water Street, just before reaching the wharf and harbor off to the right. A car approaching from the opposite direction was turning onto Pearl Street. The driver of the truck glanced at it and recognized the young girl sitting in the back seat. They made eye contact, and she glared back at him. Then, after the car had turned, she stared out the back window, her eyes intently fixed on the truck.

Damn, it's that kid, and she probably recognized me. He'd been to their house and knew they didn't live on Pearl Street. *Where the hell are they going?* He was aware that a child psychologist had an office and lived in one of the houses on that street. *If they're going there, this could be trouble. The kid could talk.*

He quickly turned right onto the road leading down onto the wharf, then circled back up to Water Street, turned left, then stopped at the beginning of Pearl Street. He watched as the car pulled into a driveway partway down on the left.

He waited a minute, then slowly drove up the street.

Crap, I was right.

Their car was parked in the driveway of a house that had a sign hanging from a post in front of it: Carla Vierra – Child Psychologist.

If this kid rats on me I'll be back in prison. That ain't gonna happen.

He continued up the street, turned right onto Church Street, and drove home.

After he arrived, he sat in his truck for a while, sorting out his options.

There's only one way to save my ass.

♦

COLLEEN BROUGHT KATIE TO THERAPY EVERY TUESDAY.

For the first few sessions, Carla worked with Katie alone. Her training was in nondirective play therapy, using a group treatment approach in cases where the children have disclosed sexual abuse. Although Katie had presented with symptoms, she hadn't mentioned anything or displayed any overt behavior that would be indicative of sexual abuse.

Carla's goals for Katie were twofold, focusing on safety and empowerment. She wanted to create a space where Katie felt accepted, believed, and supported. It was also important that she felt safe in expressing her feelings.

For the past several sessions, Katie had been drawn to the same two items in Carla's therapy room—a truck and a fish. She had observed Katie picking them up and studying them, then banging them together and pushing them off the mat that she was sitting on. Carla had gently asked her about that on several occasions, but Katie wouldn't make eye contact with her and didn't answer.

For most of their session today, Katie avoided the truck and the fish, occupying herself instead by conversing with two puppets and then creating an elaborate farm in the sandbox. As they neared the end of their hour, Katie suddenly stopped and looked around. She spotted the truck and the fish and slid over and picked them up. She held one in each hand, then angrily banged them together while yelling, "Bad, bad, bad." Then she threw them across the room.

"Can you tell me why they are bad, Katie?" Carla quietly asked.

"Bad. I want to go home."

Carla was convinced that there was a connection between the truck, the fish, and Katie's abuse.

"Okay Katie, we can stop for today. Maybe next week we can talk some more about the truck and the fish, okay?"

"No, they're bad."

"I believe you, Katie."

Carla opened the door to her office and motioned for Colleen to come in.

"Colleen, based on what I've observed of Katie, especially today, I'm certain she has been abused."

"Are you sure? How do you know that? What did she say?"

"The training that we go through teaches us the common signs exhibited by victims of abuse. Katie has demonstrated several of them."

Colleen began to cry. Carla reached over to the table next to her, removed a tissue from a box, and handed it to Colleen."

"I feel so guilty, Doctor Vierra. How could I have let this happen to my Katie? What will happen to her? Will she be okay?" Colleen said as she wiped the tears off her cheeks.

"Colleen, don't blame yourself. You're doing the right thing. After I have a few more sessions with Katie, I'll bring you in to join us. I think that will helpful. I'll do my very best for Katie. In the meantime, I'm going to give you a card for a therapist I know. I think that will be helpful for you to call her and set up an appointment to meet with her to explore if she might be able to help you with this. Would you be interested in doing that?"

"Yes, if you think it will help. Thank you so much."

Carla went over to her desk and pulled out the middle drawer. In the front of the drawer, she had several of Dr. Carney's cards, wrapped with a rubber band. For nearly a year she had been seeing her to work on her own challenges with relationships and alcoholism. She was a good therapist, and Carla knew she could help Colleen.

"Here's her card," Carla said, as she offered it to Colleen.

"Thank you. Should I bring Katie next Tuesday?"

269

"Yes, absolutely. And just so you know, I'll need to make a follow up call to Protection and Advocacy to give them some additional information I learned today. They'll probably contact the police again. Hopefully, they can catch the person who did this and put him away. Children are resilient and they can grow and change. Katie is a smart girl and I'm sure I can help her with that. I think it's important that we keep our regular Tuesday meetings so that I can help her healing."

"Yes, I'll keep bringing her. I'm not sure what I'd do without you. I feel so guilty that I let this happen to her."

"Don't blame yourself, Colleen. Let's focus on helping Katie. And yes, I'll definitely see you next week."

The man in the black truck parked at the end of the street watched as Colleen backed her car out of Carla's driveway and headed away from him on the one-way street. He had observed her three times now. *Predictable. Every Tuesday. Why else would she be going there? And if she follows the same pattern, the bitch will leave her house in a few minutes and walk to the coffee shop.*

♦

HE WAS A WRECK AND HAD HARDLY SLEPT FOR A WEEK.

He was supposed to meet with Codfather today to give him the 100K. He didn't have it. The most he could come up with was twenty thousand dollars, and he got that by draining all of his bank accounts. He spent the night trying to decide whether he'd be better off showing up with what he had, or not meet with him. He felt like he was being squeezed in a vice, and not just by the Codfather.

They're after me for messing with that kid, and they're getting closer to figuring out that I killed the harbormaster. Now, I've got that Codfather guy after me. Someone will get me soon.

270

He searched for a way out, but couldn't find one. Deep inside he knew this day would come. Desperation took over, and he knew what he had to do.

◆

CODFATHER PULLED INTO NED POINT PARK AT EXACTLY 8 a.m. *No need to be late this time.* He scanned the row of picnic tables. They were empty. He waited five minutes, then drove back up Ned's Point Road. A short time later, he walked up to the front door and knocked. No answer. He returned to his truck, reached under the driver's seat and pulled out a large knife. Then, he went back to the house, raised his hand, and drove the knife deep into the door.

◆

GOOD BARTENDERS DON'T JUDGE, THEY LISTEN. NOELLE was a good bartender. That's why so many of her customers at the Inn confided in her. Once in a while, if she thought it was important or interesting, she would share what she learned with Manny. Now, he was sitting across the bar from her—listening.

"I hear that you and Kendra are doing well," said Noelle.

"And you know that, how?" Manny asked.

"Kendra was in here the other day. Sitting right where you are now. I had mixed her three cosmopolitans and was going to cut her off. Then she started talking about you."

Noelle filled a frosted mug with the porter that I had ordered and set it in front of me. I took a sip. It was a fresh tap and hit the spot.

"And?" I asked.

271

"I probably shouldn't tell you this, but I don't know who else she's sharing it with and you probably won't like it. She told me more details about your sex life than I wanted to know. I told her that, yet she kept talking. I'm sure other customers overheard her. Finally, I told her that she was cut off and needed to leave. I was hoping you'd come in so that I could tell you. I wouldn't want the details of my sex life spread around town. It's bad enough what some people make up."

I thought back to one of my earlier conversations with Kendra, not long after we had started seeing each other. I had made it very clear to her that my privacy was very important to me, for a lot of reasons, especially my work. She told me that she respected that and that I could trust her. She obviously didn't respect me or my privacy if she so willingly violated that trust.

I took a sip of my beer, then another, trying to figure out why she would betray me. *To impress people? Feed her ego? She certainly knew what she was doing, even with a few drinks in her. It really didn't make a difference why. It was wrong.*

Noelle didn't say anything. She busied herself cutting lemons and limes into pieces that would be used to garnish drinks later that evening. She was good that way. She gave me time to think.

Had she planned trying to get me all along? Did she discourage Carla from marrying me? I didn't have answers, but I did make a decision.

"Thanks for sharing that with me, Noelle. I really appreciate it. I won't bring your name up when I talk to Kendra."

"You're a good guy, Manny, and I don't want to see you get hurt. That's why I had to tell you."

I looked at the clock on the wall behind her. They are always a little fast in bars. That way they can get customers out

272

before the legal closing time, avoiding lengthy arguments, especially with the drunks. It read one-thirty.

There were only a few weeks left in the school year, and I knew that Kendra would be teaching until 2:30. I hadn't eaten, so I ordered a lobster roll from Noelle, and she went to the kitchen to place my order. When she returned, she glanced at my glass and gave me a "refill?" look. I nodded, and she poured me another and set it on the coaster in front of me.

"The summer crowd will be flooding into town soon. That should help your tips," I said, to change the subject.

"It would be nice if they tipped fairly, but often they don't. The tips get worse as the night wears on. I don't think it's because they can't do the math."

Noelle went to get my lobster roll. It was packed with all lobster meat, light on the mayo, no lettuce and no fillers like celery—the way a lobster roll should be.

I ate my lunch while Noelle busied herself behind the bar. It gave me time to think about the conversation I would have with Kendra. Short and to the point. No need for an extended discussion. There was nothing to discuss.

I picked up the latest copy of the *Presto Press* from the end of the bar and glanced through it. A report on the school committee meeting, other town news, ads, and an announcement about summer band concerts starting up on the wharf in a few weeks. Reading about the band concerts reminded me that I needed to pull out my trumpet and music and get a little practice in. I'd be sitting in the first chair again this year, and would be playing another solo, Leroy Anderson's *Bugler's Holiday,* a little later in the summer. I'd played with the town band for several years and enjoyed seeing the crowds gathered on the lawn of Shipyard Park every Wednesday night listening to Sousa marches, Broadway tunes, and a mix of other music.

273

I finished my lobster roll and beer, and checked the clock again. Kendra should be home by now, so I paid my bill and thanked Noelle again for filling me in on her conversation with Kendra.

I left the Inn and headed straight for Kendra's house. Her car was in the driveway, so I parked behind it and went up and knocked on the front door. I had no second thoughts about what I was about to do. The way Kendra betrayed me is unforgivable. There is only one thing to do when someone betrays you, and I was on my way to do it.

"Hi lover," Kendra said as she opened the door. "What a nice surprise, come on in. Looking for an afternoon delight?"

She must have read my face, because all of a sudden the brightness on hers disappeared.

"Are you okay?" she asked. "Come on in."

We went into her living room and I sat on a chair, deliberately, so that she couldn't sit next to me.

"Remember when we talked about my need for privacy?"

"Yes, why?"

"Have you shared anything about our intimate times with other people?"

"No, why do you ask?"

I was silent for a minute. She was either too drunk at the time to remember, or she wasn't drunk and still violated our trust. Neither one was acceptable.

"You know, Kendra, I learned a phrase in my ninth grade Latin class, 'Falsus in Uno, Falsus in Omnibus,' — 'False in One Thing, False in All.' You should have learned that too. You're lying to me when you say that you didn't share our private life with others. I'm telling you that, it's not up for debate. Once you're caught in a lie, from then on, even if you tell the truth, it will always be suspect. I can't trust you Kendra, so we're finished."

She started to say something, but I was already out of my chair and headed to the door. She was still protesting when I closed the door behind me. I quickly got into my car and drove home.

◆

RONNIE PENDERGAST WAS VISITING HIS GRANDPARENTS, Winston and Mallory Pendergast, for the summer. They lived on Pearl Street, a few houses up from the harbor. On sunny days he and his grandmother went to the town beach, a ten-minute walk away. Several times a week, in the late afternoon, he and his grandfather walked to the town wharf and dropped their fishing lines into the water. His catch of the summer was a small, but legal-size, bluefish that he had struggled to pull out of the harbor. When he got home, his grandfather took a picture of him holding it up by the tail, a big smile on his face. He was looking forward to showing it to all his classmates when he returned home to East Hampton, Connecticut, at the end of the summer.

At least once a week he and his grandmother went to the town library. It was a short walk away. Ronnie loved books, and during every visit he picked out ten to take home. His grandmother insisted on always checking out ten books. That way they knew how many they had to gather up to return when they went on their next visit.

It had been raining off and on throughout the day and Ronnie had spent the last hour reading on the couch in front of the window that overlooked Pearl Street. He loved biographies and had read more than a dozen since arriving in

Mattapoisett for his summer vacation. Today, he was learning about George Washington Carver.

Pearl Street is a very old street, dating back to whaling days. Traffic was one way, away from the harbor. The old houses along the street butted up against the sidewalks and sat only a few feet from the street. Little had changed since horse drawn carriages had travelled on them.

The sun had come out and Ronnie put his book down and was looking out the window at the butterflies flitting about the liatris that were blooming in the flower beds in front of the house. Monarchs and Eastern swallowtails were pulling the nectar and pollen from the purple flowers.

A woman walked by on the other side of the street. Ronnie waved to her, but she didn't see him.

He was sitting in his pickup truck, parked at the beginning of Pearl Street. He could see her house a few doors down. *People shouldn't be so predictable.* He had watched her pattern for several weeks, and knew she'd be out soon, once the kid and her mother left, which was a few minutes ago. Almost on cue, she stepped out of her house and walked up the sidewalk, away from the harbor. He started up his truck and turned onto Pearl Street.

She heard a vehicle approaching from behind her and instinctively stepped away from the edge of the narrow sidewalk.

It's picking up speed—way too fast for this street.

Just as she turned to look, the front wheel of the truck bounced over the edge of the curb a few feet from her.

It's going to hit me!

She froze and instinctively stretched her hands out in front of her. Pain ripped through her legs as the truck slammed into her. She was thrown through the air and crashed against a house. She dropped to the ground and collapsed, unconscious, in a bed of orange and yellow marigolds.

Ronnie saw the truck hit her.

"Grandma, Grandpa, come quick, a lady got hit by a truck!"

"Where?" asked his grandfather.

"Right over there," said Ronnie, as he pointed across the street to his right.

"Call the police, Mallory!" Winston shouted.

"You stay here, Ronnie," he said as he rushed out the door and ran across the street to where the woman was lying crumpled on the ground.

Another couple came out of the house behind the marigolds.

"What happened?" the elderly man asked.

"My grandson says she was hit by a truck. The driver had to know he hit her, but he didn't stop. My wife is calling the police."

Just then they could hear the sirens off in the distance. They grew louder. A minute later a police car and ambulance came to a stop where a crowd had gathered. Two EMT's knelt over the unconscious woman and conducted a quick assessment.

"I have a pulse, but a weak one. She's breathing. It looks like two broken legs and probably a broken collar bone. Possible head, neck and internal injuries. She has numerous cuts on her face and head."

During the next few minutes they applied a C-collar to stabilize her head and neck. Then they hooked up an oxygen mask. At the request of Officer Townsend, one of the EMT's searched her pockets for any identification. All they found was a twenty-dollar bill and some keys. Townsend took the keys. The EMT's pulled a long spineboard out of the ambulance, gently slid it under her, lifted her onto a stretcher, then slid her into the back of the ambulance. One EMT climbed in with her, started an IV and administered morphine to lessen her pain. The other EMT jumped into the driver's seat, activated the red lights, and headed to New Bedford Memorial Hospital.

"Another case for our esteemed cops. It's been almost a year and they still haven't solved the harbormaster's murder," said one of the bystanders.

Officer Townsend ignored the comment. He'd heard it before. Townspeople were getting antsy for an arrest and conviction.

"Did anyone see this happen?" he asked.

"My grandson saw it," said Winston.

"Where is he? I'd like to talk with him."

"Yes, come with me."

Detective Aiello searched the area around the accident for any possible evidence while Townsend went to talk with Ronnie. He was sitting on the porch on the swing and saw them coming.

"Ronnie, this is Officer Townsend. He'd like to ask you a few questions about the accident."

"Okay."

"Hi Ronnie, how are you? Your grandfather says you saw the accident happen. Can I ask you some questions?"

"Yes."

"Well, first, how old are you?

"Seven"

"Do you live here?"

"Just for the summer. I'm visiting my grandparents. I live in Connecticut."

278

"Are you having a good time?"

"Yes, we go to the beach every day, and I caught a fish. Want to see my picture?"

"Sure."

Townsend had learned to have patience when interviewing kids.

Ronnie ran off to his bedroom to get the picture of himself holding his catch. He was back in a minute.

"Wow, that's a big one.

"Ronnie, you said you saw the accident happen?"

"Yes."

"Can you tell me what you saw?"

"A woman was walking down the sidewalk, right there," he said, indicating across the street. "She went that way," he said, pointing to his right. "Then a truck hit her."

"Was she in the street?"

"No, she was on the sidewalk. The truck went on the sidewalk and hit her. Then I yelled for my grandmother and grandfather."

"Could you see who was driving? A man or a woman?"

"No."

"What color was the truck?"

"I think it was black."

"Did you remember anything else about the truck?"

"I don't remember."

"Did you see what house she came out of?"

"No."

"Can you tell me anything else about what you saw?"

Ronnie thought a moment before saying, "It was going fast."

"Anything else?"

He squeezed his eyelids together briefly, then opened them and said, "Nope."

"Ronnie, you've been a big help. If you think of anything else please be sure to tell your grandparents."

"I will. Is the lady okay?"

"We hope so, she's on her way to the hospital. Thank you for your help."

Officer Townsend shook hands with Winston and handed him a business card.

"Give me a call if he remembers anything else."

He left and headed over to where Detective Aiello had finished his search for evidence. They climbed into the cruiser and went back to the police station to write their report.

◆

I'D BEEN IN A LOT OF DISTRESSFUL SITUATIONS IN MY LIFE, but I'm not sure that any were more so than what I was about to encounter as I approached Carla's room at New Bedford Memorial Hospital. I knew she had been badly hurt in the accident, but I wasn't sure just how bad. I walked into the lobby and knew that I was about to find out, and, frankly, I was scared. I had seen plenty of dead bodies in Vietnam, arms and legs missing, torsos ripped apart, bodies burned beyond recognition, faces obliterated. But those were people who, for the most part, I never knew. This time was different. I was about to see someone I loved who was suffering badly.

I stopped at the receptionist desk, and the woman sitting there looked up Carla's room number and gave it to me. Third floor, but not intensive care. I guess that was good news. Just before I reached the elevator I spotted the café and went in to get her something before going to her floor.

The bell dinged three times to let us know that we had arrived at the third floor, and I stepped out of the elevator and

280

looked at the sign on the wall across from me. An arrow indicated that her room was to the right, and I walked in that direction.

I stopped at the nurses station. Two nurses were sitting there working on patient charts. Their nametags said they were Jessica and Jennifer.

"Can I help you?" asked Jessica.

"I came to visit Carla Vierra. How is she?"

"She's doing better. She has two broken legs and a broken collarbone. She's bruised up pretty badly, but we have a good plastic surgeon. In a few months you won't even know she'd been in an accident."

I stopped outside her door and took a deep breath. Then I walked in. I winced when I saw her. My eyes got misty. Her black and blue face was badly swollen and stitches held her skin together. Her left arm was in a sling that was wrapped around her body, and both legs had casts on them. Her appearance affected me more than anything I had seen in Vietnam.

She was awake. As I pulled a chair up to her bed I reached over and rested my hand on hers. She attempted to smile at me, and I could see that it hurt. I wanted to kiss her on her forehead, but there wasn't a spot that wasn't bruised or stitched, so I gently squeezed her hand instead.

"How are you doing?"

Her voice was nearly a whisper as she replied, "It hurts, but thankfully the meds help a lot. I'm glad you came to visit. I've been worrying about you."

Just like Carla, severely injured, in a hospital bed with broken legs and a broken collar bone, and she's worried about someone else. I couldn't envision anyone more special than she is. Empathetic at a time when she was the one who needed caring.

281

"Brought you something, if you think you can eat it. It's not from Frates Ice Cream Shop, but it's the best I could find."

I scooped a small amount out of the cup and held it up to her dried and cracked lips. I hesitated to touch them with the spoon. She stuck out her tongue and tasted the chocolate ice cream, then opened her mouth for me to feed her. I watched her carefully as she closed her eyes and savored her treat. Her mouth curled into a smile, and when she opened her eyes they had regained a little of their sparkle. Perhaps I was imagining it, or hoping for it, but her spirits seemed to lift a little bit.

Carla had just finished her ice cream and I had thrown the container in the trash can when the charge nurse, Yvonne, walked in.

"She's doing well," she said as she gave Carla a reassuring smile. Should be pretty well healed in about eight weeks, though she'll go home long before then. She'll need to use crutches and maybe a wheelchair for a while though. The best news is that she doesn't have any brain injury. Considering how they described her accident, that's pretty amazing. We'll take good care of her and get her back to new real soon."

Yvonne left the room and I felt a little better. There wouldn't be any permanent damage, and hopefully each day she'd regain more strength and soon be back on her feet.

I could see that Carla was getting tired, probably as much from the drugs as her injuries.

"I'm going to go now, but I'll be back soon. You take care of yourself and listen to your doctors and nurses. No heroics, okay?"

Before I could stand up Carla said, "Come closer, I need to tell you something."

I leaned in, and in a soft voice she told me about her client, Katie.

"I shouldn't tell you this because it violates confidentiality, but just before I was hurt Katie's behavior in therapy revealed something else important that I think P&A should know, as well as the police."

During the next few minutes Carla told me about Katie throwing the truck and the fish and her interpretation of it. I promised to call P&A to let them know and to inform the chief. I also knew how I could use the information without breaching confidentiality.

I gently squeezed her hand then stood up to leave. When I reached the doorway, I stopped and looked back at her.

"I'd love to get you out of here right now, but you don't have a leg to stand on!"

I caught her smiling just before I disappeared around the corner.

◆

THREE BUILDINGS SIT SIDE-BY-SIDE ACROSS THE STREET from the Whaler's Inn. All are clad in weathered white cedar shingles. An oval sign protrudes above the doorway of the middle building, and gold lettering advertises it as ArtSea.

Inside, two women with heavy New Jersey accents were leaning over the glass cases that were filled with jewelry. For the past twenty minutes they had stood there in their Birkenstocks, with matching crocodile textured, glazed leather Brahmin handbags draped over their shoulders, asking Bella to show them piece after piece of wampum jewelry.

"Wampum is made from the quahog shells found in Southern New England waters and on the beaches. For hundreds of years the Wampanoag tribe in our area used it for trade," Bella said.

"I can't believe what they charge for shells they find on the beach," the woman with four rings on her left hand said.

If you want cheap, go buy the Chinese stuff.

Bella smiled at the two women and said, "My wampum is made by Sisika, a Wampanoag woman who lives in Gay Head, on Martha's Vineyard. She's one of only a few thousand Wampanoags still remaining, and her family has made wampum jewelry for several generations.

"You can see that her earrings are very well-matched. Each pair comes from two halves of the same quahog that she precision cuts, grinds, drills, and polishes, all by hand. She makes every piece herself, and Sisika is one of the best wampum artisans in the world."

"Overpriced," the woman with the rings mumbled as she decided on a piece.

At that moment, the front door opened and in walked Freddie, carrying a small box.

"Hi Freddie, be right with you," Bella said as she wrapped up the purchases of the two women and handed them their bags and credit card slips.

They walked towards the door, still complaining about the prices.

"I hate the tourists," Bella said with exasperation in her voice.

Many of the locals called them 'summer trash,' but Bella didn't.

"They can be so obnoxious. They move into the expensive homes along the shoreline as soon as the weather gets warm, then act like they own the town and that the people who live here year-round are their hired help. But, I know I need them to make a living. Enough of my complaining. What have you got there, Freddie?"

284

Freddie carefully set the box down on top of the display case and slowly opened it. He gently lifted out a small object wrapped in cloth, set it on the counter, and unwrapped it.

Bella gasped. "Where did you get that," she asked, looking at the large tooth that had an intricate carving of the Whaleship Wanderer etched into it?

"I made it."

"How . . . what . . . I don't understand."

For the next five minutes Freddie proceeded to tell Bella about how he had found all the teeth on his property after the storm. She listened in stunned silence.

"After I found them, I thought of all the scrimshaw that sailors had done on whale teeth when they were out at sea. I decided to try it. I went back to the whaling museum and found a description of how they did it. I used a small knife and some other sharp needles that I had and just carved the boat into the tooth. I used some of my ink and rubbed it all over the tooth, then wiped it off so that it only filled in the lines. I think it came out pretty good."

"Pretty good?" Bella said. "This is amazing, Freddie. It's as good as what the sailors used to create."

Freddie was beaming as he listened to her praise of his work.

"And you found the tooth on your property?"

"Yes, about five hundred of them. The river washed away a bluff and uncovered some white sand. I found them in the white sand."

"They must have been there for millions of years. This is hard to believe."

"I was surprised too, but it will be fun to do scrimshaw on them. Do you think it's okay for me to keep them?"

"Well, that's a hard question, and I don't really know the answer. I know you can't own whale teeth, but I don't know if that's true if you found them on your own property. But as I look at it, I'm not so sure it's a whale tooth because it's so flat. Whale teeth tend to be more rounded and curved. Tell you what, let me do some research for you. Can you stop back in a few days?"

"Sure. Do you want to try to sell my tooth? I can make more."

"Freddie, I think I will be able to sell this very quickly. First, let me find out if it's legal to do that. Then, if it is, let me figure out how much we should charge. Oh, and speaking of that, stay here for a minute."

Bella walked back into her office then returned and handed Freddie an envelope.

He opened it. "What's this for?" he asked, looking at the money inside.

"I sold one of your drawings. That's yours."

"You sold one? I can't believe it. Thank you so much."

"Come back in a few days and we'll figure out what to do with your tooth."

◆

Three days later, Freddie walked into ArtSea.

"Hi Bella, how are you today?"

"I'm fine Freddie, thanks. I've got some very interesting information for you. I visited a good friend of mine who deals in old whaling memorabilia. I showed him your tooth and he said it wasn't from a whale, but rather a megalodon. He told me they became extinct millions of years ago, but that they still find a lot of their teeth out in the ocean, especially off the coast of North and South Carolina. He was surprised they were here in Mattapoisett. He told me that based on the number of teeth you found that they probably came from two megalodons. And the good news is, they aren't illegal to own. So, they are yours."

"And I have five hundred of them. That's a lot of scrimshaw work for me."

"I'll be happy to try to sell whatever you make, Freddie. You are so talented."

All of a sudden Freddie gave Bella a big hug. He hadn't been respected that much since his mother passed away, and it felt good.

He hugged her for nearly a minute, and Bella was fine with it. It felt good to her too.

Finally, Freddie said, "I should go now. I'll stop by as soon as I have another tooth carved for you. What kind of a tooth did you call it?"

"A megalodon tooth."

"Bye Bella."

◆

A LARGE CROWD WAS GATHERED AT SHIPYARD PARK FOR the first band concert of the season. Families were sitting on blankets on the lawn, some eating picnic dinners, while others were enjoying ice cream cones they bought at Frates Ice Cream Shop at the top of the hill. Cars with windows down filled the parking lot adjacent to the bandstand, their occupants waiting for the concert to begin. A gentle warm breeze blew onshore, a comfortable evening for the concertgoers and musicians alike.

Forty or so of us were sitting on the bandstand, warming up, and making sure our music was in the order of tonight's program. I occupied first chair in the trumpet section, my second season in that seat. Three other trumpeters were sitting next to me, and there was a buzz of excitement among the musicians as Zavan Randolfi, our conductor, took his place at the podium in front of us, picked up his white baton, and mouthed the question, "Ready?"

We picked up our instruments and the conductor's baton cued us to begin the National Anthem, our traditional start to each concert. Most of the concertgoers stood and faced the flag at the top of the tall pole in the center of the park, their hands over their hearts. As the last note of the anthem drifted away in the evening air, the crowd applauded, and those sitting in their cars blew their horns.

Our next piece was a John Philip Sousa march, *El Capitan*. Three bars in, the audience began clapping in time with the music and several young children formed a line and marched around the bandstand like proud soldiers. Next, we played several selections from the musical, *South Pacific – Some Enchanted Evening, There is Nothing Like a Dame, and I'm Gonna Wash That Man Right Outa My Hair*. I thought of Carla as we played the last piece.

Finlandia was next up. Before we began playing, we did a quick tuning of our instruments, brass players pulling slides in and out, musicians from the woodwind section adjusting the barrels of their clarinets and saxophones. Just as we were ready to begin, there was a commotion under the bandstand. Seven-year-old Davy Thorndike crawled out from directly below us, carrying something that was almost as big as she was.

"Look what I found, look what I found," she yelled as she ran over towards her parents who were sitting on a blanket not far from the bandstand.

Our conductor lowered his baton and turned to look at the distraction. I looked too, and a knot formed in the pit of my stomach. *Not another body part!*

I set my trumpet in its case, then hurried down the steps of the bandstand over to where the family was now standing. A small crowd had gathered around them, and I pushed my way through. There in front of her parents was the young girl who had created the ruckus. She was holding a human arm, with a missing hand.

"Please set that on the blanket," I said to her.

She dropped it from her hands at my request.

I turned to her father and said, "Go find a phone and call the police."

As I knelt to look at the arm, I stopped short. A slit had been cut into the bicep, and inserted into it was a Teaberry gum wrapper, his calling card. The presence of gum wrappers was no accident.

While I waited for the police to arrive, I directed concertgoers away from the blanket as well as the bandstand. I needed to try to preserve any evidence that might exist.

The members of the band were all standing on the bandstand, looking out at what was unfolding in the park. Soon we heard sirens, and a minute later two police cars pulled down onto the wharf and parked. Chief Fernandez and Officer Townsend arrived at the same time and were hurrying over to where we were standing.

"This young lady," I said pointing to the girl who discovered the arm, "found this under the bandstand. We've got another severed arm, minus the hand. And, look at the bicep."

She looked, and couldn't miss the gum wrapper poking through the flesh. She gave me a knowing look.

"Go get a bag," she instructed Townsend.

He ran to his car and returned a minute later with an evidence bag.

"Take it over to forensics."

He knew the routine. Townsend carefully put the arm in the bag, tied it closed, then brought it back to his car and started off towards New Bedford.

"Let's check around and under the bandstand," I said.

We spent the next twenty minutes scouring the area, but came up empty. No clues, no prints, no possible evidence. There was nothing left to investigate, at least for now.

Zavan came over to where we were standing.

"Think we should cancel the concert?"

"That's a tough call," said the chief. "I guess if we're through with our work there's no reason not to continue. First, let us cordon off the area around the bandshell. Do you think the musicians are up to it?"

They both looked at me.

"Since I'll be involved with this, I'm not sure I can speak for the other musicians. But, I guess it's a good idea to continue. There's nothing to gain by ending it now. And, it might be a good distraction for our audience."

"All right, let's get started," said Randolfi as he turned and headed to the bandstand.

I followed him.

"Ladies and Gentlemen, it's very unfortunate we had such a tragic disruption to our concert, but after a thoughtful discussion, we've decided to resume tonight's performance. He pointed to the oboe player who set the A, the note the other musicians used to tune their instruments against. After a few seconds had elapsed, all the instruments were in tune.

Randolfi mouthed '*Finlandia*' to us, and, with a wave of his baton, the first band concert of the summer continued.

◆

290

WITH BLUE AND RED LIGHTS FLASHING, DETECTIVE AIELLO slowly led two town employees driving backhoes up Acushnet Road and onto Crystal Spring Road. The lights really weren't necessary as they hadn't seen a car since they pulled out of the town's public works grounds next to Cushing Cemetery on Mendell Road. A few minutes later, Aiello knocked on the front door of an old white farmhouse. When the door opened he handed Freddie Texeira a search warrant.

"We're going to have another look around your place, and this time we'll find what we're looking for. It's best that you stay in your house. You can serve time for interfering."

The selectmen had authorized the use of town employees for the search and the police had enough information to convince a judge to issue a search warrant. Now, Aiello turned and motioned for the two employees to follow him. He knew where they'd start, and he led them to the back of the pig field where a large trench had recently been filled in.

"Start here, and dig up this trench. Go slowly 'cause I have to look through everything you bring up. Just dump it on the side, then spread it out a bit."

The two men hadn't been told what they were looking for, but they had a pretty good idea.

They started digging thirty feet apart, facing each other, and then slowly worked their way towards the middle. After they had dug down about a foot, they began bringing up bucket loads of pig remains. They spread it out with their buckets and Aiello took a rake and sifted through it.

I just ruined my shoes and these pants will have to be trashed, but it will be worth it if I can find some evidence on this guy.

Aiello wasn't happy.

After the first day he complained to Chief Fernandez that this wasn't in his job description. She pulled a signed copy of it from his file and pointed out the bottom line that read, ". . . and other duties as assigned." Aiello went back to the fields the following day.

They dug up the trenches for seven straight days, leaving piles of pig entrails alongside where they had dug. At the end of each day's work the area was roped off and an auxiliary officer was assigned to preserve the scene until they resumed their search the next day. After a week of digging they came up empty and gave up. They left a mess behind, and when Freddie complained, Aiello told him that the search warrant didn't say they had to clean up after they were done.

"So, we're not," was his answer to Freddie's complaint.

◆

THE CHIEF AND I GOT TOGETHER AT THE END OF THE week. The forensic report came back and the findings were about as we expected, a human arm severed from a body. B-negative blood. Townsend had searched the area under and around the bandstand again, but didn't discover anything helpful.

"We tore up Texeira's farm as much as we could, but we didn't find anything. It's so big we certainly could have missed something."

In a way, I was hoping they'd find the rest of the body and that maybe it wouldn't be the harbormaster's. But, no luck on either count.

I tiptoed around Carla's experience with her client and the truck and fish incident. I wanted to be careful about breaching confidentiality, but I shared what I could.

"There could be a possible connection there," said the chief. "It's a long shot, but we don't have much else to go on, so it makes sense to follow up on it. How's Carla doing, by the way?"

"She's in tough shape, pretty beat up, but, thank God, no permanent damage. She's a trooper and her doctor said he'll let her out of the hospital next week. Her casts will be on for another few weeks, and then she'll have some rehab to do. By then she'll be able to walk, though probably with crutches."

"Well, that's good. Please give her my best when you see her again."

"Thanks, I sure will. I want to find the guy who did this to her. It's personal. If you can get the Department of Motor Vehicles to run a list of the trucks in town, I'll check them out one-by-one. If I do find it, you'd better have one of your boys with me."

◆

THE CODFATHER HAD DONE A LOT OF FAVORS FOR people. He had money and he had connections. Often, those he helped repaid him—sometimes in unusual ways. He had just received a call from one of those people and was on his way to the Whaler's Inn. *He'll learn not to blow off a meeting with me.*

He pulled into the parking lot behind the Inn then walked around to the front and entered the restaurant. He didn't stop at the hostess' desk; he continued on in and scanned the tables. He saw the guy sitting by himself at a corner table and started towards him.

The guy looked up from his fish and chips and saw the Codfather just about the same time that the Codfather spotted him. His hands shook and he dropped his fork. Although it was comfortable inside the restaurant, beads of sweat formed on the diner's forehead and more sweat ran from his neck down the center of his chest. *How did he find me? Will he create a scene? Is he going to assault me?* He thought about trying to escape but knew he'd only be followed out the door, and there wouldn't be any witnesses there. *He'll probably threaten me, but as long as I'm in here he probably won't attack me.*

"Did you forget our meeting?" he asked as he pulled out a chair and sat down.

The guy didn't reply.

"I asked you a question and I expect an answer. Why didn't you show up?"

Hope was the bartender today. She had long wavy dark hair and a sparkle in her eyes. That didn't hurt her tips. She picked up a menu from behind the bar and walked over to their table.

"Can I get you something to drink?" she asked as she offered the new customer a menu.

"Just a beer. This is a business meeting. I won't be having anything else. It'll be short."

Hope set the menu on the table and looked at the two men.

Fish and chips guy looks scared. It shows in his eyes and on his face. He isn't eating. When I took his order, he was joking and flirting with me. Talking about liking younger women. Something changed, and the only thing that was different was the guy sitting across from him.

Hope returned to the bar and poured a draft Dawson beer, then brought it over to him.

"Are you sure you don't want something to eat?"

"Positive."

Hope picked up the menu and returned to the bar and busied herself putting more beer into the coolers. She was curious, but acted like she was focused on stocking the coolers while she listened to their conversation. They were far enough away that she could only hear bits and pieces of it, *crates . . . money . . . cops . . . reward . . . .* She glanced over at them. Fish

294

and chips guy wasn't eating. He was paying attention to the new guy. He still looked scared. The new guy was pointing a finger in his face.

I know, thought the fish and chips guy.

"Here's how I can pay you," Hope overheard him say. She didn't hear what was said after that.

Fish and chips guy leaned over and whispered, "The crates that you brought me contain famous old paintings worth millions of dollars. I'll give you one and you can sell it. It's worth a lot more than what you're asking me for."

Codfather was quiet as he thought for a minute before answering.

"How the hell will I sell a stolen old painting? Run an ad in the *New Bedford Tribune*? Forget it. Get me my 100K or you are going for a one-way ride on my boat."

Abruptly, new guy got up and went over to the bar and threw a dollar on it.

"Here's for the beer."

He walked out the front door leaving fish and chips guy staring at his back.

Hope waited awhile before she went over and asked, "Can I get you anything else?"

Fish and chips guy unwrapped a piece of gum, put it in his mouth, and just shook his head no.

"I'll bring you your check then."

After he paid his bill and left the restaurant, Hope grabbed a tray and went over to their table. She picked up the empty bottles, dishes and utensils and put them on the tray. She studied the pink gum wrapper for a minute, then, thinking about what she had overheard, went back to the bar and got a clean napkin. When she returned to the table she picked up the gum wrapper with it and put it in her pocket.

◆

HOPE WAS MIXING A MIMOSA FOR THE COUPLE AT THE bar at the Inn. It was their second one as they waited for their Mattapoisett Benedicts to arrive from the kitchen. The 'bene' was created by the Inn's long-time chef, Dana, who graduated from Johnson and Wales Culinary school in Providence. Lobster, scallops, and fresh spinach were stacked on top of the English muffins and poached eggs. It was a favorite with the locals and the tourists had recently caught on to it.

Sometimes you felt it in your gut when something was wrong. Hope had that feeling about the conversation she had overheard between the stranger and the fish and chips guy.

Hope was one of the regular bartenders at Whaler's Inn, and she often had conversations with Manny about detective work. She knew that sometimes the smallest piece of information or evidence could help solve the biggest crime. That had stuck with her. That's why she picked up the gum wrapper that the fish and chips guy had left on the table. *Manny will probably think I'm silly and maybe I should just throw it away. But, he's the one who always talked about the smallest pieces.*

Hope had tried calling Manny several times during the past few days, but he didn't answer.

He's probably with Carla.

Finally, a week later, she reached him early in the morning.

"Hi Manny, it's Hope. I have something I need to talk with you about. You'll probably think I'm stupid, but I remember you always talk about how important little details are, and I have something I think I should share with you. Can we get together sometime?"

"Absolutely. You're a good student. What time do you get out of work tonight?"

"I'm off at six, when Megan comes in."

"Okay, how about we meet at the bench across the street near the bandstand after you get out of work?"

"Good. I'll see you there."

♦

It was a busy day, and Hope had just finished restocking the bar for Megan when she walked in to relieve her.

"Hi Hope. Quiet afternoon?" Megan asked, looking around the empty bar.

"Actually, it's been pretty busy. It's slow right now, but will probably pick up tonight. Have fun," she said as she headed out of the Inn and walked across the street to meet Manny.

She spotted him sitting on the bench and walked down to join him.

"Hi Manny. How are you, and how is Carla?"

"I'm fine, Hope, but Carla's pretty badly injured. Both legs and her collarbone are broken. Fortunately, she doesn't have any head injuries. She's in rehab, but making good progress."

"Please tell her that I'm thinking about her the next time you see her. Tell her to stop by when she's doing better."

"I'll be sure to tell her. Maybe we'll come for dinner sometime soon. What do you have for me?"

"A week ago, a guy was having lunch at the Inn. He comes in once in a while, but I don't know his name. I'm pretty sure he lives in town. Anyway, he was eating fish and chips when another guy came in. I never saw him before. He went over and sat down with the guy having fish and chips. He seemed pretty angry and was pointing his finger in his face. The fish

297

and chips guy looked pretty scared. I could only hear parts of their conversation from the bar, but the angry guy said things like cops, money, crates, reward. I'm not really sure what he was talking about. I couldn't hear much else. After they left I cleared the table and remembered what you said about the little things often being important, so I picked this up and saved it."

Hope handed me a napkin. I carefully unwrapped it, and inside found a pink Teaberry gum wrapper.

"Hope, this could be far more important than you realize. You really should get your degree in criminal justice. One thing is very important, Hope. You can't share the information about the gum wrapper with anyone else. Sometimes, what seems to be insignificant can help us set a trap that implicates a suspect. If they somehow learned about it, it could hamper our investigation. I'm sure you understand that. Thank you so much for sharing this with me. It's important."

I paused. "Can you describe the two people?"

For the next few minutes Hope gave me a description of her two customers. I recognized one of them, but would have to do some digging on the other. We stood up and I gave her a big hug.

"Good work, detective."

◆

IN ADDITION TO BEGINNING HER PHYSICAL THERAPY, Carla had resumed her appointments with Dr. Carney to continue working on her relationship issues. Today she was sitting in her office. During their last few sessions Carla had made great strides in regaining trust. Dr. Carney's plan for today was to help her continue that progress.

"Carla, you've been seeing Manny for a long time, and you

298

went back to him after you broke up with him. Does that tell you anything?"

"I like him and I enjoy spending time with him."

"Do you get tired of being with him?"

Carla thought a moment before saying, "No."

"Do you look forward to being with him."

"Yes."

"Tell me what you don't like about him."

Carla was quiet for a minute and didn't offer an answer.

"Okay, now tell me what you *do* like about him."

"Well, he's always been very good to me. He came to see me every day when I was in the hospital."

"And at other times?"

"Oh yes, always."

"What else?"

"He's honest and very ethical."

"And?"

"We get along well together. We almost never have an argument, and when we do we usually resolve it very quickly and without a lot of yelling and screaming."

"Do you trust him?"

Carla knew where Dr. Carney was going. Her problem with trust issues had been the focus of many of their sessions. Carla sat silently for a minute. Reflecting.

"I do trust him, more than anyone else in my life."

"Are you happy when you are with him?"

"Yes, almost always."

For the rest of their session Dr. Carney explored Carla's progress dealing with her alcoholism. She had made great strides towards sobriety, and Dr. Carney reinforced her progress.

The hour passed and they ended their session, agreeing to meet again in one week.

◆

RONNIE PENDERGAST AND HIS GRANDFATHER WERE
fishing off the end of Makuch Wharf. A small scup was slowly
moving its tail back and forth in the bucket of salt water next
to Ronnie. It was the only fish they had caught that afternoon.
Several boats were returning to the wharf after spending a day
out on Buzzards Bay, sailing and fishing.

All of a sudden, Ronnie looked at his grandfather and said,
"There was a fish!"

"When that happens, just give your line a quick tug and you'll
set the hook in its mouth. Then you just have to pull it up."

"No, no, no. I mean there was a fish on the back of the
truck that hit that lady. I just remembered it."

"Are you sure?"

"Yes, it was a blue fish on the window. The back one."

"It's great that you remembered that Ronnie. We should
go and tell the police. They will be happy to know that. Then
we'll go and get an ice cream cone. Want to?"

"Okay."

"Let's pack up our stuff and go to the station."

Ronnie looked at the scup in his bucket.

"I don't need that fish."

He reached down, picked it up, and threw it off the end of
the wharf.

They walked back home, dropped off their fishing gear,
and then drove over to the police station.

Detective Aiello was sitting behind the desk when they
walked in.

"Can I help you?" he asked.

"Ronnie has something to tell you. Go ahead Ronnie."

300

"There was a fish on the back of the truck that hit that lady. I just remembered it when we were fishing. It was a blue fish, and it was on the back window. I saw it when it started to drive away, but I just remembered it."

"It's good that you remembered that Ronnie. That will be a big help to us."

"You're really sure that you saw a fish on the window?"

"Yes, I saw it."

"You're a good detective. Maybe you'll be a policeman someday."

Ronnie grinned from ear to ear. "And I could have my own car with lights and sirens?"

"You sure could."

"Can we go get ice cream now?"

◆

HE HAD FEW FRIENDS. OTHER PRISONERS DON'T LIKE pedophiles. That caused him problems, and for that he hated the cops.

Bastards set me up when they couldn't prove a thing. They rigged the damn lineup! Someday they'll pay for that, or I'll die trying.

Fifteen years ago, it took the jury only thirty minutes to convict him of indecent assault and battery on a child under fourteen. Up to ten years. He got five, then moved back to town after he got out.

The girl could only tell them the color of the truck and she picked me out of six dark skinned Cape Verdeans and another guy twice my age. And they still sent me to prison!

Berkshire Federal Prison is located in the hills of Western Massachusetts. He had been there for a little over a year and pretty much

301

stayed to himself. It was safer that way. The only friend he made was a guy from Pittsfield who was serving two years for drug dealing. Willie Morin was his name. He trusted Willie.

Twelve prisoners were outside in the courtyard for their one hour 'recreation period.'

"I got some weed stashed in the toolshed, want some?" Willie asked.

"Sure, how will we get in? They keep it locked."

"Easy. When I was in the kitchen I went through the back door near the freezer and it opens right into the shed. I opened the door and stuck a piece of cardboard between the lock and the doorjamb. Fools don't even use padlocks or deadbolts."

They waited until the lone guard was at the far end of the yard then casually walked over to the shed, looked around, then slipped inside. The shed was dark and empty except for a metal workbench in the middle of the room.

"Over here," motioned Willie to the far side of the room.

He followed Willie.

Seconds later the door opened and four inmates burst into the room.

"Get him! Gag him!" said one of the inmates as they rushed over, grabbed him, and threw him face down over the table.

He was terrified. He had heard the stories and in the back of his mind knew that this might happen to him. It usually does to pedophiles. He tried to fight, but it was useless. Two men held his arms over his head and stretched them across the table while another forced part of a towel into his mouth. He broke into a sweat, his heart pounded, he tried to fight back, but it was useless. They had him. Another man wrapped tape around his head, securing the towel in his mouth. He gagged and dry heaved, again, and again, and again. He felt hands pulling his prison uniform down until it reached his ankles. He was bent over the table, helpless. Fear took over. He knew what was coming next.

He was dizzy, disoriented and then in pain as the first prisoner took him. He felt searing pain, humiliating pain, pain he had never felt before.

Over the next fifteen minutes each of the men, including Willie, violated him. He grew numb to it, hoping that he would pass out, but he didn't. He stopped counting the number of men after the third. Finally, it was over. He lay across the table, in pain, unable to move. Light entered the room as the men opened the door to leave.

One turned back to him, "You talk, you'll take the elevator down from the second floor, 'cept we ain't got no elevator," he said with a laugh as he exited the shed and slammed the door behind him.

◆

NED'S POINT ROAD IS JUST UNDER A MILE LONG. IT follows the east side of Mattapoisett Harbor and ends at the white lighthouse at the entrance to the harbor. Ned Point lighthouse was built of stone in 1838, but was deactivated a few years ago due to the emerging use of GPS devices by boatsmen. Just inside the black, steel doorway, a spiral staircase leads to the top of the lighthouse and the lights and reflectors that were once used to inform sailors of the location of the entrance to the harbor. The grounds around the lighthouse are a favorite spot of picnickers, families flying kites, and those who liked to fish from the large boulders stacked against the banks that prevent the waves from washing away the land that the lighthouse sits on.

Freddie Texeira didn't fish from the rocks. Instead he often took his boat to the waters just off Pico Beach, near the lighthouse. It was late in the afternoon, and it had been a good day for fishing. It was his third trip this week, and all had been productive. This afternoon he had hooked several scup, a tautaug, and a small bluefish. They now lay lifeless in the hull of his boat.

He was about ready to call it a day when, off in the distance, he spotted a truck parked next to the lighthouse. It wasn't a typical place to park, so out of curiosity he picked up his binoculars and took a closer look.

The door to the lighthouse is open. That's odd.

He adjusted the focus on his binoculars and observed a man struggling to lift something large out of the back of the truck. He turned, then carried it a few steps and entered the lighthouse. A minute later he emerged, closed the heavy black door, and walked to his truck. Freddie watched as the man got into his truck then drove towards the beginning of Ned's Point Road. As the truck turned to leave the park, Freddie recognized it by the sticker of a blue fish on the rear window.

What was he doing there?

Freddie pulled his boat near the small beach and anchored. He took his shoes off, rolled up his pants, then jumped into the shallow water and waded ashore. He walked across the park until he reached the lighthouse, then grabbed the door handle and gave it a pull. It was locked.

He must have had a key. Where did he get it? And what did he leave inside?

Freddie looked at the door for a minute, trying to decide if it was worth getting involved with this. If he went to the police, more likely than not he would be harassed and tied up for lengthy questioning. *I've wasted enough of my time in lineups and sitting across from cops defending myself from things I never did.* He paused. *But what's on the other side of this door?*

He made his decision, went back to his boat and drove it to his mooring spot at Mello Wharf. Thirty minutes later he walked into the police station.

"Well, if it isn't Wharf Rat," said Detective Aiello from behind the desk in the lobby. "What brings you here? Finally have something to tell us?" his comment not-so-thinly-veiled mockery.

"Actually, I do," said Freddie.

"I was fishing just off Pico Beach when I saw a truck at the lighthouse. The door was open, and a guy took something out of the back of his truck and put it inside. After he left, I anchored my boat and went over to see what was going on, but the door was locked."

"Can you describe the truck?"

"As a matter of fact, I can. And I can tell you who it belongs to."

He waited for Aiello to ask.

"Who was it?"

"Art Nunes."

"Are you sure?"

"Positive. I recognized his truck by the sticker of a blue fish on the rear window. That's the only truck I've ever seen with that sticker."

"Anything else you can tell me?"

Freddie thought for a minute, then said, "No, that's about it. I was offshore and that's all I could see through my binoculars."

Aiello's attitude changed. "Thank you very much Mr. Texeira. We'll follow up on it. We might have some more questions for you later on, once we get over there and see what's inside."

He extended his hand to Freddie. Freddie looked down at it. *That's a first!*

They shook hands and Freddie left. *My first visit to the station when I wasn't being interrogated for something.*

Aiello picked up the phone and called the chief. She picked up on the second ring.

Before she could say hello, Aiello blurted, "Art Nunes just dumped something inside the lighthouse. Wharf Rat, I mean

305

Freddie Texeira, just came to the station and told me that he witnessed it. He was sure it was Nunes. We need to get over there to investigate, but I don't know where to get a key. Would it be in the harbormaster's office?"

"Whoa, slow down. Are you confident in what he told you?"

"Yes, I'm very sure he was telling the truth."

"Okay, let me see if I can track down a key. Why don't you head over to the lighthouse to keep an eye on things in case he goes back there? I'll meet up with you as soon as I can find a key."

"Okay, Chief."

Her next call was to me. She caught me just before I left for New Bedford for dinner and the State Theater to see the movie *Patton*.

"We've got a situation at the lighthouse. I'll pick you up in ten minutes."

So much for dinner and a movie. Hopefully it's nothing and I can catch a later show. Maybe I can guilt the chief into buying dinner.

Chief picked me up and drove us out to Ned Point. She was able to get a key from the first selectman, which led to a lot of questions about where the harbormaster's keys were. Another thing on her list. We pulled into the park and saw Aiello sitting in his cruiser in front of the door to the lighthouse. We drove over and pulled up next to him.

"Anyone come by?" Chief asked as she inserted the key into the door of the lighthouse.

"Nobody."

I could sense her hesitation to turn the key and open the door.

"Open it up. I'll check it out," I said.

That's all she needed to turn the key and unlock the door. I took the handle, opened it, and stepped inside. Once inside,

306

I didn't have far to go. A bundle the size of a large dressed hog was wrapped in a tarp and lying on the floor. I looked around out of habit and, seeing nothing out of the ordinary, knelt down and carefully began to unwrap the tarp.

My mind flashed back to Vietnam. I'd seen a lot of bodies, decomposed and otherwise. Inside the tarp was a human torso. No arms, legs, or head. I immediately knew where the arms and legs we had discovered came from. The answer was right here in front of me. I gently touched the torso with the fingertips of my right hand, then quickly pulled them away, as much in surprise as anything else. It certainly wasn't like anything I had witnessed during my two years in the one hundred plus degree days in the Mekong Delta. The body was ice cold – frozen – solid.

The chief and Aiello were still outside and hadn't said a word. Dozens of questions flashed through my mind. Some I could answer, some I couldn't. One I couldn't answer was, "Where's the head?" We had the arms, legs, and torso, but no head. We could probably make an ID if we had it, dental records and so on, but it wasn't here. The bigger question was, where's Nunes?

Partway down my list of questions I thought about the calling cards the murderer had left behind—a Teaberry gum wrapper. I carefully looked under the tarp and the body, but didn't find one. That still didn't rule out a connection. Odds were, the parts all fit.

"Chief, come on in, we've got a torso."

She stepped inside. This was the second body she had encountered since coming to Mattapoisett. Her first was at the Ellis-Bowles cemetery a few years back.

"It's frozen solid," I told her. "And we don't have a head. Most likely the arms and legs we found came from this. And, it's definitely a male."

I had taken pictures as I unwrapped the torso, and I felt that I had seen all that I needed to see. "You can have one of your men take it over to the Medical Examiner."

The ground was dry in front of the lighthouse and I couldn't spot any tire tracks or footprints. Since we had a tentative ID on the truck and driver, it wasn't as important. We'll be able to check out the tires on the truck with the pictures of the tracks that I took at the fair and the cranberry bogs. With any luck, we'll have a match and the murderer.

Aiello drove off towards New Bedford with the torso. Chief called Townsend on her radio and told him to meet us here.

Townsend arrived a short time later. Chief directed him to search the rest of the lighthouse and then to secure the scene until the auxiliary officer showed up.

"You're coming with me," Chief said as she looked at me.

◆

TWICE AROUND TO 1, THEN L3 – R8 – L9. I FELT THE tumblers fall into place and I pulled the door to open my safe. I hadn't been in it for a long time, but the call from the chief before we headed to the lighthouse changed all that. She was waiting outside for me as I took out my Smith and Wesson Model 36, a "Chief's Special." I removed five cartridges from the ammunition box and loaded them into the chamber. I shouldn't need any more than that. I was hoping that I wouldn't need any of them. I strapped my shoulder holster on, then went down to my cellar to grab a crowbar. We might need it. A minute later we were backing out of my driveway.

"We'll swing by the station and pick up Townsend. He just got back from the lighthouse and can follow us over."

A short time later we were heading down Ned's Point Road. Chief had tracked down Nunes' house number and we counted the numbers down on the houses we passed by on our left side.

We pulled into the boat yard that was part way down the road so that we could decide on a strategy before arriving at his house. Chief looked at me, and since my life could also be on the line, I had no problem taking charge.

It really was simple. Secure the back and come in through the front. Because we were pursuing a suspect, we didn't need to obtain a warrant and follow the law that would have required us to knock, announce, and then wait a reasonable amount of time before entering.

We found the house. Carla had been right when she followed the truck back from the fair. His truck wasn't there, but that didn't mean he wasn't home.

We parked on the street a few doors down from his house and gave Townsend several minutes to cut through backyards and station himself behind a shed in back of Art's house. It was broad daylight and we were easy targets if he saw us and had a gun. While keeping my eyes on the windows on the front of the house, I noted where the trees were that could provide some cover. I had my S&W in my right hand, and the crowbar in my left. I motioned to the chief to pull hers out as well, but she was ahead of me on that one.

We reached the front door without any new holes in our clothing. I nodded to the chief then knocked. No answer. I knocked again.

"Open the door or we'll break in."

No answer.

One more time.

"Open the door or we'll break in."

I glanced at the windows to see if he was watching. I didn't see him.

"Keep your gun pointed at the front door, and be ready in case he appears."

I took my crowbar, inserted it at the lock point, then leaned on it until the force pushed the strike plate right through the wood. I dropped the crowbar, then slowly opened the door, my revolver leading the way.

"This is the police. If you're here, come out with your hands up."

At least one of us was a cop.

No answer, so we cautiously stepped inside. I was reminded of my days in Vietnam. We never knew when someone might be hiding in the bushes, waiting for us. The tension I felt now wasn't unlike the tension I had felt back then. And I lost a leg over there.

We slowly searched the rooms on the first floor. My heart pounded as I pulled open each closet door. I was drenched in sweat. If he *was* here, he'd more likely be on the second floor or in the cellar. Somehow, he'd think that was safer.

I motioned for the chief to stay on the first floor and pointed to the stairs, indicating that I was going up. As I took the first step, I knew I was an easy target. All he'd have to do is come around the corner at the top of the stairs and start firing.

I hope I'm faster and more accurate than he is.

I reached the top of the stairs and quickly checked to my left and right. No Nunes. I checked the first two rooms. He wasn't there. My gun led the way into the last room, which appeared to be his office. For what, I wasn't sure. Not here. Ten large wooden crates over in the corner caught my eye. *That's odd. I'll come back later for a closer look.*

I was pretty confident that he wasn't on the two floors we had searched, so that only left the cellar. I went back down and joined the chief, and nodded towards the cellar door.

Just then there was a loud crash below us. We both jumped and then looked at each other.

"He's down there," I whispered.

I motioned the chief over to the right side of the cellar door. I wanted to be on the left side so that my gun hand would be closest to the doorway when I opened it.

Could he be at the top of the stairs, with a gun pointing our way?

If he was, I knew I had to be ready to fire instantly.

I had to decide whether to swing the door open or to announce and order him to drop his weapon. I opted for the element of surprise. That came from my military training. Surprise was always better. I pointed to the doorknob, then nodded to the chief. She understood. With her gun drawn, she reached down with her left hand and quickly opened and pulled the door inward. I tensed and was ready to fire, but he wasn't there.

He must be downstairs.

I reached around the corner and flipped on the light switch with my left hand. I was ready to shoot if I needed to.

"Drop your weapon and crawl to the bottom of the stairs," I yelled.

I waited for a reply, but there wasn't one.

Was he looking for a shootout?

I knew that some criminals liked going out in a blaze of glory.

I hope he's not one of them.

My unit had searched a lot of buildings and caves in Vietnam, and I had a pretty good idea as to how to approach this. I led with my gun and protected myself with the walls as much as I could. I had motioned for the chief to stay upstairs. I didn't want to be the recipient of friendly fire. I reached the spot where I could peer under the ceiling, and I quickly scanned the room. I didn't see him, but that didn't mean he wasn't hiding. Then I saw some movement and quickly swung my gun around, ready to squeeze the trigger—until I saw that it was a cat, sitting on a workbench. I slowly exhaled.

For what seemed an eternity, I scoured the room, sweeping back and forth from side to side with my eyes and my gun. Finally, I was convinced that Nunes wasn't in the house. I let out a long, slow breath and relaxed.

"All clear down here, Chief. Come on down."

When the chief joined me I pointed at a large chest freezer against the wall. I knew we were still missing some body parts, and that the ones we had found had been frozen.

We walked over and I lifted the cover, knowing what we'd probably find. To our surprise, it was empty. We stared into the empty freezer, and that's when I noticed the dark reddish-black tar-like stains on the bottom. I'd seen enough of it in the past to be pretty certain that it was blood.

"Looks like blood," said the chief. "We'll have to get that checked out. A good chance it's Tinkham's. I'll let the forensic team know as soon as we get back to the office."

I scanned the rest of the cellar. Two large jars sitting on a shelf behind a workbench caught my eye. I walked over to them, and as I got closer my pace slowed. I could see what they contained from ten feet away, and I got an uneasy feeling in the pit of my stomach. I stepped closer and confirmed my suspicion. Each jar contained a human hand. I had no doubt whose they were.

"Chief, come over here."

She walked over to where I was standing and I pointed to

312

the jars. We looked at each other, knowingly.

I carefully took each jar down from the shelf and set them on the workbench. I was especially interested in the one that held the left hand. I slowly turned that jar until the knuckles were pointing at me.

L-O-V-E. It was Tinkham's.

Until this moment we all had hoped that he was away somewhere and would suddenly show up at his office, unaware of the anxiety he had caused for the people of the town. Now, that hope was gone. We were quiet for a minute, in part out of respect, as we looked at the two hands.

Chief broke the silence.

"Why would he do such a thing? Cut off his hands and keep them in jars?"

"Trophies."

I waited for the chief to ask, but she didn't, so I continued. "Sometimes killers keep a trophy to remember their kills. Native Americans used to take scalps, and mass murderers have kept body parts as trophies. Others have kept articles of clothing. It's pathological, and this guy clearly fits the diagnosis."

The chief thought a minute.

"Let's get Townsend in here, I don't think we need him outside any more. When Aiello gets back, I'll have him take the hands over to the forensic lab."

"And, I'll get an all-points bulletin out for his truck. Hopefully he's still in the area and we can pick him up," said the chief.

"While you're working on that, I want to check something out upstairs."

Chief went out the back door and hollered for Townsend while I climbed the stairs to the second floor. I entered the room that I thought might be his office so I could check out the crates I had seen. This wasn't the first time that the issue of crates had come up. The Codfather had told me about them when I saw him on the wharf in New Bedford, and Hope mentioned them to me when we had our conversation about the two men she had overheard at the Whaler's Inn. Now, I was curious. I walked into the room and went over to where they were stacked end-to-end against the wall. I counted ten of them, and each was numbered. They all had swastikas on them.

An envelope was lying on top of the crates. I picked it up and opened it, then pulled out an old, hand-written letter. At the top of the letter was the address and phone number for Antone Nunes in Praia da Vitoria, in the Azores.

Portuguese. Maybe a relative?

Then I was puzzled. Beneath the address was a list of paintings—old ones—famous ones:

1. Painter on His Way to Work
   Van Gogh

2. Silent Sea with Sailboats
   Jan van de Capelle

3. Portrait of the Venetian Admiral Giovanni Moro
   Titian

4. Portrait of a Courtesan
   Caravaggio

5. Saint Agnes
   Cano

6. Still Life with Copper Kettle, Bottle, Bowl
   with Eggs and Two Leeks
   Chardin

7. Virgin Mary and Child and baby Saint John
   Lucas Cranach the Elder

8. The Murder of Julius Caesar
   Del Sellaio

9. Madame Boone and Her Daughter
   Sir Joshua Reynolds

10. Martyrdom of Saint Lucy
    Beccafumi

11. The Vision of Saint Bruno
    Jordaens

I looked at the crates, then back at the list.

Could these crates contain the paintings on this list? Impossible.

I went back downstairs and picked up the crowbar that I had left on the front steps. When I got back to the room I looked at the first crate, then at the list.

Painter on His Way to Work. Van Gogh. I know of Van Gogh. This can't be.

I carefully inserted the crowbar under the slat that covered the top of the crate. I was both nervous and excited as I pried it open, removed it, and set it on top of the other crates. I looked inside and saw the top of a frame, surrounded by crumpled brown paper. I reached in, almost afraid to touch it, and carefully pulled it out of the crate.

It was a picture of a man in a blue suit with a white package tucked under his left arm. His shadow was cast on the road beside him, and he was walking towards the left. Behind him, two trees stood at the edge of a field. I was pretty sure that I was looking at a masterpiece.

"Chief, get up here!"

A moment later she was standing beside me, looking at the painting. I glanced at the list in my hand and said, "I'm almost certain that this is an incredibly valuable painting, *Painter on His Way to Work,* by Van Gogh.

Chief was speechless.

"This is beyond us. We need to get in touch with Interpol. They have to be stolen, but from where? They'll have to figure that out. I'll bet you dinner that the other crates contain other paintings."

I looked at the list. Eleven paintings were on it, though only ten crates rested against the wall. I put the letter back into the envelope and slipped it into my pocket. I had a hunch, and I wanted to do it quietly.

"Chief, we've got some work to do. We have to get the hands over to forensics along with a sample of the blood in the freezer. We need to track down Nunes, and we need to contact INTERPOL and get them to deal with the paintings."

"Okay, as soon as he gets here I'll have Aiello collect specimens of the blood in the freezer and take them along with the hands over to forensics. I'll assign an auxiliary officer over here to relieve Townsend and secure the house. Then I'll get my two men looking for Nunes."

For the next fifteen minutes I took pictures of all the evidence, then said to the chief, "Let's get back to your office. We can call INTERPOL from there and get that one off our list."

316

♦

The phone rang at the National Central Bureau (NCB) for the United States, the point of contact for INTERPOL. Three days later, after the investigation had been completed, a black car pulled into Nunes' driveway. Soon after that, a van arrived and the ten crates were removed from the house and taken away.

♦

AFTER HE DROPPED THE TORSO AT THE LIGHTHOUSE, Nunes drove his truck to Cushing Cemetery. He turned off Mendell Road into the cemetery and headed to an isolated spot at the back of the burial grounds. He spotted a large old oak tree and eased the front bumper of his truck up against it. Then he shifted his truck into third gear and pushed the gas pedal to the floor, full throttle, while using the clutch to keep the engine revving. In two minutes he accomplished his goal, when the clutch overheated.

He stepped on the gas as he left the cemetery on his way back to town, less than a mile away. The truck wouldn't accelerate and he had difficulty shifting gears.

Five minutes later he pulled into Linhares' Garage on Route 6. The owner, Joe Linhares, was pumping gas for a customer.

Art walked over to him and said, "My clutch is burned out. It's got a bad smell and I'm having trouble shifting into gear."

"Pull it into the farthest bay," Linhares said, pointing towards his garage. "I'll take it apart and have a look at it. If I have to order parts it could be tied up for a few days."

317

"Well, if I can't drive it I'll just have to do without it for a bit. Can I use your phone to call a friend for a ride?"

"Sure thing, come on inside with me."

Linhares led Nunes into his office.

"There's the phone," he said, pointing to his desk.

Nunes picked up the phone and dialed his own number. After a few rings he said to no one on the other end, "Hey, I need a ride. Can you pick me up at the drug store? Okay, I'll see you there in a few minutes."

He hung up the phone, gave his phone number to Linhares, then left and walked to the wharf.

That will be out of sight for a few days.

◆

ART RELEASED THE STERN AND BOW LINES, THEN CLIMBED aboard his red boat, the *Arte Perdida.* he would be alone on this trip. Nudging the bow away from Makuch's Wharf, he glanced up at the swordfish weathervane before heading out into the harbor.

His running lights were on as he cut through the water at four knots, one below the speed limit for the harbor. He didn't want to call attention to himself. As the wharves receded to his stern, he passed Rob Boardman's Herreshoff 30. Art hated sailboats and much preferred his stinkpot, as those who owned sailboats called them.

He pushed the throttle ahead as he passed Ned Point Light, then turned to the starboard and headed down Buzzards Bay towards Cuttyhunk, at the Southerly end of the Elizabeth Islands, about twenty miles away. The string of islands, that extended southwesterly from Woods Hole, were discovered in 1602 by the English Explorer Bartholomew Gosnold. The

318

name Cuttyhunk comes from an Algonquin Indian word meaning point of departure or land's end. *Pretty fitting*, thought Art.

Off in the distance he spotted Gosnold light and the Gosnold Monument. The monument was a small, round tower that stood on a remote spot on the island. Most people thought it was a pretty lousy tribute to the man who discovered the Elizabeth Islands, Martha's Vineyard, and Nantucket.

A few hours earlier Art had called a friend, Joshua Slocum, a descendent of one of the original settlers of the island. He was one of the few dozen residents who lived on the island year-round. No one ever called him anything but Captain, and only a few long-timers even knew his first name. Captain had served a stint as a selectman, but wasn't re-elected for a second term. Art never asked why.

He made his living as a commercial fisherman, and was one of the few residents who had their own dock with an attached, covered boat shelter. Art had asked him if he could use the shelter for a few days, and Captain had agreed. Prior to Art's arrival, he had pulled his own boat out of the shelter and tied it to the dock. He was there to greet Art, and motioned for him to nudge the *Arte Perdida* into the shelter. It would be out of sight while Art was on the island.

"So, you need a place to camp out, huh?"

"Yes, I do."

"I won't ask why. I'm sure I don't want to know."

"You're right."

They walked up to his house and sat on the deck, taking in the view of some of the nine islands in the Elizabeth chain. His house sat on a hill not far from where the first non-native inhabitant, Francis Usselton had lived. He was banished there by the Governor of Massachusetts for trading with the

Wampanoags without the Governor's permission. Captain didn't think being banished to Cuttyhunk was such a bad thing. Lots of peace and quiet, and no one snooping into his business.

"How long are you planning to stay?" Captain asked as he cracked open his third beer and tossed another one to Art.

"Probably head out in a few days, maybe a week. I've got a few things to take care of."

Captain didn't ask what those 'few things' were. Not snooping into his business. That's how it worked on Cuttyhunk.

"I've got some bluefish marinating in red wine vinegar. Grab your beer and let's go broil it. I've got some kale I'm going to sauté with some Spanish onions."

After dinner, they sat out on the porch watching the reds and oranges of the sunset slowly disappear until all that remained was a thin vermilion line separating the sky from the bay. They each had a beer in hand and a lot of empties littered the deck.

"That bluefish was so good I don't care if I never have another meal. Usually it's so damn oily and fishy that I just cut it up and use it for bait and chum."

"It's a recipe that has been around the island for generations. Only way to cook it."

"Well, I think I'm going to call it a night," said Art. "I'll sleep on my boat, so that I don't bother you."

They shook hands and said goodnight. Captain headed into the house, while Art walked down to the dock, into the garage, then jumped onto the deck of the *Arte Perdida*.

He stayed for a week, enjoying the solace of the island. He went fishing with the Captain, and enjoyed being on someone else's boat for a change. During the evening they sat on the porch and reminisced. They had a lot of stories, some that they had never shared with each other. A week had passed, and as they sat on the deck after dinner the sky looked as if it were a slowly changing kaleidoscope of bright reds, oranges, and purples. *Red sky at night, sailor's delight. Tomorrow will be one bloody red day.*

♦

Praia da Vitoria, Azores

THE POLICE WERE TRYING TO TRACK DOWN ART, AND, ironically, I was on my way to do the same, though mine was the kind that hung on museum walls. After finding the crates containing the ten paintings, and a letter from the Azores listing eleven paintings, I had some questions. *What's the connection to the Azores? Where did they come from originally? How did they get to Mattapoisett? What happened to the eleventh painting?* Perhaps number eleven had been sold. Interpol will look into that, but for now, I needed to get to the Azores.

It would be a quick trip, and I planned to be back in Mattapoisett in a few days. Carla had a friend staying with her and Chief said she wouldn't need my help to track down Art Nunes. The State Police had been brought in to help with that.

Southeastern Massachusetts has a large population of people whose roots are in the Azores Islands. I'm one of them. My grandfather was from the island of Terceira and my grandmother was from the island of Pico. Because so many people in the area have connections to the Azores, there are daily flights from Boston to the islands. I was able to book one for early the next day.

I was pensive as my plane approached Lages Airfield after crossing the Atlantic. In the early 1950's my uncle had died there while working on rebuilding the airfield with the U. S. Army Corps of Engineers. He was operating a stone-crushing machine when he tried to loosen a stone that had been jammed in the crusher. The machine caught his shirtsleeve and he was pulled in and died quickly, according to the letters I had read about the accident. I couldn't help but visualize that day as I stared down at the runway as our plane began its descent.

After entering the small terminal, I retrieved my luggage, caught a taxi, and was on my way to Praia da Vitoria, a small town on the east coast of the island of Terceira, a few miles from the airport.

The taxi turned down a cobblestone street, took a quick right, then immediately pulled to a stop. I handed the driver several escudos, Portuguese currency that I had picked up at the New Bedford Maritime Bank before I left on my trip. After paying my fare, I pulled a slip of paper from my shirt pocket and double-checked the number on the door, 7 Rua Padre Cruz, a short street on the north side of the small natural harbor at Praia da Vitoria. The house was made of white stucco and had an orange tiled roof, similar to most of those in the town. The trim was painted gold and the yard was blooming with colorful flowers. The few houses on the street were all well-kept, and most had small sheds behind them. I put the slip of paper back in my pocket and knocked on the door. Moments later it was opened by a young woman in her twenties. She had long dark hair and the darker complexion typical of the Azorean people.

She looked at me questioningly, and, before I could introduce myself, asked, "Posso te ajudar?"

"I don't speak Portuguese, but I'm looking for Antone Nunes."

"Antone was my father, but he died several years ago, she replied in English. We believe he was lost at sea. My mom, Heda, died last year. I'm Anna Grazia, their daughter, is there something I can help you with?"

Certainly a friendlier reception than I would have gotten back in the States.

"I'd like to talk with you about a letter that was sent to a relative of yours in the United States."

"Come in," she said, cautiously pulling the door open and stepping aside to let me enter. She was certainly far less concerned about letting a stranger into her house than people back home would be.

Her home was a modest one, neat and clean. A large cross hung on the wall over the couch in the living room, where we were standing, and numerous religious pictures and statues adorned the tables and shelves around the room.

My eyes were immediately drawn to an oil painting that hung on a wall in front of a small table with several candles on it. The painting depicted a man with outstretched arms, wearing a priestly robe, kneeling in front of a depiction of Jesus Christ. The two men were surrounded by angels above and nine figures below, all of which were bathed in the soft sunlight streaming from the windows of the ornate dome overhead. A large, lit candle sat on the small altar on the right side of the painting, in front of the outstretched hands of the kneeling man in the robe.

"What happened to your parents," I asked.

Anna Grazia spoke softly.

"My father left in his boat with my cousin, Caetano. He told my mom and me that they were going on a long fishing trip. He was often gone for several days at a time, and once in a while for a week or two. After two weeks, when he hadn't returned, my mother reported it to the local police. They didn't do much to try to find him, and after more than a year they declared my father and cousin dead. We never found out what happened to them, and, as I told you, my mom died last year."

Anna Grazia sat in silence for a minute, her eyes closed, before she asked, "Would you like some coffee or a glass of wine?"

Her question interrupted my study of the painting.

"I have some new vinho verde."

"Yes, thank you. We have that back home and it's my favorite white wine."

Anna Grazia retreated to the kitchen and a few minutes later returned with two glasses of the light, fresh, straw-colored white wine, handed me one, and set the other on a table next to the couch.

"Sit," she told me, pointing to a large overstuffed chair facing the couch.

Anna Grazia went back to the kitchen and then returned with two small plates, each with a pastry on it. "These are queijadas de nata. They are filled with whipped cream, lemon rind, eggs and sugar. My mother used to make them and this is her recipe."

I settled into the chair as Anna Grazia took a seat at the end of the couch.

"These are delicious; they go nicely with the vinho verde."

I hadn't eaten since having a pre-packaged sandwich and a beer somewhere over the Atlantic Ocean, and this was a treat.

"Why are you really here? Do you have any information about my father?"

I took a deep breath and began. Twenty minutes later I finished telling her about the missing art, the murder in Mattapoisett, and finding her father's letter on the desk at Art

Nunes' house. When I was finished, we both sat in silence. Anna Grazia was in deep thought, and I gave her all the time she needed. Finally, she took a sip of wine, followed by a deep breath.

"I never heard that story, and I don't know anything about missing art, but I do know that my mother's brother, my uncle Ulbrecht, worked at the Kaiser Friedrich Museum in Berlin."

Perhaps another piece of the puzzle.

"Tell me about Art and your father."

"It's a long story."

"Take your time," I said reassuringly.

"Art is my uncle, my father's brother. I was told that he left Terceira with his father, my Grandfather, many years ago. My mother only heard from them once every year or so, and after a while, not at all. I don't even know where to begin."

I let her sit in silence for a few minutes. She was sorting out what I told her and piecing it together with what she knew.

Finally, I decided to break the silence.

"Where did you get the painting on the wall?" I asked, pointing at the oil painting over the table with the candles on it.

"My mother told me that it was given to her by my grandfather, Heinrich Schiffer, who was the captain of a German submarine."

"Do you know where he got it from?"

"No, I don't. My mother said he gave it to her as a gift for her birthday a long time ago. She told me it was called *The Vision of Saint Bruno* and that he knew it would be special to her. That's another long story that she told me many times.

"My mother's grandparents, my great-grandparents, Antonio and Anna Costantin, lived in the village of Roccaforte del Greco in the Southern part of Italy, the toe of the boot, in an area called Calabria. They were known as Griko people because their ancestors migrated from Greece, and along with many other families settled in communities in Southern Italy. This was during the Roman Empire.

"My grandmother spoke Italian, because that's what she learned in school. She only knew a few words and phrases in Greek. My mother once told me that we have relatives who are also Grikos who crossed over the Strait of Messina, the Stretto di Messina as she called it, and live in Sicily. I have never met them.

"Anyway, when their daughter, my grandmother, Grazia, was young, her parents sent her to the convent at the Sanctuary of Santa Marie de Polsi, which means Our Lady of the Mountain. It's near San Luca not too far from where they lived, in a valley between the mountains. My mother told me that my grandmother was put on the train to San Luca. She told me that her parents said she was young and beautiful and that could become a problem with the boys in the village. I always thought that was funny. Anyway, nuns met her there and they walked several miles to get to the convent. She became a nun, but really didn't like being in the convent and was constantly getting into trouble. When she was eighteen, she and several of the other nuns snuck out of the convent, walked to the train station, and took the train to Reggio Calabria, a large town on the west coast of Italy, for the celebration of the Feast of Saint Bruno, the Patron Saint of Calabria.

"During the celebration she met a German man who was there on vacation. Being a bit impetuous, at least that's what my mother told me, she snuck off to a restaurant with him. After several hours of conversation and a few glasses of the local wine, he convinced her to return to Germany with him.

"My grandmother hid in his hotel room until the celebration was over and the other nuns returned to Santa

Marie without her. Two days later they took a ferry across the Strait of Messina to Sicily and then another boat to Hamburg in Germany. They were married two months after they arrived there. My grandfather's name was Heinrich Schiffer and he was in the German Navy, but I think I already told you that.

"His son, my uncle, Ulbrecht, worked at the Kaiser Friedrich Museum, in Berlin, but I never met him and have never heard from him. Two of my cousins died when they were infants. My mother always said that the two angels in that painting," she said as she gestured towards *The Vision of Saint Bruno*, "were my two cousins.

"I've been rambling on, but that's why I love that painting. I'm *here* because my grandmother went to the celebration of the Feast of Saint Bruno."

"That is a quite a story. I understand why that painting is so important to you and your family. Would you mind if I look at it more closely?"

"Why no, you are most welcome to, but please be careful with it."

I walked over to the painting and looked at it for a full minute, almost reverently, studying what might be the work of Jacob Jordaens, a Flemish Baroque painter. Bella did a little research for me before I left for the Azores, and told me that Jordaens was known for his oil paintings of altarpieces.

Jordaens painted more than one hundred pieces, and one of them might be hanging on the wall in front of me. I reached up and carefully lifted the painting by its sides and gently carried it over and set it on the chair I had been sitting in. I was nervous as I slowly turned the painting around. There, on the top left corner, clearly marked, was the number eleven!

I took my time hanging it back on the wall as I thought about how to continue our conversation.

"Anna Grazia, can we go for a walk? I would love to see a bit of Praia da Vitoria."

She seemed happy with the suggestion, and we got up and walked outside. She didn't lock the door, even with a masterpiece hanging on a wall inside. *The Azores must be like it was back in the States decades ago.*

We walked up a slight hill across the street, then up seven steps to a white church with blue trim. A sign on the front read 'Edificada Em 1521.'

This church was here before Europeans settled in North America.

We sat on the steps in front of the church, and I finished the story that she had started. I was connecting dots, for her and for me.

"Anna Grazia, your grandfather, Captain Schiffer, apparently brought eleven pieces of art to your parents, here in Praia da Vitoria. From what you told me, it might have been taken from the Kaiser Friedrich Museum in Berlin during the bombing of Berlin at the end of World War II. He probably saved it from being destroyed. It seems that your father later brought the paintings to your uncle, Art, in Mattapoisett, in the United States. I think they somehow went through Newfoundland. Anyway, the police are looking for him and he will likely be arrested, for something else he did." I hoped she wouldn't ask.

"While we were searching Art's house we discovered a letter from your father that had your address on it, and that's how I came to be here with you. The letter had a list of the eleven paintings on it. Ten of the eleven pieces were at Art's house."

I paused, giving her time to think. She was wrestling with a moral dilemma.

"And *The Vision of Saint Bruno* is the eleventh painting?" she asked.

"Yes," I said, "and that's why I looked at the back of the painting. The paintings we found in Mattapoisett were all numbered on the top left corner. The number eleven is written on the back of *The Vision of Saint Bruno*. It's the missing painting."

I paused again. It was a nice day and the warm sun felt good. There was no need to rush. Anna closed her eyes and I sensed that she was praying.

"The painting is so special to me. In some ways, it's the story of my life, and certainly my mother's."

She was quiet again. She was struggling. I didn't interrupt her silence.

"As much as I love it, it really doesn't belong to me."

I gave her time. I knew this was difficult for her.

Minutes passed, and more minutes.

Then, with slight hesitation she said, "It should be returned. But, how do I do that? Where does it go?"

She paused, seemingly to confirm her decision to herself.

I waited.

Finally, after several minutes, I answered her questions.

"I can have the International Police, Interpol, pick it up. They'll determine where it belongs, though it certainly seems like it will be the Kaiser Friedrich Museum, though it's called the Bode Museum now. If it came from there, they'll return it to them."

"Well, it will be there for the whole world to see, though they won't know my family's connection to it."

I thought a minute.

"You know, the people who run the museum might be so happy that the painting has been returned to them that they might consider putting your story next to it when they hang it. Why don't you write it up and send it to them? I'll send you the address."

Anna Grazia smiled a big smile at the same time soft tears formed at the corner of her eyes. But, they were happy tears, and I could see the relief on her face.

◆

IT WAS SHORTLY AFTER SUNRISE AND THE RED BOAT WAS heading northeasterly up Buzzards Bay. It cut through Quick's Hole, between Nashawena and Pasque Islands, and on into Vineyard Sound.

He turned the boat to starboard, and a little over an hour later was passing between Woods Hole and Martha's Vineyard.

He checked his navigational chart and saw he was in six fathoms of water as he turned to run parallel to the Atlantic side of Cape Cod. The Martha's Vineyard Ferry was approaching, heading towards Woods Hole, bringing tired visitors back from their summer vacation on the island. He cut close in front of the ferry and received a long steady blast from its horn for doing so.

He kept the throttle wide open as he steered the boat along the lower Cape, past Hyannis, West Dennis, Harwichport. He reached the elbow of the Cape about two hours after leaving Cuttyhunk, then rounded Orleans and headed northward towards his destination.

Almost there.

Seagulls began to follow him, hoping for the small pieces of fish, or chum, that were often tossed off the stern of boats to attract fish. Their meal would come later. Art wouldn't be fishing today.

As he moved past Chatham Harbor he spotted Coast Guard Beach up ahead. Thousands of summer vacationers were enjoying the Cape Cod National Seashore, working on their melanomas, cooking in the sun before heading to Arnold's for the best seafood and fried onions on the Cape.

On the beach, near the water's edge, Bryson Morton was an hour into building a large crocodile sand sculpture. His two children, Madison and Ava, had begged him to sculpt it, as they had every summer for the past three years since they began coming to the Cape for their vacation. He was shaping the teeth with a small plastic shovel, his kids oblivious to his efforts. He'd be glad when he was done with this annual tradition. He had suggested sculpting a sea turtle this year, but Madison and Ava protested that idea so much that he again gave in and was in the middle of creating his third crocodile in three years.

Bryson's wife, Jocelyn, was sitting under a blue and white striped umbrella, reading the latest romance novel, an Elsa Kurt romance. She slid her red-rimmed Cartier sunglasses over her forehead as she glanced at the Vacheron Constantin on her wrist.

It's almost lunch time.

She scanned the shoreline for Madison and Ava and spotted them running along the edge of the waves, throwing their skimboards down and shooting across the shallow water.

Farther down the beach an overweight guy in an undersized bathing suit sat in a beach chair training his binoculars on the three young women in tiny bikinis bouncing along the edge of the water. He hadn't put the binoculars down for hours, not even to apply some sunscreen, and now he looked like the twin lobsters he had eaten at the Eastham Lobster Shack the night before. Something in the background caught his eye and he raised his binoculars slowly away from the young women to look at the sailboat that poked above the line of the horizon off to the south.

Onboard the 28-foot Triton, Mike Hinkley, his wife Kathy and their two boys, Alan and Drake, were enjoying the moderate winds that had pushed their masthead sloop along the shoreline from Chatham Harbor, a few miles to the south. They were heading towards Provincetown where they would dock for the night and enjoy dinner and people-watching on Commercial Street. The Hinkleys had bought their boat in 1968 from a boatyard in Barnegat Light, New Jersey. Kathy immediately named it *Pier Pressure*. Mike spent a week sailing it home to Chatham with his friend Skip Chase. The Triton had its mainsail and yellow and orange striped spinnaker raised and was catching some good wind this sunny afternoon.

Not long after the *Pier Pressure* sailed from Chatham Harbor, Mike spotted the red fishing boat off his stern. He thought nothing of it as many fishing boats worked the shoreline this time of year, while others took fishing parties out to the Stellwagon Banks, a rich fishing ground between P-Town and Boston.

A little while later the *Pier Pressure* passed Coast Guard Beach, one of the three main beaches of the Cape Cod National Seashore. Next, they'd sail by Nauset Beach, the middle of the three beaches, then farther on to Marconi Beach, named after the Italian inventor, Guglielmo Marconi, who, from that spot in 1903, sent the first transatlantic wireless message from Theodore Roosevelt to King Edward VII in England.

"Alan," Mike shouted to his oldest son, "trim the mainsail. It's luffing a bit."

Alan pulled in the sheet until the mainsail was filled with wind, proud that he knew his way around the boat.

Onboard the *Arte Perdida*, Art had hardly noticed the Triton ahead of him. He was looking for something else. He stared through his binoculars, scanning the water in front of him.

332

Nothing. Hopefully farther ahead.

He knew they were out there.

He followed the Triton past Coast Guard Beach and on towards Nauset Beach. He again lifted his binoculars to search the surface of the ocean but still didn't find what he was looking for, so he continued ahead, about four hundred yards offshore.

Amber Monroe was sitting in the lifeguard tower at Nauset Beach, wearing her red sweatshirt with a white cross and the word "lifeguard" on the front of it. She had watched the red boat approach, but wasn't concerned since it was far enough offshore that it wouldn't be a danger to the swimmers. Amber was one of many college students who took jobs as lifeguards for the National Park Service each summer on the Cape Cod National Seashore beaches. She was in her junior year, an art major at the University of Connecticut, and this was her second summer working at the beach. Her boyfriend, a pre-med student and captain of the Yale football team, was in a lifeguard chair two hundred yards down the beach from hers. They had met here on Cape Cod during lifeguard orientation in January before the beaches opened.

There they are!

Through his binoculars, Art finally found what he was looking for. The small round heads of seals bobbing in the ocean, looking for fish. Tourists on the beach crowded the edge of the water, looking out at the seals ducking under the water then surfacing many yards away, their mouths filled with small fish. The food chain. Small bottom fish were food for the seals. The seals were food for larger predators. *This is it.*

Art looked at the sunbathers on the beach. *They're really going to get a show today.* He cut the engine, walked forward and picked up the Danforth anchor, then dropped it into the water. He went back to the stern and lifted a small plastic bag off the deck. It contained a heavy object the size of a soccer ball. Holding it over the port gunwale, he dropped it into the water. As it sank towards the bottom, his eyes followed it until it was no longer visible. *Good luck finding that!*

He examined the filleting knives lying on the cutting board that was stained black and green from the blood and guts of all the fish and chum that had been sliced there over the years. He picked one up, and, running his thumb over the blade, decided that this was the one. He looked at the crowds once again, and for a brief moment thought it was too bad that there were kids there. *Who cares? Their parents can deal with it.*

He looked out at the water, reaffirming his decision. He thought back to his time in prison and the horrific and demeaning abuse he had suffered by the other prisoners.

I'm sure the cops are on to me. They must have searched my house by now. Found the art. If I go back to prison, it will be for the rest of my life. And I know the other prisoners will find out that I molested that kid. They have ways of finding things out. And when they do, my life will be hell every day that I'm there. Then the damn cops will win again. This is my only choice.

Holding the knife in his right hand, he laid his left arm across the cutting board with his palm facing upward. Slowly, he lowered the blade and drew it across his wrist, feeling a sharp sting as it opened a thin cut through his flesh and several veins. *Not so bad.* Switching hands, he did the same to his right wrist, cutting a little deeper. He dropped the knife, then walked a few steps to the stern of the boat. The seals had returned and surrounded the boat. *This is it.*

Blood dripped onto the deck, bright red in contrast to the dark stains accumulated there during so many fishing trips. He

334

climbed onto the rail, looked around, and then stepped off into the warm water.

His clothing quickly absorbed the salt water and pulled him towards the bottom. He didn't struggle. Two lines of blood paralleled his descent, like the contrails of a fighter plane. He hadn't thought to grab a breath of air before he jumped, not that it would have made a difference. He bottomed out, but the weight of his water-logged clothing slowed his ascent, and he never reached the surface.

The great white shark was swimming a few hundred yards from his boat when it sensed a threat to its food source. Feeding is not the reason sharks attack humans. It had been scouting its preferred food, the seals bobbing in the ocean just off the beach, when it detected blood in the water and picked up the scent of an intruder. With a few whips of its tail, it was alongside the boat, ready to defend its territory.

Art felt strong turbulence in the water around him. Suddenly, the two-ton shark grabbed his legs between its jaws and quickly pulled him downward towards the ocean floor. The pain was excruciating. He tried to scream, but his mouth filled with salt water and no sound came out. He felt his body being whipped back and forth like a ragdoll in the grip of a playful dog and knew that he had only a few seconds before the last bit of air in his lungs would be gone and salt water would flow through his nostrils and into his lungs.

He went into shock just as his left leg was torn from his hip socket. The great white released its grip, then quickly grabbed him again, ripping away a large part of his midsection. His flesh and blood slowly spread outward from his body, creating a red and green saltwater soup. He began to hallucinate and saw a beautiful mermaid with long-flowing reddish-blond hair swimming towards him. Unconscious, what

335

was left of his body slowly drifted downward and settled on the ocean floor.

Amber stood on her lifeguard chair and watched the boat while checking regularly on the swimmers in the water in front of her. She glanced back at the boat, then suddenly realized that someone out there was likely in trouble. A minute earlier she had seen a man standing near the side of the boat. Now, he wasn't there. The turbulent water all around the boat convinced her that he had fallen overboard. She picked up her walkie-talkie and called her supervisor.

Vacationers on the beach pointed towards the boat, not quite certain what was causing the commotion in the water. Amber and the other lifeguards blew their whistles and frantically waved for everyone to get out of the water. Parents scurried to pull their children back onto the beach. A crowd of tourists stood at the edge of the water, looking out at the scene before them, puzzled by what they were seeing.

Its territory successfully defended, the great white finally swam away in search of a seal. Smaller fish, the scup, tautaug, and blues, moved into the maelstrom to clean up the remnants of blood, flesh, and bone. Seagulls hovered overhead, occasionally swooping down to scoop up a piece of the remains. Thirty minutes later, all that was left was a slick of blood that gradually dissipated into the warm ocean waters. The *Arte Perdida* lay at anchor, without its captain.

◆

"COAST GUARD STATION CHATHAM, THIS IS LIEUTENANT Raul Figueiredo, aboard the Coast Guard Cutter Recovery. We are proceeding North from Chatham towards Nauset Beach following up on a report of a possible attack by a great white. Please confirm that an ambulance has been dispatched to the scene. Over."

"Recovery, confirm, ambulance is on its way. Over."

A short time later, the Recovery came upon the scene. The name on the transom of the red boat was *Arte Perdida*. A crewman jumped aboard and searched it. No one was there, but fresh blood was on the cutting board and a trail of blood was splattered on the deck.

"Coast Guard Station Chatham, this is Lieutenant Raul Figueiredo, aboard the Coast Guard Cutter Recovery. It looks like we have a possible suicide. There's a red and yellow slick next to the boat. It appears a person was attacked by a shark, probably on the bottom. We won't be sending a diver down due to the danger of sharks. Contact the State Police and National Park Service. We're towing the boat back to station. Over."

"Roger."

"Coast Guard Station Chatham, this is Lieutenant Raul Figueiredo, aboard the Coast Guard Cutter Recovery. Please run a boat registry check on the *Arte Perdida*. That's Portuguese for Lost Art."

◆

A LONG DAY. MORE LIKE A LONG YEAR, I THOUGHT AS I walked down Mahoney's Lane and stepped onto my porch. I had spent the last several hours at the police station wrapping up the loose ends of the case. *Art Nunes, murderer and holder of stolen antiquities, is gone. Arte Perdida—Lost Art. How ironic.*

I picked up the newspaper that had been left on my front steps, knowing how tomorrow's headlines would read. As I stepped into the dark entrance way and reached for the light switch, I was immediately engulfed by the scent of parfume de baunilha.

EPILOGUE
1971

"He that can have patience can have what he will."

— Benjamin Franklin

THE INVESTIGATION HAD BEEN COMPLETED. FORENSICS confirmed that the body parts were those of Eddie Tinkham. His killer was dead. Interpol, the International Criminal Police Organization, had been contacted and had removed the paintings from Arthur Nunes' house and returned them to the Bode Museum, the former Kaiser-Friedrich Museum, in Berlin. Anna Grazia had surrendered *The Vision of Saint Bruno*. It now hung in the Bode Museum, alongside the story of the Saint's influence on her life.

◆

SEVERAL WEEKS AFTER THE MURDER CASE WAS CLOSED, A crowd gathered at the end of Freddie Brownell Wharf. A public address system had been set up, and Larry Benham, the first selectman, was eulogizing Eddie Tinkham. Carla and I watched as he dropped a wreath from the end of the wharf into the harbor. The high school band played the Navy Hymn, *Eternal Father Strong to Save,* as others in attendance walked one by one to the end of the wharf and dropped a white carnation into the harbor in Eddie's memory.

After everyone had paid their respects, the first selectman returned to the microphone and asked those in attendance to turn towards the harbormaster's office behind them on the wharf.

"At this time, I'd like to introduce our new harbormaster. This man is extraordinarily knowledgeable of the harbor, wharf, mooring and anchorage rules and regulations. He's lived in town all of his life and has spent countless hours on his own boat out in our harbor. He's also served as a deckhand for numerous charter fishing trips. He knows almost every boat in the harbor and almost every owner, though perhaps not personally. In addition to possessing such outstanding qualifications, he was instrumental in solving the murder of his predecessor. There is no person more qualified for this position than the man I'm proud to introduce as our new harbormaster, Freddie Texeira."

With that, Freddie stepped out of the harbormaster's office. He was sporting a fresh haircut, a clean shave, neatly pressed tan slacks, and a black shirt with a patch on the left sleeve proclaiming him Mattapoisett's Harbormaster. A gold shield was pinned to his left shirt pocket. The crowd was silent for a few seconds. Most weren't overly familiar with the name, having referred to him as Wharf Rat for so long. Then the crowd erupted with sustained applause and cheers.

"That's a lot of guilt being exorcised," I said to Carla.

"You're right about that," she said.

The crowd moved towards the new harbormaster, shaking his hand and patting him on the back. More than one person offered an embarrassed apology. Freddie soaked up the new-found recognition and friendship. He was beaming from ear to ear as person after person stepped forward to congratulate him and wish him well in his new position.

Finally, the crowd began to dissipate and Freddie went back into his office to begin his first official day of work. After work, he would return to the new home he had built out on Mattapoisett Neck. He had been presented with the reward money for his role in solving the murder, and had given Ronnie Pendergast a thousand dollars for his part in helping to solve the case. When he combined the reward money with the money he received from his younger brother when he sold him his share of the pig farm, he had enough to build a comfortable house overlooking Mattapoisett Harbor. A large table sat in front of the picture window of his new home across the harbor from Ned Point Lighthouse. Dozens of boxes containing various sized megalodon teeth were scattered around the room. When he wasn't performing his duties as harbormaster, he was etching nautical scenes into the teeth to sell at ArtSea.

◆

The last of the crowd was leaving the wharf as Carla and I walked down the grassy hill of Shipyard Park. We sat on a bench in front of the bandstand, looking out at the harbor as we ate the ice cream cones we had just purchased at Frates Ice Cream Shop. A gentle onshore breeze was blowing warm salty air across our skin, and the large swordfish weathervane atop the pole at the end of the wharf indicated it was out of the southeast. A man and a boy were fishing off the end of the wharf, not far from where the *Arte Perdida* had, until recently, been moored.

"Why don't we get married," asked Manny.

Far out in the harbor sails were being raised on a Herreshoff Rozinante. The large mainsail caught the wind and the boat was underway, perhaps heading to Nantucket for the annual Nantucket to Block Island race being held in two days. A lobster boat was passing Ned Point Lighthouse on its way to check the pots it had set off Cormorant Rock.

"Why not?" said Carla.

Her reply didn't immediately register with Manny. Then, realizing what she had said, he turned to her and asked, "Do you mean it? Please don't toy with me."

"I mean it."

◆

343

ON THE FIRST SATURDAY IN OCTOBER WE WERE MARRIED in the Congregational Church. The next day we flew out of Logan Airport on our way to Calabria, Italy. Now, after making several connections, we were waiting for our ride at the train station in San Luca. It took a lot of persuasion on my part, not to mention the promise of a sizeable donation, to arrange our honeymoon at the convent at the Sanctuary of Santa Marie de Polsi.

Shortly after we stepped outside the train station, a nun pulled up in a small black Fiat. Her only acknowledgment was a nod of her head as she opened the trunk for our luggage. Carla and I sat in the back seat and held hands as we began our drive, winding through a large gorge between the mountains of the Aspromonte range. It was said that the convent, established in 1144 by Roger II of Sicily, was built in such a remote location to discourage any impetuous young novices from sneaking into town to partake in sinful activities. For the most part, it had worked.

The convent came into view, and a minute later we were parked in front of the main entrance. At our driver's beckoning, we retrieved our luggage and followed her through the front door. She led us to the second floor, then turned a key that opened the door to a small room overlooking the mountains.

"Perfect," Carla and I said at the same time. We looked at each other and smiled.

"No one will find us here," I said as I handed the nun a plain white envelope. She nodded her thanks as she gave us the key to the room.

"This week we're celebrating the Feast of Saint Bruno, in Calabria. His feast day is October 6th. Will you be going?"

Carla and I looked at each other.

344

"We're not sure," I said. "We might have had enough of Saint Bruno."

A puzzled look crossed the nun's face, but she didn't ask.

"If you need anything, just come downstairs and someone will help you. I hope you enjoy your stay with us."

Carla pulled me into the room, turned, put her arms around my neck, then kissed me. At the same time, she lifted her right leg, and with her foot pushed the door closed. She winced a little, then reached behind me and turned the lock.

"How nice," I said. "A week with no investigations for me, no clients for you. No questions, no press. I won't have to chase philanderers."

"You'd better not become one of them," she said with a wink.

"Why would I do that? There wouldn't be anyone as capable as me to investigate."

"Are you talking to yourself again?"

"Yes, I need an expert opinion."

Carla mockingly gave my face a light slap, followed by a big smile, and then a kiss.

She took both of my hands in hers and said, "Mr. and Mrs. Pereira. I like that."

Outside in the hallway, a young novice peeked around the corner, tiptoed up to their door, then giggled as she hung a sign on the door knob:

DO NOT DISTURB!

Recipes from *Arte Perdida*

DENNIS'S STUFFIES

Ingredients

3 large diced onions (Vadilla's are best)
Celery equal to the amount of onion, diced
5 cloves of minced garlic
2 packages diced hot chourico
2 packages Arnold seasoned stuffing
1 bottle Samuel Adams Summer Ale
1 1/2 quarts fresh minced clams
Clam juice to make the mix moist
60 large scallop shells (you can find them online)

Directions

1. Saute onions and celery in olive oil until translucent
2. Add minced garlic to onions and celery just before they become translucent
3. Separately, saute hot chourico in olive oil until just starting to brown
4. Combine the vegetables with the chourico, including the oil – let cool
5. Add the beer to the stuffing
6. After stuffing mix has thoroughly cooled, add the clams and the juice they are packed in
7. You may need to add more stuffing or clam juice to make the mix soft and moist
8. Put in the fridge overnight, to let the flavors "get happy".
9. Portion into shells. You can freeze at this point
10. When ready to serve, cook 45 - 60 minutes, checking for top crispiness

Makes about 60 stuffies.

MARY'S CLAM CHOWDER ("Chowda")

Ingredients

2 quarts fresh chopped clams in their juice
1/2 lb bacon
3 large yellow onions
3 – 46 oz. cans of clam juice
10 lbs. Yukon gold potatoes
2 - 3 T dill weed
pepper or hot pepper sauce to taste
heavy cream

Directions

1. Fry the bacon until crisp. Remove from pan and save
2. Dice onion and fry in bacon fat until translucent
3. Pour clam juice into a large stock pot
4. Peel and dice potato, boil in the clam juice until fork tender, then bring the broth to a simmer
5. Thicken the broth: remove 2 cups of cooked potato and 1 cup of broth. Blend in a food processor until smooth, then return mixture to the pot
6. Add onion
7. Continue cooking chowder at a low simmer
8. Add the clams and juice. When the clams turn white they are cooked through
9. Add dill weed
10. Ladle into bowls and add a dollop of heavy cream to each bowl, then stir
11. Top with crumbled bacon
12. Sprinkle with pepper- or take it up a notch and use a few shakes of hot pepper sauce

TIA MARY'S KALE SOUP

Ingredients

2 T unsalted butter

1 onion, finely diced

3 cloves garlic, sliced

black pepper (to taste)

6 T extra virgin olive oil

3 medium potatoes, peeled and cut into ½ inch cubes (mix of Russets and Yukon Golds works best, but not necessary to have these two)

1 can white beans, drained and rinsed

6 cups low sodium chicken stock

1 bunch of kale with stems removed, leaves rough chopped into large pieces

Small link of linguica (Portuguese sausage), cooked and cut into ¼ - ½ inch pieces

¼ - ½ pound stew beef, cut into small pieces

Directions

1. Heat butter in large Dutch oven or saucepan over medium heat until melted. Add onion and saute until soft and translucent, but not browned. Add a little olive oil if necessary to keep onions from sticking.
2. Add chicken stock and remaining ingredients except for the kale, then simmer for thirty minutes.
3. Add kale and simmer for twenty more minutes, until kale is cooked and tender.
4. Add salt and pepper to taste
5. Serve with Portuguese bread/rolls

ABOUT THE AUTHOR

Jack Matthews, a retired college professor, spent seven years writing his first novel—*Arte Perdida*. Research for this historically rich work of fiction took him throughout Germany and the Azores. He also spent a week in Portugal Cove, Newfoundland, exploring background material for the book.

Matthews grew up in Mattapoisett, Massachusetts, where he sailed and fished on Buzzards Bay, the setting for much of the novel. He is also a crew member of the Half Moon, an 85-foot replica of the ship that Henry Hudson sailed on the river that now bears his name. On one cruise, Matthews served as the ship's cook on this square-rigged, three-masted wooden sailing vessel. He also sings with several groups and plays the trumpet, cornet, and flugelhorn.

Matthews is available for author talks and book signings at libraries, book clubs, book stores, seminars, and other venues. He can be contacted at:

belltownpress@gmail.com
or
On Facebook: jack matthews author

♦

To order additional copies of this novel, please contact the author at the above email address.